p m

SONS AND DAUGHTERS

Charlotte is an only child, reared by a domineering father who cannot forgive her for not being the son he desires. Charlotte has a gift for friendship and when Charlotte meets Miles Thornton she is instantly drawn to him. He is new to the area and a widower, with three young sons to look after. His youngest son Georgie, only six, adores Charlotte while his middle son Ben is mature well beyond his twelve years. It is Philip, the sixteen year old who attracts the interest of Charlotte's father, who believes he has at last a son to take over his farm.

SONS AND DAUGHTERS

SONS AND DAUGHTERS

by

Margaret Dickinson

Magna Large Print Books
Long Preston, North Yorkshire,
BD23 4ND, England.

British Library Cataloguing in Publication Data.

Dickinson, Margaret
    Sons and daughters.

    A catalogue record of this book is
    available from the British Library

    ISBN   978-0-7505-3549-6

First published in Great Britain 2010 by Pan Books
an imprint of Pan Macmillan Publishers Ltd.

Copyright © Margaret Dickinson 2010

Cover illustration © Gordon Crabb by arrangement with
Alison Eldred

The right of Margaret Dickinson to be identified as the author of this
work has been asserted by her in accordance with the Copyright,
Designs and Patents Act, 1988

Published in Large Print 2012 by arrangement with
Pan Macmillan Publishers Limited

Magna Large Print is an imprint of Library Magna Books Ltd.

Printed and bound in Great Britain by
T.J. (International) Ltd., Cornwall, PL28 8RW

For Mandi

ACKNOWLEDGEMENTS

My grateful thanks to Eric and Mervyn Griggs for a lovely day out around Wainfleet All Saints and district. Thank you for sharing all your memories with me.

Many thanks to David Henson, Chairman at the Magdalen College Museum, Wainfleet All Saints, for a warm welcome at the museum and to David Turner for his kind interest and knowledge of the area in times past.

And as always my love and thanks to my family and friends for their continuing support and encouragement, especially to those who read the typescript: Fred Hill, David Dickinson and Pauline Griggs.

One

LINCOLNSHIRE, 1905

'Is that the – the coffin?'

'Yes, Charlotte dear.'

'And is – is Mama lying inside it?'

Mary, standing beside the child and holding her hand tightly, gasped and covered her mouth with her handkerchief, her eyes brimming with tears. She could not answer.

From an upstairs window of the farmhouse, Charlotte watched the cortège move away from the front door with sadness in her dark, violet eyes. But she did not weep. The coffin, smothered with wreaths of white lilies, lay in a glass hearse drawn by four black horses. Behind it walked her father, Osbert Crawford, and behind him were the men who worked for him. Charlotte – even at five – knew them all. First there was Edward Morgan. He was their household manservant. His wife, Mary, was their housekeeper and cook with only a young girl, Sarah, who came in daily to help her. Between the three of them they took care of everything and everyone in the household. Papa, Mama and Charlotte.

Only now there would just be Charlotte and her father.

Harry Warren, Osbert Crawford's farm foreman, walked beside Edward. Though still

11

only in his mid-fifties, he suffered from arthritis and needed a stick. Usually he rode his chestnut horse around the fields and lanes overseeing the farm workers. But today he was obliged to walk with the rest of the mourners and every step looked painful. Just behind him and ready to help if he was needed was Harry's son, Joe. He'd worked on the land since leaving school and even before that he'd worked during the holidays, at weekends and most evenings, always ready to do his father's bidding, always eager to learn the ways of Buckthorn Farm and to please its master, Osbert Crawford. No doubt, Joe would take over his father's job when the older man retired. The Warren family lived in one of the two semi-detached cottages two hundred yards down the lane from the farm. Charlotte wondered where they all slept, for now there were not only Mr and Mrs Warren and their son Joe, but also Joe's wife, Peggy, their two sons and a little baby girl, Lily, who'd been born two weeks ago.

Charlotte bit her lip. Was it really only such a short time ago that she'd walked down the lane to the cottage holding her mama's hand and taking a large basket of food for the family and gifts for the new baby?

So how, the child puzzled, could her mama have got so poorly so quickly that she'd died?

Mary had tried to explain it gently. 'Your mama's gone away, sweetheart.'

Mama never went away. Charlotte had never known a night when her mother had not been there to tuck her into bed. She'd been there a few days before, had bent to kiss Charlotte gently and whisper 'My darling daughter' before tiptoeing from the bedroom. The last sound Charlotte remembered had been the rustle of her mama's silk gown and the soft closing of the door. Even after she'd gone, Alice's perfume still lingered, enveloping the child in her mama's reassuring presence. But in the cold light of morning, Charlotte's world had fallen apart.

'When is she coming back?' Charlotte had asked.

Mary had dabbed her eyes with the corner of her apron. 'She won't be coming back, lovey.'

'Not – ever?'

The woman had shaken her head and glanced up at her husband, Edward, standing solemnly beside her. 'No,' she'd whispered. 'Not ever.'

The child had asked no more. Despite Mary trying to break the news gently, Charlotte knew her mother was dead. Living on a farm, she'd seen dead animals. She'd sat on a stool at Mary's kitchen table often enough, watching the cook pluck a chicken, skin a rabbit or a hare. She'd seen the pheasants hanging in the barn – row upon row of them – after one of her father's shooting parties. She knew full well what 'dead' meant. And now – though she couldn't see her – she knew her mother was lying silent and still in that coffin disappearing down the lane on its way to the churchyard.

'No women,' Osbert Crawford had instructed harshly. 'I don't want unseemly weeping and wailing. My wife's funeral will be conducted with dignity.'

So even the faithful Mary, who'd come to

Buckthorn Farm ten years earlier when Osbert had brought his bride home, was not allowed to attend her mistress's funeral.

Two years after Mary's arrival, Edward Morgan, already employed at the farm, had asked her to marry him. At first, Osbert had forbidden the match, but when both had threatened to leave, he'd been forced to capitulate, aware that good and loyal servants were hard to find for the lonely farm set amidst the flat Lincolnshire marshland near the Wash.

So, Edward and Mary had married and continued to live at Buckthorn Farm, serving their strict master and caring for his lovely, dutiful bride. And so it was Mary Morgan's hand that Charlotte now grasped as she watched her mother leaving home for the last time.

All the other men and boys who worked on the farm lined up behind Harry and Joe Warren. Charlotte knew them all and they all knew her. They always smiled and waved and raised their caps to her when they saw her. Today, they were not smiling or waving. They were walking with their caps in their hands and their heads bowed. Today, they didn't even look up at the window.

'Come, child,' Mary said, trying to pull her away from the scene below, but Charlotte stayed, obstinately watching until she could no longer see the procession. Only then did she allow the woman to lead her downstairs to the comforting warmth of the huge kitchen.

And through all her growing years it was the only place she was ever to find warmth and comfort and affection.

14

Two

LADY DAY, 1926

'I hear the kitchen maid's gone from the farmhouse, then?'

Peggy Warren straightened up from bending over the range and turned towards her husband as he sat down heavily at the table. As she placed his dinner in front of him she sighed. 'Not another one!'

'Aye.' Joe picked up his knife and fork. 'But who can blame 'em, eh?'

Peggy sat down before her own meal. 'Not me, for one.'

Joe chuckled. 'Don't fancy havin' a go yarsen, then? Earn yarsen a bit o' pin money?'

Peggy stared at him. 'Joe Warren, have you taken leave of your senses? Haven't I enough to do looking after you and your two strapping sons who refuse to find themselves wives and leave home? To say nothing of your poor old dad, who can hardly get out of his bed these days. And then there's Lily, who still comes home now and again from her job at the manor, and as for our Tommy—' Peggy cast a despairing glance to the whitewashed ceiling. 'Always in some scrape or other.'

At seven, Tommy was the youngest of the Warren family. His arrival had been a 'surprise'

15

to the 44-year-old Peggy, who'd thought her childbearing days were over. Indulged by his parents and three older siblings, the boy ran wild.

Joe's smile widened. 'I was only teasing, lass. I wouldn't want you working in that miserable place.'

Peggy was thoughtful. 'If things were different, I wouldn't mind. Me an' Mary Morgan have been friends ever since she came here. We'd work well together, I know. And Edward's a lovely feller. Still,' she sighed, 'I can't and that's that. Has his lordship–' this was Peggy's scathing nickname for Osbert Crawford – 'gone into town today to hire someone else?'

Joe glanced at her briefly. When he'd swallowed a mouthful, he said shortly, 'No. Rumour has it, he's expecting Miss Charlotte to do the work.'

Peggy's fork clattered on to her plate as she gaped at him. 'Miss Charlotte? You're joking.'

'I only wish I was.'

'His own daughter? Working as a kitchen maid as well as all the work she does on the farm?'

'Daughter, you say? Huh! Now tell me, Peg–' he waved his fork at her – 'has that man ever – *ever* – treated that lass of his as a daughter? A *proper* daughter?'

Peggy sighed. 'No, he hasn't. But that's just it, isn't it, Joe? It's because she *is* a daughter...' She paused and, as she met his gaze, whispered, 'And not a son.'

Joe placed his knife and fork neatly together on the empty plate and leaned back in his chair. 'Aye,' he said softly. 'That's the tragedy of it. Poor Mrs Crawford miscarrying three bairns, all boys,

16

and the first two in the same years as our lads were born.' He shook his head. 'That must have hurt. Seein' his farm worker the proud father of two healthy lads and him havin' to bury his sons in the churchyard. You've got to feel sorry for the feller, Peg.'

'I suppose so. The last one – two years after Charlotte was born – went full term, but he was stillborn. Poor little mite. Mary told me once, he was a bonny baby – just perfect. But he never even drew breath.'

'Aye, the master was distraught, they said. Locked himself in his room for days and wouldn't come out.'

Peggy rose and gathered the plates, clattering them together with swift, angry movements. 'But he's got a daughter. A lovely girl, if only he'd see it. But d'you know summat, Joe.' She stood very still for a moment as she added quietly, 'I reckon he'd willingly sacrifice her if it'd give him just one of his sons back.'

'Poor lass,' Joe sighed. 'She hasn't got a lot going for her. Plain little thing, isn't she?'

'Not so little now, Joe. She's twenty-six next month. But she doesn't make the best of herself, I'll grant you. Shapeless, drab clothes; round, steel-rimmed spectacles; and her shining black hair always scraped back into a plait and covered with an old-fashioned bonnet. And have you seen the shoes she wears? They're like a man's.'

Joe grinned. 'Well, not all lasses can be as pretty as you, my love.' His tender glance roamed over Peggy's face, as lovely to him as the day he'd married her despite the fact that she had borne

17

him four children and led such a busy life. There were only a few strands of grey in the curly brown hair and her figure was as slim and lithe as a young girl's.

'But he treats her like a boy,' Peggy was still preoccupied with thoughts of Charlotte. 'Worse than a lad, if you think about it. He never lets her out to enjoy herself. She's never even been to the annual Harvest Supper at the manor, now has she?'

After her mother's death, Mary and Edward had cared for Charlotte. She'd been kept firmly within the confines of Buckthorn Farm, not even allowed to attend the local village school. A governess, Miss Helen Proudley, had taken care of her education. Living in, even sleeping in the same large bedroom, she'd become a companion to the girl too, but it'd always been Mary who'd mothered Charlotte and she who was the constant in the girl's life. At fifteen, Charlotte's formal education had ended.

'You're old enough to work now,' her father had said, dismissing the governess at the end of July 1915. 'With all the young men off to war, you'd better help about the farm.'

From that day forward, Charlotte had spent most of her waking hours out of doors working alongside Joe and his two sons. Now her education was the farming way of life. In her bedroom at night, she would write in a journal all that she had learned that day from old Harry. Though retired through ill health by that time, Harry still lived with his family in the cottage at the end of the track where it joined the long lane

18

running from the sea to the small town of Ravensfleet. Before long, Joe, who as expected had taken his father's position as foreman, could be heard telling anyone who'd listen that Miss Charlotte knew as much as he did about the workings of the farm. 'Though mebbe not quite as much as me dad,' he would add in deference to the man who'd taught him, 'but, you mark my words, she'll be as good as any lad when her turn comes to tek over the farm.'

It was the greatest compliment Joe could pay Charlotte and he said it again now as he rose and kissed Peggy, adding, 'I'd best be off. Doesn't do for the foreman to be seen slacking.'

Peggy laughed. 'That'll be the day any of us on Buckthorn Farm is seen slacking. Not even Miss Charlotte. Poor lass.'

'Aye, poor lass indeed.'

At that moment, the 'poor lass' was laughing her head off in the farmhouse kitchen.

'Stop it, Jackson Warren. You're making my sides ache.' She took off her glasses and wiped her eyes. 'I've got work to do in the dairy. Butter won't churn itself.'

Rolling pastry at the table, Mary Morgan chuckled too. It was good to see the girl laughing and her kitchen was the only room in the house where merriment was ever to be found. The older woman watched as the young man stood by the table looking down at Charlotte.

'You know, you've got pretty eyes, miss. Violet, they are. Shame you have to wear them specs. They hide them.'

19

'Go on with you, you and your flirting.' Charlotte perched the spectacles back on the end of her nose and looked at him over them like a severe school marm. 'I've heard about you and all the village girls. And I've seen you after church on a Sunday, walking with your arm round the waist of some unsuspecting lass.' She chuckled and glanced at Mary. 'I think we should put up a warning notice to all the town's maidens, don't you, Mary?'

'Oh, I think they all know about Jackson Warren. That's why he can't find himself a nice girl to settle down with. Not like his brother.'

Jackson threw back his head and laughed heartily. 'Our John? Get married? He's been walking out with Grace Whitehead for years. Why she dun't give him the boot, I don't know.'

'They'll marry when they're good an' ready.' Mary nodded wisely. 'It dun't do to rush into things.'

'I don't call five years courting rushing,' Jackson countered. 'He's thirty next month and Grace must be twenty-six if she's a day. She'll be an old maid if she dun't watch out.'

Charlotte's smile faltered.

'You mind your tongue, Jackson Warren,' Mary said tartly. 'And you'd best be off about your work. If the master hears all this noise–'

'I'm goin', I'm goin'.' He pulled on his cap and touched it in farewell to both women. 'Thanks for the tea, missus. And you, Miss Charlotte.'

They both nodded acknowledgement at him, Mary with pursed lips and Charlotte with the ghost of a smile.

After the back door had banged behind him, there was silence in the kitchen except for the thumping of Mary's rolling pin.

'That boy,' she declared, 'will be the death of his poor mam! Unless, of course, their Tommy gets there first.' She laughed wryly. 'And that wouldn't surprise me one bit.'

'Jackson's all right,' Charlotte said softly. 'He's a lot of spirit about him. I like to see that. And young Tommy has, too. He's very like Jackson.'

'Aye well, mebbe so. He's a little scallywag, that Tommy. But then, so was Jackson at the same age. But now it's spirit that's mostly out of a bottle on a Saturday night in Jackson's case, so I've heard tell.'

'He's only young.'

'Twenty-eight. He's ready to call others, but he doesn't take a look at himself and realize it's high time he settled down an' all.'

Now Charlotte laughed. 'Peggy looks after him far too well for him to leave home. And as for settling down, I doubt he ever will. He's having too much fun.'

'And whose fault is that, might I ask? Them silly girls who let themselves be charmed by his flirting ways. I just hope none of 'em gets themselves into trouble 'cos it'd break poor Peggy's heart if her lad were to be chased with a shotgun by an angry father.'

She glanced at Charlotte, who was still sitting pensively at the table, lost in thought, scarcely listening to the housekeeper's chatter.

'Don't you mind now, lovey. What he said. He dun't mean no harm. He didn't stop to think

21

what he was saying.' She sniffed disapprovingly. 'He never does.'

Charlotte sighed. 'I know. I'm quite resigned to the thought that I'll never get married. I'll be here in this dusty old house, dreaming of a wedding day that never happened and was never going to.' She chuckled suddenly. 'Another Miss Havisham – that's what I'll be. No, it's not that. It's just – it's just that when Jackson talks about all the *fun* he has, I – well – it's only then I feel the loneliness.'

'But you've a busy life. All the kiddies at the Sunday school love you. And you're always out an' about the farm – you laugh and joke with the hands, now, don't you?'

'I know, I know. Everyone's very kind, but there's always this sort of – barrier, you know. I'm their master's daughter. They're always so polite. *Too* polite, if you know what I mean. And–'

There was a pause before Mary prompted quietly, 'Go on. What is it?'

The words came out in a rush. 'I think they feel sorry for me.'

'Oh lovey, no!' Mary dropped her rolling pin with a clatter and moved to put her arm round the girl's shoulders, leaving a floury smudge on Charlotte's grey dress. 'That's not true.'

Charlotte turned slowly to look at the woman who'd brought her up from the age of five. It was a kind face; round, with soft, smooth skin, though there were a few wrinkles there now and grey strands in the once dark hair. Her hazel eyes were honest and direct – and Charlotte trusted her with her life. Now she smiled. 'Mary Morgan, you are one terrible liar.'

Mary swallowed hard. Oh my dear girl, she was thinking, if only you knew the terrible lie I've been forced to live all these years.

Three

Buckthorn Farm lay in Fleet Marsh, a flat, fertile land on the edge of the Wash. The nearest small town, Ravensfleet, had a long history, a close-knit community, and was the centre of the surrounding farmland. Though several farms and cottages were some miles from the town, they still came within the parish boundary. Most farmers and their workers made the effort, whatever the weather, to attend church every week travelling on foot, by farm cart or pony and trap. It was a chance to meet their neighbours and the townsfolk – the blacksmith, the wheelwright and all those who were a vital part of their own lives. Most of the farms around the town were part of the Ravensfleet Estate, owned by the acknowledged squire of the district, who lived at the manor. A large, rambling house on the outskirts of the town, its windows overlooked the land belonging to its owner. By tradition, Home Farm was farmed by the squire, whilst the rest of the estate was divided up into tenanted farms. Only Buckthorn Farm had been owned outright by the Crawford family for four generations. The farmhouse, with outbuildings clustered around it, faced towards the coast. To the north was the growing seaside resort of Lynthorpe; to the south, the historic town of Boston.

Mary had been right when she said that all the village children loved their Sunday school teacher and Sunday was Charlotte's favourite day.

Come rain or shine, she and Mary walked along the straight track westwards through the fields to the church near the railway station in Ravensfleet, whilst Edward drove Osbert Crawford in the pony and trap. They aimed to reach the church gate as Edward drew the conveyance to a halt. Then they'd wait until Osbert had descended and, without a word or even a glance at his daughter, walked up the path between the lines of his farm workers, their wives and families. Again, without a word to anyone, or even a glance, he'd enter the church and make his way to the front pew on the left-hand side whilst the rest trooped in to take up the pews behind him. Charlotte, with Edward and Mary Morgan, sat in the seat directly behind him. No one, not even his own daughter, sat with Osbert.

The squire from Ravensfleet Manor had always occupied the right-hand-side front pew. But on this last Sunday in March the pew was empty. Old Mr Davenport had died some months before without close relatives and his heir – a second cousin once removed – lived abroad and had no intention of taking up occupancy. So, the manor, along with the whole of the Ravensfleet Estate, had been sold and a new family was expected. Indeed, the whispers running amongst the congregation said that the new owner had arrived and taken up residence on Lady Day, three days ago. So now they all waited, craning their necks, to see if anyone would arrive for the service.

As the vicar, Cuthbert Iveson, young, eager and newly ordained and inducted into the parish of Ravensfleet, moved forward to begin the service, there was a disturbance at the back of the church. The door opened and a blast of the cold wind from the sea swept into the church skittering around the ankles of the worshippers, so that they all frowned and turned to see who had caused their discomfort.

A man – tall and broad shouldered, with dark brown hair smoothed back and dressed in a smart three-piece suit – walked down the aisle. He nodded to either side and then gave a little bow towards the vicar as he took up his place in the right-hand side front pew. Three boys followed him. The first – who perhaps by now considered himself a young man – was about sixteen. Tall and thin, with straight fair hair and cold blue eyes, his fine, handsome young face was spoilt by a petulant pout to his mouth. The middle boy – about twelve or so – walked with his head bent, his shy gaze upon the floor. But the youngest of the trio skipped down the aisle, grinning up at the people on either side.

'Hello,' he said, his piping voice echoing to the rafters. 'How do you do? I'm Georgie. I'm six and we've come to live at the manor.'

Smothered laughter rippled amongst the congregation and all eyes turned towards the little chap and his round, cherubic face to return his friendly smile. Blond, unruly curls and bright blue

25

inquisitive eyes brought soft 'Ahs' from the women.

'Come along, Georgie,' his brother murmured, ushering the younger boy with a little push into the pew to sit between himself and the eldest boy.

Whispering broke out until Mr Iveson cleared his throat and his parishioners settled down. But their curiosity had been aroused and, throughout the service, necks craned to catch sight of the new arrivals. Charlotte was entranced. She could hardly concentrate on her hymn book. The little boy in a smart little sailor suit fascinated her. The middle boy, with dark colouring like his father and soft, dark brown eyes, was having difficulty in keeping a straight face himself. But the eldest boy, now he was a different kettle of fish altogether, Charlotte thought. He frowned down at Georgie and once bent to whisper in his ear. The little boy was immediately subdued, but only for a few minutes before he began to twist round in his seat and smile at those sitting behind him. His gaze wandered all around the church and at last came to rest upon the pale face of the vicar in his pulpit. The little boy swung his legs, his heels drumming on the pew until, once again, the eldest brother frowned at him.

Charlotte tore her eyes away and tried to concentrate on what Mr Iveson was saying. As she brought her gaze to the front again, she saw with surprise – indeed, with a sense of shock – that her father, sitting directly in front of her, was not paying attention to the vicar either.

He was watching the man with his family of sons.

26

As the service ended, the congregation filed out from the back with the occupants of the two front pews leaving last. Just outside the porch, Mr Iveson stood shaking each and every hand, but his flock was in no hurry to depart. Not this morning. They hung about in little groups, spilling out on to the road, pretending to talk to one another, whilst their children chased each other amongst the gravestones. But their glances kept coming back to the church door watching for the newcomers to emerge.

'That must be our new squire and his family, then.'

'Where've they come from?'

'Why is there no woman with him? Where's his wife?'

'He's a widower, I've heard tell.'

'Are those three boys his sons, d'you suppose? Aren't they handsome young fellers?'

''Cept that oldest one. He looks a mardy 'un.'

'Snooty, if you ask me.'

'But the master looks nice. Not uppity. He was pleasant enough, now, wasn't he? Nodding and smiling to us all.'

'And the youngest – what a little cherub he is.'

Charlotte, Mary and Edward walked down the aisle towards the door, where Charlotte paused and glanced back over her shoulder to see her father hovering at the end of his pew and holding out his hand.

'Osbert Crawford, sir, of Buckthorn Farm. And, by what your young son said, you must be the new owner of the Ravensfleet Estate?'

27

The dark-haired man smiled. Laughter lines crinkled his eyes. 'There are no secrets when Georgie is around,' he said in a deep voice. 'And yes, we moved into the manor on Lady Day.' He shook Osbert's hand and introduced himself. 'Miles Thornton.'

Osbert inclined his head. 'And these' – he waved his hand towards the three boys already walking – or, in Georgie's case, skipping – down the aisle – 'are your sons?'

'Yes, they are.'

There was a slight pause before Osbert, with undeniable envy in his tone, murmured, 'You are indeed a fortunate fellow.'

There was a fleeting bleakness on the other man's face as if he carried some secret sorrow. Then he seemed to force a small smile but, to Charlotte's surprise, he made no comment, no murmur of agreement with her father's statement.

She smiled at the three boys moving towards her. The eldest, leading the way, looked her up and down with such disdain that Charlotte almost felt the urge to curtsy under his superior glance. He passed her by without a word, put on his hat and marched out of the church. The second son smiled before following his brother, but did not speak. Georgie, however, stopped and beamed up at her.

'Hello. What's your name?'

Charlotte smiled, her eyes sparkling behind her spectacles. 'Miss Charlotte.'

The young boy put his head on one side. *'Miss Charlotte?'* His smooth forehead puckered in a puzzled frown. 'Who d'you work for?'

Now Charlotte was puzzled. 'Work for? How – how do you mean?'

'You're a maid, aren't you? So, who d'you work for? The gentleman you were sitting behind?'

Charlotte almost gasped aloud and then she realized. In the young boy's mind, she had every appearance of a maid. In her dowdy clothes and seated behind her father alongside his household staff, she appeared to be a servant too. For a brief moment, she was hurt, but then her natural sense of humour and the realization of how she must look to anyone who did not know her – and her circumstances – came to her rescue. She chuckled and bent down towards him.

'The gentleman talking to your father – the one I was sitting behind – is my father.'

Georgie blinked and for a brief moment seemed lost for words. 'Oh,' was all he said.

Charlotte straightened up and put her head on one side, regarding the boy with wry amusement. 'But I suppose you're right. I do work for someone. I work for my father on his farm and about the house. And I suppose I work for the church, too. I teach at the Sunday school. Would you like to come?'

'Ooh, yes please. When is it?'

'Well, right now, after Morning Service, but–'

Georgie held up his hand and, almost without realizing how it had happened, Charlotte found his warm little hand grasping hers. 'I'll come now.'

The two men were walking towards them and Charlotte turned anxious eyes to the stranger.

'I'm sorry, I–'

'Georgie,' his father said easily, 'are you misbehaving?'

The child turned his blue eyes and his beatific smile on his father. 'No, Papa. This nice lady's called Miss Charlotte and she's the Sunday school teacher. And I'm going with her to Sunday school.' He turned back to Charlotte. 'What time do we finish, Miss Charlotte, so that Brewster may come back in the motor to fetch me?'

'Well – I – er–' Again she cast an anxious, questioning gaze at the boy's father. He was watching her with amusement.

'This, Mr Thornton,' Osbert said grudgingly, 'to my eternal disappointment, is my daughter.' He waved his hand towards her. 'So now that you see her in all her *glory*–' his mouth curled with sarcasm – 'dithering like some halfwit, perhaps you can understand why I called you "a fortunate fellow".'

Mr Thornton seemed startled and a small frown deepened the creases in his forehead. Then he gave a courteous little bow towards her and said quietly, 'I'm happy for Georgie to come with you, Miss Charlotte. Shall I send my man back for him at twelve?'

'That – that would be fine,' Charlotte found herself stammering and blushing, not only from embarrassment at her father's cruel words, but also as, under the soft brown gaze of the stranger, she found the colour rising in her face and her pulse racing.

As she led the little boy to the room at the back of the church where the Sunday school was held,

Charlotte heard her father say, 'I was not blessed with sons like you, sir, and, as you can see for yourself, with her looks, it's most unlikely she'll marry and present me with a grandson.'

To Charlotte's surprise, the little chap walking sedately beside her now, suddenly squeezed her hand, looked up at her and smiled, and her father's words – true though they undoubtedly were – lost some of their sting.

Four

The children came running from all directions into the schoolroom. Georgie had seated himself in the centre of the front row. He sat on the small chair swinging his legs and smiling up at Charlotte. The others jostled each other to sit beside him. They all wanted to know about the newcomers. Charlotte sighed inwardly. She could see she was going to have a battle this morning to keep order and gain their attention.

She opened the children's book of Bible stories that formed the basis of her Sunday school teaching and stood in front of them, waiting patiently until the shuffling stopped and silence reigned. She had to wait quite a while, for there was a lot of nudging and whispering.

At last she said, 'Quiet now, children, please. We must begin. Today, as it's Palm Sunday, I'm going to read you the story of how Jesus rode on a donkey into Jerusalem.'

31

For the next half an hour she read the story of Palm Sunday to them and then asked questions, but the children were still inattentive and fidgeting.

Then, in the second row, a hand shot into the air. 'Please, miss,' Tommy Warren – with a cheeky grin so like Jackson's – asked, 'can we do a play? Like we did last week with the loaves and fishes?'

Charlotte smiled. The children loved to act out whatever story she'd read. They got rather excited and noisy, but Mr Iveson didn't seem to mind. He encouraged it. Sometimes, if he arrived to visit the class, he joined in and took one of the parts. Not like the previous vicar – old, crusty and certainly of the 'children should be seen and not heard' brigade. He'd heartily disapproved of her even reading anything that was not straight out of the Bible itself. He hadn't liked her reading the simplified stories, but Charlotte knew the children could understand them so much better and that performing them brought the tales to life. They really remembered them.

'So, you want to act out the story of Jesus riding into–?'

'No, miss. Can we do the story you read us last week? About the Good Samaritan. It were brilliant, miss.'

'Well...' Charlotte said, but, glancing around the class, she saw that all the scuffling and the chatter had ceased and they were sitting up straight, their innocent eyes turned towards her. 'Very well, then.'

She was organizing who was to play which part when Tommy piped up again. 'A' ya goin' to let

Georgie have a part, miss?' Two other boys beside him giggled and clapped their hands to their mouths to stifle the sound.

How thoughtful they are, Charlotte thought, to include the new little boy so soon. 'That's a very good idea, Tommy. Now–' she turned towards Georgie – 'what part would you like to play?'

'He could be the chap who gets set upon by thieves, miss,' Sammy Barker, one of Tommy's friends, suggested.

The golden-haired little boy nodded eagerly and slid off his chair. When all the parts had been arranged, Georgie and Tommy and his two friends, who were to be the robbers, took their places at the front of the room.

'Now,' Charlotte directed, 'you go over there, Georgie, and you three go to the opposite side of the room. Now, you're travelling along a road, Georgie, and these three robbers jump out and attack you. We're just pretending, of course...'

Scarcely had the words left her mouth, before the three boys launched themselves at Georgie, punching and kicking him. Fists flailed as the small boy fought back. He landed a punch in Tommy's eye but he was no match for the three of them. They wrestled him to the ground as Charlotte rushed forward. 'No, no!'

Horrified, Charlotte dragged them away. It had all happened so quickly. 'Sit down at once,' she cried. The three boys returned to their seats with Tommy holding his eye. But they were all grinning.

'That'll show the "little cherub",' she heard Sammy mutter. She'd deal with the three of them in a minute, but first she bent down in front of Georgie. A cut on his lip was oozing blood. Charlotte's heart missed a beat. Oh, dear Lord, the child was hurt, but to her surprise, Georgie was grinning. 'What did you stop us for, Miss Charlotte? They were robbing me like the story said.'

'Yes, I know, but they were only supposed to *act* it, Georgie, not do it really.' She took a clean hanky from her pocket and dabbed at his lip. 'Whatever will your father say?' she murmured, mortified to think what a bad impression the locals would have made on their new squire.

At that moment, Mr Iveson chose to appear. He entered at the back of the room and strode to the front. Charlotte looked up at him with worried eyes. She hated telling tales, but it would be obvious to him at once that all was not well in her class this morning. She gave her handkerchief to Georgie. 'Keep pressing that on your lip, dear. It'll stop the bleeding.'

The little boy shrugged. 'It's nothing, Miss Charlotte. Honest. I'm always in the wars. Father says I'm–' he paused, his smooth brow wrinkling in thought – 'I'm accident prone.'

The child was nonchalant about the whole incident and comical too, but Charlotte didn't feel like laughing. The naughty boys had attacked the newcomer deliberately and she was very angry with them.

She sighed as she stood up and turned towards the vicar.

'What happened?' Cuthbert asked.

Before she could speak, Georgie piped up. 'We

were doing a play, sir. The Good Samaritan. Please may we carry on now?'

'But you've hurt your mouth,' Mr Iveson began, but Georgie ignored him and beckoned the three boys to come to the front again. 'Let's show the vicar.'

Tommy, Sammy and Michael sidled out of their seats once more, glancing at one another uncomfortably. What was the new boy playing at? Now the vicar had arrived, they were going to be in such trouble.

'Right–' Now it was Georgie directing. 'Let's start again and–' Charlotte saw him glare at the other three boys in turn – 'let's do it properly.'

She almost gasped aloud. His fierce look was warning them. She couldn't believe a boy of six could act with such maturity. But the three miscreants were meekly taking up their places again. Georgie turned to her. 'Tell us what to do, Miss Charlotte.'

Charlotte swallowed, embarrassed under Mr Iveson's watchful eye. 'Er – well,' she stammered, her usual composure quite deserting her. She took a deep breath to calm her jangling nerves. 'You're walking along the road when three robbers jump out at you and' – Charlotte turned what she hoped was a stern gaze on the other three boys – 'you three attack him but you're only *pretending*.'

Out of the corner of her eye, she saw Cuthbert raise his eyebrows, but he said nothing and the three urchins looked suitably chastised.

This time they threw mock punches at Georgie but not one of them touched him, though the younger boy cried out with realistic terror as Tommy pulled his off his sailor jacket. Georgie fell to the ground, but intentionally now. Michael pulled off Georgie's boots.

'That's enough,' Charlotte cried, suddenly afraid that the three boys were going to strip the child naked in the interests of authenticity. The three 'robbers' ran to the back of the room, whilst Charlotte beckoned the two children who were to act out the roles of the priest and the Levite, who 'passed by on the other side'.

Georgie lay on the floor, moaning and reaching out with pleading hands. 'Help me, oh please help me.'

'He's a good little actor, isn't he?' Cuthbert murmured, coming to stand beside Charlotte.

'Now you, Phoebe,' Charlotte instructed. 'You're the Good Samaritan...'

The girl walked shyly towards Georgie and held out her hand to help him up. Then she put her own shawl round him and led him off to the side of the room.

All the other children clapped.

Cuthbert moved to the front of the class and began to ask questions about what they had all learned from the story. The children glanced at each other and then one or two hands were raised tentatively. Then, with growing enthusiasm, the answers and comments came thick and fast, with the vicar nodding and smiling, pleased at such a good response.

As the hands on the clock on the wall reached twelve, Mr Iveson dismissed the class, but Charlotte raised her voice above the scraping chairs and scuffling boots. 'Tommy, Sammy and Michael – I want a word with you. Stay here until I come back.' She held out her hand towards Georgie. 'We'll see if your father's motor car has come back for you.'

They went outside to see Brewster leaning against the vehicle, reading a newspaper whilst he waited for his young master.

'I'm so sorry about what happened,' Charlotte said to the boy. 'I – I'll come and see your father later to explain.'

Georgie grinned up at her. 'There's no need really, Miss Charlotte. Father always says we must stick up for ourselves and fight our own battles. And not be a telltale,' he added.

'You're certainly not that. But I feel I must explain to your father. I'm responsible for all the children while they're in Sunday school.'

Georgie was thoughtful for a moment. Then he nodded. 'Just so long as you promise not to tell him their names.'

Charlotte sighed. It would be a difficult interview with the new squire but she felt duty bound to see him. She felt it was all her fault.

'Very well,' she promised and the little boy's grin widened.

As the motor drew away, Charlotte returned to the schoolroom. Cuthbert had disappeared back into the church, but the three boys were waiting for her looking ill at ease. Sammy – not so brave now – looked as if he might cry at any moment. His father would give him a beating if he found out what had happened. And what on earth Joe would do to his son, Charlotte dared not think.

'Now,' Charlotte said severely, 'what you did was very naughty. You know very well when we do our little plays about the Bible stories, we are pretending. So why did you all hit Georgie?'

Even as the question came out of her lips, Charlotte already half guessed the answer herself. Their action had been a kind of primeval instinctive reaction against someone who was different. Georgie was from a privileged home. He wore a smart suit. He was articulate and bright and outgoing. And hearing their mothers gushing over the angelic-looking little chap, the local boys had taken an instant dislike to him. Luckily, Charlotte thought, it was most unlikely that Georgie would be attending the village school. And he probably wouldn't want to attend Sunday school again.

She turned towards the one she knew had been the ringleader. 'Tommy Warren, I'm surprised at you. Whatever were you thinking of?'

Tommy went red and hung his head, afraid that Miss Charlotte would tell his father. 'I'm sorry, miss. I didn't think.'

'And you, Sammy. Your father is now Mr Thornton's tenant.' Saltwort Farm, where the Barkers lived, was part of the Ravensfleet Estate.

Tears were running down Sammy's face now. 'Please don't tell me dad, Miss Charlotte. He'll whip me.'

'So'll mine when he finds out,' Tommy muttered.

Charlotte bit her lip. She so wanted to tell them that she thought it unlikely that their fathers would get to know of their escapade. But a few

38

hours, days maybe, of fear would be an apt punishment.

'Well, I hope you've learned your lesson. And the next time you see young Georgie Thornton, you apologize to him. D'you hear me?'

Three heads nodded vigorously. 'We're sorry, Miss Charlotte.'

'Just mind you tell that to Georgie, too. You may go now.'

She watched them walk out of the schoolroom and down the path through the churchyard. There was no running and whooping and yelling. They were suitably subdued, their heads together, no doubt swapping stories of what punishment awaited them. She felt mean but was determined to stick to her resolve.

Besides, the little rascals had put her in an unenviable position. Feeling responsible for what had happened to his son, she felt obliged to face Miles Thornton.

Five

As Charlotte walked up the long lane leading to the manor on the edge of the town the following morning, she was trembling all over. Her palms were sweaty and her stomach churned.

Knowing some of the servants there, she went round to the back door.

'Miss Charlotte,' Lily Warren cried, 'whatever are you doing here?' The girl's welcoming smile

39

faded suddenly. 'Oh!' She clapped her hand to her mouth. 'Nothing's wrong at home, is it? Don't say it's me grandad!'

'No, no, Lily,' Charlotte reassured her swiftly. 'Nothing's wrong. I'm so sorry – I never thought.'

Lily breathed a sigh of relief. 'It's all right, miss. It's just me being silly. But you know how bad me grandad gets.'

'I do and I'm sorry. I'll call at the cottage on my way home and see your mother. See how things are.'

'Would you, miss? Oh, that is kind. We've been so busy just lately with the new family arriving.' But Lily was smiling as she said it, as if the changes in their lives were very welcome. Lily had worked at the manor since the age of fourteen, starting as a scullery maid and working up to become first housemaid. Now she wore a black dress, a frilly white apron and cap. Servants were fast becoming a dying breed since the end of the Great War. Women had begun to look for work in offices, shops and even factories. Menial housework was beneath them, they felt, but Lily liked her life at the manor. She loved living in the grand house and she could see her family often. Any other employment would have meant her leaving the countryside she loved.

There was a pause before the girl asked again, 'So – what are you doing here?'

Charlotte pulled in a deep breath. 'I've come to see Mr Thornton.'

'Oh – right. Come away in, then. I'll introduce you to Cook. Mr Thornton brought his own cook.'

'What's happened to Mrs Overton? Has she

40

been dismissed?'

Lily laughed. 'No, no, nothing like that. When old Mr Davenport died, Mrs Overton left to go an' live with her widowed sister in Bognor. She was getting on a bit anyway and her legs were bad. So it all worked out well.'

'What about the rest of you?'

'We've all been kept on, miss. 'Course, when the old man died it was a bit worrying, like. Not knowing who might buy the place and if we'd all still have jobs. But the master only brought Cook and his chauffeur with him and a tutor for the two younger boys. But of course we hadn't got one of them anyway.'

Charlotte was relieved. The manor had a large household of servants, some of whom would have been hard pressed to find new employment locally either because of their age or the scarcity of jobs available.

'And the oldest son–' Lily went on. Did Charlotte fancy it, or did the girl's tone of voice alter? She glanced at the housemaid to see a pink tinge in the girl's cheeks. 'Goes to boarding school, but he's home for Easter just now.'

Lily opened the kitchen door and ushered Charlotte inside. Cook was standing in front of the huge range but she turned at the sound of the door opening and smiled a welcome.

'Cook, this is Miss Charlotte Crawford from Buckthorn Farm. This is Mrs Beddows, Miss Charlotte.'

The cook wiped her hands on her apron and came forward. 'I'm pleased to meet you, Miss Crawford.'

Charlotte took the plump hand. 'Please call me Miss Charlotte. Everybody does.'

Mrs Beddows smiled, invited her to sit down at the table and take a cup of tea and a slice of her chocolate cake, but all the while Charlotte was uncomfortable under the woman's scrutiny. Not that the cook was being impolite, just curious. Charlotte wondered what she'd been told. She could imagine what might have been said. 'Miss Charlotte's plain as a pikestaff. She'll die an old maid at the beck and call of that miserable old devil of a father.'

It was not how she would have chosen to be described, but Charlotte was honest enough to realize that it was the truth.

'You go an' get on with your work, Lily, whilst me an' Miss Charlotte here have a nice little chat.'

When the girl had left the room, Mrs Beddows said, 'I didn't know how they'd all accept me, to tell you the truth. But since the last cook left of her own accord, it's been easy. They're a nice bunch what works here.' She leaned forward, confiding. 'And they can't get enough of my chocolate cake – it's a speciality of mine.' She nodded towards the half-eaten piece in Charlotte's fingers. 'All right, is it?'

'All right? It's delicious.'

Mrs Beddows smiled and sat back. 'So, what brings you to the manor?'

'I've come to apologize to Mr Thornton.'

'Apologize? Whatever for?'

Charlotte sighed. 'Georgie stayed on yesterday after Morning Service to attend my Sunday school. We were acting out the Good Samaritan and the three "robbers" got a little – well – shall we say over enthusiastic.'

'Ah, so that's how he got a cut lip?'

'I'm afraid so.' There was a moment's pause before Charlotte asked, 'He didn't say?'

'Little Georgie wouldn't tell tales and his father wouldn't encourage it, I assure you. In fact, my dear, if you'll take my advice, you'll not give the master any names either.'

'I wasn't going to. Georgie asked me not to and I admire him for that. I'm just here to apologize for not keeping better control of my class.'

Mrs Beddows laughed. 'Boys will be boys. It's not the first time Master Georgie's been in a scrape and it'll not be the last.'

Charlotte began to feel a little easier, but she was still determined to see the boy's father. 'Is Mr Thornton at home?'

'I believe so. He'll be in the room he's had fitted out as his study.' Her face clouded. 'He spends a lot of his time on his own since his poor wife died.'

'You've been with him a long time?'

'Ever since they were married. Mrs Thornton appointed me when she set up house. Lovely lady, she was. So sad.'

'What – I mean – when did she die?'

'Three days after little Georgie was born. She got the childbed fever.'

'How dreadful.'

'The master's never got over it and I don't think he ever will.'

'He must have loved her very much,' Charlotte

said huskily.

'Oh he did, he did.' The cook sat a moment, lost in memories in which Charlotte could have no part. Then she shook herself and heaved herself to her feet as Lily came back into the room.

'I've told the master you're here, miss, and he says to take you up.'

Suddenly, the churning stomach and the sweaty palms were back, but Charlotte rose, thanked the cook for her hospitality, and followed Lily up the back stairs and into the hallway. The housemaid led the way to a door on the right-hand side and knocked. She opened the door and announced, 'Miss Charlotte Crawford, sir.'

Charlotte stepped into the room and the door closed behind her.

Miles Thornton was seated behind a large mahogany desk, with his back to the long windows overlooking the front lawns. The room was more like a small library than a study, for most of the wall space was lined from floor to ceiling with shelves of books. There was a large marble fireplace on one wall. Above it hung a huge oil painting of a beautiful woman. Charlotte couldn't help staring at the lovely face framed by blond curling hair. The woman's mouth curved in a sweet smile and her blue eyes seemed to follow everyone in the room. This was Miles Thornton's late wife and Georgie's likeness to her was unmistakable.

Charlotte tore her gaze away and let her glance rest on the big dog stretched full length on the rug. It raised its head and growled softly, but at a word from its master it was silent, though it remained watchful and wary.

Miles rose, came around the desk and held out his hand. His face creased in a smile, but Charlotte noticed that the sadness deep in his brown eyes didn't quite disappear. Now she knew why. This man was still mourning the loss of his beloved wife six years earlier.

'Good morning, Miss Crawford. Please come and sit down – if you can find your way around Duke.' Miles gestured towards one of the two wing chairs that were placed one on either side of the hearth.

Charlotte smiled nervously and went towards one of the chairs. It was not the dog of whom she was afraid, but the man. She bent and held out her hand towards the animal.

'I wouldn't. He's not very friendly towards strangers. He's–' Miles stopped mid-sentence and stared in astonishment. His temperamental guard dog was actually licking the hand of this woman.

'Well, I'll be damned,' he muttered. 'I'd never have believed it if I hadn't seen it with my own eyes.'

Mesmerized, he sat down in the other chair, still staring at his dog. Now, Charlotte was scratching Duke's head and the animal was gazing up at her with a bemused expression.

Miles chuckled suddenly; a deep, infectious sound. 'Are you a witch?'

Charlotte relaxed a little. 'No. I just seem to have an affinity with animals.' She forbore to add that she felt more at ease with animals and children than she did with adults. Especially strangers and, even more particularly, men. The thought reminded her of the reason for her visit and nerves gripped her once more.

'I've come to apologize,' she began, never one to put off doing whatever had to be done. 'Georgie got into a fight yesterday at Sunday school and I feel responsible.'

'You? How come?'

She repeated what she had said to Mrs Beddows.

'Ah, so that's why three urchins presented themselves at my front door this morning asking to see Georgie?'

Charlotte gasped in surprise. 'They – they did?'

'They did indeed. In fact, they're still here somewhere – outside in the grounds, I think – playing with him.'

'Oh!' Charlotte could not hide her surprise and a sliver of anxiety. Was little Georgie safe? What if...?

As if reading her thoughts, Miles said quietly, 'Have no fear for my son, Miss Crawford. Though I didn't interfere, I heard them apologizing to Georgie and he invited them to play with him in the orchard. Cowboys and Indians, I think he suggested. So I'm sure all is well.'

'I – do hope so,' Charlotte said fervently.

'And you have no need to feel guilty any more. They're just being what they are. Boys.'

Charlotte smiled wanly. 'Yes,' she whispered. 'I suppose so.'

He watched the pain in her face and knew from his brief conversation with her father that he was approaching delicate ground. Charlotte gave the dog a final pat and stood up. 'I mustn't take up any more of your time. You must be very busy. Thank you for seeing me.'

Miles rose too. 'It's been a pleasure.' His deep tone was warm and genuine. He opened the door for her. 'And I'll be seeing you again very soon. Tomorrow evening, in fact.'

Charlotte stared up at him. 'T-tomorrow?'

'Hasn't your father told you? He's invited us all – even Georgie – to dinner.'

Six

'I don't believe it. I *can't* believe it.'

Charlotte had still not recovered from the shock by the time she reached home and went straight to the kitchen. Mary was in a blind panic.

'He's just told me,' she said. 'It's more than twenty years since I cooked for a dinner party. Not since–' She paused and glanced at Charlotte. 'Well – not for a long time. Dear, oh dear. I'll have to get Joe to take me on the cart into town. We've nothing in but the plain fare we normally have. "The best, Mary." That's what he said. "The best." Whatever's he thinking of? And with such short notice, an' all. I'll have to have some help, Miss Charlotte.'

'Yes, yes, of course. I'll help you.'

'Oh, more'n that. I'll have to ask Peggy Warren to come. That'll be all right, won't it?'

47

'Of course. If she can leave the old man.'

'She'll just have to – for once,' Mary said firmly. She stopped her agitated pacing and sat down at the table. 'But why? Why now and why them?'

Charlotte was silent for a moment. Then she said in a flat voice, 'Because Mr Thornton has three sons, Mary, that's why.'

Mary gaped at her and couldn't think of a word to say.

By the time Mary and Edward were in their own bedroom that night, however, Mary could think of plenty to say.

'All these years he's been a recluse and kept that lovely girl away from any kind of society 'cept his farm workers and their families,' she whispered angrily, to avoid being overheard. There were three large bedrooms on the first floor of the farmhouse. Osbert slept in the biggest, reached by the main staircase, and Charlotte in the one on the opposite side of the landing. The third room, beyond Charlotte's, was where Mary and Edward slept and it was reached by a narrow back staircase from the corner of the huge kitchen. 'So why does he suddenly want to start entertaining now?' Mary was still ranting. 'Miss Charlotte reckons it's because of the boys. Mr Thornton's sons. But I don't see why he wants to befriend them?'

'Wouldn't put owt past that old devil,' Edward muttered. 'He's got a devious mind. I wouldn't like to even try to guess what be goin' on in his head.'

'So why've we stayed here all these years?'

'You know as well as I do, love. We've only put

48

up with him for Miss Charlotte's sake. If it hadn't been for her, I'd've been long gone.'

Mary smiled. 'Aye, me an' all.' She sighed. 'But we've stayed and now we're too old to move on. Who'd want us now?'

The two glanced at each other. What Mary said was true. They were probably too old now to find domestic work elsewhere, but not for one moment did they regret their decision to stay here. For it was Miss Charlotte who would own the farm one day, and she would see them all right.

Of that, they had no doubt.

'I don't want you at the dinner party,' Osbert told Charlotte the following morning. 'I shall inform our guests that you have a headache and have begged to be excused. You can either stay in your room or help Mary in the kitchen.' He gave a snort of derision. 'Yes, you'd better do that. She's going to need all the help she can get. I hope she's up to the task. I don't want to be shamed in front of our new squire and his sons.'

Charlotte stared at her father. Had his disappointment in her festered for so long that it was now akin to hatred? She'd no choice but to obey him, but, once over the initial surprise, she'd been looking forward to the dinner party. Now, it seemed, she was to be kept in the background like some mad woman in the attic.

Her father was ashamed of her. She sighed inwardly as she left the sitting room. If you could call it that for *she* never sat in it. Her father had made it his own sanctuary, surrounding himself with his books. He spent most of his days in the room now, scarcely venturing out except to church and the occasional visit to the market. Once he had been a regular public figure, had attended shooting parties and had even hosted such events on his own land. But after his wife had died, he'd ceased to socialize.

Back in the kitchen, Charlotte found Edward opening the door to Joe Warren.

Seeing her, Joe pulled off his cap. ''Morning, miss. Could I have a word?'

'Of course.' She led the way from the back door to the outbuildings running at right angles to the house and to the former tool shed that had been converted into a farm office.

'Sit down, Joe.'

'No, 'tis all right, miss. I mun't stay long. I just wondered if you'd come and have a look at one of the 'osses, miss. He seems lame and old Matty said to ask you afore we call the vet.'

Living alone in the cottage next door to the Warrens, Matty Whitehead had worked for the Crawfords all his life, working his way up to become a waggoner. What he didn't know about horses wasn't worth knowing.

Charlotte nodded as she sat down behind the desk. For the last seven years, this room had been her domain. As she'd grown up, Osbert had passed more and more of the running of the farm to his daughter. The foreman now came to Charlotte for instruction and advice. But very few people knew the truth; Mary and Edward, of course, and Joe and Harry Warren. But no one else. Not even Peggy and the rest of the Warren

50

family. Some of the farmhands might have guessed if they'd stopped to think about it. But few did. They'd been so used to seeing the young miss about the place all her life and took her interest and involvement as natural. What they did not realize was that the farm was hers now – in all but name. And her father did nothing to disillusion them. In his twisted mind, he still ran things and his daughter was less than useless.

'I'll meet you at the stables in ten minutes,' Charlotte said.

'There's nothing in his hoof. I think he's pulled a muscle or a tendon. Rest him for a few days and I'll come and massage it twice a day. Can you manage with the other two until he's better?' There were four horses on Buckthorn Farm – three shires and a pony that pulled Osbert's trap.

'Oh-ar, miss.' Matty nodded.

'There, there old boy.' Charlotte ran her gentle fingers down the horse's right front leg. The animal flinched and moved restlessly but seemed to sense that she was trying to help him. 'There doesn't seem to be anything out of place,' she murmured. 'Just a strain.' She straightened up. 'But we'll get the vet if you think it best, Matty.'

'Aw no, miss.' He grinned toothlessly at her. 'You're as good as any vet I've seen. You should have been one.'

Charlotte smiled sadly, reminded once more that if only she'd been a man, she could have done or become anything she liked.

But the truth was, she wasn't even thought enough of by her own father to sit at his table

51

when he entertained.

'That's an absolute disgrace.'

Edward didn't think he'd ever heard his wife so angry. 'I've a good mind to go on strike just like them miners are threatening.'

The newspapers had been full of the coal crisis and rumours were spreading that if the miners went on strike, the whole country would soon come out in support of them. Edward had followed the news avidly, reading snippets out to Mary.

'Wouldn't do you any good, love,' he said mildly now. 'You'd just get the sack. And me along with you.'

Mary's eyes glittered. 'And right this minute, I wouldn't mind if I did.'

'Aye well, it wouldn't help Miss Charlotte, now, would it?'

'But have you ever heard the like? Banning his own daughter from a dinner party and suggesting she work like some skivvy in the kitchen!'

'Likely she'll be happier down here with us than up there.'

'Mebbe so, but it's the principle of the thing. What on earth will Mr Thornton think?'

'I doubt he'll ever know. He'll have no reason to doubt the master's word and he's not likely to venture down into the kitchen. Unless, of course, he comes to compliment the cook.'

Mary gave him a wry glance and continued to beat the batter for Yorkshire puddings. The back door opened and Peggy Warren came in with the breeze.

'By, but it's blowy today, Mary. Nearly lost my wig on the way here.' She laughed. 'That's if I'd got one.' She hung her coat and scarf on the peg behind the door and tied a white apron round her waist. Washing her hands at the kitchen sink, she asked, 'Now, Mary love, what can I do to help?'

'Mek us a cuppa, there's a dear. Edward's tongue's hanging out and I haven't a moment to stop. Then you can start on the veg over there on the draining board.'

'Where's Miss Charlotte? Prettying hersen' for tonight?'

Husband and wife exchanged a glance that was not lost on Peggy. 'What? What have I said?'

Mary explained.

'Not being allowed to join the dinner party?' Peggy's voice was high-pitched with indignation. 'Well, I've heard it all now. Wait till I tell our Joe. He'll never believe it. Not this, he won't.'

Peggy and Mary carried on grumbling to each other about the unfairness of Charlotte's life long after Edward had escaped upstairs to lay the dining table. There was no separate dining room at Buckthorn Farm, but the long sitting room was spacious enough for a seating area around the fireplace and for the dining table and chairs and a sideboard to be placed near the front window overlooking the lawn.

He found Charlotte, a scarf around her hair and a copious apron covering her dress, dusting and polishing the furniture. Any stranger arriving at that moment could certainly be forgiven for taking her for a housemaid.

'Father's gone upstairs for a rest, so I thought I'd give the whole room a good going over before he comes down again.' She stood back and surveyed the whole room. 'There, what do you think, Edward?'

'Looks grand, Miss Charlotte.'

'What about the china and the glassware?'

'All done, miss. And the cutlery. Everything fair sparkles. I'll lay the table now, if you've finished kicking up a dust.'

Charlotte laughed. 'I have. I'll go and see if I can help Mary.'

'Peggy's here, so they're fine if there's anything else you need to be doing.' Edward bit his tongue, longing to add, 'Like getting yourself ready for the dinner party.' But he didn't want to hurt the girl's feelings any more than they had already been wounded.

'If everything's under control, then, I'll just nip down to the stables and check on Tobias,' she added, referring to the lame horse.

She left the house by the back door, wearing a long trench coat, wellingtons and her headscarf. She lifted her head to the breeze and tasted the salt air blowing in from the sea. It was surprisingly warm for early April and promised fine weather for Easter weekend.

Charlotte would have loved a walk to the sea, but with Father's unexpected dinner party, there was no time today. Perhaps tomorrow.

Turning to the left, she crossed the path that ran down the side of the house and the farm buildings, walked past the greenhouse and entered the paddock, where Joe was watching Matty leading the horse in gentle circles.

'Hello, Miss Charlotte.' Joe touched his cap and Matty nodded to her.

'How is he?'

They stood side by side watching the horse.

'Improving already we think, miss. What d'you say?'

Slowly, Charlotte nodded. 'Yes, he's definitely not limping as much as he was this morning. But I think you should rest him for at least a week.'

He grinned at her. 'Better'n a vet, you are. It's them healing hands you've got.'

Charlotte laughed aloud, the sound carrying on the breeze so that the horse pricked up his ears and whinnied softly. Matty brought the animal to a standstill and Charlotte moved forward to pat the horse's neck and feed him a carrot from her pocket. 'Good boy,' she soothed. 'You'll soon be better. What about Jacob and Lightning?' Charlotte was referring to the other two shires.

'They're fine.'

'Another day or so and I'll take Tobias for a short walk, Matty. Then later on, maybe as far as the beach before we let him on the land again.'

When there was little work on the farm for the horses – which wasn't often throughout the farming year – Charlotte took them to the beach further north near the seaside resort where the sand was safer and firmer for the horses. In the warmer weather, they loved a paddle. It would have done the horse good now, she thought, and today would have been warm enough, but she daren't risk the horse on the soft sand yet and it was too far away, anyway, and there was no time.

She bent and ran her hand down the animal's leg. Tobias whinnied again, but he did not flinch or move away from her touch. 'There, boy, there.'

She straightened up. 'I'd best get back to the house. There's a lot to do.' She turned to Joe. 'Peggy's come to help. I expect you know?'

Joe nodded, his mouth tight. He'd called into the farmhouse kitchen only minutes before and heard that Charlotte was to be kept out of sight that evening. His anger threatened to spill over and he literally bit down on his lower lip to stop the words coming out of his mouth. It was a disgrace. An absolute disgrace. A travesty. Charlotte was speaking again and he dragged his angry thoughts back to what she was saying.

'But are you sure your father's all right, Joe? Is he well enough to be left?'

'Our Tommy's there, Miss Charlotte. He's to stay in all day. The little scamp's been fightin' again. He's sporting a shiner of a black eye.'

Charlotte glanced away, avoiding his gaze as Joe went on, 'So I've told him he's to stay at home and watch over his granda. He'll run and fetch me if there's owt wrong.'

Charlotte turned away, her heart thumping in fear lest Joe should say more about the 'fight'. But, rationally, she knew there was no earthly reason why he should think she'd know anything about it.

As she began to walk away, Joe called after her. 'I'll be up to see you in the morning, miss, if that's convenient. There're one or two matters I need your say-so on.'

'That'll be fine, Joe. About ten. See you then.'

But before that, she thought as she walked back to the house, there's this dinner party to get through.

I'll be glad when it's all over.

Seven

'Where's Miss Charlotte? I want to see Miss Charlotte.'

From the kitchen, Charlotte heard the little boy's piping voice in the hallway as the Thornton family arrived and, then, her father's answer.

'I'm very sorry, young man, but Miss Charlotte has a headache and has begged to be excused.'

'But I've brought her some flowers. Father said I might.'

'And magnificent they are, too. I'll see that they're taken to her room. Morgan,' Osbert addressed Edward, 'see to it at once. Now, if you'll come this way, dinner is about to be served.'

The voices died away as Osbert and his guests moved into the room and Edward pushed his way through the door from the hall, carrying the biggest bouquet of flowers Charlotte had ever seen in her life.

'I expect they're from the greenhouses at the manor, miss.'

With trembling fingers, she touched the lovely blooms – daffodils, tulips, iris and even roses.

'No one's ever given me flowers before,' she

murmured. 'How thoughtful. How kind.'

And how sad, Edward was thinking, that they come from a six-year-old!

The dinner party was going well. Osbert sat at the head of the table looking around with deep satisfaction. Three sons. How lucky the man was. And he didn't even seem to appreciate it. If only... Osbert's attention was drawn, not to the little chatterbox, whom his father made no attempt to quieten, but to the eldest of the three boys.

Philip Thornton was everything that Osbert looked for in a young man and everything that he'd desired in a son of his own. At sixteen, the youth was tall and slim, with handsome, even features. His blond hair – so fair it was almost white – was smoothed back from his broad forehead. His blue eyes were intelligent, if a trifle cold and calculating. But even that was a quality Osbert esteemed. He liked the steely look of determination. The young man would go far in life.

Osbert felt an unaccustomed thrill and his heart quickened its beat as an idea began to form in his mind. A preposterous idea, but a wonderful one. He continued to regard Philip through narrowed eyes, assessing him, judging him. The boy caught his gaze and held it with a haughty arrogance that further increased the older man's admiration.

What a splendid young man! What a son!

He leaned towards him. 'And what do you hope to do, Philip? I understand that you're at boarding school at present?'

Philip smiled stiffly. 'Yes, sir.' He answered politely enough, but he was not enjoying the evening. He'd been aware of their host's gaze upon him and had found it disconcerting.

'And after school?' Osbert prompted. 'What then?'

'I'd like to read law at university.'

Osbert felt a flash of disappointment. 'Indeed? So you do not intend to take over the running of the Ravensfleet Estate from your father?' He smiled, though the smile did not reach his eyes. For many years Osbert's smile had been a mere stretching of the lips. No humour or kindliness ever reached his eyes. 'Though, of course, that should be many years off.'

Philip glanced across the table at his father. There was a slight sneer to his mouth as he said, 'I don't think farming is for me. Besides, as you say, that's many years off. And there are two more sons–' he gestured towards his siblings – 'who are probably more suited to–' he paused and added sarcastically, 'more suited to the bucolic life.'

Osbert's eyes narrowed. It was a blow to his idea, but merely a setback. Far from being put off by the young man's arrogance, he liked him even more.

'I – see,' he said slowly. 'But you wouldn't – surely – be averse to being a land*owner*, would you? Even if you didn't want to till the soil with your own bare hands, as it were, you'd like to be a man of property?'

Philip shrugged nonchalantly, not quite sure what their host was driving at. 'I suppose so. But the estate my father's just bought is hardly vast.

Certainly not large enough to divide amongst three sons.'

'Precisely so,' Osbert murmured, his gaze still on Philip. His glance went next to the middle son, sitting so quietly. He'd hardly spoken the whole evening and then only when directly addressed. He did not attract Osbert's admiration like his elder brother did.

Benjamin Thornton was the quiet one of the three. At twelve, he was still a little shy and would have been far happier visiting the stables at Buckthorn Farm and seeing all the animals than sitting in this stranger's shadowy front room with its heavy, dark furniture.

'And you, my boy?'

Benjamin started as he realized their host was addressing him directly. 'What do you hope to do when you leave school?'

The boy ran his tongue nervously around his lips and glanced at his father. Miles Thornton smiled and came to his son's rescue. 'Ben is the one who is most likely to take over the running of the estate. His ambition is to go to a good agricultural college when he leaves school. It's one of the reasons we've come to Lincolnshire. The move doesn't affect Philip, of course. He'll still attend the same boarding school and as for Georgie–' His smile was indulgent. 'Well, he's a little young to worry about what he'll do when he's grown.'

'I shall be a soldier,' the little boy piped up. 'Like you, Papa.'

Osbert raised his eyebrows as his gaze now shifted to the man sitting at the opposite end of the table.

'Is that what you were, Mr Thornton?'

Before his father could reply, Georgie spoke up again. 'He was a colonel in the war, weren't you, Papa?'

For a moment, Miles's eyes clouded as he remembered the terrible days of the Great War. He did nothing – at present – to discourage the little boy's dreams, but he fervently hoped that no son of his would ever have to fight in another war.

'Yes,' he replied heavily, 'I was. But it's not a time I care to remember.'

'Quite so,' Osbert replied stiffly. 'But now you are the country gentleman? Have you any experience of running a large estate?'

Miles smiled and his eyes crinkled merrily. Like his sons, he hadn't quite worked out why the invitation to dine at Buckthorn Farm had been so swiftly forthcoming. He'd suspected – though with her absence from the dinner table perhaps he'd been wrong – that the man had designs on him as suitable marriage material for his spinster daughter. Unless, of course, that *was* the case and the girl herself had made her excuses out of embarrassment. If so, Charlotte Crawford went up in his estimation.

Having been devoted to his beautiful and vivacious wife, Miles had no desire to even think of remarrying. Already he'd fended off several designing females and had no wish to be the object of Osbert Crawford's plans for his daughter.

Answering the older man's question, Miles shook his head. 'I come from a family of soldiers and that's what was expected of both my brother and me.' For a moment, his face was suddenly bleak. 'My brother was killed at Ypres in 1915.'

There was a moment's pause before Osbert asked, 'But you've finished with the army now?'

Now there was a bitter tone to Miles's voice. 'Most definitely.'

'So,' Osbert leaned back and steepled his fingers together as Edward began to serve the pudding, 'how do you expect to run the Ravensfleet Estate with little – er – training or knowledge?'

'Well, as you will know, most of my land is divided up into four farms, three of which are run by tenants, with only Home Farm attached to the manor and left to my tender mercies.'

'Pah! You can't trust tenants to farm properly. You should oversee everything they do. Keep your eye on them – all the time. My own foreman – Joe Warren – is a good man. His father, who preceded him in the job, trained him from a young age. I can confidently leave everything to him. Of course, he consults me, but I have great faith in his abilities.' He waved his hand benevolently. 'If you have any problems, speak to Warren.'

Miles inclined his head politely but said nothing. Only the tightening of his mouth told his sons of his outrage at Osbert's superior attitude.

Georgie, spooning pineapple pudding into his eager mouth, broke the tension. 'I say, this is jolly stuff. We must get Mrs Beddows to make this, Papa.'

Miles Thornton's mood lifted and he chuckled. 'You should know, Georgie, that a lot of cooks guard their secrets very jealously. Perhaps Mr Crawford's cook wouldn't want to hand out her family recipes.'

Osbert laughed, but it was a humourless sound, sarcastic and with a bitter note. 'Cook? Mary Morgan?' Again he laughed but then nodded towards Georgie. 'But if you like her pudding, my boy, I'll see she sends the recipe to the manor.'

The boy scraped the spoon on the plate, criss-crossing it until every drop was gone. He stood up and turned towards their host. 'Thank you for my dinner. Please may I leave the table?'

At least the little rascal has manners, Osbert thought, as he inclined his head giving permission.

Georgie pushed back his chair and marched towards the door, which was opened for him by Edward hovering close by. The young boy beamed up at him. 'Thank you, Mr Morgan. Which way is it to the kitchen? I want to see Mrs Morgan.'

A perverse pleasure shot through Edward Morgan as he pointed across the hall. Let them find out, he was thinking, just how their precious host treats his own daughter.

'Now, Georgie,' his father began, 'you mustn't go wandering about the house. It isn't polite.'

But the child was already skipping across the polished floor of the hall.

'Stop him, Morgan,' Osbert bellowed, suddenly realizing that Charlotte was probably still in the kitchen, dressed in her skivvy's clothes. But the boy paid no heed, and pushed open the door leading directly into the huge kitchen that ran the full width of the house.

Behind him, Edward hid his smile.

Georgie stepped into the kitchen, a ready smile on his face. He glanced around at the three shocked faces. Mary Morgan, Peggy Warren – and Charlotte.

For a brief moment the young boy's smile wavered. Then it broadened again. 'Miss Charlotte! You're feeling better. I'm so glad.' He went to her and took her hand, gazing up at her. 'Why didn't you come to see us? Even if you didn't feel like eating.' He grimaced. 'Headaches can make you feel you don't want to eat, can't they? I had one once and I was sick, too. Were you sick, Miss Charlotte?'

Lost for words, Charlotte shook her head. But she put trembling fingers to her forehead. She was about to get a headache for real any moment now.

Eight

By the time Georgie had finished chattering to the three women in the kitchen, Osbert had led his guests to the chairs and settee around the fire. Though he was agitated by the young boy's action – behaviour he firmly believed should have been checked by the over-indulgent father – he managed to steer the conversation towards the news of the day.

Once again, he addressed his remarks to Philip. 'And what do you make of this threat of a miners' strike and the call for other unions to follow suit in support?'

'If it happens, I think they should send the

army in to break it up,' the young man replied at once. 'They'd be holding the whole country to ransom.'

Osbert's eyes gleamed. The boy talked sense. Good sense, in his opinion. But it seemed the father was softer.

'I think,' Miles said, 'that you should consider what is being done to the miners and their families before you make such a statement, Philip. They're trying to reduce their wages and increase their hours of working. Now that doesn't seem fair to me.'

Philip shrugged as if the folk affected by such an action were of no consequence. Miles frowned, disappointed by his eldest son's lack of thought for others. It was not how he and his beloved Louisa had brought up their boys. But, as he glanced across at their host, he could see that Osbert delighted in Philip's reply and said as much.

'Well said, my boy. Well said.' He even patted Philip's shoulder.

At that moment, Georgie returned and sat beside his father. His cheeks were pink, his eyes bright and he was strangely subdued.

Miles rose. 'I think it's high time this young man was in his bed. Thank you for a most enjoyable evening,' he said evenly. 'And for your hospitality. You – and your daughter – must dine with us some time.'

In the motor car on the way home, Georgie sat in the front seat beside his father who was driving.

'Papa–' Georgie was the only one to still call

their father by that name. The older boys now addressed him as 'Father'.

'Yes, Georgie,' Miles shouted above the noisy engine.

'You know when I went to the kitchen...?'

Miles tried to hide his amused smile. He knew he should reprimand the boy for having gone there without their host's permission. But he felt a perverse devilment and said nothing.

'And you know he told us that Miss Charlotte had a headache...?'

'Ye-es,' Miles said slowly, wondering what was coming.

'Well, she was in the kitchen. Dressed like a maid and doing the washing-up. Now, why do you think that was, Papa?'

'I don't know, Georgie,' Miles said thoughtfully. 'I really don't know.'

As he drew the car to a halt in front of the manor, the two boys in the back seat got out. Just before he shut the door with a slam, Philip answered his little brother's question. 'Because she's drab, uninteresting and no better than a maid. No wonder he didn't want her "gracing" his dinner table.'

Miles and his youngest son stayed where they were, gazing out of the windscreen into the darkness, a thoughtful silence between them.

'Joe, ya dad's taken a turn for the worse. Ya'd best fetch the doctor.'

Joe stared at Peggy, his eyes widening. Over Easter his father had seemed much better. He'd even struggled downstairs to join the rest of the

66

family for their Easter Sunday dinner. During the week since then, the old man had stayed in his bedroom. That was nothing unusual so Joe had thought nothing of it. But now, for Peggy to ask for the doctor to be called, it had to be serious.

'I'll send our Jackson. He'll ride like the wind on his bike. D'ya think...?' His voice trailed away but they continued to stare at each other with serious faces.

Slowly, Peggy nodded and said huskily, ''Fraid so, love. He's got steadily worse this last week.'

The doctor confirmed their fears. 'His heart's giving out.' He put his hand on Joe's shoulder. 'I'm sorry, lad.'

Dr Markham had been in Ravensfleet since arriving as a newly qualified young doctor. He'd served the small-town and the nearby villages, to say nothing of the outlying farms and cottages, for over thirty years. Sprightly and energetic in his mid-fifties, he showed no sign of wanting to retire. A widower for the past five years and his family grown and flown, his patients were his life.

'What would I do with myself?' he'd say, spreading his hands in a gesture of helplessness to the unanswerable question of impending retirement.

He knew all the families around here, had delivered their babies, watched them grow, and seen them leave the world, too. And now one of his oldest friends was about to depart.

'Something seems to be bothering him.' Dr Markham eyed both Joe and Peggy quizzically. 'Do you know what it could be? He's asking for the vicar.'

Joe and Peggy glanced at each other. 'I'd guess,' Joe said slowly, 'it's about where he's to be buried.'

'Ah, yes. I remember now. Your mother's not buried here, is she? Taken to – Lincoln, was it?'

Joe nodded slowly, his brow creasing. 'He – wouldn't let – any of us go,' he said haltingly. 'He reckoned Ma wanted to be with her own folks. She was from near Lincoln. He insisted that only he accompanied her coffin to the interment there.'

'You had a service in the church here, though, didn't you? I seem to remember it was somewhere around the same time that poor Alice Crawford died. Didn't we have two funerals within a couple of days of each other?'

'That's right. Mam died two days before Mrs Crawford.'

'I wasn't called to Buckthorn Farm when she died so suddenly.'

Joe detected the note of bewilderment, even hurt, in the devoted doctor's tone, even after all these years. 'I'd always been the family's doctor, yet Osbert Crawford chose to call a doctor from Lynthorpe. I never did understand why.'

'Aye, he's an odd one, doctor, I don't mind telling you, even though I work for him. I could never understand why he wouldn't let any women go to his wife's funeral. Poor Mary Morgan was heartbroken, so my Peg said at the time.'

'Ah well,' Dr Markham shrugged philosophically, 'ours not to reason why, eh, Joe? Long time ago now. What we've to do now is to find out

68

what's troubling your poor old dad. I'd like to see him go peacefully. Go in and have a word. If it's Iveson he needs to see, then send for him. But' – his voice dropped – 'don't delay, lad. Don't delay.'

As the doctor left, Joe and Peggy went upstairs to Harry Warren's bedroom. The old man had suffered cruelly over several years with arthritis and he was a shrunken, pain-racked shadow of his former self. Now Harry clutched Peggy's apron with a skeletal hand. 'Get the vicar,' he rasped. 'I need – to speak to him.'

'I'll go, Dad,' Joe answered him. 'I'll go this minute. Don't fret. Lie quietly. I'll get him.'

Reminded of his mother's passing by his conversation with the doctor, Joe realized that Harry's health had deteriorated from that time. Only five years after her death Harry had handed the foreman's reins to Joe and for the last sixteen years he'd lived the life of an invalid, sitting hunched in his chair by the fire or lying in bed. The only person able to raise a smile, apart from his own grandchildren, had been Miss Charlotte. He'd relished her visits, transported back to happier times in his reminiscing.

Joe touched Peggy's shoulder lightly as he hurried from the room, murmuring, 'I won't be long, love.'

Mr Iveson arrived, his pale, round face solemn, ready to take the dying man's confession. Though neither he nor many of the locals were of the Catholic faith, he'd already found during his short ministry that the dying often wished to confide in him in their last, frightening moments.

As he sat down beside the bed, Harry, calling on his last reserves of strength, pulled himself up. He waved Joe and Peggy away. 'Go. This is – private.'

Joe shrugged. 'We'll be just downstairs, Vicar, if you need us.'

Cuthbert Iveson nodded and took the old man's hand in his.

Joe closed the door and he and Peggy went down the narrow stairs.

'We should get Jackson to fetch Lily home. And find John too?' Peggy said. 'They'd never forgive us if–'

'You're right. I'll call him. He's digging the vegetable patch as if there's no tomorrow.'

'He likes to keep busy when there's trouble,' Peggy murmured. 'It's his way of coping.'

'Me an' all. I'd like nothing better than to get on me horse and gallop round the farm. But I know me duty's to stay here. I wouldn't leave ya on yar own, lass, to cope with...' His voice faltered. Peggy squeezed his arm comfortingly.

She mashed a pot of tea and they sat either side of the range waiting for what seemed a long time before they heard the vicar's footsteps on the stairs. Cuthbert came into the room looking white faced and slightly dazed. Peggy rose at once and poured him a cup of tea. He sank down into a chair at the table and gulped it gratefully. Then he sat, staring into the middle distance, almost as if he was unaware of the other two people in the room.

'So, Vicar,' Joe prompted at last. 'Where's he

want to be buried, then? Lincoln, with me mam?'

Cuthbert jumped visibly and blinked rapidly. 'Er – well – no,' he stuttered, avoiding meeting their eyes. 'Er – it seems he has a plot already purchased in the churchyard. Next to Mrs Crawford.'

'Next to Mrs Crawford?' Joe was shocked. 'A' ya sure?'

Cuthbert pursed his mouth. 'Oh yes. He was adamant. I must look it up in the records, he said. It was all done properly over twenty years ago.'

'But surely, Mr Crawford must have reserved a plot next to his wife? I mean...' Peggy faltered.

Cuthbert shrugged, but still he avoided meeting their gaze. 'I presume he's reserved one on the other side, perhaps. I – don't know. I'll need to look it up.' He rose hurriedly, took his leave and was gone.

Through the window, Joe watched him go. 'Ya know summat, our Peg. I'd say yon vicar couldn't get out of here fast enough.'

'He's only young. Mebbe he's not got used to attending the dying yet.'

'Mm,' Joe said, but the sound expressed his doubt.

The Warren family gathered around old Harry's bed as he slipped away. Lily cried openly and there were tears in the boys' eyes, though they fought hard not to let them fall. Young Tommy was dry eyed but solemn faced. It was the first time someone close to him had died, but he couldn't remember his grandfather as anything

71

other than a grumpy, bedridden invalid. He had no memories of happier times as had John and Jackson, and even Lily. Peggy and Joe, though sad, couldn't help but feel a sense of relief, too. The old man had suffered dreadfully, but now he was at peace.

'You know, love,' Joe said later that night, 'if you want to help Mary Morgan out now and again, I wouldn't mind.'

'What about Tommy? He needs a firm hand. He runs wild as it is.'

Joe smiled. 'He's all right. He can't get up to much mischief that one of us won't hear about.' He lowered his voice. 'Lily was telling me that he arrived at the manor the other week with two other lads, looking very sheepish. She reckons they'd got into a fight with young Georgie Thornton.'

Peggy gasped. 'Oh no! We don't want to make an enemy of the new squire.'

Joe chuckled softly. 'Seems the boys all ended up playing together, so no harm done, eh?'

'Not this time, mebbe. But we'd better keep our eye on him. He's Jackson all over again. Allus in trouble.'

'Well, Jackson's not turned out so bad, now, has he?'

'No,' Peggy agreed. 'But even so...' She said no more, but Joe's approval of her helping out at Buckthorn Farm had made her think. If it gave that poor lass a bit more freedom, then she'd do it willingly. The thing was, would that miserly old devil agree to it?

Nine

The church was packed for Harry Warren's funeral. Foreman for Buckthorn Farm for much of his adult life, he'd been well known and liked in the district. Farmers whom he'd met at the weekly markets years before in Ravensfleet, and even from farther afield, attended. Miles Thornton was there as a mark of respect for the family, even though he'd never known Harry.

Osbert Crawford did not attend. His absence was whispered about, but when they surrounded the newly dug grave, many thought that perhaps he couldn't bear to see his wife's grave right next to the yawning hole.

The headstone bore the wording: *Alice, beloved wife of Osbert Crawford. Born 1 August 1876, died 6 June 1905.*

'Two days after our mam,' Joe murmured, standing with Peggy and his family as they lowered Harry's coffin into the ground. He glanced across at Charlotte, who, white faced, couldn't help glancing at the place where her mother lay. She'd not attended that burial but the fleeting images of watching the cortège leaving the farmyard still haunted her.

It was something she knew she'd never forget.

The committal, spoken by an obviously nervous Cuthbert Iveson, was over. Once the earth had been scattered by members of old Harry's family

73

on to the coffin, the mourners began to move away.

'A grand feller.' One burly farmer put his hand on Joe's shoulder. 'But you'm following in his footsteps and meking a good job on it, by all accounts. Funny your boss hasn't come,' he added, looking round. 'Old Harry served him well. I'd've thought the least he could do was to come to his funeral.'

Joe gave a wan smile 'Well, Miss Charlotte's here and it's her that...' He stopped, not wanting to give away the truth about the running of Buckthorn Farm nowadays. Charlotte had always made it very clear to him that no one was to know. Swiftly, Joe altered what he'd been going to say. 'She's here to represent them both. Mebbe her father isn't too well,' he added, making an excuse.

The farmer eyed him speculatively, but said no more. He went away muttering, 'There's summat funny there. Still, none o' my business, an' I'd best be on me way. Me cows'll be burstin' to be milked.'

Charlotte was still standing near her mother's grave when Peggy touched her arm. 'We'd like you to come back to the cottage, Miss Charlotte. We can't ask everyone, but we've put a bit of a spread on. Just for the family, old Matty, the Morgans and you.'

Charlotte turned to her and smiled. 'I'd love to, Peggy. Thank you.' She glanced down at the coffin now lying deep in the hole. 'Your father-in-law was always so kind to me. I'll miss him too. I used to love our little chats. He taught me so

74

much about farming and country ways.'

'He always said you should've been a boy, that you–' Peggy stopped, appalled at her own thoughtlessness. 'Oh, miss, I'm so sorry. I wasn't thinking. Me an' my mouth. Joe allus ses it'll get me into trouble one of these days.'

Charlotte smiled and patted Peggy's arm. 'Don't worry, Peggy. It was what Harry used to say to me, though I don't think he realized just how very true his words were.'

'What he meant, miss, was that you'd be as capable as any man to run the farm. And one day – you will.'

Charlotte glanced at her briefly and then looked away. So, she thought, Joe had kept his promise. Not even his wife knew that Charlotte already ran the farm.

Peggy's voice butted into her thoughts again. 'Dad was a good man and your visits to the cottage, even after he'd given up work, always brightened his day. But there was something troubling him at the end, and we've no idea what it was. He told the vicar that last day, but he wouldn't tell us.'

Charlotte glanced again at her mother's grave. 'Perhaps it was because he couldn't be buried beside his wife, d'you think?'

Peggy sighed. 'Maybe so, but he could've been if he'd asked. At least, we could've found out if it was possible, but he never asked. He never asked,' she repeated, the unspoken question hanging between them. Why?

Far from being a sad occasion, the little gathering

at the Warrens' cottage drank a toast to Harry and reminisced about the years they'd all worked alongside him. Charlotte recalled him teaching her to ride and instilling in her a love for all the animals in their care.

'He always said,' she reminded those present, 'that it was a funny mixture being a farmer. We breed and raise animals sometimes to be slaughtered, but we should always respect and care for them. He couldn't abide cruelty to animals in any form and he would travel miles to find the best slaughterhouse.'

'He always told us you had a gift with animals, miss,' Mary told her. 'Healing hands, he said you'd got. And he was right.'

Charlotte's cheeks were pink with a quiet pleasure. She wasn't used to compliments or praise.

Peggy touched her arm and drew her a little aside. 'Mebbe I shouldn't say this so soon, miss, but – well – now poor old Harry's gone and my boys are old enough to fend for themselves a bit ... I mean, even young Tommy's always out with his pals. What I'm trying to say, Miss Charlotte, is that if ever you need any help at the house, I'll be only too glad.'

'That'd be wonderful, Peggy. I must ask Mary, of course. I wouldn't like her to think I felt she wasn't coping.'

'She'd not think that, miss, I promise you. Why, she said–' Peggy stopped and bit her lip. Perhaps she was betraying a confidence by repeating what the older woman had said on the night of the dinner party.

'It's not fair,' Mary had muttered to Peggy

when she'd thought Charlotte was out of earshot. 'That lass should be in there sitting in a pretty frock and playing the hostess. But no, he's ordered that she's here in the kitchen working like a scullery maid.'

Charlotte smiled, patted Peggy's hand and said softly, 'I know exactly what Mary thinks. In fact, let's go and ask her now.'

'Shouldn't you talk about it without me there? I mean...'

Now Charlotte chuckled. 'No, no, Mary Morgan has never been afraid to speak her mind. If she doesn't want you there, she'll say. Have no fear.'

But Mary was delighted, as Charlotte had known she would be. 'That's a lovely idea, Peggy. And it'll give you more time, Miss Charlotte, to keep up with the books and such.'

Charlotte actually giggled and put her finger to her lips. 'Shush, Mary, no one's supposed to know.' Until a few moments ago, Charlotte had presumed that Joe would have confided in his wife about the unusual set-up at the farm. Obviously, he had not.

Peggy blinked and glanced from one to another. 'Know? Know what?'

Charlotte and Mary exchanged a glance. 'Well, if you're coming to work at Buckthorn Farm, you'll soon find out. But you're sworn to secrecy. Isn't she, Mary?'

Mary shrugged as if she didn't agree, but she murmured, 'Aye well, if it keeps his lordship happy...'

Peggy almost laughed aloud to hear that Mary

77

Morgan had the very same nickname for Osbert Crawford as she did.

What Peggy found out after working a few days at the farmhouse was that Osbert Crawford idled away his days reading and smoking in the sitting room.

'I can't believe it, Joe. Why did you never tell me that it's Miss Charlotte who runs the farm?'

'Not allowed, love. There's only me an' the Morgans know.'

'What about John and Jackson?'

Joe shook his head. 'No, they haven't guessed. An' as far as I know, neither's Matty, for all that he's worked there for years. Me dad knew, 'cos he was the one who taught her the most when she was a young lass growing up and taking on more and more. She's always asked his advice right up until he got so ill. When he was still foreman, of course, Miss Charlotte wasn't old enough, but since I took over, Mr Crawford has left more and more to her and now she's running the whole place.'

'With your help, of course,' Peggy said proudly.

'Well, yes, that's what his lordship tells everyone. He doesn't give her an ounce of credit. Not for anything. But it's her I go to now for advice. And when we go to market, although I do the bidding, it's always been talked over between us afore the sale starts. She's done the picking and choosing *and* she tells me what price I'm to go to.'

'Really? Well, I never!'

'And I'll tell you summat else not many know.

She's a very good little artist.'

'An artist?'

Joe nodded. 'Sometimes when she's riding around the farm, she brings her sketchpad with her and her Brownie Box camera.'

'What does she paint?'

'Scenery mostly, I reckon. The fields, the marsh, the farmhouse – but I caught her one day in the stable yard doing a lovely sketch of one of the shires. I'd love to know if she ever did a proper painting.' He sighed. 'It's another little secret she's got. I asked Mary about it once and you should have seen her face.'

'Why? What d'you mean?'

'Frightened to death, she was, that I was going to let the cat out of the bag.'

'I don't understand.'

Joe sighed. 'Evidently, the old man doesn't approve. Ses Charlotte's wasting her time. A *woman* will never become a famous painter. So, the lass has to keep her drawing books and paints in her bedroom.'

Peggy shook her head slowly. 'That man's not right in the head, if you ask me. Fancy denying the poor girl a bit of pleasure. I don't expect she even thinks about being famous. She just does it as a hobby. Like I do me knitting.'

'True, but your hobby keeps us warm in winter with all the lovely jumpers you knit. I suppose he thinks painting pretty pictures doesn't produce anything useful.'

Peggy glanced around the rather bare walls of their cottage. 'Well, I wouldn't mind one of her pretty pictures on my wall if she's as good as you say she is, and that's a fact.'

'She's good all right,' Joe said firmly. 'Just a pity her father doesn't appreciate her a bit more. And not just for her painting, either.'

Ten

The return invitation to dine at the manor came towards the end of May. And this time, because Miles had insisted on Charlotte being present, Osbert could not avoid taking her.

Charlotte had no choice of fine gowns to wear. Her one good dress – a deep purple, plain, shapeless garment that reached to her ankles and had not a scrap of likeness to the fashionable shorter skirts that were all the rage of the mid-twenties – would have to suffice. She scraped her shining black hair back from her face and plaited it, coiling it up into the nape of her neck. She did not possess even one item of jewellery to brighten the drab garment and what she thought of as her one good feature was masked by her round, steel-framed spectacles. No wonder, she thought as she regarded herself solemnly in the mirror, her father didn't want to take her anywhere. She was a sad disappointment, as he never tired of telling her. Not only was she not the son he so obviously desired, but she was also plain and had inherited none of her mother's beauty. With a sigh, she left her room and went down the stairs to find him waiting impatiently in the hall.

'I don't know why it takes you so long to get ready,' he grumbled. 'However long you spend in front of the mirror you're not going to make a silk purse out of a sow's ear. Come on, we don't want to be late. It's impolite. And I don't want to offend the Thorntons.'

Charlotte handled the reins of the pony and trap, whilst her father clung on to the sides.

'Not so fast, girl. Are you trying to have me thrown out?'

Charlotte pulled the horse to a slower speed as they entered the gates of the manor and trotted up the drive. Coming to a halt outside the front door, Osbert clambered down.

'Take it round to the stables,' he ordered. 'You can come in the back way.'

Grousing under his breath, he mounted the steps up to the front door and rang the bell. As Charlotte manoeuvred the vehicle round the side of the house to the stable yard, Miles Thornton's manservant, Wilkins, opened the door.

As Osbert stepped inside, Georgie ran towards him across the wide hallway. 'Good evening, Mr Crawford,' the boy began, smiling a welcome. Then his face fell. 'Where's Miss Charlotte? Hasn't she come?'

'Yes, yes,' the older man said irritably. 'She's taken the pony and trap round to the stables.'

Georgie beamed once more. 'That's all right, then. I'll go and meet her.' He skipped towards the front door, which Wilkins began to open for him. But Osbert's next words stopped the boy in his tracks. With a growl he said, 'I've told her to come in the back way.'

Georgie turned and stared at the man for a moment before marching purposefully back across the hall towards the door leading to the kitchens.

'Wilkins, please show Mr Crawford into the drawing room,' the young boy said with a maturity exceeding his tender years, 'whilst I find Miss Charlotte.'

'Certainly, Master Georgie. May I take your hat and coat, sir, and then if you'd come this way...?'

When Georgie burst into the kitchen, he found Charlotte already there talking to Mrs Beddows and Lily Warren.

'*There* you are. I've come to find you,' Georgie said. 'I thought you might get lost.'

The cook turned to smile at him. 'Master Georgie, Miss Charlotte has brought the recipe for that pineapple pudding you liked so much.'

The boy clapped his hands together. 'Oh thank you. Please thank Mrs Morgan, too, won't you?'

'Of course, I will.' Charlotte held out her hand. 'And now we'd better go up.' She glanced at Mrs Beddows and Lily and they were in no doubt that she'd be much happier down there with them in the kitchen than facing the ordeal of a formal dinner party upstairs.

But with the excitable Georgie at the table there was little formality. He'd arranged the seating to his own liking. He'd seated Charlotte at one end of the polished mahogany dining table, with his father at the opposite end. Georgie sat on Charlotte's right-hand side and opposite him, was his brother, Ben. Osbert and Philip sat on either side of their host.

Miles smiled. 'I'm not sure my son has complied with the rules of etiquette.'

But Osbert was not going to criticize. He was where he wanted to be – sitting opposite the eldest son.

As they sat down, Charlotte glanced around her. The dining room was spacious, with gleaming mahogany furniture, lovingly polished by Lily, no doubt. The table sparkled with cut glassware and silver cutlery. A square of thick, luxurious carpet covered the floor and over the fireplace was another portrait of Louisa. This one, unlike the one in Miles's study, showed an older woman with her children. Leaning against her knee was a golden-haired child of five or so, and sitting on her lap was a baby. Seeing her staring at the picture, Ben leaned forward and whispered. 'That's our mother – with Philip and me.'

'She's lovely,' Charlotte said, smiling at him. She could see the sadness in Ben's eyes. He would have been about six, she reckoned, when Louisa died and he would have only fleeting, disjointed memories of her. Just as Charlotte had of her own mother. She glanced down the table towards Philip and saw that his gaze, too, lingered on the portrait every so often. Aged ten or so when she died, he would have much sharper memories of the beautiful woman. Perhaps that was the reason for his abrasive manner; he still missed her dreadfully.

'So, the General Strike didn't last long, then, Philip,' Osbert opened the conversation.

Philip actually smiled. 'No, sir. It did not. Just

as you predicted.'

'But the miners are carrying on their strike, aren't they?' Before she'd stopped to think, Charlotte, who'd followed the news avidly during the strike, which had affected the whole country for nine days at the beginning of May, spoke up.

There was a moment's awkward silence. The girl held her breath, expecting to be banished from the table for her impudence in daring to join in the conversation. She heard her father's sharp intake of breath and waited for his wrath to descend. But before he could speak, Miles said softly in his deep voice, 'You're quite right, Miss Charlotte, and I can't say I blame them. It seems hardly fair to dock their pay and then expect them to work longer hours, too. And it's one of the most dangerous and unhealthy jobs I can think of.'

Charlotte cast him a grateful glance down the table.

'I wouldn't want to be a miner,' Ben said quietly at her side. 'I'd hate to have to work in total blackness like that.' He shuddered.

'Do you know,' Georgie piped up, 'they take a canary down there just to make sure the air's good. If it isn't, the poor bird might die. Don't you think that's cruel, Miss Charlotte? To the canary, I mean.'

Osbert and Philip laughed, but Ben and Charlotte – and even Miles – took Georgie's comment seriously.

After that, whilst the meal was served and eaten, the table seemed to divide into two. The two adults and Philip at one end talked politics,

84

whilst Charlotte, Ben and Georgie talked about the local countryside.

'I haven't seen the sea yet,' Georgie said. 'And we've been here two months already.'

'Then perhaps your papa would allow me to take you one day,' Charlotte offered. 'Do you ride a pony?'

'Papa's just bought one for me to ride. She's called Gypsy. Philip has a big horse called Midnight, but he's rather wild at the moment. Phil can't ride him yet.'

'I'd love to see them.'

'Why don't you come over tomorrow after Sunday school?' Georgie suggested excitedly. 'You could come back in the motor car with Brewster and me.'

'Well, I...' Charlotte hesitated and glanced down the table to their host, but Miles was listening intently to something Osbert was saying and she couldn't catch his eye.

'That's settled then,' Georgie said firmly and there seemed no point in arguing with the determined little chap. Charlotte hid her smile.

As the meal ended, Georgie raised his voice again. 'Papa, thank you for my dinner. Please may I leave the table?'

'You may, Georgie.'

'And may Miss Charlotte and Ben come up to the playroom?'

'I'm not sure that Miss Charlotte–' Miles began, but she interrupted swiftly.

'I'd be happy to, Mr Thornton.'

The three made their escape from the solemn talk at the opposite end of the table, giggling as

85

Georgie led the way to the second floor of the big house.

'Oh my!' Charlotte gasped as the boy flung open the door of what had once been the nursery. 'I've never seen so many toys.'

In pride of place in the centre of the room stood a huge rocking horse, looking very much the worse for wear. It had obviously been ridden and played with so often that its mane was shaggy, its paint peeling.

'This is Starlight,' Georgie said, patting the horse's neck. 'He was father's when he was a little boy, but now he's ours.'

Charlotte stroked the toy's nose just as if it was a real animal.

'And this is Georgie's new toy,' Ben said softly. 'He got it for his birthday recently.'

Charlotte turned to see a motor car that Georgie was able to sit in and pedal.

'He frightens us all to death tearing up and down the landings.'

'I bet!' Charlotte laughed.

There were teddies, mechanical toys and games galore. Georgie ran around picking up one thing after another. At last he said, 'What shall we play, Miss Charlotte? Snakes and ladders? Ludo?'

'I...' Charlotte faltered. She wasn't very good at games. She had never had any playmates during her childhood – only her governess and Mary. Her upbringing had been severe. Miss Proudley had been told that her sole purpose was to instruct the child, whilst poor Mary was kept fully occupied running the house. So games and play had not figured very much in Charlotte's childhood. Only at Sunday school had she learned how to act out the Bible stories, as she did now with her own class. Though sometimes, she remembered ruefully, even that went wrong.

But now she smiled. 'We'll play whatever you want. You can teach me.'

'Ludo, then,' Georgie said promptly. 'Me 'n' Ben play it, but it's better with three or four.'

'Phil won't play now,' Ben whispered. 'He says he's too old for puerile games.'

Charlotte chuckled inwardly, not in the least surprised that the superior young man had abandoned such childish pursuits. As for herself, she couldn't wait to play.

They were in the middle of a second noisy game of Ludo, Charlotte having surprisingly won the first, when Lily came to say that her father was ready to leave.

Charlotte scrambled up from the floor at once, but Georgie cried, 'Do let's finish the game first. Your papa won't mind, will he?' Without waiting for Charlotte's reply he addressed the maid. 'Please tell Mr Crawford we're just finishing a game. We won't be long.' He grinned. 'Because I'm winning.'

'I really don't think...' Charlotte began but Lily had already disappeared.

Five minutes later, Georgie whooped with glee as his last counter arrived 'home'.

'Now, I must go,' Charlotte said standing up. 'Thank you so much for a lovely evening, I–' Georgie launched himself at her, flinging his arms round her and pressing his cheek against her waist. 'You'll come tomorrow and see Gypsy

87

and Midnight, won't you?'

'Yes, yes,' she said, stroking the child's hair with gentle fingers. She was touched by his affectionate gesture. 'I promise.'

As she turned towards the door, her glance caught sight of a magnificent dolls' house sitting in the corner of the room. Her eyes widened and she stopped. 'What a beautiful dolls' house. I – I always wanted one.' She forgot her father waiting impatiently below. She forgot that their host might want them to leave. She forgot that it was perhaps way past Georgie's bedtime. She forgot everything except the sight of the magnificent toy. She crossed the floor, drawn to it against her will.

Georgie got there first. 'We don't play with this,' he said, opening the front of the house to reveal the tiny, perfectly replicated furniture and the family of dolls in residence. He laughed delightedly. 'Father was so sure I was going to be a girl that he bought this in readiness. I think he really wanted a girl, didn't he, Ben?' Gleefully, almost as if he had engineered it personally, he added, – 'But I was a boy.'

Charlotte glanced at him but the child had no sense of being a disappointment to his father. He knew himself dearly loved. Not like... Charlotte pushed away the unwelcome thoughts. Enchanted, she fell to her knees in front of the house and touched the furniture and the dolls with gentle fingers.

'You can come and play with it, Miss Charlotte, if you like,' Georgie offered generously, but Ben nudged him.

'Miss Charlotte's too old to play with toys,' he said, but fell silent as he watched her rearranging the furniture and putting one of the dolls into the bed in one of the upstairs rooms. 'Or maybe not,' he murmured under his breath.

The two boys watched as Charlotte continued to kneel in front of the house, taking in every little detail.

'It's lovely,' she whispered at last, 'but I really should go.'

But for several more minutes she made no move to leave.

As they hurried down the stairs at last, Charlotte could see her father waiting impatiently in the hallway. He scowled up at her, but Georgie explained guilelessly, 'It was my fault. I made Miss Charlotte stay to finish the game of Ludo. You see–' He spread his hands and widened his eyes as if it explained – and excused – everything. 'I was winning.'

Charlotte saw Miles hide his smile, but her father merely transferred his glare to the boy.

As Wilkins opened the front door, they saw that it was raining hard.

'You can't drive home in the pony and trap in this,' Miles insisted. 'You'll get soaked. I'll get Brewster to drive you home in the motor car. Your pony will be fine in our stables and I won't take "no" for an answer.'

The Thorntons' chauffeur drove them home but once inside his own door, Osbert still complained. 'Noisy contraptions. Don't you go getting ideas we shall ever have a motor car, girl.'

'No, Father,' Charlotte said obediently. But it was not something that worried her. She much preferred riding a horse anyway, even if it was only the pony or one of the huge, cumbersome shires.

And tomorrow, on Georgie's invitation, she was to visit the manor again.

Her heart lifted with excitement, anticipating the pleasure in store.

Eleven

'I won't be in for lunch today, Mary,' Charlotte said as they got ready for church the following morning. 'I'm going over to the manor straight after Sunday school.'

Mary cast her a quizzical look but didn't ask questions. Charlotte smiled. 'On Georgie's invitation. He wants me to see his pony.'

Mary smiled and nodded. 'That'll be nice.' There was a pause before she added, 'Are you telling your father?'

Charlotte shrugged. 'I don't think he'll notice.' The remark was made without self-pity, which, to Mary, was remarkable. She couldn't understand why the girl couldn't see that she was treated like a servant. Less than a servant, Mary thought bitterly. At least employees got paid, pittance though it was.

Charlotte never took meals with her father but always ate in the kitchen with Mary, Edward and

90

the kitchen maid if there was one. It had always been so. Osbert had never wanted the child at his table and the practice had not changed even now that his daughter was an adult.

Mary sighed. She supposed Charlotte accepted it because she'd never known any different.

'Right, are we ready?' Charlotte asked, pulling on her coat and jamming her hat on to her head. 'Where's Edward?'

'He fetched the pony and trap back from the manor first thing this morning, so they've gone already.'

'Oh heck! We'll be late.'

As usual, the women walked down the long lane together to the church in Ravensfleet. On a normal Sunday, the pews were comfortably full and the Sunday school in the little room at the back of the church was well attended. But at Christmas, Easter and especially at harvest time when the congregation swelled, it threatened to burst at the seams.

'Your father's already there,' Mary panted as they came in sight of the gate.

Charlotte bit her lip but said nothing. Father didn't like them to be late. He was waiting in the porch, scowling. He opened his mouth to say something, no doubt to berate them, but then his gaze moved beyond them. To her surprise, Charlotte saw him begin to smile as she heard the sound of the motor car from the manor pulling up at the gate.

Briefly, his gaze came back to his daughter. 'Get inside,' he snarled. 'And don't let this happen again.'

Charlotte's mouth dropped open. Her father always demanded that she and his servants enter church following meekly in his wake. Yet now he was sending them in ahead whilst he waited to greet the Thornton family.

She glanced at Mary, but she was already marching through the door, a grim expression on her face. As she made to follow, Charlotte looked back over her shoulder to see Georgie wave and begin to run towards her. She hesitated.

'Get in!' her father hissed and, raising his stick, hit her across the shoulders. Mortified that the young boy had witnessed his action, Charlotte hurried into the church, her back smarting. Red faced with shame, she sat beside Mary, and bowed her head. She heard quick footsteps coming down the tiled aisle. They stopped beside her and Georgie's small hand crept into hers.

'Miss Charlotte,' he whispered anxiously. 'Are you all right?'

She took a deep breath. 'Yes, dear. I'm fine.'

'Can I sit with you?'

'Well, yes, but won't your father–?'

'Papa won't mind.' He grinned mischievously. 'And you'll keep me in order, won't you?'

Despite her humiliation, Charlotte smiled down at him. He was such a dear little imp. Her golden boy. How she wished he really was hers.

He slid in beside her and bowed his head in prayer as he'd been taught to do on taking his place in the church. Charlotte watched him, longing to stroke his blond curls. As the rest of his family passed her and entered their own pew, she caught Miles Thornton's eyes and raised her eyebrows in a silent question. His glance rested briefly on his small son. He smiled and nodded his approval. But when her father sat down in front of them, Osbert glared round at her and muttered, 'I'll see you at home, miss.'

Just as before, Georgie's tiny hand crept into Charlotte's and held it tightly all through the service.

'Papa, Papa.'

Georgie ran down the church path to his father and brothers as they were leaving after the service.

Miles turned. 'What is it? Aren't you staying for Sunday school this morning?'

'Yes, Papa, but last night I invited Miss Charlotte to come back with me afterwards to see my pony. And she'd like to see Midnight, too,' he said beaming up at Philip. 'She likes horses.' He turned back to Miles. 'May she stay to luncheon, too, Papa?'

'Of course.' Miles nodded.

'Thank you, Papa,' the boy shouted back over his shoulder as he ran back to Charlotte.

'Did you really have to invite that dreary creature again, Father?' Philip muttered. 'Wasn't last night enough?'

'Now, now, Philip,' Miles admonished gently. 'Don't be unkind.'

'Philip's always unkind, Father,' Ben said. Shocked, his father and brother stared at him. 'Haven't you noticed?' He turned away. 'I think I'll go to Sunday school too.'

'Well, well, well,' Miles murmured, his gaze still

93

on his middle son as he walked away. So, the quiet, shy one of the trio did have some spirit after all. The man felt a warm glow.

'Huh,' Philip muttered, his mouth twisting cruelly. 'The worm turns, does it? He'd better watch it.'

The glow in Miles Thornton's heart died instantly.

'So, Ben, have you got a pony or a horse?'

They were sitting in the motor car on their way to the manor after Sunday school had ended.

'I did have a pony.' The boy's eyes were bleak. 'But he had to be put down just before we moved here.'

'He was very old and got sick,' Georgie put in. 'Father said we shouldn't let him suffer.'

'That's quite right,' Charlotte said gently. 'But it doesn't make it any easier, does it?'

Ben smiled at her.

'Father promised to get Ben a bigger horse when we moved.'

'There's a horse fair at Horncastle. It's not until August, but that's only ten weeks or so away,' Charlotte said. 'Would you like me to have a word with your father? Tell him about it?'

'Would you?' Ben looked up eagerly.

'Of course.'

The car chugged up the drive and around the side of the house, coming to a halt in the yard.

The boys scrambled out.

'This way, Miss Charlotte. The stables are this way,' Georgie said excitedly. 'Look, Philip's got Midnight in the training ring.'

94

They walked through the yard lined with stables on either side to where, beyond it, was an area of open ground. A huge circle was fenced off. In the centre of the circle stood Philip, with a whip in his hand. Near the fence was a magnificent black stallion. Charlotte gasped in horror. The animal was sweating, his eyes wild and frightened. He was snorting and stamping his feet. Every so often he whinnied and reared up on his hind legs.

Philip approached the animal slowly, menace in every step. 'I'll teach you to obey me, if it's the last thing I do,' he yelled. The horse whinnied again and cantered away. But there was no escape from the circle and the young man, whip in hand at the ready, followed.

Appalled, Charlotte, Ben and Georgie watched as Philip raised his whip and lunged towards Midnight, beating him once, twice, three times on his flank.

'No – no, Philip. Not like that.' Lifting her skirt, Charlotte climbed the fence, threw her leg over the top and jumped down inside the ring. She had begun to run towards them when the horse turned towards his attacker and reared, his front hooves pedalling the air. He came down heavily, his left hoof catching Philip on the shoulder and knocking him to the ground.

Charlotte reached the horse and, unafraid, caught hold of the bridle and led him away to the side of the ring, throwing the reins over the top bar of the fence to tether him there. Then she ran back to the inert figure on the ground and fell to her knees beside him. Philip opened his eyes and his face twisted, with both pain and anger. 'See what you've done? Get away from me and mind your own business – ah!' His words ended in a cry of pain as he tried to raise himself from the ground.

'Lie still,' Charlotte commanded and began to feel around the young man's shoulder.

'I said, get away from me–'

'And I told you to lie still and let me help you. I think you've dislocated your shoulder.'

'Oho, a doctor are we now?' Despite the pain he could still raise a sneer.

A shadow fell across them and Charlotte glanced up to see Eddie Norton, the stable lad at the manor, standing there. 'You'd do well to listen to her, Master Philip. Miss Charlotte's clever like that. Knows about animals and bones and such. Not much of a jump to a human.' His face darkened as he added, 'At least – not in your case.'

'Why, you impudent young – ah!' Again, whatever Philip had been going to say was lost in a pain-ridden yelp.

'For goodness' sake, lie still,' Charlotte said sharply. 'Eddie – get something to use as a stretcher. We must get him to the house quickly.'

'Is he all right?' Georgie's voice, quavering with fright, called from the other side of the fence as Eddie hurried away. 'Ben's gone to fetch Papa.'

'He'll be fine,' Charlotte called back. 'Don't worry.'

'This is all your fault. If you hadn't come into the ring shouting your head off, he'd never have reared.'

'Nonsense,' Charlotte countered sharply. 'That's no way to train a horse. Cruelty will get you nowhere with any animal.'

'He needs to be broken.'

'But not like that.'

'What's happened?' Miles Thornton vaulted the fence with the agility of a man half his age and ran towards them.

'That horse is a vicious beast, Father. I want him shot.'

'No – no,' Charlotte cried in dismay. 'It was Philip's treatment of him, Mr Thornton. He whipped him. That's no way to break a young horse in. He's a magnificent animal–'

'I want him shot,' Philip repeated through clenched teeth.

'Never mind about that now. What about you? Are you hurt?'

'It's his shoulder. It's dislocated.'

'Thinks she's a bloody doctor,' Philip muttered then groaned in agony, his face white.

Eddie returned with an old door and set it down beside the injured young man. He went to Philip's head and bent as if to lift him on to it.

'Wait, Eddie. We should bind his arm to his side first. Any movement will be very painful. Here, we'll use my scarf.'

Charlotte unwound the cotton scarf from her neck. 'Just raise him gently.'

Though Philip cried out again, Charlotte managed to get the scarf beneath his shoulders and tie it across his chest, fastening his arm to his side.

'Now, lift him gently on to the door.'

97

'Let me,' Miles said, moving to his son's feet.

Eddie pushed his arm under Philip's shoulders whilst Charlotte supported his back as the three of them slid him on to the door.

'Father – look out,' Ben called. 'Midnight's pulled free.'

Startled, Charlotte, Miles and Eddie looked round. The horse had somehow pulled and pulled until the reins had slid off the fence.

'You carry him to the house. I'll see to Midnight.'

'Don't go anywhere near him, Miss Charlotte,' Miles said at once. 'I'll get the vet to come and put him down. I–'

'No, you will not!' Charlotte rounded on him, forgetting in her anger just to whom she was talking.

'I think,' Miles said stiffly, 'I can be allowed to make my own decision on that matter. For the moment, my son is my concern.' He bent and grasped the end of the door. At the opposite end, Eddie did the same.

'Lift,' Miles ordered.

As they carried Philip away, Charlotte moved slowly towards the horse. As she neared him, she spoke quietly and soothingly. At last she was able to grasp the bridle and lead him out of the ring. There was no one about now – they'd all gone up to the house – so she led the animal to the nearest empty stable, settled him as best she could and closed the door on him.

She paused a moment, watching him. He was calmer now, but there was still terror in his eyes.

'Poor old fellow,' she murmured. 'I'll not let

98

them hurt you.' Then she turned and made her way to the back door of the house.

Entering the kitchen, she found the servants in turmoil and Lily in floods of tears.

'Oh, Miss Charlotte. What's happened? Is he badly hurt?'

Despite her anxiety, Charlotte blinked in surprise. She glanced around. Cook's face was anxious, the little kitchen maid's fearful, but Lily's agitation was excessive. But it was Eddie's grim expression that startled Charlotte the most as he watched Lily's weeping and wailing.

'Calm down, girl,' Cook snapped at last. 'Miss Charlotte – tell us what happened. Please.'

Swiftly, she explained and then added, 'I should go upstairs and see how he is.'

'The master's telled me to fetch Dr Markham,' Eddie muttered.

Lily gasped and cried out. 'Then what are you waiting for?' She ran to him and dragged him by the arm towards the door. 'Go on, go on – fetch him.'

'I'm going,' the young man said morosely, his furious gaze still on Lily's face. 'But there's nowt wrong wi' him that Miss Charlotte couldn't put right in a jiffy.'

'Go *on*,' Lily cried again, pushing him out of the door.

'I'll go up,' Charlotte murmured and turned towards the door leading upstairs, amazed to find that Lily was following her.

'You stay here, girl,' Cook snapped.

'But–'

'No "buts".'

Crestfallen, Lily turned away, wiping the tears from her eyes. Charlotte glanced at the cook, but Mrs Beddows avoided meeting her gaze.

Thoughtfully, Charlotte made her way upstairs.

'Keep her away from me. I don't want her anywhere near me,' Philip spat as Charlotte entered the morning room where the young man lay on the couch. 'She's done quite enough damage for one day.'

'You brought it on yourself,' Charlotte said quietly. 'Like I said before, whipping a horse is no way to break him in. You'll make him wilder.'

'Father, just get her out of here, will you?'

Miles frowned. 'That's enough, Philip.' Now he could see his son was not seriously hurt, he would no longer tolerate the boy's rudeness to Charlotte. He turned towards Ben. 'Will you tell me what happened?'

For once Georgie was silent, standing white faced beside his father, his gaze on his brother lying on the couch.

'We were taking Miss Charlotte to see the horses. Phil was in the training ring with Midnight.' Ben paused and bit his lip. 'We stood by the rail to watch. The horse was–' again he paused briefly – 'very agitated. It was sweating and snorting and – and trying to get away from Phil.'

'That's a lie. It's a disobedient beast that needs disciplining,' Philip spat out, but his words ended in groan. He winced and closed his eyes.

'Phil went after him – with the whip. He hit him three times on his flank. Then – then–' The boy glanced at Charlotte with an apologetic look.

100

'Miss Charlotte shouted "no – no" and climbed over the fence. She was running towards them both when Midnight reared. His hoof caught Phil on the shoulder and he fell down.'

Georgie slipped his hand into Miles's. Tears filled his eyes and his voice trembled as he said, 'It wasn't Miss Charlotte's fault. It was Phil's. He shouldn't have hit Midnight, Papa.'

Philip opened his eyes again. 'It was all her fault. If she hadn't shouted–'

At that moment, Wilkins opened the door and ushered the doctor into the room. 'Dr Markham, sir.'

'Now, what have we here?' The portly, bewhiskered man's eyes twinkled through his spectacles. 'Nothing too serious, I trust. Ah,' he said, spying Philip on the sofa. 'This is the patient, I presume.'

Swiftly, Miles explained what had happened and the doctor examined the young man gently. 'Dislocated shoulder,' he pronounced. He glanced around the room and spotted Charlotte. 'Ah, the very person. Charlotte, if you'd assist me, we'll soon have–'

'I don't want her anywhere near me. Get – her – out – of – here.'

'My dear boy,' Dr Markham regarded him benignly over his spectacles, 'there is no one better to help me put your shoulder back in place than Miss Crawford, I can assure you. And unless you want a very uncomfortable half-hour ride in your father's motor car to the nearest hospital and a possible wait of anything up to an hour, then I suggest you let us help you.'

101

'Father – are you going to stand there and let these – these *yokels* pull me limb from limb?'

Before Miles could answer, Dr Markham laughed. 'Come now, my boy, that's a trifle harsh. Country folk we may be, but we know a thing or two when it comes to dislocated bones, now don't we, Charlotte? Now–' a note of firmness crept into the man's tone as he beckoned Charlotte to his side – 'this may hurt a bit...'

They heard Philip's scream down in the kitchens as between them the doctor and Charlotte clicked his dislocated shoulder back into place.

'Now – we need to bind it to keep it in place. See he takes two of these...' Dr Markham pulled a bottle of tablets from his bag and handed it to Miles – 'every four hours. That'll ease the pain. Rest and quiet for a day or two. I'll call in again.'

When the doctor had departed, Charlotte faced Miles. 'Mr Thornton, if you are seriously contemplating getting rid of Midnight, then let me have him. I'll buy him from you.'

Miles stared at her. 'You know someone who can tame him?'

Charlotte hid her smile. 'I do,' was all she said quietly.

'The damned animal needs putting down,' Philip muttered.

'Papa,' Georgie tugged on Miles's hand, 'don't have Midnight killed. He's not old and ill like Ben's pony was. Let Miss Charlotte have him. Please, Papa. Or–' his face brightened as another idea came to him – 'sell him at the horse fair.'

'The – the what?'

'The horse fair. Miss Charlotte told me about

it. She said you might be able to get a horse from there for Ben. You promised he could have another when we got settled in here.'

'And you can get me another. I don't want that devil,' Philip muttered.

'Where is this horse fair?' Miles asked.

'It's at Horncastle at the beginning of August,' Charlotte said.

Miles appeared to consider. 'I only bought Midnight recently,' he murmured. 'Perhaps I should sell him and get Philip something more – suitable.'

'I'd still like to buy Midnight from you. I'll give you whatever you paid for him.' She held out her right hand to him. After a moment's hesitation, Miles took it and she felt his firm, warm grasp.

'Very well,' he said. 'If you're sure.'

'Oh, I am. In fact, I'll take him home with me now.'

'Don't you have to ask your father first?' Now Miles was puzzled. The girl had seemed so down-trodden, so meek and subservient. And yet, here she was giving her word to buy the unbroken animal without even conferring with her father. And she'd taken charge over Philip, telling every-one – even him – what to do. And, it seemed, she'd been right about the dislocated shoulder too.

He was even more puzzled when she said quietly, 'Not on this occasion – no.'

Twelve

A week later, on the last day of May, Joe came to the farm office.

Charlotte was seated behind the desk and looked up as he entered. 'Good morning, Joe. Please sit down.' She waved towards the chair in front of the desk. They talked for a while about the farm.

'It'll be haymaking before we know it,' Charlotte said. 'And then harvest.'

'Aye, and talking of August time, there's something else I'd like to ask you, Miss Charlotte. Mr Thornton drove over yesterday to ask my advice about buying a couple of horses for his sons.' Joe smiled. 'To replace the one you brought back from there and another for the middle boy – Benjamin, is it?'

'That's right. But everyone calls him Ben.'

'He said you'd mentioned the horse fair at Horncastle in August. I was wondering if we could take Mr Thornton. I mean, you could look over the horses there and then...' His voice petered out.

Charlotte was thoughtful before she said, 'Can we do it without him guessing?'

'Would it really matter, miss, if he did find out?'

She sighed. 'My father...' she murmured and needed to say no more.

Joe's mouth tightened. 'It's high time you got

the credit, Miss Charlotte, for everything you do, if you'll forgive me saying so.'

Charlotte's smile was pensive. 'It's kind of you to say so, Joe, but you know that's not possible. There's only you and the Morgans who know the truth.' She sighed. 'And that's the way it's got to stay.'

'Miss Charlotte, it's 1926 for heaven's sake. You're living the life of a daughter in the Victorian age.' He bit back the words, 'And dressing like one too.'

'I can't see a way out, Joe. Unless I pack my bags and leave. And where would I go? I've no money of my own. No relatives. No–' There was a catch in her voice as she realized just what an isolated, lonely life she led. 'No friends.' Then she added swiftly, 'Apart from everyone around here, of course. And besides,' she added with wry amusement, 'who'd care for my father? Mary and Edward only stay here because of me. If I went, they'd go too. They've told me so.'

'I know that,' Joe said boldly. 'And my Peg only comes to help out here because of you, an' all. By heck, I'm opening me mouth and letting me tongue run away with itsen'. I don't mean no disrespect, miss, but all of us don't like to see you treated the way you are. And him hitting you last week at morning service, well, it riled us all.' He leaned forward. 'Don't think it wasn't noticed, 'cos it was. Does he often hit you, Miss Charlotte?'

'Not – often. Not now, anyway. Only when I anger him. His punishment when I was younger was to lock me in my room for hours on end. If it hadn't been for Mary and Edward...'

Joe's face was grim.

'Please, Joe, not a word to anyone. I've said more than I should. Promise me.'

Reluctantly, Joe nodded, hoping that his promise didn't include keeping secrets from his Peggy, because he had no intention of doing that. Not any more. Now she, too, worked at Buckthorn Farm occasionally, she was seeing for herself how things were.

'So,' Charlotte went on, briskly bringing them back to the topic that had caused the shared confidences, 'Mr Thornton and the Horncastle horse fair. I suggest you offer to go with him and just ask, casually, if he minds if I come along. He knows of my fondness for horses–' she grimaced comically, 'so I don't think he'll be surprised to see me amongst them. And, somehow, I will communicate to you which animals I think might be suitable. It's worth a try. I'd like to see Ben with a nice mount.' Her mouth tightened. 'But as for Philip, I'm not sure he deserves to be in charge of a horse. Still, perhaps I can find him a nice docile one.'

Joe laughed. 'There's nothing docile about that young man. Anyway, we can but try.'

June was a busy month for haymaking and all the farmers in the district helped each other not only with machinery and horses, but also with manpower. It was a time of the year that Charlotte loved, for it gave her an excuse to work alongside the farm labourers each day, spreading the cut grass out to dry and then, just before nightfall,

106

raking it into long rows down the fields.

Eddie Norton and two other workers from Home Farm, the farm attached to the manor, came to help at Buckthorn Farm and, in turn, the Warren family and old Matty went to work on Miles Thornton's fields. Even her father had not been able to stop Charlotte mixing with the workers on neighbouring farms at haymaking and, later, at harvest time. Her help was needed.

'The new master dun't know the first thing about farming, Joe,' Charlotte overheard Eddie say as she raked the cut grass into windrows alongside Peggy. 'But Master Thornton's such a nice feller. We all like him. And we know how lucky we are to've been kept on. And I'll tell you summat else an' all, that second son of his – Ben, is it? He'll mek a grand farmer one day. He listens and learns and he's been working out in the fields as good as any man.'

As they worked, Georgie and his three friends scampered about the field, playing.

'Now, Master Georgie,' Jackson warned, 'don't you go trampling down the grass before the mower comes, else it won't get cut proper.' He frowned at his own brother and the other two local lads. 'You should 'a known better, our Tommy. Don't go leading this little lad into bother. He dun't know country ways. Not yet.'

Georgie stood still and regarded Jackson solemnly. 'Why mustn't we trample it?'

Jackson leaned on the wide rake he was using and smiled at the boy, whose golden curls glinted in the sunlight.

'Because,' Jackson explained patiently, 'if the

107

grass is lying flat, the mower can't cut it. You go and watch it, Master Georgie, then you'll see what I mean. But don't get in the way of the cutter bar.'

The boys ran to where the mower was cutting the grass on the far side of the field, drawn by two of the farm's shires. A little later the boys returned and now, Charlotte noticed, they were skirting carefully round the uncut grass. The workers had all been at Buckthorn Farm for several days and today, by mid afternoon, they were almost finished here. Charlotte stood up and eased her aching back. She glanced across the flat fields and smiled with satisfaction at the long rows of cut grass. Then, suddenly, she felt a little hand creep into hers.

'Are you tired, Miss Charlotte?' Georgie asked.

'A little. We all work very hard at this time of the year. And soon it will be the corn harvest. That's an even busier time.'

The boy's face fell.

'Why do you ask?'

'I – I just wondered if we could go to the beach. You – you did promise to take me.'

Charlotte's smile broadened 'So I did. Then we'll go.'

'Now?'

'Yes, now. But first, we must ask Eddie to take a message to your father that–'

'Papa's over there. We can ask him.' And before she could say another word, he was capering across the field towards his father, but still, she noticed with a smile, avoiding the grass that was yet to be cut. Georgie was hopping up and down excitedly in front of Miles as Charlotte walked towards them.

'Please may I go, Papa? Miss Charlotte will bring me home before bedtime.'

Miles looked up. 'I'm sure Miss Charlotte's tired. Another day perhaps...'

'I don't mind. Any excuse to go to the shore.'

'Then of course he may go with you.' He paused and she felt his brown gaze upon her. 'Would you mind if I came too?'

'Of course not. And if we can find a sack, we can collect samphire.'

'Samphire? What's that?'

Charlotte laughed. 'Poor man's asparagus. It grows on the saltmarsh, even where the tide covers it. You should try it.'

Miles laughed. 'I doubt Mrs Beddows would know how to cook it. You do cook it, I take it?'

She nodded. 'I'll get Mary to send you the recipe.' Moments later, when they'd collected a sack, the three walked along the lane towards the sea.

'Oh look, Papa. The sea!' The boy stood on top of the bank, his eyes wide in wonder as he took in the vast expanse of marshland, mudflats, sand and the North Sea beyond.

'Now,' Charlotte said, bending down, 'you must never come here on your own, Georgie. The tides can be very treacherous. It's coming in now and you see how the water is swirling round and forming creeks–'

'What's a creek?'

Charlotte pointed. 'There, that water that looks like a pond just now, but watch, you see the strip of marshland beyond it – between it and the sea?'

'Yes.'

'Now see how the water starts to cover the land?'

They watched for several minutes until the piece of marsh disappeared beneath the encroaching waves and the creek became one with the sea.

'I think I understand what you mean, Miss Charlotte,' Miles said. 'You see, Georgie, if you'd been standing on that bit of marsh and the sea had come swirling in around you, perhaps by the time you'd realized you were getting cut off, the water in the creek would have been too deep for you to get across. Do you understand?'

The boy nodded solemnly.

'I've always been told that if you walk that way,' Charlotte gestured to the left, 'towards the north, you can beat the water coming in from the right, but it'd be safer not to risk it. I never go beyond the creeks when the tide's coming in. Now, will you remember what I've said, Georgie?'

'Do Tommy and the others know?'

'All the children living here are told as soon as they're old enough to understand. And another thing–' she turned and pointed inland – 'you see that windmill over there? That's Webster's Mill. You can see it from the marsh, but as soon as it disappears from view we mark our path across the mudflats with thakking pegs, so that when the tide starts to come in you can see your way back. We won't need to do that today, but you will remember what I've said, won't you? And you must be wary of sea frets, too. A sea mist. They roll in very quickly sometimes.'

'I'll tell Ben – and Phil,' Georgie promised solemnly.

'What on earth is a thakking peg?' Miles asked, amused.

'It's something that thatchers use to hold the thatch in place whilst they're working.'

'Ah.' Miles chuckled. 'Maybe one day I'll learn all these Lincolnshire words.'

'Now can we collect samphire?' Georgie demanded.

For the next hour or so, until the sun began to sink behind the sandbank, streaking the sky with red and gold and the tide crept nearer, the three of them picked the fleshy-leafed plant to carry back to the farm. As they left, they paused at the top of the bank to look back across the marsh, listening to the soft sound of the sea.

'In a month or so,' Charlotte told Georgie, 'the marsh will be covered with lilac sea lavender, and later yellow and mauve sea asters. There are all sort of plants that grow on the marsh. It's really very pretty. I'll bring you again. We'll look for crabs or just watch the birds feeding on the mud-flats when the tide's out. That's if–' she paused and glanced at Miles – 'your father doesn't mind.'

'Any time, Miss Charlotte.' She heard his low chuckle. 'Just so long as I can come too.'

'We wondered where you were, Miss Charlotte,' Mary greeted them at the back door. 'Good evening, sir – Master Georgie. Would you care for something to drink before you go home? A nice glass of my elderflower wine, perhaps? And lemonade for Master Georgie?'

'That'd be very nice,' Miles said, stepping over the threshold.

'Mrs Morgan,' Georgie piped up, 'we've collected some samphire. Will you cook it for us?'

'I will indeed, Master Georgie. I'll show you what to do and then you can tell Mrs Beddows. It's very easy, but she might not have heard of it, not being from these parts. First you wash it well, then boil or steam it for about ten minutes. Serve it with a knob of butter and season it with black pepper and vinegar. Now, Master Georgie, can you remember that?'

Solemnly, Georgie nodded whilst Miles looked on with an amused smile.

'It goes nicely with fish or meat,' Mary went on. 'And you can pickle it, too, so you've got supplies through the winter.'

It was a very tired, but happy little boy who travelled home in the pony and trap driven by Edward, tightly clutching the tureen of samphire Mary had shown him how to cook.

Thirteen

August arrived and, with it, Georgie's excitement reached fever pitch at the anticipated trip to the horse fair.

It was arranged that Mr Thornton, his two younger sons, Joe and Charlotte should all travel to Horncastle in Mr Thornton's motor car.

'Would you like to go on the Sunday?' Charlotte asked Miles. 'A lot of the dealers and their horses start arriving immediately after Bank Holiday Monday. There'll have been some buying and selling even in that first week, but the following Sunday is what they call show day and the fair starts in earnest on Monday, the ninth. The boys would love it.'

'You've been before?' There was a surprised note in his tone.

'Joe's father, Harry Warren, used to take me. I was only ten the first time I went.' She bit her lip, resisting the urge to confide in him that trips to the horse fair had been the only outings she'd ever known, except for the occasional visit to the optician in Lincoln. For some reason, her father had never stopped her going to the annual fair. No doubt it had been because it all added to her farming knowledge.

So the trip was arranged for the second Sunday in August, with another visit to buy two horses the next day.

'A lot more arrive then and the best 'osses are snapped up quickly,' Joe explained, winking at Georgie. 'So we need to go again.'

He was rewarded by a beaming smile from the excited little boy.

'I hope you don't mind squashing in the back seat with the two boys, Miss Charlotte.' Miles Thornton smiled as he held open the car door for her.

'Of course not.' She'd been looking forward to this day ever since it had been suggested and her heart lifted even further when she saw that Philip was not joining the outing. There was only one thing that might prove difficult. She was worried that Georgie – and possibly Ben too – would stay with her and she wouldn't have the chance to look over the horses and indicate her choices to Joe. But, unwittingly, Miles came to her rescue. 'If you need to go off on personal matters, Miss Charlotte, just say so. We don't want to spoil your plans.'

But then Charlotte thought that having the two boys alongside her might be a good idea. Perhaps she could glean which animals took Ben's eye, since one of them was to be for him. She would have plenty of time that evening to talk to Joe before their buying trip the next day. She'd already primed Joe that he should ask Miles how much he wanted to pay. As they travelled, she heard snatches of the conversation from the front seats and knew they were discussing the details.

'I thought it'd be an auction,' she heard Miles say. 'But Miss Charlotte mentioned "dealing". What actually happens?'

'The fair's not so big now as it used to be. Years ago, the town was packed, but it's still a good place to buy a horse; that's if you watch out for the scams.'

'Scams?'

'Oh aye, not all dealers are honest, Mr Thornton, but don't you worry, we can usually spot 'em. When me dad first brought me here,' Joe went on, 'there used to be a couple of fellers held auctions in the yard of the Reindeer and used the paddock to put their 'osses through their paces. We allus went to them. Honest as the day is long, they were. They're not there now, more's the pity, 'cos I'm talking twenty years or more ago. Still, we'll have a good look around for you.'

Charlotte caught her breath, wanting to say, 'Don't say "we", Joe.'

Innocently, Georgie came to her rescue by interrupting. 'Ben doesn't mind what colour 'oss he has. But he doesn't want a big one like Midnight, do you, Ben?'

Charlotte felt the urge to giggle at Georgie copying Joe's Lincolnshire dialect, but Ben, seeming not to notice, shuddered and shook his head. 'No – nor one so wild.' He glanced sideways at Charlotte. 'Where's Midnight now, Miss Charlotte?'

'Still in our stables at Buckthorn Farm. He's being schooled,' she added. It was the truth, but not the whole truth. The horse had indeed been broken in – and was making good progress – by Charlotte herself with old Matty's help. But again, this was one of the secrets of Buckthorn Farm. In the summer evenings, when all but perhaps Joe had left work, Charlotte worked with the horse.

Sunday was, as Charlotte had said, show day. Stalls had been set up in the inn yards in readiness for the days ahead and dealers were already showing off their horses, running them up and down the street or on the nearest piece of grass, hoping to secure early interest in their animals.

'Oh look – do look!' Georgie exclaimed as Miles parked the car and they all scrambled out. 'I've never seen so many horses. How are you ever going to choose one, Ben? You'll have to come with us, Miss Charlotte, and help us.'

Charlotte and Joe exchanged a swift glance. It couldn't have worked out better. She held out her hand to him. 'Come, let's see if we can find a horse Ben might like.'

They wandered through the Bull Ring, where the main concentration of business would be, but the dealing spilled over into the surrounding streets and inn yards. There were more public houses than normal for the size of the town, but these stabled the horses and provided accommodation, food and drink for the dealers and buyers. August was a busy month and usually a profitable one for the town even though, as Joe had said, the heyday of the fair had been years earlier. But there was still much business to be done and many of the local residents relied on the fair. Even the surrounding farms grew oats especially to provide feed for the horses at this time of the year.

They all enjoyed the day; even Ben forgot to be a sedate twelve-year-old and ran around excitedly with Georgie.

'Mind where you're stepping,' Joe warned them both. 'I dun't reckon your Pa'd like 'oss muck in his car.'

'Have you seen anything you like?' Charlotte asked Ben. 'Because if you have, Joe could have a word with the owner.'

'He likes them all!' Georgie piped up before his brother could answer. They laughed and Miles said, 'I don't think I could afford to buy *all* of them, Georgie.'

'Couldn't you, Papa?' the young boy asked innocently. Then, suddenly, his attention was caught by the sound of music. 'What's that?'

'That'll be the Methodists,' Joe said. 'They hold an open-air service in the Bull Ring after the normal evening service. They have speakers and singers and–'

Georgie caught hold of Charlotte's hand and began to drag her along the street towards the sound. 'Let's go and listen.'

Laughingly, they all followed his lead.

Charlotte couldn't remember such a perfect day and it was almost dark by the time Miles left them at the gateway to Buckthorn Farm, promising, 'We'll be here bright and early in the morning.' He nodded to the back seat, where Georgie had been asleep against Charlotte's shoulder. 'If we can get Georgie to wake up, that is.'

The following day, Charlotte and Joe were waiting by the gate, almost as if they'd never left it, when the car bowled into view. Georgie was wide awake bouncing up and down on the back seat. 'Are we going to deal, Joe, or go to an auction?'

'We might do both, Master Georgie. It depends on what we see.'

They wandered through the streets that were even more crowded than the day before. There were men in suits and bowler hats or caps, but few women.

'Joe – the one over there.' Charlotte touched his arm and whispered. 'The bay.'

'Master Ben,' Joe said at once, taking the hint. 'Let's go and have a look at this one.' As the five of them wove their way through the throng, Georgie asked, 'Is this one for Ben or Phil? Isn't it a lovely colour?'

'He is,' Charlotte said and, forgetting for a moment to hide her interest, she stepped forward and ran her hand over the horse's back. Then she patted his nose and murmured soothingly, 'Now, feller, now then.'

The dark-haired man holding the reins greeted her, 'Hello, Miss Crawford. Nice to see you again. Looking for a mount for yarsen, a' ya?'

Charlotte smiled and blushed. Her secret could be out any minute. 'Not today, Ned, but Mr Thornton here is looking for two horses for his sons.' She turned quickly before the man could say more. 'Joe – what do you think?'

Joe was pretending to examine the animal closely, but he knew that Miss Charlotte approved of this horse, otherwise she would already have moved away.

'He looks all right,' Joe said carefully.

'He's a good trotter,' the man said. 'Like to see?'

Joe nodded and Charlotte stepped back as Ned ran with the horse up and down the short stretch of available street.

Charlotte and Joe exchanged a glance and, when everyone else was watching the horse, she gave Joe a slight nod. As the dealer slowed the animal to a walk and came back to them, Joe said, 'Are you putting him through the auction?'

'Nah,' Ned said dismissively. 'I know there's not the dealing done in the streets now like there used to be.' He sniffed. 'More's the pity, I reckon.

But I like to do me own selling, see who me 'osses are going to. And strike a fair bargain.'

'How much?' Joe asked bluntly.

'Sixteen guineas.' The man held out his hand as if to strike a deal, but Joe only grinned. 'Now, Ned, you know you'll never get that for this 'oss. Not these days, you won't. 'Tis not like the old days. Prices have gone down since the war.'

Ned laughed, took off his cap, scratched his head and then replaced it. 'Fourteen, then; I can't go no lower, Joe. Not even for you.'

Joe pretended to consider and then slowly shook his head again.

'Papa – Papa.' Georgie tugged at his father's sleeve. 'Can't you buy him? Ben likes this one.'

'Shush, Georgie. Leave it to Joe,' Miles whispered.

But Joe seemed lost and could do no other than look to Charlotte. With an inward sigh, she was obliged to take the risk. 'Twelve guineas, Ned,' she said firmly. 'You know that's a fair price.'

The man grinned, spat on his hand and held it out to her. 'I'll not argue with a lady. 'Specially not you, Miss Crawford. I could never fool you, now, could I?'

Charlotte took his hand and the deal was made.

Leaving Joe to make the arrangements, the others walked away.

'Ugh, he spat on his hand, Miss Charlotte. And you shook it.'

'That's the way Ned makes his deals, Georgie. It means he gives his promise to sell the horse to us. Even if he got a better offer, he won't break his word. That horse is Ben's now.'

After a few moments Joe caught them up. 'Ned says there's an auction in one of the inn yards at two o'clock. He reckons we might find a good mount there for Master Philip.'

Charlotte glanced at Miles to find him watching her. 'Is that all right?' she asked him.

'Whatever you say, Miss Charlotte.' He smiled and she had the uncomfortable feeling that he was beginning to guess just exactly who was choosing the horses – and striking the deals.

When the auction began, Georgie got very excited. 'I can't see, I can't see. I want to see when our horse comes up.'

They'd already viewed all the horses due to go through the auction and had picked out one they liked for Philip. A grey, docile-looking animal.

'Sh,' Charlotte whispered, hiding her laughter. 'You mustn't say which one you like.'

He turned his innocent blue eyes on her. 'Why?'

'Because,' she explained softly, 'it lets other people know the one you're interested in and it might make someone bid against your father and drive the price up. You don't want your papa to have to pay more than he needs to, do you?'

Georgie shook his head and pressed his lips together as if to stop himself speaking. Then unable to help himself he said, 'But I still want to see.'

'All right, then. I'll lift you on to the wall, but you mustn't say anything or wave your hands because the auctioneer might think you're making a bid.'

120

Charlotte sat on the wall beside Georgie and Ben climbed up beside her. Miles and Joe were standing close by. Miles, under Joe's guidance, was to do the bidding. The two boys were lost in the proceedings, whispering every now and again to Charlotte, asking her questions. Then Georgie wriggled with excitement and squeezed Charlotte's hand. 'This is Phil's.'

The horse was paraded in front of the crowd and the bidding began. As Miles watched and waited but made no move, Georgie became agitated.

'It's all right,' she murmured to the boys. 'Just wait and see.'

The bidding slowed and two of the men, who'd been making bids, shook their heads. Now there was only one man left who'd made the last bid. The auctioneer raised his gavel, his gaze travelling around the faces in front of him. Georgie, his eyes wide and fearful, drew in a deep breath, just as, close by, they heard Joe mutter, 'Now, sir. Raise your hand...' And Miles's hand shot high in the air. The gavel was lowered as the auctioneer nodded towards Miles in acknowledgement. Now bidding between Miles and the other man continued backwards and forwards until, at last, the other man shook his head. The gavel fell and Joe turned with a wide grin to Georgie and Ben. 'And he's a fine mount, but gentle. I think he'll suit your brother.'

Ben nodded and Georgie clapped his hands in glee. 'What shall we call him, Ben?'

'I don't know. Maybe he's got a name already – like Ned said mine's called Blaze. Besides, Phil should decide.'

'It's Prince,' Charlotte said, quite forgetting in the excitement, that she was not supposed to know. But having looked around at all the horses together, the boys didn't seem to notice her slip and question how she came to know the name of the horse.

Only Miles glanced over his shoulder and regarded her curiously yet again.

'I just hope Philip's going to take better care of him than he did of Midnight,' Charlotte said later to Joe, as they waved the family off outside Buckthorn Farm.

'I had a word with the master. He's going make sure he does.'

'Mm.' Charlotte was doubtful. Miles couldn't supervise his eldest son every minute of the day. There were bound to be times when the young man was riding alone, and what would happen then?

Fourteen

Two days after the horse fair, Charlotte took Midnight to the beach further north to avoid the treacherous marsh. It was the first time she'd ridden him any distance from the farm. Gentle patience coupled with a firm hand had earned the animal's trust. Old Matty had always been on hand to offer his advice, but he'd hardly been needed. He'd merely nodded his approval. It had been a few weeks before she could put a saddle on the horse's back and another week or so before he would let her ride him.

'You've worked wonders with that 'oss, miss,' Joe marvelled. 'And in such a short time an' all. It takes some o' them so-called experts months sometimes.'

Charlotte smiled and glowed inwardly at his praise as she stroked Midnight's face. 'He's a beautiful animal. All he needed was to be treated with kindness and he responded. That's all, Joe.'

She made it sound so simple, but all Joe could think was that it was a pity she didn't receive that same kindness from a certain person. But he held his tongue.

Now Charlotte felt confident enough to take Midnight to the sea. 'A good canter along the beach will do him the world of good. He's a big horse and could do with the exercise.' And it would do her good, too, she couldn't help thinking, to get away from the gloomy house.

'Want me to come with you, Miss Charlotte?'

'I'll be fine, Joe.'

He nodded. 'If you say so, miss, but if you're not back in – let's say three hours – I'll come looking for you. I know where you're going.'

She smiled down at him from her lofty seat on the horse's back, but she was touched by the man's concern. At walking pace, she and Midnight left the stable yard, but she could feel Joe's anxious eyes watching her a long way into the distance.

She turned north, along the lanes, until she came to the area near the seaside town's golf course where there was no marsh between the sea bank and the beach. The stretch of hard sand left by the receding tide was firm enough for the horse to feel surefooted. As she urged him up the sand hill and on to the beach, Midnight whinnied, unused to the softness beneath his hooves. But she soothed him gently and, trusting her, he obeyed her commands. Gaining the top of the rise, Charlotte lifted her face to the sea breeze and breathed in deeply. How she loved the sea! She loved it in all its moods. Calm, like today, when the waves seemed almost too lazy to lap the shoreline, or ferocious, when the gales whipped the waves into a raging frenzy, crashing on to the beach in fury. But she loved it best when its mood was somewhere between the two extremes; when the waters seemed playful, the waves bowling to the shore, trying to catch anyone unawares who dared to step too close.

Charlotte encouraged Midnight down the slope. When they gained the firmer sand near the water's edge, she urged him into a brisk trot, then a canter and, finally, a gallop.

Breathless but exhilarated she reined the horse in and slowed him to a walk again.

She saw three horses in the distance coming towards her. As they drew nearer, she could see the little figure on the smallest mount, waving excitedly. Georgie, she thought, and then recognized Ben and Miles Thornton alongside him.

'Did you see, Miss Charlotte? Did you see me riding Gypsy?'

Charlotte laughed, her face pink from the fresh air. 'I did indeed, Georgie. And very well you ride, too. Good afternoon, Mr Thornton – Ben.'

They were staring at her, but both of them touched their caps with their riding crops, which Charlotte fervently hoped were more for show than use.

'You're not wearing your spectacles,' Georgie said suddenly.

'Now, son, don't make personal remarks,' his father rebuked gently. 'It's not gentlemanly.' But the young boy only grinned.

'Then is it gentlemanly, Papa, to tell her she looks so much prettier without them?'

'Well...'

'I take it as a lovely compliment,' Charlotte put in swiftly to save them any further embarrassment. 'Thank you.' She forbore to say that this was the only time she was sure her father wouldn't find out that she'd taken them off. She hoped fervently that the little chatterbox would not let her secret slip out.

'I say,' Ben said, 'I've just realized. You're riding Midnight. Father – she's riding Phil's horse.'

'So I see,' Miles said quietly. 'But it's no longer Philip's horse. It's Miss Charlotte's.'

'Except that you haven't let me pay you for it yet.' She laughed, then turned to ask Ben, 'How are you getting along with Blaze?'

She turned Midnight round and they began to walk alongside each other back the way Charlotte had come.

'He's great,' Ben said.

'And the horse you got for Philip?' She wanted to ask if the young man was treating the animal kindly. She hesitated and bit her lip. But Georgie came to her rescue.

'He's being good with him, Miss Charlotte,' he giggled, 'but he calls him an old nag and doesn't ride him much. He wanted Ben's horse instead, but Papa said no.'

'He's decided he wants a motorcycle or a car,' Miles put in. 'But I shall hold out against that as long as I can. I don't think he'd be safe with either.'

They rode together companionably until they came to the end of the short lane where Charlotte turned for home.

'I must get back or Joe will be worried. This is the first time I've brought Midnight away from the farm.' She leaned forward and patted his neck. 'But he's done very well, haven't you, old feller?'

Having bade them goodbye, Charlotte rode towards Buckthorn Farm, unaware of Miles's thoughtful gaze following her.

'But she *was* prettier without her glasses,' Georgie said to no one in particular.

The wheat was ready for cutting and the extra hands arrived at Buckthorn Farm. Mary and Peggy had been baking for a week to provide food for the workers, but on the days when the corn was cut even they went out into the fields to help put the sheaves into stooks. Then, when all the fields at Buckthorn Farm had been cut, everyone moved on to the other farms to help out where needed.

On the following Monday morning, Joe knocked on the door of Charlotte's office and then poked his head round it. 'Could I have a word, miss?'

She smiled a welcome and gestured towards the chair he always sat in.

'It's about Dan Bailey at Purslane Farm, Miss Charlotte. He's not well again and he'll be struggling to get his harvest in. I was wondering if you'd mind us helping him out. A bit more than usual, I mean.'

'Of course not, Joe. Have you told Mr Thornton?'

Joe shrugged. 'I don't like to. It'd seem like telling tales. I'm not one to kick a man when he's down. Dan Bailey's a good man. He's just hit a bad patch of illness and his farm's suffering, that's all.'

Charlotte smiled. 'I'll let Mr Thornton know we'll all be helping out there now that we've finished here. He needn't know it's any different from normal.'

'We'll need the threshing tackle from Home Farm,' Joe warned. 'Dan's let his gear get into bad repair, so his farmhand, Jim, was telling me in the pub last night.'

Home Farm had its own traction engine and threshing drum that the estate's tenant farmers had the use of if they needed them. Buckthorn Farm, too, had always hired the gear but Dan Bailey, although a tenant of the estate, had his own. Until now, it seemed.

'And can me and the lads lend a hand with his threshing through the winter? We're used to the squire's engine.'

'Of course. We'll all help whenever it's needed. Just one thing, Joe,' she added as he got up to leave. 'Don't forget to save me some of the last

127

sheaf of wheat from our fields when it's brought to the stack yard. I must make a corn dolly for the Harvest Supper as usual.'

Joe nodded, unable to speak for the lump in his throat. This poor lass, he was thinking. Ever since she'd learned how to make a corn dolly as a little girl, she'd made one to be carried to the Harvest Supper celebrations at the manor. The irony of it was that the girl had never been allowed to join in the festivities.

Her father had seen to that!

Harvest time in the rural area around Ravensfleet had always been a big celebration. Almost as big as Christmas. Until recently, when the largest landowner in the district, Mr Davenport of Ravensfleet Manor, had fallen ill and died, the festivities had always been held in one of his huge barns and people had travelled for miles to attend the Harvest Supper. Farmers and labourers mingled freely, forgetting, for one night, their 'place'. Landowner served his tenants and, in turn, tenant farmers served their workers. All the workers on Buckthorn Farm attended, even though they were not part of the Ravensfleet Estate, for Osbert Crawford owned his farm. But Osbert himself never joined in the revelry.

Only Charlotte Crawford had never been allowed to attend a Harvest Supper.

'It'll be different this year.' Mary nodded sagely to Peggy. 'You'll see, that owd beezum'll go to the manor this year. You mark my words.'

'Thing is,' Peggy remarked thoughtfully, 'does Mr Thornton know what's expected of him? I mean, it's obvious to us – me 'n Joe – that he's new to this game. He's always asking my Joe for advice.'

'Is he?'

The two women exchanged a look of understanding, but it was Mary, greatly daring, who murmured softly so that only Peggy might hear. 'And your Joe asks Miss Charlotte, I suppose?'

Peggy nodded, her mouth a tight line. 'But Mr Thornton dun't know that.'

'Of course not,' Mary said on a sigh. There was a pause before she added, 'And is Joe going to tell him?'

Peggy sighed. 'I expect he'll have to be the one to say summat. About what's expected of him as regards the harvest celebrations. We can't expect Miss Charlotte to do it.' Again there was a hard edge to her tone as she added, 'Seein' as the poor lass never even gets the chance to go.'

Fifteen

The only place where Charlotte did have some say in the celebrations for a harvest safely gathered in was in Sunday school. And Cuthbert Iveson also relied upon her to explain to him what was expected of him in the church services, this being his first year.

'I don't know what I'd do without you, Miss Crawford. Your advice ever since I came here has been an enormous help to me. And your work with the children – well – I've never seen anyone

129

so universally loved by the little ones.'

Charlotte blushed under the unexpected compliment. 'Well, I love them all dearly,' she said and added impishly, 'even the naughty ones.'

Cuthbert smiled too. 'And there are certainly one or two of those in your class. But you do seem to have a wonderful way of handling them. I hear you have an amazing affinity with animals, too. It must be a gift.'

She blinked behind her spectacles. 'I – I'd never thought of it like that.'

'Then I think you should,' Cuthbert said solemnly. 'It's not something given to everyone.'

He paused and then added. 'You're well liked in the community. Have you – I mean – would you ever consider becoming–' he paused again and ran his tongue nervously round his lips – 'more involved with parish work.'

Suddenly Charlotte felt uncomfortable. How could she be involved in church work more than she already was, unless...? She forced a laugh and hoped he wouldn't notice the blush creeping up her face. 'I'm sorry, Mr Iveson, but I really couldn't. My father would never allow it.'

There, she thought, that should put a stop to what ever he might have been about to say.

'But what am I going to say to Mr Thornton, Peg?' Joe asked his wife worriedly. 'You've got to spend a lot of money throwing a party for a lot of people you don't even know?'

Peggy laughed at Joe's worried expression. 'I'm sure – from what you've told me about the new squire – that he'd be more than willing to do it.

130

It'll be a way for him to meet all his tenants in a friendly atmosphere and to get to know a lot of the other landowners and farmers around here, too.'

Joe wasn't so sure. 'Don't forget half the folk from the village come an' all.'

'I hadn't forgotten. But they're all part of this community. They may not actually work on the land themselves, but they're involved. Where would the greengrocer be without his supply of fresh vegetables straight off the land? Where would all the little shops be without the custom of all the farm workers and their families? I don't think you need worry about Mr Thornton, Joe. But,' she added, putting her head on one side and smiling mischievously at him, 'you could always get Miss Charlotte to speak to him herself.'

Joe shook his head vehemently. 'Oh no. Any advice Mr Thornton asks for has to seem to come from me. She made that quite clear at the horse fair.' He chuckled. 'You should have seen us. Never knew I could be so – what's the word? – furtive.'

'Well, well, I shall have to watch you, Joe Warren.'

'It's only to protect Miss Charlotte, love. I'm an honest sort of bloke most of the time. But I wouldn't want to bring more trouble on her head, poor lass.'

When he'd finished work that evening, Joe walked the mile or so to the manor. It was growing dusk when he reached the back door. He'd already raised his hand to knock, when he heard a scuffling in one of the outhouses nearby. He paused, listening. Then he heard girlish laughter. He stiffened. *That's our Lily's laugh*, he thought. *I'd know it anywhere*. He'd already turned, ready to stride towards the outhouse, when the girl herself appeared, straightening her apron and smoothing her hair. At the sight of her father, even through the gloom, her eyes widened and colour suffused her face.

'Dad! What are you doing here?'

'I might ask you the same question, girl.' He nodded to the door behind her. 'What are you up to in there? One of the farm lads, is it? If it's young Eddie Norton, I'll–' He took a step forward.

'No, Dad. No, it isn't,' Lily said quickly, linking her arm through his and urging him away from the outhouse and towards the back door leading into the kitchen.

'But I heard you laughing. There's someone in there.'

Lily laughed, still a little nervously, Joe thought. 'It's – it's only the farm cat. She's got some kittens. I – I was playing with them, that's all.'

Joe's eyes narrowed. He didn't like to think that his daughter would lie to him, but somehow he couldn't quite believe her. When he said nothing, Lily asked again, 'What are you doing here?'

'I've come to see the master. Is he in?'

'I'll see. But it's almost dinner time.'

'Dinner?'

'Oh aye, we're posh here, Dad. Dinner's in the evening, not midday.'

Joe grinned ruefully. 'Aye, well, 'tis tea or supper in our house, now, ain't it? And I'm ready for mine. But I need to see Mr Thornton and I can't come in the day.'

He didn't need to explain to his daughter what would happen if Osbert Crawford found out he'd been visiting the manor in working hours.

'I'll see if he's free, Dad. Come on in...' She skirted round him, opened the back door and held it for him to enter.

Just before the door closed behind him, Joe heard the squeak of the door across the yard. That's no cat, he thought grimly. He said no more for the moment, but he'd tell Peg about what he'd heard. Lily was of age, but she was still his little girl. However, maybe such matters were best spoken of between mother and daughter.

A few minutes later he was standing in Mr Thornton's study and the man was leading him to a chair by the fire and bidding him to sit down. It was a courtesy that was never extended to him on the rare occasions he saw Osbert, though Charlotte always treated him with this same respect.

'A drink, Joe? You've no doubt finished for the day?'

'Aye, well, I have an' I haven't, Mr Thornton.' He chuckled. 'I suppose I'm a bit like our local bobby. I'm never really off-duty.'

'You're a good man, Joe.' Miles wrinkled his forehead. 'D'you think I should employ a foreman here? Obviously, my predecessor didn't find it necessary, as most of the land is worked by the tenant farmers, but – just sometimes – I feel a bit at a loss to know what to do, especially around Home Farm which I'm *supposed* to manage.' He grinned ruefully. 'As I think you know by the number of occasions on which I've sought your advice.'

Gently, Joe said, 'Well, the old squire's family had lived here a long time. So he was brought up to it.'

'Mm,' Miles said thoughtfully and Joe put in, 'But I'm sure we – that is, Mr Crawford – would always be willing to help you out.'

Miles nodded. 'He's said as much, but...' He stopped and held Joe's gaze steadily. 'Is it *really* Mr Crawford who runs Buckthorn Farm?' Joe held his breath, fearing the end to the question. 'Or you?'

Joe breathed again and smiled lopsidedly. 'Well, without wanting to sound conceited, Mr Thornton, I suppose it's me. Though I always ask for advice when I need it,' he added, choosing his words carefully.

'Mm.' The other man was still thoughtful. 'You took over the position from your late father, didn't you?'

Now Joe was on more comfortable ground. 'That's right, sir. I was born in the cottage where we still live.'

'So, he taught you everything you know, eh?'

Again, Joe was cautious. 'Something like that, sir.'

Miles crossed the room to the sideboard, poured generous measures of whisky into two glasses and brought them back to the fire. Handing one to Joe, he sat down opposite him.

'Now, what is it you've come to see me about?'

'I'm not keeping you from your – dinner, sir, am I?'

'No, no. Another half an hour or so yet. We dine a little earlier, perhaps, than most households. I like all the family to be present and Georgie is only young. You have a young son too, I believe. He and Georgie have become friends. Young Tommy often comes to play here.'

'Does he?' Joe couldn't hide his surprise. 'I hope he's no trouble.'

'Good heavens, no. My boys are free to make their own friends and anyone they choose is always welcome here.'

There was a moment's pause before Joe began, haltingly, to explain the reason for his visit. 'Except for the past two years, sir, when old Mr Davenport was too ill, it's always been the tradition that the squire – and that's really what you're thought of, living at the manor – has held the harvest supper in the big barn at the back of the house.'

'Really?' Miles's eyes lit up. 'That sounds a splendid idea. What do I have to do?'

Joe breathed a silent sigh of relief. He hadn't expected it to be so easy. The two men spent the next half-hour happily discussing plans for the festivities. As the gong sounded, Joe said, 'I should be going and let you get to your dinner, sir.' They both stood up as Miles said, 'Won't you stay and eat with us?'

'That's very kind of you, sir.' Joe was touched by the man's magnanimity. 'But Peg – my wife – will have my supper all ready and waiting.'

'Of course.' Miles held out his hand. 'Thank you so much for coming to see me. We must talk again. I'll be very grateful for your guidance.

135

Perhaps I could see Miss Charlotte, too–'

'Oh no, sir,' Joe said swiftly. 'Miss Charlotte isn't allowed to attend the harvest supper.'

'Isn't *allowed?*'

The two men stared at each other, both realizing that perhaps they had said – or implied – too much already.

'Good night, sir. I'll see mesen out the back way.'

Joe almost hurried from the room, still afraid that Miles Thornton would voice the question that was in his eyes.

Sixteen

The preparations for the harvest supper were well underway by the day that Miles rode over on horseback to Buckthorn Farm to invite Osbert and his daughter to attend. All the sheaves of wheat had stood in the fields to dry for three weeks and then had been brought to the stack yard. Threshing would go on through the winter months, a little at a time on each farm in turn, but now it was time to think of celebrating a harvest safely gathered in.

'I understand it's a tradition that the squire should host the harvest supper in the big barn at the manor.'

'Huh!' Osbert grunted. 'A waste of good money, if you ask me. We never go.'

'But I'd very much like you and Miss Charlotte

to come this year. I believe all your workers attend.'

'Aye, they do,' Osbert said bitterly. 'And a fat lot of use they are for work the next day after all that free beer.'

Miles sighed, thinking the man had a very Scrooge-like attitude, even though it wasn't Christmas. But maybe he had the same outlook on those festivities, too. 'Well, I'm sorry you feel that way,' he began, but, suddenly, Osbert smiled.

'Your sons will all be there, I take it?'

'I hope so.'

'Hmm.' There was a pause before Osbert said, 'In that case, I'll be glad to come.'

'And Miss Charlotte?'

'No.' His mouth was a hard line. 'Not her.'

'I – see,' Miles said, though he didn't see at all. Instead, he added firmly, 'Well, I hope very much that she will come. I'd like to see her there and,' he added pointedly, 'I'm sure my sons would too.'

With that, he gave a curt but polite bow and strode from the room.

The harvest festival service took place in September. Under Charlotte's guidance, the children brought vegetables, fruit and two sheaves of wheat. On the previous Sunday, Charlotte had worked on her corn dolly at Sunday school, showing the children how to plait and weave the straw into the shape of a doll. Now this sat in the centre of the display on the altar steps. The service was a joyous occasion with everyone singing lustily the hymns they knew so well.

During the next week, several of Miles's workers readied the barn for the celebrations on the following Friday evening. They decorated it with flowers and replicated the display of produce that had been in the church. Mrs Beddows, Lily and the kitchen maid were run off their feet cooking and baking and Brewster was dispatched to the town to buy ale from the local brewery.

To everyone's surprise, Osbert Crawford was one of the first guests to arrive at the supper and, to their shock but enormous delight, walking in behind him, came Charlotte, shyly carrying the corn dolly she'd made to take pride of place in the celebrations.

Sadly, she was still dressed in her drab Sunday purple with a long dark coat over her dress, but before many minutes had passed Jackson had grabbed her hand and whisked her away from her father.

'Here, let me take your coat, Miss Charlotte. Biddy!' he called to one of the villages lasses. 'Take care of Miss Charlotte's coat, will you?'

The girl smiled, dimpling prettily. 'Hello, Miss Charlotte. Nice you could come,' she said diplomatically. The villagers were whispering to each other.

'He's let her come.'

'Fancy, after all these years.'

'Why now, d'you suppose?'

'He's all over the new feller at the manor like a rash, that's why. An' Mary Morgan says the squire rode over to Buckthorn Farm last week and invited them both to come, an' he wouldn't take "no" for an answer.'

'Well, good for 'im then, I say. I'll raise me glass to Mr Thornton and drink 'is health. 'Specially as it's 'is beer I'm drinking!' The blacksmith from Ravensfleet laughed raucously and drank the squire's health. Those nearby joined him. 'Good health, Squire.'

'And hers,' someone else added. 'Let's drink to the lass, an' all.' With one accord they all raised the tankards or glasses they held and turned towards Charlotte.

'Good health, miss, and happiness to you.'

Hearing them, Jackson touched her arm and nodded towards the four or five men. 'They're toasting you, Miss Charlotte.'

She turned and smiled and bobbed a little curtsy of thanks.

'Aye,' muttered one of the drinkers. 'An' no one deserves it more'n you, lass.' But he didn't speak aloud the words that were in everyone's mind: 'But you'll not find happiness whilst yon miserable devil you call "Father" still has you in his clutches.'

Miles had seen the Crawfords arrive and noticed how Jackson went at once to Charlotte's side and drew her into the gathering of the younger folk at one end of the barn. He'd heard the toast to her and seen her smile and the pink tinge of pleasure – and perhaps a little embarrassment – touch her cheeks. And now Georgie, too, had seen her and was running across the barn towards her. Then he noticed that Osbert Crawford was standing alone near the door, leaning heavily on his walking stick and glaring

139

around him with a morose frown on his face. No one had gone to him to take his coat or welcome him to the proceedings. Always aware of his position as host, Miles moved towards him and held out his hand.

'I'm so glad to see you both. Come, this way. I'm sure you'll know most of the men here...' He led Osbert to the corner where other farmers from the district were gathered. They nodded towards him, but not one of them made any effort to engage him in conversation. Miles felt a distinct chill in the atmosphere now that Osbert had arrived which had nothing to do with the autumnal evening. But he pressed on, offering him a drink and something to eat. The man and his daughter were here at his express invitation and it was his duty to see that they had a pleasant evening.

It was not until Philip appeared that Osbert smiled, excused himself from the gathering and moved towards the young man.

'Thank God for that,' muttered Roland Thompson into his beer. 'Can't abide the man. No offence, Squire, but as you've mebbe gathered, Osbert Crawford in't exactly popular round here.'

'No,' Miles said thoughtfully, his gaze still on the older man now talking to Philip. 'So it would seem.'

But, even though he waited, no one volunteered any further information.

When the dancing started, Jackson drew Charlotte into the throng.

'Oh, but I can't dance.'

'Neither can I, miss,' he grinned, 'but all we've got to do is jig about a bit.'

She laughed and put her hands into his.

It was all right whilst the merry dances were playing, but when it came to a slow waltz, after treading on her toes three times, Jackson said, 'This has got me beat an' all. I reckon we'd best sit this one out.'

Charlotte, fanning her hot face, agreed. But she'd not been sitting down for many seconds when a diffident Cuthbert Iveson approached her and asked if he 'might have the pleasure of this dance'.

'Go on, miss,' Jackson urged. 'Mebbe Vicar can mek a better fist of it than I can.'

Charlotte rose and put her hand shyly into Cuthbert's. Together they stepped in amongst the dancers. Cuthbert put his arm about her waist and whispered, 'Just relax and let me lead you.'

Now he was holding her firmly against him. Her body moulded to his so that when he moved, she automatically followed his steps.

'One, two, three. One, two, three,' he murmured in her ear and smiled down at her.

The other dancers, seeing Charlotte and the vicar together, smiled and nodded. Gradually, couple by couple, they stopped dancing and stepped to the side. At last, only Cuthbert and Charlotte were left in the centre of the floor. As the music came to an end, applause burst out spontaneously. Cuthbert bowed and Charlotte curtsied. They were laughing and moving to the side, when there was an angry roar as Osbert

141

pushed his way through the throng, brandishing his walking stick. He stopped in front of his daughter and the vicar.

'How dare you disgrace yourself, girl? And you, sir.' He turned his venom on the timid man. 'Cavorting in public in such a manner. You dishonour your cloth. I shall report you to the bishop.'

'But, sir...'

'Father...' Charlotte began, but Osbert grasped her arm roughly and dragged her after him towards the door. In disbelief, the revellers parted to let them through, too stunned to move to help her. He pushed her through the door into the dark night. 'Get yourself home, this instant. I should never have let you come. I knew it was a mistake. You can't be trusted.' His raised his stick and struck her viciously on the side of her face.

There was a cry from the women watching and one or two men moved forward, but before anyone had time to come to her aid, Charlotte picked up her long skirt and ran out into the night.

Jackson pushed his way through the throng and ran outside, Georgie beside him. But already Charlotte had fled into the darkness.

'He hit her,' the little boy said, tears choking his throat. 'He hit her again.'

Jackson looked down at the young boy. 'Again? What do you mean "again"?'

'I saw him hit her with his walking stick once before. At church. Why, Jackson? What's she done wrong?'

Jackson put his hand on the boy's shoulder, his mouth a grim line as he muttered, 'God only knows, Master Georgie. God only knows.'

Seventeen

After the incident, the merriment seemed to die. Even though the musicians – locals who played an instrument and got together to entertain at such gatherings – struck up once more, no one had the heart for dancing now. Georgie was in tears and was carried off to bed by the house-keeper at the manor, Mrs Harkness. Ben soon followed of his own accord and only Miles and Philip were left of the Thorntons. Miles would have liked to escape too, but seeing as he was the host, he knew his departure would be seen as a signal for the party to break up.

'Come on, Lily,' Philip said, grabbing her hand and pulling her towards the empty space which served as a dance floor. 'Let's liven things up a bit. Let's get their tongues wagging. We'll do the Charleston. D'you know it?'

'Well, a bit, Master Philip. Someone tried to teach us it at the Valentine's Dance in Ravensfleet village hall, but I–'

'Let's give it a go then. Now, I wonder if this motley crew can play the music.'

'Eddie Norton on the fiddle can, Master Philip.'

'Right, I'll ask him. But stop all this "master"

stuff. It's Philip.'

Lily blushed but as the music began, she kicked her legs in a pretty fair go at the dance that was sweeping the aristocratic parties of the 'flappers'.

From the sidelines, Miles watched with amusement, but in Joe's eyes there was a wary, anxious look.

'She's only having a bit of fun, love,' Peggy whispered at his side. 'She's a good girl.'

Joe said nothing. He buried his nose in his beer, but his gaze never left the gyrating couple.

As the festivities came to their natural end just after midnight, Jackson said, 'Miss Charlotte left her coat and hat. Shall I take them to the farm tomorrow, Dad?'

Miles, overhearing, butted in before Joe could reply. 'It's all right, Jackson. I'll see they're returned to Miss Charlotte first thing in the morning.'

A swift look of disappointment crossed the young man's face, but, dutifully, he nodded. 'Right you are, sir.'

The following morning Miles mounted his horse and took the package his groom handed up to him. He lifted his face and breathed in the autumn air. He loved September and never more so now that he had been introduced to the traditional harvest celebrations. There was a special smell to autumn and the colours were so glorious, though here on the flat open land there were few trees. That was the only thing he missed about his previous home in Derbyshire, the abundance of tree-laden slopes in all their wonderful greens and browns and golds. But in compensation, he revelled in the magnificent Lincolnshire sunsets. Never had he seen such skies. The glowing pinks, mauves and bright oranges of the setting sun. He was so thankful that he and his family had been accepted into the community and he felt a moment's sadness when he thought how his dear wife would have loved it all too.

At Buckthorn Farm, Edward opened the front door.

'Is Miss Charlotte at home?' Miles asked. 'I've come to return her hat and coat.'

'Yes, sir, but she's – er – indisposed this morning.'

A concerned frown furrowed Miles's forehead. 'She's ill?'

'Not – exactly, sir.'

The man said no more, but from his grim expression Miles deduced that she was perhaps suffering the ill effects of the incident the previous evening. Perhaps her problem was more emotional than physical harm.

'And Mr Crawford? Would he see me?'

Edward inclined his head in his best butler manner. 'If you'd care to step inside, sir, I will enquire.'

Edward took the package from his hands. A few moments later, Miles was being shown into the sitting room; not, as he had expected, into a study.

Osbert was sitting by the fire, a book in his lap. He rose as Miles entered and waved him towards a chair on the opposite side of the fireplace. 'I'm glad you've called, Mr Thornton. I planned to call upon you later today myself.'

Miles sat down whilst Osbert instructed Edward to bring coffee. When the door closed behind the manservant, Osbert said, 'I must apologize for my daughter's disgraceful behaviour last evening. As for the vicar, I shall take steps to get him removed from his post. Dancing, indeed!'

'I saw no harm in Mr Iveson enjoying himself amongst his parishioners. Surely, it helps him get to know them and vice versa.'

Osbert glared at him. 'You think so. I'm afraid I cannot agree. A man of the cloth should keep himself aloof – be an example – not be cavorting like a village lad. And I shall have to have words with Joe about his son, Jackson, too, I can see.'

Miles stared at the bitter, twisted man and couldn't stop the question. 'Why?'

'Why?' Osbert barked. 'Do you really need to ask?'

'Yes, I do.'

'Making a fool of my daughter.'

Miles shook his head. 'He did no such thing. He danced with her, that's all.'

'Well, she made a fool of herself, then. I won't have it.'

There was no persuading the man that it had been harmless enjoyment.

'There's one good thing come out of it, though,' Osbert went on, his mouth a hard, bitter, un-forgiving line. 'It's made me come to a decision. That's what I was coming to see you about.'

Miles waited.

'I have realized that I am getting on in years and I need to make a will if I am to safeguard the

146

future of Buckthorn Farm. Since I have no son of my own to carry on the family farm, I intend to bequeath my farm and all my possessions to your eldest son, Philip. I've taken a liking to the young man and he will be a worthy landowner and employer, I've no doubt.'

Miles's jaw dropped open. 'But – but what about your daughter?' he spluttered. 'It's her inheritance.'

Osbert glared at him but offered no explanation. 'What I want to do with my farm – and the reasons for it – is my business,' he said tartly.

'But you hardly know us.'

Osbert shrugged. 'That's of no consequence. As I say, I've taken a liking to your boy. If it should come about that he proves unworthy of my confidence in him, then I can always change my will.' He stared at Miles with cold, hard eyes that defied contradiction.

'But – but Philip made it clear that he has no interest in the land. He wants to become a lawyer and I intend to help him achieve it if that's his ambition.'

'You don't wish to hand your estate on to your eldest son?' Osbert was surprised and it showed.

'I–' Miles hesitated. He'd been going to say that he had two other sons, both of whom might prefer to be gentleman farmers. But it seemed a cruel remark to make to the man who had no son and was so obviously disappointed. He altered what he'd been about to say. 'Ben seems more interested in the land than his brother.'

'Hmm.' Osbert frowned. 'He seems a sensible young fellow, I grant you. Quiet and well man-

147

nered, but as for your youngest boy, God knows what will become of him.'

The note of disparagement in Osbert's tone was not lost on Miles, but he smiled quietly to himself at the thought of Georgie. Then he brought his wandering thoughts back to the amazing – and to his mind ridiculous – suggestion.

As if sensing the other man's doubts, Osbert leaned forward to press home his point of view. 'Even if Philip doesn't want to manage the farm himself, I'm sure his brother would oversee it for him. Just think how the addition of Buckthorn Farm would enhance the Ravensfleet Estate. Between them, your sons would be the biggest landowners for miles.'

'But – your daughter...?'

Osbert leaned back. 'Ah, now there is a proviso. As you can see for yourself, she is unlikely ever to attract a suitable marriage partner. She is plain, dull and useless. But I suppose I must make provision for her in some way.' His eyes narrowed. 'In return for me leaving my farm to a member of your family – most likely Philip – I would expect you to marry her.'

Miles stared at him. Was he in a dream? Or rather a nightmare? The man must be crazy to think up such a preposterous scheme. It was tantamount to being back to the days of arranged marriages amongst the landed gentry, when unions were sought for reasons of wealth, possessions or power. Well, he would have none of it. He stood up suddenly, the coffee cup he still held clattering in its saucer.

'I'm sorry. I cannot agree to such a suggestion.

148

It is totally unacceptable to me, my family and, I'm sure, to Miss Charlotte, whom I presume you have not even consulted.' He gave a small bow. 'I wish you good-day, sir.'

As he turned away, Osbert said in a silky tone, 'I beg you not to be so hasty. You are throwing away a superb opportunity for your son.'

But Miles, incensed by the man's arrogance, marched towards the door, flung it open and left the house, passing a surprised Edward in the hallway without a word.

Eighteen

That evening, after work had finished for the day, Miles again rode over towards Buckthorn Farm. He would have enjoyed the gentle ride through the dusk of the balmy September evening, but his mind was still reeling. This time he did not go to the farmhouse, but stopped at the farm workers' cottages. The two semi-detached cottages each had a piece of ground at the back cultivated as a vegetable garden and room at the far end for chickens and a pig.

Horse and rider came to a halt outside the Warrens' cottage. Through the lighted window Miles could see the five members of the family sitting down to their evening meal. Only Lily was missing. Whilst he had no wish to interrupt them, the matter he wished to discuss with Joe – and possibly with Peggy too – was gnawing at him. As

149

he watched, he saw John, the eldest son, come to the window and peer out. Then the young man turned back towards those still sitting around the table, presumably to say something, for Joe got up. Moments later, he was opening the front door and coming down the short path. Miles sighed and dismounted.

'Mr Thornton?' Joe's tone was worried. 'Is owt wrong?'

'No, no, man. It's just – well, I'd like a private word with you and your wife, but I see you are eating. I didn't want to interrupt–'

'Think nowt of that. Come away in. We've almost finished and Peg will make us all a cup of tea. That is–' Joe hesitated as he realized he was speaking to this man as if he were an equal. Miles Thornton – and his family – were so friendly, it was easy to forget the differences between them. 'If – if you'd like one, sir?'

Miles smiled. 'That would be most welcome. Thank you.'

He tethered his horse to the fence and followed Joe up the path, to be greeted a little anxiously by Peg and her two sons.

John and Jackson exchanged a glance and raised their eyebrows. Jackson could contain the question no longer. 'Is it our Lily? Is summat wrong?'

Miles blinked and then said swiftly, 'Good heavens, no. Oh dear, I never thought my coming here might make you think that. No, no, Lily is fine.'

The tension in the room relaxed and Peggy bade her surprise visitor sit down in Joe's chair by

150

the range whilst she made tea.

'Away to your bed, Tommy,' Joe said to the youngest boy.

'Aw, Dad,' he began to protest, but Jackson put his hand on his young brother's shoulder and, without another word being spoken, steered him towards the door leading to the staircase. As the door closed behind him and they heard his footsteps thumping up the stairs, they all exchanged a smile.

'Boys!' Peggy said and raised her eyes to the ceiling.

'Now, Ma,' Jackson teased. 'You'd not be without any one of us.'

When they had all been served with tea, the four remaining members of the family looked towards Mr Thornton expectantly. Under their scrutiny his resolve wavered. He glanced at John and Jackson, a little unsure whether he could trust them. But they were grown men, one thirty already and the other in his mid-twenties.

'I would be very grateful if you would keep this conversation confidential.' His gaze swept them all. Joe turned towards his boys and seemed to be about to ask them to leave, too, but Miles held up his hand. 'No, I'd like you all to hear what I've got to say – or rather to ask.' The family members glanced at each other but their gaze came back to the squire.

Miles took a deep breath and smiled a little sheepishly. 'This is difficult. If you don't wish to answer my questions, please say so. I shall quite understand.'

Joe frowned, growing more mystified by the

minute. He felt like saying, 'Get on with it, man,' but of course he said nothing.

'Joe, just what is going on at Buckthorn Farm?'

Joe blinked. Whatever he'd thought the purpose of Miles's visit might be, it wasn't this. 'I – er – don't understand what you mean?'

'Mr Crawford's treatment of his daughter doesn't seem – well, normal.'

Now Joe understood and his face was grim. For a moment the man sitting opposite him believed he was about to get short shrift and asked – politely, no doubt – to leave. But to his surprise, the four all spoke at once.

'No, sir, it isn't–'

'You're right there–'

'That poor lass–'

'It's a bloody disgrace–'

This last remark from Jackson earned him a glare from his mother. The young man apologized at once. 'Beggin' your pardon, sir, but it is. She's a lovely girl and she's been held down and used – yes, used – all her life. He treats her like a skivvy–'

'That'll do, Jackson,' Joe said quietly. For a long moment, he looked into Miles's face, wondering if he dare trust the man. He was still a stranger to them. If Joe spoke out of turn and it got back to Osbert Crawford, the whole family could find themselves in serious trouble. And not even Miss Charlotte would be able to save them.

He glanced at Peggy and, seeing her silent nod of agreement, he cleared his throat. 'I'd better explain it as I see it, sir, but it's only as I see it, mind.'

'We, Dad,' Jackson put in. 'As we all see it.' And his brother nodded agreement.

'Our family have lived in this cottage and worked on Buckthorn Farm for four generations now, if you count the boys.' He nodded towards his sons. 'It started with my grandfather who came to work for Mr Osbert's grandfather. I reckon it was *his* father who bought the farm. Now, grandfather came here in the late forties, because my father, Harry, was born here just after they arrived. His father died when he was about twenty, I think, and he stepped into his dad's position.' Here Joe paused and smiled. 'Didn't go down too well with some of the older workers, so he used to tell me. Him being made up to foreman at such a young age. But there you are; he was, and he made a damned good job of it.'

Miles nodded. 'If your expertise and knowledge come from him, then he certainly did.'

Joe's smile faded. 'Ah well, I'm coming to that in a bit, Mr Thornton. I'm sorry it's taking a while to tell you it all, but I want you to understand everything.'

'That's quite all right. I *want* to hear it all.'

'More tea?' Peggy asked, taking the chance of the pause in Joe's tale.

'Thank you,' Miles murmured, but his attention was still wholly on Joe. Whilst Peggy moved about quietly, pouring them all more tea, Joe went on.

'Mr Hubert Crawford – that's Mr Osbert's father – took over the farm when *his* father died in – let's see–' Joe wrinkled his forehead.

'In 1870,' Peggy put in helpfully, 'because it

153

was the same year as Mr Osbert was born. I remember your mam telling me, Joe.' She turned to Miles. 'Joe's mam loved relating family history. Not only her own family, but everybody else's as well. And I suppose it was natural she should take an interest in the Crawfords. Their two families had been – what's the word – entwined, is that it? – for so long.'

'That's right, love. And then Mr Hubert died fairly young really. Only forty-eight, he was. I remember that. I was about sixteen and Mr Osbert was only twenty and, of course, he had to take over the farm there and then. That was in 1890. Five years later he brought home a bride.'

'Alice Hall.' Peggy took up the tale briefly. 'But where she came from and how he met her and courted her, none of us ever knew and never have known.' She glanced at Joe and murmured, 'That's when it all began to get a bit mysterious. They were married the same year as us – '95. She had a baby boy same year as John was born and another the same year as our Jackson. But she miscarried them both at about seven months. I felt dreadful, I don't mind admitting, that there I was with two healthy strapping lads and that poor lass couldn't give her husband the sons he craved. And I mean *craved*.'

'She had another boy, didn't she, Ma, before Miss Charlotte came along?' Jackson said.

'No, that was after, but poor little mite was stillborn.'

'But they had a daughter by then?' Miles looked around the faces before him, seeing the family glance at each other, their expressions a mixture of sadness and anger.

Quietly, Joe took up the tale once more. 'And that was the tragedy of it. All Osbert Crawford wanted was a son to carry on the farm and the family name. That's all he's ever wanted and he treats that lass – well, I don't rightly know how to say he treats her, but it's not like a daughter. If it hadn't been for Mary and Edward Morgan looking out for her, I don't know what might have happened to the little lass, 'specially after her mam died. Charlotte was only five.'

'But she seems – well – all right. I mean, she doesn't have pretty clothes, I grant you, and those glasses–'

'She doesn't need no glasses,' Jackson burst out. 'They're made out of plain glass. He makes her wear 'em because – because it makes her look even more plain and – and unattractive.'

Miles stared at him, unable to believe that a man would do such a cruel thing. He remembered now how, when they'd met her riding on the beach, sharp-eyed little Georgie had said with the guileless candour of the young that she was prettier without her spectacles.

'And now we come to the crux of it all, sir,' Joe went on. 'And here I must ask you in return, most sincerely and respectfully, to keep what I am about to say to yourself, else my family could all find themselves thrown out of their jobs and home.'

'Of course,' Miles said quietly. 'You have my word.'

Joe met and held the other man's steady gaze and then gave a small, satisfied nod. He believed

155

he could trust him. 'As you've seen for yourself, sir, Miss Charlotte is kept downtrodden. It's as if he's punishing her for not being a boy. Thing is–' Even now he hesitated in telling the secret he'd held for years. He glanced once more at Peggy for her reassurance, but then, taking a deep breath, said, 'The thing is, it's Miss Charlotte who runs Buckthorn Farm. You say I'm knowledgeable, well yes, I've learned a bit about running the farm from me dad, like you say, but I still go to her for a lot of help and advice about things. And it was her that chose them 'osses for you at the fair. We 'ad to be careful you didn't see.'

'I didn't, not really, and yet there was something about that day I didn't quite understand,' Miles murmured, amused and yet appalled at what he was hearing. 'Now I do.' If the girl was clever enough to run the large farm, knowledgeable about horseflesh, then why...?

'The master does nothing, sir, not a thing now. He did in the early days, of course, but for the last – oh, almost ten years – he's done nowt. It's her sits in the office at the back of the house, her does all the books, pays the wages, buys everything we need. Together – her and me – we plan the crops, buy and sell beast, sheep and pigs at market. And yet he treats her as if she's worth nothing.'

'And she works out on the farm alongside us, an' not just at harvest,' John said. 'She's first up in a morning to do the milking and last to bed at night when she's shut up the chickens.'

'And I'll tell you summat else, an' all,' Jackson put in. 'She's a clever artist. I've seen her out with her sketchbook, drawing. Painting too, sometimes. But she has to keep it all hidden – secret.'

There was silence before Peggy spoke. Now it was she who was a little hesitant and she glanced towards Joe for support. 'There's another bit of a mystery, Mr Thornton, that we don't understand. You know that Joe's dad died in April – just after you came to live at the manor?'

Miles nodded.

'Well, he was very agitated just before he passed away. Had us send for the vicar and insisted on speaking to him alone.' A flicker of a smile crossed her face. 'God only knows what he said to the poor chap, 'cos the young feller came out white as a sheet and scuttled off.'

'Dad died without telling us owt,' Joe added. 'And we can't expect the vicar to break a confidence, now, can we?'

Miles shook his head.

'We did find out a bit, though, and that was what was odd, you see.' Jackson now took up the tale. 'Me grandad had bought a plot in the churchyard – a grave – next to Mrs Crawford.'

'Osbert's wife,' Peggy put in, 'died two days after Joe's mother back in '05.'

Miles frowned in puzzlement. 'I don't understand...'

'Me mother was buried in Lincoln,' Joe explained. 'Dad said at the time that she wanted to be buried with her own folk and that's where she'd come from.'

'Was that true? I mean – did her folks come from Lincoln?'

'Oh yes. We used to go there to see me grandad and grandma. And Mam had brothers and sisters

157

there too, though we've lost touch now.'

'So what are you saying, exactly?'

'It just seemed odd that me dad didn't want to be buried alongside her. They were a loving couple, none closer, but he bought a plot here in the churchyard at Ravensfleet.'

'Presumably you went to your mother's funeral in Lincoln, so you know–'

'No, sir, that's just it. None of the family went from here. Dad insisted he went alone. After Jack Layton, the undertaker in Ravensfleet, took her from here, we never saw her again.'

'And when was Mrs Crawford buried?'

'Two days after Mother.'

'It does sound a little odd, as you say. And maybe Reverend Iveson knows more, but like you say, we can't expect him to divulge whatever it was your father confided in him.'

Miles stared round at them, biting his lip. Slowly, he said, 'Thank you for your confidence in me. And now, it's only fair that I explain the reason for my visit.'

Nineteen

All four members of the Warren family sat waiting expectantly. But now it was Miles who sought their reassurance that they would not betray his trust. 'I went to Buckthorn Farm this morning, mainly to enquire after Miss Charlotte.' He glanced at Jackson. 'And to return her hat and

158

coat. Edward said that she was indisposed, so I asked to see Mr Crawford.' Miles shook his head wonderingly, still unable to believe it had not all been a dream. 'He was obviously still very angry with Miss Charlotte for her "unseemly behaviour", as he called it. And then–' he glanced round at them all – 'he came out with the most preposterous suggestion I've ever heard in my life. It seems' – he ran his tongue nervously round his lips – 'that he's taken a fancy to my sons, especially my eldest, Philip.' He paused a moment, overcome by the enormity of what he was about to tell them. 'Mr Crawford tells me that he plans to make a will leaving everything he possesses – land, buildings, livestock, everything – to Philip.'

There were shocked gasps from each and every member of the Warren family. They stared at him in disbelief. 'Can he do that?' Jackson blurted out.

Miles shrugged. 'I think a man may do anything he wants in his will.'

'Would she be able to contest it?' John asked thoughtfully.

'She could. But it would take money to do that and – as far as I see it – he intends to leave her penniless. I know,' he said simply, as if reading their minds, 'it's outrageous, isn't it? But that's not all. In return for my son being left such an inheritance, I have to marry Miss Charlotte.'

Now their mouths dropped open.

'That's – that's blackmail,' Jackson burst out. Then he blinked and glanced around him, seeking confirmation. 'Isn't it?'

Miles sighed. 'I agree with you. It *is* a sort of blackmail.'

'But – but–' Even Joe was spluttering with indignation. 'I mean – do you *want* to marry Miss Charlotte? Does she want to marry you?'

Miles's face was suddenly grey with sadness. 'I – I'd never looked to marry again. I lost my beloved wife, Louisa, when Georgie was born. I adored her and I still miss her every day.' He bit his lower lip. 'I'd never even thought about it.'

'Then you don't love Miss Charlotte,' Jackson burst out. 'It'd be a marriage of – of – what is it they call it, Mam?'

'A marriage of convenience,' Peggy said quietly, her gaze on the squire. Surely, he wouldn't think of doing such a thing, just to gain land and property for his son? He would plummet in her estimation if he were seriously to contemplate it.

'Jackson,' Joe said warningly and the young man apologized swiftly.

'Begging your pardon, sir. I meant no disrespect. But I'm fond of Miss Charlotte. We're friends. I'd not like to see her forced to marry someone who doesn't love her.'

'Your defence of her does you credit, young man. And no offence taken, I assure you. And I have no intention of agreeing to his absurd suggestion.'

Peggy breathed a sigh of relief. She'd not been wrong in her estimation of the new squire. He was, as she'd thought, a man of honour.

'According to her father,' Miles murmured, musing aloud, 'she's never had any suitors and,' his tone hardened, 'in his opinion, is never likely

160

to have.'

Jackson sprang to his feet. 'That's a cruel thing to say.'

'His words, not mine, I assure you.'

'Sit down, son,' Joe said softly and Jackson sank back into his seat.

'Her father has never allowed her to have a young man,' Peggy put in quietly. 'She's never had the chance to meet anyone other than the young fellows who work on the farm.' She nodded towards her own son. 'Like Jackson says, Mr Thornton, him and Miss Charlotte are friends – have been since they were little – but if the old man got wind of it, he'd sack Jackson on the spot and likely throw us out an' all.'

'We don't want him to hear about it,' Jackson said shortly and glared at Miles almost warningly.

Miles grimaced. 'He's none too pleased about you dancing with her last night,' he warned. 'He'll be having a word with your father, he said.'

Jackson groaned and muttered, 'Oh, heck! I didn't mean to get her into more trouble. I was just so pleased to see her there.'

'So,' Miles said slowly, his gaze still on the hot-headed young man, 'would you *like* to court Miss Charlotte? Are you fond enough of her to want to propose to her?'

Jackson stared at him. The thought had quite obviously never crossed his mind. 'Um – er – well, I am fond of her,' he stuttered, forced suddenly to examine his feelings for Charlotte. 'Very fond, but I don't think I'd call it the sort of love you should feel for the girl you want to marry.' Now he shook

161

his head in a swift decision. 'No – no, I don't think of her like that.'

'So – is there anyone else who's shown an interest in her?'

The Warrens glanced at each other.

'What about the vicar?' John suggested. 'He was dancing with her last night.'

Miles laughed wryly. 'Her father noticed that, too. I think that's what incensed him. He's threatening to have him removed from his living here. But, as it happens–' he smiled at them – 'I know the bishop. I can put in a good word for him if necessary.'

There was silence for a moment. Joe shook his head in disbelief. 'I've never heard the like. Really I haven't.'

'Of course,' Miles said, thinking aloud, 'years ago marriages were arranged amongst the gentry to unite families for money, possessions or power. And widowers often married again to give their children a mother.' He sighed. 'Just between ourselves, I get lonely. I thought it might be better when we moved here, away from the house that held all the poignant memories. But it isn't. It's worse, if anything.'

'But you have your boys,' Peggy said softly. 'You seem to have a wonderful relationship with them.'

'Oh I do, I do. But it's not the same, is it? They'll grow up and lead their own lives. I hope we'll always be close, but it's not like having a – a wife.'

Peggy and Joe glanced at each other. They understood – even if their sons didn't at this

162

moment. They couldn't imagine what it would be like for either them if something happened and one of them was left alone. They couldn't even bear to think about it.

Miles said no more. Though he felt that Joe and Peggy perhaps understood, he could see from their faces that the two young men thought it incredible that anyone should marry other than for love. He smiled sadly to himself, thinking of all the arranged marriages that had taken place through all the different cultures – and were still taking place in some parts of the world. Even here in Britain, particularly amongst the aristocracy, he was sure that parents still decreed that their offspring should marry 'suitably'.

'I mustn't keep you good folk any longer. Thank you for your time.'

They all rose and Joe held out his hand. 'And thank you for your trust in us, Mr Thornton. That means a lot.'

Miles took his hand and shook it warmly. 'If there's anything I can ever do, you'll let me know, now, won't you?'

'Thank you, sir.'

'And now I must go home and break the news to my eldest son that I have just refused a handsome inheritance.'

'You're going to tell him about it?' Joe was surprised.

Miles nodded. 'I try to instil honesty and trust in all my boys and therefore I always try to be open and truthful with them. I know Philip's still only young, but when his mother died, being the eldest, he had to grow up quickly.' He sighed and murmured, more to himself, 'Maybe too quickly.'

'You mean you said "no"?' Philip spluttered. 'You'd no right to do that. It's me he wants to have his farm. What right have you got to deny me an inheritance?'

He'd listened to his father's explanation with growing excitement, but Miles's final words had shattered his hopes. Philip faced him angrily across the broad surface of the leather-topped desk. Outside the door of their father's study, Ben and Georgie crept closer to listen. Seeing them, Wilkins smiled and tiptoed away, wishing he could eavesdrop too.

'I've every right,' Miles said mildly, not rising to anger like his son. 'For several reasons.'

'Name them,' Philip snapped.

'One,' Miles ticked them off on his fingers, 'the farm should go to Charlotte, his daughter.'

'But he doesn't want her to have it. You've just said so yourself.'

Ignoring him, Miles went on. 'Two, part of this – this bargain is that I should marry Charlotte. Do you want me to do that?'

Philip glared at him, hesitating. His glance strayed to the portrait of his mother, which had hung over the fireplace in his father's study in whatever house they'd lived in for as long as he could remember. He stared at the lovely face. The portrait had been painted at the time of her engagement to his father. She'd been eighteen then, young and lovely, and her sweet smile, captured for ever on the canvas, was like no other he'd ever seen. And it wasn't just the portrait that reminded him of his mother, for Philip, being the eldest, could remember her well. He could remember her voice, her laughter and, if he closed his eyes, he could almost feel her love for him reaching out even from beyond the grave.

Seeing the torment on his son's face, Miles said softly. 'Do you really want me to marry Charlotte Crawford?'

The fight and the anger drained out of the young man and he sought the armchair behind him and sank down into it. 'No,' he said huskily. 'No, I don't.' He saw his dream of becoming a landowner fading into the distance.

There was silence and Miles heard a scuffle outside the door. He raised his voice and called, 'Come in, you two scallywags. I know you're there.'

Sheepishly, the two boys entered the room.

Georgie, the bolder of the two, approached his father's desk. 'I wouldn't mind if you married Miss Charlotte, Papa. I think she's lovely.'

Miles noticed Philip's lip curl disdainfully. 'That's only because you don't remember our mother. But then, you wouldn't, would you? Seeing as she died having you.'

'Philip!' his father roared, for once roused to swift anger. 'That's enough.'

He glanced at his little son and saw Georgie's mouth quivering. 'Come here,' he said gently. The boy moved round the desk and clambered on to his father's knee. Miles stroked the boy's fair curls. 'You should all know, but especially you, Georgie, that each of you was a much-wanted child. You all were. And yes, your mother

165

did die just after giving birth to you, Georgie, but she was willing to sacrifice her own life to bring you – to bring *any* of you – into the world.' He glanced at her portrait. 'See, she's smiling down at us. She's watching over us. All of us.'

'But,' Georgie's eyes were still brimming with tears, 'you wanted a girl, didn't you? Not another boy?'

Miles smiled sadly. 'I'll not lie to you, Georgie. I hope I'll never have cause to lie to my sons. It would've been nice to have had a daughter, yes. I think all men dream of the day they'll walk their daughter down the aisle. But no, you're very precious to us all, Georgie, and I wouldn't change a hair of your head.'

Now the little boy beamed as he said, 'But you could walk me down the aisle, Papa, because when I'm grown up, I'm going to marry Miss Charlotte.'

There was a moment's stillness before they all burst out laughing.

The following morning neither Osbert nor Charlotte was at church. Nor were Edward and Mary.

Cuthbert Iveson, his pale faced blotched with patches of pink, conducted a nervous service and then dismissed the children.

'Papa, Papa!' Georgie cried, running after the rest of the family as the Thorntons climbed into their car. 'Miss Charlotte's not here to take the Sunday school. Mr Iveson says we're all to go home.'

He scrambled into the front seat beside his

father. 'Papa, could we drive to Buckthorn Farm and see if she's all right?'

'I don't think that would be a very good idea, Georgie. Not today.'

The boy's face fell. 'Oh.'

Miles smiled gently at him. He was proud that Georgie cared so much about others. It was a trait that seemed to be sadly lacking in his eldest son. As for Ben, the boy was so quiet and reserved that Miles hardly knew what he was thinking most of the time.

'I'll have a word with the vicar,' Miles murmured, climbing out of the vehicle again. 'Perhaps he'll know something.'

'Oh, for heaven's sake!' he heard Philip mutter impatiently, but chose to ignore the remark. As the last member of the congregation shook Cuthbert's hand and left, Miles approached him.

'Mr Iveson – a word, if you please.'

The vicar, about to turn away to go back into the church, hesitated. 'Mr Thornton...' He ran his tongue nervously around his lips.

'Have you heard anything from Buckthorn Farm? I'm concerned for Miss Charlotte.'

For a moment, Cuthbert stared at him before saying hesitantly, 'Would you step into the church a moment? There is something I would like to tell you.'

Together they stepped into the dim interior once more. Sitting down in one of the pews, they faced each other.

'I had a hand-delivered note from Mr Crawford this morning,' Cuthbert began, his already high colour deepening yet further, 'informing me that

167

he intends to write to the bishop about my dis-
reputable behaviour at the Harvest Supper and
asking – no, demanding – my dismissal from this
living.'

'Then I will also write to the bishop and tell him
that your behaviour was perfectly correct. You
were merely joining in the harvest celebrations.
And even dancing with Miss Charlotte–' Miles
spread his hands. 'Well, that's perfectly in order. I
mean, you're not married, engaged or anything,
are you?'

Cuthbert shook his head. 'No – no. There's no
one.'

There was a slight pause before Miles asked,
'But are you – shall we say – interested in Miss
Charlotte?'

Cuthbert sighed. 'In a way. It's best if a young
vicar is married, you see. And I thought she
might make a suitable wife for me.'

Poor Charlotte, Miles thought with com-
passion. No declaration of love or even affection.
Just that she would make a 'suitable' wife for
him. How cold and calculating. The man was
almost as bad as the girl's father. Miles bit back a
retort and, instead, asked, 'And was there any
indication in his letter as to how Miss Charlotte
is?'

Cuthbert shook his head. 'No, none. I suppose
we'll just have to wait and see what happens,' he
murmured, but Miles had the distinct feeling
that the young man was more concerned for his
own future than for Charlotte's. He almost regretted his promise to write to the bishop on his
behalf, but his innate sense of fair play came to

168

the fore once again. The vicar had done nothing wrong and it was only right that the bishop should hear the truth.

Miles rose. 'I'll visit Buckthorn Farm again. See what I can find out.'

Cuthbert rose too. 'He's a manipulative and dangerous man,' he burst out suddenly. 'He seems to think he can run the lives of all those around him. Certainly, the lives of the people who work for him.'

Miles stared at him. 'What d'you mean?'

Cuthbert turned away. 'I'm sorry,' he muttered. 'I've said too much already.'

Miles watched him as he hurried up the aisle towards the altar steps where he knelt and bowed his head in prayer.

Twenty

In the afternoon, Philip was missing.

'I think he's gone to Buckthorn Farm, Papa. I saw him riding in that direction.'

'Has he indeed?' Miles said grimly. He suspected his son had gone to plead with his benefactor to lift the condition attached to his inheritance. Miles had to admit, with sadness in his heart, that his eldest son was utterly selfish. Ruthless, even. After a moment's hesitation, he left the room. Minutes later, Georgie, watching from the window, saw his father galloping in the same direction.

'Oh, Georgie,' Ben murmured, 'now what have you done?'

Miles was shown into the sitting room at the farm to find his son and Osbert sitting opposite each other on either side of the fireplace. They both turned to look at him as he strode towards them. 'This nonsense has to stop. I shall not allow you to make Philip your heir.'

Philip sprang to his feet, 'Father...' he began, but Miles held up his hand to silence him, his gaze on the older man.

Osbert merely smiled. 'I don't think there's anything you can do to stop me, Thornton. A man can will his possessions where he wishes. That is the law and, hopefully, by the time I meet my Maker, the boy will be of age and you will no longer have any say in the matter.'

'But your daughter–' Miles began.

Osbert's eyes narrowed. 'If you're so concerned about the girl, then do as I suggest.'

Miles let out a breath and shook his head. 'I don't believe you,' he muttered. 'I really don't. What sort of a father are you?' When Osbert did not answer, Miles asked huskily, 'Where is she? Where is Charlotte?'

Osbert raised his eyebrows. 'Coming round to it, are we?'

'Most certainly not,' Miles snapped. 'I just want to see for myself that she's all right.'

'She's all right,' Osbert said dismissively. 'Locked herself in her bedroom, that's all.'

Miles stared at him as he asked icily, 'And why would she need to do that?'

170

'Who knows what foolish girls will do or why they do it?' He glared at Miles as he added bitterly, 'But then you wouldn't know that, would you, being blessed with *sons?*'

Miles grunted and marched from the room, across the hall and through the door leading to the kitchen. As he entered the room, Mary threw up her hands in surprise, flour from the bowl in which she was mixing pastry scattering everywhere. 'Oh, Mr Thornton!'

With wide eyes, Peggy turned from the sink where she was peeling apples, but Edward, carrying logs in through the back door, merely nodded and greeted him as if it was the most natural thing in the world to see him there. 'Good afternoon, sir.'

Miles took a deep breath, wondering if he'd overstepped the line of propriety. But for once, he didn't care. He was encouraged when Peggy dried her hands and indicated a Windsor chair set near the range. 'Please – sit down, sir. I'll make a cup of tea.'

'It would be very welcome, Mrs Warren, but please don't go to any trouble.'

'No trouble, sir.' She smiled. 'Edward and Mary never say no to a cuppa.'

As he sat down he said, 'I just wanted to know how Miss Charlotte is. I can't seem to get any kind of answer from her father.'

The other three in the room glanced at each other uncomfortably. Mary spoke up. 'To tell you the truth, sir, we don't rightly know ourselves and we're worried about her.'

Shocked, Miles glanced from one to the other.

171

'You – you don't know?'

Edward dropped the logs into the hearth. 'When she got home from the harvest supper on Friday night, she ran upstairs and locked herself in her bedroom. We haven't seen her since.'

'We've left trays outside her room,' Mary said. 'But she's touched nothing.'

'Only a jug of water I took up – and a glass. She's taken that in,' Peggy put in. 'But she's eaten nothing.'

'But you've spoken to her?'

'We've tried, sir, but she won't answer.'

'But – but she might be ill. Have you a key for the door?'

Edward shook his head. 'We've knocked and called, but there's no answer. We've all tried.'

'Her father too?'

Mary snorted. 'Not him! No. He wouldn't care if she were alive or dead. An' he's up to summat. I know he is.'

'Mary,' Edward said softly, warningly. Miles and Peggy exchanged a glance and he knew she'd done as he'd asked. She'd kept the conversation he'd shared with her family to herself. But perhaps it was time that these good people – the Morgans – who obviously had Charlotte's welfare at heart, knew, too, just how devious their master was.

Mary covered her face with her apron and sobbed. 'I'm out of me mind wi' worry, sir. We don't know what to do.'

Peggy handed a cup of tea to Miles and turned to Mary. Gently she pushed her into a chair at the table and placed a cup of tea in front of her.

'Here, Mary love, drink this. It'll be all right now Mr Thornton's here. He'll help us. He'll tell us what to do.'

There was a long silence in the kitchen whilst they all drank their tea.

'We must do something,' Miles said. 'She might be ill.'

'That's what I'm afraid of, sir,' Mary said, recovering a little. 'She walked all the way home from the manor on Friday night with no coat or hat. I'm so afraid she might have taken a chill.'

Miles stood up and set his empty cup down on the table. He glanced round at the three anxious faces. 'I'm willing to do whatever it takes, but you do realize, don't you, that this could cause trouble for you? All of you. Because if I get involved, he'll know it's come from you.'

Edward nodded. 'We know that, sir, and we're not bothered for ourselves. Just Miss Charlotte. Though mebbe Peggy should go home. Keep out of it. She's her family to think of.'

But Peggy shook her head adamantly. 'No, Joe would back me up. And so would the boys. If he turns us all out, then so be it. We've that poor lass to think of.'

Miles nodded grimly. 'Very well. First of all, Mrs Morgan, you go upstairs and have one last try to get her to open the door. If only she would, it would make things a lot easier.'

Mary got up eagerly. 'You come an' all, Peggy.'

'Shall we tell her you're here, sir, and want to see her?'

'Of course, if you think it'll help.'

The two women disappeared and the two men

173

were left to wait anxiously in the kitchen. Several minutes passed before Mary and Peggy returned, shaking their heads.

'No sound, sir. We can't hear a thing.'

Miles smacked his fist into the palm of his other hand. 'Then we must take drastic action.' He looked at Edward again. 'You really haven't got a key?'

'As far as I know, there's only the one and she's got that.'

Miles turned on his heel. 'I'll ask her father.'

'Sir, I wouldn't...' Edward began, but Miles had already gone and was striding through the house back to the sitting room. Edward gave a helpless shrug and followed him.

Without even knocking, Miles marched into the room. Osbert and Philip were still seated as he had left them, leaning towards each other, deep in conversation. They both looked up in surprise as the door was flung open and Miles entered like a whirlwind.

'It seems, Mr Crawford, that Charlotte might be ill. She's locked herself in her room and won't answer. Have you another key?'

'Let her be.' The man waved his hand. 'She'll come out when she's hungry.'

'It's been two days. If she was all right, she'd surely have come out by now.' He glared at the man who was lying back in his chair. Anger boiled up inside him. 'Have you a key, sir?' he shouted.

Slowly, Osbert turned his head. 'No, I have not. And even if I had, I wouldn't give it to you.'

'Then you have two choices,' Miles burst out.

174

'Either I break the door down, or I call the police.'

'Father–' Philip was on his feet.

'Be quiet, boy! You're partly the cause of all this. If you were man enough, you'd refuse his ridiculous suggestion, but no, you're too selfish and greedy.' There, it was said, and whilst he was sorry, it had needed saying, he didn't regret it for it was the truth.

White-faced with shock, Philip sank back into his chair. He couldn't remember his father ever speaking to him so harshly.

Miles's attention turned back to Osbert Crawford. 'Very well. You leave me no alternative.' He turned and left the room once more, taking the stairs two at a time. Mary, Peggy and even Edward were waiting for him at the top.

'This is her door, sir,' Mary said, gesturing to her right.

He knocked gently on the door and called out. 'Miss Charlotte. It's Miles Thornton. We are all anxious about you. If you can, please open the door.'

There was silence, not even the sound of movement from within the room.

Miles turned the doorknob, though he knew it was futile. 'Charlotte,' he called now with more firmness in his tone. 'If you don't open the door, I shall break it down. Can you hear me?'

Still, there was no response.

Mary moved close to the door and cried, 'Please, Miss Charlotte, open the door. Mr Thornton means what he says.'

Silence.

Miles turned and nodded towards Edward. 'Right, let's give it a go.'

Edward looked at the door doubtfully. 'I don't reckon we can brek it open wi' just our shoulders, sir. 'Tis a solid door and the lock's sturdy.'

'We'll try. If we can't we'll have to fetch something to use as a battering ram. Right,' Miles said, putting his shoulder to the door. 'Are you ready?'

But as Edward stood beside him, they all heard the key turn in the lock. They glanced at each other in surprise and relief. Miles stood aside and motioned for Mary to go in first. 'See if she's all right first, before we all troop in,' Miles said, though in his growing anxiety for the girl, he would readily have charged in first.

Entering, Mary stood a moment, glancing round the room. Miles saw her eyes widen and her mouth fall open. 'What is it?' he demanded urgently. 'What's the matter?' Unable to contain his impatience any longer, Miles pushed the door wider and stepped into the room. With like urgency, Edward and Peggy were close behind him.

Charlotte was sitting in the far corner at a small table, a paintbrush in her hand, her head bowed in concentration.

'Miss Charlotte,' Mary said tentatively, 'why didn't you open the door? It's been two whole days. We've been that worried...' Now a note of reproach crept into the woman's tone. The girl seemed in perfect health, calmly pursuing her hobby as if nothing was wrong. And yet...

Miles touched Mary's arm. 'Gently, Mrs Morgan. There must be something...'

'Charlotte?' Mary tried again, but it was Peggy who pushed the others aside and crossed the room towards Charlotte.

'Now, miss,' she began gently, but with a note of firmness, 'you've had us all worried and here's Mr Thornton – oh!' Her words ended on a startled cry and her hand flew to cover her mouth. She glanced back at the others still standing near the door. Then she turned back to the young woman, knelt down beside her and put her arms round her waist.

'Oh, Miss Charlotte. Whatever happened?'

Now Mary rushed forward and she, too, stood staring down at Charlotte, her hand to her mouth. Miles and Edward glanced at each other before also moving towards her.

With a sigh, Charlotte laid down her brush and turned to face them all. Down the left-hand side of her face was an ugly weal and her eye was swollen until it was all but closed, the bruise blackening the tender area around her eye.

'My God!' Miles muttered. 'When did that happen? And how?' He already guessed the answer, but he had to be sure. He'd heard Georgie saying that Mr Crawford had hit Charlotte. He'd thought his son must have been mistaken, but now the evidence was before him.

Charlotte bowed her head. 'I – I'm sorry to have worried you all, but I didn't want anyone to see. I – I'm so ashamed.'

Peggy, still kneeling beside her and looking up into her face, said, 'Ashamed? Why should you be ashamed?'

'I – I made a fool of myself at the Harvest

Supper. I–'

Four voices spoke at once, refuting her.

'Nonsense!' Miles Thornton's voice rose above the rest and then asked the question, the answer to which they had all guessed already. 'Did he do that to you? Your father? Did it happen as you were leaving the other night?'

Miserably, Charlotte nodded. Silently, Miles made a vow never to disregard anything Georgie said again.

'Mary, pack her clothes. I'm taking her back to the manor with me. I'll have the doctor look at her and then–'

Charlotte looked up in fear. 'No – no, I can't do that. I can't leave here. Who would–?' She stopped whatever she had been going to say and bit her lip, lowering her head again. 'It's very kind of you, but I can't leave. It's not possible.'

Anger surged through Miles. The girl's loyalty to her father and to Buckthorn Farm was admirable – but sadly misplaced. He was sure that she was totally unaware of her father's schemes. She could have no idea that he intended to leave her penniless when he died. He ran his fingers through his hair. So many underhand goings-on. And for the moment, he didn't know how to handle it. He needed time to think. And he needed to tell Philip just what sort of a man his benefactor was.

Twenty-One

Miles returned home deep in thought. He tried to tell himself it was none of his business. He was a newcomer to the district; he had no right to interfere. Yet his conscience would not let the matter rest. He could not stand by and let that poor girl be cheated out of her rightful inheritance, nor see his selfish son benefit from such an absurd and vengeful action by a man who was obviously unbalanced. Osbert Crawford's desire for a son was out of all proportion. It had been an obsession and his only issue – a daughter – was being made to pay the price for something that was not her fault.

Miles called his three sons into his study. They stood before him as he gazed at each one. Philip, the eldest, tall and slim, golden haired and handsome. But his angelic looks hid a selfish, ambitious streak. Ben – the quiet one. Dark haired with brown eyes – solemn and deep-thinking. He was perhaps the cleverest of the three, and it was to him that Miles would turn to run his affairs when he was no longer capable. He knew that already, even though the boy was still so young. There was something dependable about Ben.

And then there was Georgie. The adorable scamp. Still so young, but already showing the ebullient character he would always be. He would always – always, Miles knew – put others

179

before himself. Everyone loved Georgie – even Philip, albeit grudgingly, in spite of himself. And throughout his life, Georgie would always be loved. Miles cherished all three of his boys – he'd give his life for them, just as his beloved Louisa had given hers to bring their youngest child into the world. But there was still a tiny corner in his heart – a special place – that had always been reserved for a daughter. A little girl whom he could dote on and spoil. But it had always remained just that: a wish which had not been fulfilled, but which would never, ever, become an obsession that would overshadow and eat away his love for his sons.

Miles sighed. 'Sit down, boys. This may take a little time.' He paused whilst they settled themselves. Georgie wriggled to get himself comfortable, his legs swinging. He had a wide grin on his face; he felt important at being included in a family discussion. But Ben looked apprehensive and Philip mutinous.

Miles leaned back in his chair and linked his fingers together. 'I've seen Miss Charlotte.'

'Is she all right, Papa?' Georgie couldn't help interrupting.

'Yes – and no.' He paused, wondering how best to explain. 'She'd locked herself in her room since Friday night because she's got a nasty bruise on the left side of her face. She was ashamed to let anyone see it.'

'Why? I mean, why was she ashamed?' Georgie asked innocently.

'Because of how she got it, stupid,' Philip muttered.

Unperturbed by his brother's insult, Georgie was still anxious about Charlotte.

Ben said nothing, but he regarded his father steadily. He was taking in and digesting every word.

'I know he hit her on Friday night. I saw it,' Georgie said, tears starting in his eyes at the memory. 'What I don't understand is – why?'

Georgie, who'd never been hit by his father in his life, not even spanked, had been horrified. He'd had bad dreams about it each night since.

'It seems he thinks she misbehaved at the Harvest Supper.'

Misbehaved? The little boy frowned. That was a word that was applied to him if he was naughty, not to a grown-up like Miss Charlotte.

'He didn't like to see her dancing with the vicar,' Miles tried to explain. 'In fact, he didn't even want her to come to the festivities. He's never allowed her to attend in the past.' Now he must admit his own part in the incident. 'I'm afraid it was I who persuaded him to let her come.' He glanced uncomfortably at Philip. 'You were the bait.'

'The bait?'

Miles sighed. 'Mr Crawford wanted all three of you to be present, but especially you, Philip. I sort of implied that you would be there as long as he allowed Miss Charlotte to come too.'

'Why's he never let her go before?' Georgie asked.

'Because he's ashamed of her,' Philip said scathingly. 'She's drab and plain and never likely to find a husband. I expect he thinks everyone will

181

ridicule her, snigger about her behind her back.'

'But they *don't* laugh at her, do they?' Ben put in quietly. His father and brothers all turned to look at him. Such was the rarity of Ben putting forward his opinion that, when he did, everyone listened. 'At church all the villagers greet her and talk to her. They're fond of her. You can see they are. And the children – her Sunday school class – they all love her.' It was a long speech for Ben and by the time he'd finished, he lowered his head, his face red.

'That's right,' Georgie said excitedly. 'He's right, Papa. They do. Everyone was disappointed when she wasn't there this morning.'

'So,' Miles said slowly, 'what d'you think we should do to help her?'

'You could always marry her,' Philip said sarcastically. 'As the old man suggested.'

Miles glared at him, a jolt of anger running through him suddenly. 'I thought you said you didn't want that. Not even if it robs you of your inheritance?'

Philip smiled smugly. 'He's dropped that condition. He's promised to leave me his entire estate anyway. He told me so this morning. And yes, since you're all so concerned, he is ashamed of his daughter. She's neither use nor ornament. That's what he said.'

Miles sat forward in his chair. 'I think you'll find–' He stopped and bit back the words that, in his fury, he'd been about to unleash; the truth about Charlotte that he'd been told in confidence by the Warrens. It was a trust that he could not betray, however much he wanted to wipe the self-

182

satisfied look off his son's face.

'What?' Philip snapped.

Miles sighed, his anger dying to be replaced by a great sadness. He'd hoped never to see such greed and self-interest in any of his sons. For the first time in six years he was glad that his dear wife was not here to witness the man their eldest son was becoming. She would have been heartbroken. He leaned back in his chair and merely made a gesture with his hand, dismissing what he'd been about to say as if it was of no consequence.

'Miss Charlotte could always come here, Papa,' Georgie suggested. 'You wouldn't need to marry her. She could live with us as a friend. And she could play with me.'

Once more, it was Georgie who brought laughter back into the room

The following morning, Miles went again to Buckthorn Farm. This time, he entered by the back door and was greeted by Edward, Mary and Peggy like an old friend.

'So,' he asked, 'how is she this morning?'

'Better, sir, thank you. She's had some breakfast and–' Mary glanced at Edward – 'she's going about her daily routine as normal.' Miles hid his smile as he interpreted her words as meaning Charlotte was at her desk in the farm office. But he gave no indication that he knew and Peggy turned away lest her face should betray her.

'We don't know how to thank you, sir, for helping us yesterday,' Mary went on. 'If you hadn't come, goodness knows how long she might have stayed locked in her room.'

'Would she see me, d'you think?'

'Best not try today, sir, if you don't mind. She's still embarrassed about it all.'

'Mm. Very well, then, but will you tell her from me that if she needs any help – any help at all – she's only to ask?'

'I will indeed, sir.' Mary smiled. 'And thank you once again.'

There was nothing more he could do and Miles drove home feeling disconsolate that he'd not been able give Charlotte some practical help. He was the sort of man who, faced with a problem, was happiest if he could take some positive action to solve it. If he couldn't, the matter lay heavily on his mind. And the thought of Charlotte was beginning to fill his waking thoughts and trouble his restless nights.

Twenty-Two

The matter of the vicar's dismissal was more easily remedied. As he'd promised, Miles wrote to the bishop and received a friendly letter in return:

Every incumbent of the parish of Ravensfleet seems to displease Mr Crawford eventually. He had a previous one removed, I believe, in the days of my predecessor. Despite his complaints I shall not be taking any further action in the case of Mr Iveson – as indeed I have not on two previous occasions!

Miles folded the letter away and put it in his drawer. Later he would ride over and give the good news to the young man.

Perhaps, after all, Charlotte could do worse than become a vicar's wife.

Charlotte attended church the following week and took up her Sunday school duties once more. During the week no one, except the household staff and Joe, had seen her. The bruise had faded and was scarcely noticeable and it was to the credit of those closest to her that no one else knew the cause of her absence.

The Thornton boys – as they were becoming known throughout the neighbourhood – had been sworn to silence by their father. Even little Georgie had said nothing to his playmates. So, on the morning of her return, the villagers were fulsome in their concern for her.

'Have you been ill, Miss Charlotte?'

'We've missed you – and so have the children.'

If they'd looked closely beneath the brim of her close-fitting cloche hat, they might have seen the telltale yellowing mark. But no one did. The hat – borrowed from Peggy – was the closest Charlotte had ever come to wearing something remotely fashionable. But the plain, single plait down her back looked absurd beneath it, though the villagers made no remark upon it. Only the local dressmaker with her eye for fashion noted it and felt a rush of pity for the girl.

Charlotte smiled and thanked them all for their

185

concern and assured them she was quite well, thank you. As she sat in the pew behind her father with Mary and Edward beside her, she kept her head bowed, her gaze fixed on the floor, and never once did she meet the vicar's gaze. He, too, it seemed, was at pains to avoid her. After the service, having said his goodbyes to his parishioners in the porch, Cuthbert scurried back to the vestry and then to the vicarage.

He did not, for the first time ever, visit the Sunday school to inspect its progress and take part.

On his return home Georgie couldn't wait to tell Miles.

'Did you see, Papa, that Mr Crawford walked straight past the vicar after the service? He didn't even shake his hand. And *then*,' he added dramatically, 'he – Mr Iveson, I mean – didn't come into the Sunday school class at *all*. And he *always* does.'

Miles laid a hand on the boy's shoulder. 'Now, you mustn't speak of it to anyone else, Georgie, there's a good boy.'

The boy shook his head. 'I won't, Papa. I wouldn't do anything to hurt Miss Charlotte. Not for the world.'

Miles smiled to himself. Well, he thought, Charlotte has one champion, even if he is only six years old.

'D'you know, Miss Charlotte,' Georgie told her solemnly after Sunday school the following week, 'Tommy, Sam and Mikey can't play with me this week.'

186

'Oh dear! Why not?' she asked, suddenly afraid that there'd been yet another falling out.

'Because they're going 'tatie picking.' Charlotte hid her smile as the boy added, 'D'you think Papa would let me go, too?'

'I don't know, darling,' she replied as seriously as she could. 'You'll have to ask him.'

The following day, Charlotte was amused to see the four boys, wearing warm coats, with a piece of string tied round their waists, Wellingtons and flat caps that were several sizes too big, solemnly marching into the fields at Buckthorn Farm, armed with baskets and buckets.

'Where d'you want us to start, Miss Charlotte?' Tommy, taking the lead, asked.

'You can all work a row each near me.' She smiled.

By midday, Georgie was white-faced with tiredness and wincing with backache. As Mary and Edward appeared at the gate into the field carrying baskets of food and drink for the workers, Charlotte called a halt to the work. She turned to the boys. 'That's enough work for you boys today. Thank you for coming. Now, go back with Mary and Edward and they'll find you some scones and lemonade.'

'Oh but, Miss Charlotte...'

Forestalling the argument, she said firmly, 'See you in the morning. Eight o'clock sharp, mind.'

She watched them cross the field, trailing wearily after each other, and marvelled at how the youngsters had stuck doggedly to the back-breaking task, not wanting to be the first to give in. But she'd seen the relief on all their little faces

187

when she'd called a halt.

'Can I go an' all, miss?' Jackson mimicked a child's high-pitched tone. 'I like lemonade and scones.'

'You most certainly cannot, Jackson Warren.' She laughed and bent again to her own labours.

As the last load of potatoes trundled its way from Buckthorn Farm to the railway station in Ravensfleet, Joe said, 'That were a good 'tatie harvest this year, miss. For us, any road.'

'Mm. We've been lucky. And now we'll have to start planning what we're going to plant for next year.'

'I was talking to some of the farmers in the Mucky Duck last night...'

'The Mucky Duck' was the local nickname for the White Swan pub in Ravensfleet.

'...And some of 'em are thinking of growing sugar beet. There's a new sugar beet factory planned for Bardney. All being well, construction'll start next spring and they reckon it'll be operatin' by October for next year's crop. Now if we–' Joe broke off as he saw the smile spreading across Charlotte's face. 'What, miss?'

'Funnily enough, I've been reading up about sugar beet. It seems it's a very good crop to rotate with wheat, barley, potatoes – all the things we grow. It helps the soil, so' – she linked her fingers together – 'how about we grow a few acres for next year? And even if the Bardney factory isn't ready, there's one at Spalding, isn't there?'

'There is, miss, but the others reckon we could send our crop by train from here to Bardney.'

'Really? That'd be excellent.' She thought a moment then said, 'What do you think about five acres as a trial the first year?' When Joe nodded, she added, 'I must check up when's the best time to plant sugar beet.'

'Er – ought you to run the idea past his lordship? Oh, begging your pardon, miss.' Joe coloured at his slip of the tongue, but Charlotte only chuckled.

'No, let's just do it.'

On Christmas Eve, an unexpected visitor arrived at the manor on foot, but leading a horse. There'd been a light scattering of snow and the ground was icy.

'It's Miss Charlotte,' Georgie cried excitedly, seeing her coming up the drive. He ran to the front door before Wilkins could reach it and flung it open, rushing to meet her, slipping and sliding down the steps.

'Miss Charlotte, Miss Charlotte! You've brought Midnight.'

The horse shied a little and Georgie stopped abruptly, aware that he was frightening the animal. Charlotte patted the horse's neck and quietened him with a soothing word. She smiled down at the excited boy. 'Come and stroke him.'

Though the animal was still a little restless, and there was wariness in his eyes, Georgie approached him fearlessly. He reached up and stroked his neck. 'There, boy, there,' he murmured.

'That's good, Georgie. Very good. Now, is your father at home?'

'Yes, I'll fetch him.' He turned away and walked a little distance before he began to run. Charlotte smiled, watching him go. At least one of the Thornton boys was learning how to treat a nervous animal.

Only a moment later, Miles was coming down the steps, his feet crunching on the snow, Georgie skipping beside him. He held out his hands towards her. 'Miss Charlotte – this is a pleasant surprise. You must come in and have some mulled wine. We were just trying it out ready for the party tonight. You are coming, I hope.'

Charlotte blinked at him.

'Ah,' Miles said, understanding at once. 'You didn't receive my invitation?'

She shook her head. 'No. I – I'm sorry, we – we can't have. It must have got lost in all the Christmas mail.'

If only that was the explanation, Miles thought grimly. He'd had the invitation delivered by hand but, he realized now, he'd made the mistake of addressing it to Mr Crawford. Hence, the girl knew nothing of it.

'Then if you are free this evening, I do hope you will come.'

Now he'd embarrassed her, for she blushed and avoided his gaze. 'I – I'm sorry, I don't think we'll be able to.'

'No matter.' Miles smiled, trying to ease her discomfort. 'Perhaps at New Year?'

She smiled weakly and nodded. 'Perhaps.'

'Don't let's stand here getting chilled. And you, Georgie, out here without a coat. Dear me, Lily will have a ducky fit, as she calls it.'

'I'll take Midnight round to the stable yard, shall I?' Charlotte said.

'Yes, yes.'

Whilst Mr Thornton and Georgie returned inside, Charlotte led the horse round the side of the house. As she rounded the corner, she almost bumped into Philip and Lily, hurrying, hand in hand, in the opposite direction.

'Oh!' Lily cried and snatched her hand from Philip's, blushing a bright pink. 'Oh, miss. I–'

But, smoothly, Philip covered her embarrassment. 'Lily is going home for the afternoon as we're having a party tonight and she'll be here over Christmas too.' His eyes challenged Charlotte. 'I was just making sure she doesn't slip and fall.' Now he turned to Lily. 'You'll be all right now. I really should get one of the men to clear the path from the back door round to the front.'

'Yes – I – er – thank you, Master Philip.'

With her hat pulled down low and her scarf covering the lower half of her face, Lily hurried away.

'Take care, now,' Philip called after her before turning his attention back to Charlotte and to the horse she was leading. His face darkened. 'So, you've brought that creature back, have you?'

Charlotte regarded him with her head on one side. 'He's rightfully still yours. Your father wouldn't let me pay for him, so, I thought now that he's had a little training, it's only right that you should have him back. He'll be fine now – if he's treated properly.'

Philip's face was thunderous. 'How dare you speak to me like that? Who do you think you are?'

His mouth curled. 'I suppose,' he drawled sarcastically, 'you think that one day you'll be a woman of property because Buckthorn Farm will be yours when the old man dies. Well, let me tell you, Miss Charlotte Crawford' – he thrust his face close to hers – 'you won't inherit a penny. Not – one – penny. Not one blade of grass. The whole lot's coming to me.' He struck his chest. 'Me!'

Charlotte's face was white and she clung to Midnight's reins to keep upright. 'I – don't understand,' she whispered at last. The boy must be unhinged. She feared for his sanity. He was given to uncontrolled fits of temper. She'd seen that with his treatment of Midnight. And now she wished fervently that she'd not brought the horse back. Her sense of fairness had made her make the offer. But now she regretted it heartily. The horse might have been tamed, but she doubted the boy ever would be. The preposterous idea that he – a comparative stranger – was to be her father's heir, astounded her. Was it really possible that her father would do such a thing?

Philip's next words confirmed her worst fears. He'd plunged the knife into her heart and now he twisted it with vicious delight. 'He's taken a liking to me. He looks upon me as the son he's never had. And–' he sneered, 'you are, as he says himself, "neither use nor ornament".'

Charlotte stared at him, at the young, handsome face that was at the same time ugly with malice. With a strength and resilience that she hadn't known she possessed, she straightened her shoulders and said tightly, 'If you will let me pass, I will ask one of your men to stable Midnight. I

192

must see your father.'

A flicker of fear crossed the boy's face. His hand shot out and he gripped her arm, his fingers biting into her flesh. 'Don't you say a word to him about this. Don't you dare. You're not supposed to know.'

'Oh, I'm sure I'm not.' She shook herself free of his grasp. 'No doubt my father was saving this little piece of information for an appropriate moment.' She forced a smile. 'But I'm very grateful to you for telling me, Philip. Very grateful indeed. At least it allows me to make my own plans. I can leave now without any guilt, without any shred of filial duty left. And as for the farm, I hope you're up to running it because, unless you take over right now, by the time you inherit it, it won't be worth the paper his precious will is written on.'

'Me? Run a farm? I've no intention of running a farm.' Once more his mouth curled disdainfully. 'I'm no country yokel. But my brother, Ben, now, Father has him earmarked to take over running our lands one day.' He shrugged nonchalantly. 'Buckthorn Farm will just become part of the estate and he can pay me a fair rent.'

'You really are despicable, Philip. How you come to be the son of such a kind and caring man as your father I don't know. Now, if you'll kindly let me pass, your father is waiting for me to sample his mulled wine.'

Twenty-Three

'Come in, come in,' Miles cried when Charlotte found her way through the kitchens to the morning room. 'We thought you'd got lost.'

'I ran into Philip,' she said, taking the glass of steaming mulled wine gratefully. She'd become chilled, standing talking in the cold, but that was nothing compared to the bleakness in her heart. 'I'd come to offer you Midnight back, now he's broken in. He's a wonderful animal, but he still needs careful handling – gentle treatment. The horse is ready, but I'm not sure – now – that Philip is.'

'I give you my word–' Miles began, but at that moment Philip entered the room, a look of apprehension on his face when he saw Charlotte and his father deep in conversation. Georgie followed close behind him.

Before anyone else could say a word, Georgie piped up, 'Miss Charlotte's trained Midnight for you. She's brought him back.' Then he frowned and added as sternly as a little boy of six could manage, 'But you've got to promise not to whip him any more.'

Philip glanced from Charlotte to his father and back again. He bit his lip and muttered morosely, 'I promise.'

Miles smiled and said benignly, 'Good, good.'

But Charlotte was not so sure as she watched

the boy turn and leave the room. Philip had just proved, to her at least, that he was not capable of keeping confidences. It did not bode well for his chosen profession in the law, Charlotte thought, with a surprising hint of silent amusement, considering the disastrous news she'd just heard.

'Now, we're having a party for all the staff here tonight in the big room they tell me used to be used as a ballroom, but on New Year's Eve I'm planning a quiet dinner party. Just the family, you and your father, Mr Iveson and an artist friend of mine. He lives in London now and although we've always kept in touch, we haven't seen one another for several years. He's on his own, so I've invited him to come here for New Year. It's Ben's birthday that day and it's what he's chosen.' He smiled. 'No big birthday party for the quiet one of the family. Now, do say you'll come?'

With a defiant sparkle in her eyes, Charlotte said, 'I can't answer for my father, but yes, I'd be delighted to come to your dinner party. Thank you.'

She raised her glass to him and they smiled at each other.

'Papa,' Georgie said, 'Brewster and Wilkins have put the tree up in the hall. Please can we decorate it now?' He came to Charlotte's side and slipped his hand into hers, beaming up at her. 'And may Miss Charlotte stay and help us?'

For a brief moment, Miles hesitated, his expression suddenly melancholy, but then he forced a smile and said quietly, 'Of course.'

They went out into the hall where Philip and

195

Ben were coming down the stairs, carrying down the boxes of Christmas decorations for the tree. Georgie hopped excitedly from one foot to the other. 'Where's the fairy for the top? Papa always puts the fairy on last. We'll do the bottom branches, Miss Charlotte, and Philip and Ben–'

As Charlotte touched the paper decorations in the box, gently lifting the first one out, Philip said harshly, 'What d'you think you're doing?'

She looked up to see him glaring at her, his face thunderous.

'I–'

'Miss Charlotte's going to help us decorate the tree,' Georgie said, rummaging in each box, trying to find his favourite ornaments.

'Oh no, she isn't,' Philip snapped. 'That was always Mother's job and no one – *no one* – is ever going to take her place.'

As he glared at her, Charlotte could see that he was not just referring to the decorating of the family Christmas tree. She dropped the paper chain as if it was burning her fingers. Huskily, she said, 'I'm so sorry.'

'Phil, please–' Georgie began, but his brother rounded on him.

'You can't remember. How could you? But *I* do. And Ben does.'

Charlotte saw Ben's head drop and he said nothing. Then she saw tears start in Georgie's eyes. She squatted down in front of him. Taking a deep breath, she smiled and said as brightly as she could manage, 'I ought to go, anyway. I've so much to do at home.'

It was a lie; there was nothing to do at home. Christmas was not celebrated at Buckthorn Farm.

'I'll come and see your tree when you've got it done. I promise.'

She stood up, turned away and walked quickly to the front door and all the while she was acutely aware of Miles watching her with troubled eyes. She pulled open the door and paused, just a moment, to look back. Georgie was delving into the boxes, his excitement overcoming his brief disappointment. Ben now avoided her glance, but Philip caught and held her gaze, a smile of triumph curving his mouth. It was a double victory for the scheming young man.

The news Philip had given her stunned Charlotte and, as she walked home, she was proud of herself that she'd managed to carry off her conversation with the rest of the family without giving away the fact that she was in a state of shock. Who else knew about this? Did Mary or Edward? And how could she find out anything more without causing embarrassment to them? If nothing else, the knowledge that her father intended to leave her quite penniless strengthened her resolve. She would indeed, she told herself, need to plan her future carefully. But how – and where – to start? That was the problem.

Apart from a slight change in the usual food, Christmas at Buckthorn Farm was a dull affair. Mary cooked a goose with all the trimmings and proudly presented a plum pudding she'd made weeks earlier. Charlotte, Mary and Edward ex-

197

changed small gifts but their dinner was eaten, as always, in the kitchen whilst Osbert ate alone in the gloomy room across the hallway.

Charlotte couldn't help her thoughts returning to the manor. How she'd love to have seen Georgie opening his Christmas presents. She could imagine his excitement and his indulgent father and brothers watching. They'd make the day special for the little boy. Even Philip would unbend a little, she was sure. There'd be warmth and laughter and love in that household. How she longed to be a part of it.

But, despite the shattering news about her inheritance, Charlotte carried on as normal. She was as courteous and obedient as ever to her father, affectionate as always to Mary and Edward – and to Peggy, who'd now become a part of the household. She wondered if Joe knew about it.

And then, the day after Boxing Day, she suddenly realized that there was someone she could confide in. Someone she could trust with her life. Jackson. She could talk to him. He would tell her, if he knew anything. And if he didn't, then he was the very person to find out.

But that same morning, Peggy came with news that halted Charlotte's plan – at least for the moment.

'Our Jackson's got the influenza. He's ever so poorly.' Peggy bit her lip. 'We even had to get the doctor.'

If that was the case, Charlotte realized, then the young man must be very ill. People like the Warrens didn't often call the doctor in, if they could help it. Doctors needed paying and country folk, knowledgeable in the ways of Nature's remedies, seldom called upon Dr Markham's services.

'Jackson must stay off work as long as he needs to,' Charlotte reassured her.

'Thank you, miss. I'll tell him what you've said.'

Later that day, Charlotte inspected the contents of her wardrobe. It was dismally inadequate. There was nothing there that was suitable for another dinner party. She fingered the dress she'd worn the last time she and her father had dined at the Manor. She allowed herself a wry smile; it was the *only* dinner party she'd ever attended. She turned away with a sigh and sat down at her dressing table and regarded her reflection critically. She had a well-proportioned face, with smooth skin that was lightly tanned from being out doors in all weathers. Removing her spectacles, she leaned closer to the mirror. Her eyes were violet, with thick, black lashes. Her nose was the right size and shape for her face and her mouth generous and turned up at the corners as if she were ready to smile at any moment. And, despite the harshness of her life, she was. Until now, she'd never really stopped to compare her life with that of others. She'd always been housed, clothed and fed. She'd always had the affection of Mary and Edward, the friendship of the men and boys who worked on the nearby farms and in some cases, that of their wives too. And as for the lack of love from her father, well, she'd never known any different. So how was she to know that her life was unduly harsh, very different to what it would have been as the daughter of a loving father? But now she was becoming painfully aware of the differences. She remembered all the times she'd visited the Warrens' cottage home. How there was affection between each and every member of the family for one another. How Joe treated his daughter, Lily, with the same love he had for his boys. If anything, Charlotte thought wistfully, it was a love that was even more tender and protective. And Lily's brothers looked out for her too. Charlotte smiled at herself in the mirror. And that was how she thought of Jackson. He was like a brother to her.

Lost in thought, she didn't hear the quick footsteps on the stairs and she jumped when an urgent knock sounded on her bedroom door.

'Miss Charlotte, Miss Charlotte. Come quickly.'

Charlotte rose at once and hurried to the door, flinging it open. 'What is it? What's the matter? Is it my father?'

'No – well – yes, in a manner of speaking.' Mary was standing there, twisting her fingers together agitatedly.

'Is he ill?' Charlotte hurried to the head of the stairs and began to run down.

Mary, following close behind, said, 'No, but he will be if he carries on like he is doing.'

As they reached the hall, Charlotte heard raised voices in the sitting room, her father's voice loud and angry above another, female, voice. It was not a voice she recognized. She hurried into the room.

There were two visitors in the room with her

father, but it was immediately apparent that they were not welcome. Osbert was standing in front of the fireplace, holding on to the mantelpiece as if for support. But he was shaking his fist at the woman standing straight-backed before him and shouting, 'Get out! Get out of my house.'

The woman was middle-aged. Tall – stately, Charlotte thought irrationally – and elegantly dressed. Tiny curls of brown hair escaped from beneath her tight-fitting felt cloche hat and she wore a knee-length crossover coat trimmed with fur at the collar and cuffs and fashionable, pointed-toe T-bar shoes. Behind her, a man was standing near the window, keeping out of the altercation. Of medium build – neither fat nor thin – balding and sporting a moustache.

As Charlotte entered the room, they all turned to look at her – the man and the woman with interest, her father with anger. 'And you can keep out of this, girl. Go to your room and stay there.'

The woman was smiling and coming towards her, her arms stretched wide to embrace Charlotte. 'My dear, dear girl. We meet at last! Come, kiss your Aunt Euphemia.'

Twenty-Four

In a trance, Charlotte submitted to the woman's embrace and kiss on her cheek. Then the stranger stood back and held Charlotte at arm's length. 'Let me look at you. My, my, such a pretty little thing...'

Charlotte smiled weakly, more at the misplaced compliment than anything else. 'Did you say *aunt?*'

'I did indeed. I am your father's sister.'

Charlotte gasped in surprise. 'Father's – sister? I didn't know he had a sister.'

The woman threw back her head and laughed. 'Dear me, am I such a black sheep that he hasn't even mentioned me in all these years? I hoped you might remember us, but then you were only four – or was it five? – when we were last here.'

'Euphemia...' The warning note in Osbert's voice was unmistakable, but the woman carried on smoothly, as if she hadn't heard him and certainly as if she intended to take no notice.

'I'm the older by four years. And this is my husband, Percy. Percy Bell.' She waved her hand vaguely in the direction of the man standing near the window. He smiled towards Charlotte and gave a courteous little bow. But he made no attempt to approach her, to kiss her cheek or even to shake her hand.

'We've been abroad for many years. Percy

worked for the Foreign Office, so we've been all over the world. But we've come back home to England now Percy's retired.' Euphemia linked her arm through Charlotte's and drew her further into the room. 'Your father and I had a silly quarrel when–'

'Euphemia!' Osbert roared, this time successfully cutting off whatever she had been going to say. 'That matter is never spoken of in this house. I'll thank you to hold your tongue.'

She stared at him for a long moment, before saying, with surprising meekness, 'Very well, Osbert. If you say so.'

'I do. And you will speak to no one about it. *No one*, do you hear?'

Charlotte watched the change on the woman's face. She was staring at her brother, frowning, as if trying to read the reason behind his words – his demand. She gave a slight nod, but this time she made no promise.

Euphemia turned back to Charlotte with a bright, rather forced smile. 'We've taken rooms in Ravensfleet. At the White Swan.' She patted Charlotte's hand. 'You must come and see us there. We can go to Lincoln on a shopping spree and–'

'She'll do no such thing,' Osbert spat. 'I don't want her looking like some–' he gestured towards his sister – 'some woman of the streets.'

'Oh I say, old boy, steady on,' Percy murmured and began to move towards his wife, as if in support. But Euphemia waved him away, 'Don't worry, my dear; I'm used to my brother's insults.'

Osbert moved stiffly from his stance near the

fireplace to sit in his chair. He made no offer of refreshment for them nor did he even invite them to sit down. 'I wish you good day, Euphemia. You are not welcome in this house.'

For a moment there was stunned silence. But then the woman laughed gaily. 'Nonsense, Osbert. You are my only living relative. I want us to put the past behind us.' She released her hold on Charlotte and moved to stand on the hearthrug in front of her brother. Charlotte glanced at her uncle. He was watching the proceedings, but taking no part now.

'We were close once, Osbert,' Euphemia said softly.

'We were never close,' Osbert barked, his frown deepening. He nodded towards Percy. 'You married *him* against Father's wishes and ran off to Timbuktu or wherever it was.'

'India, actually, old boy.' Percy spoke for the first time. 'And we didn't run off, as you put it. My work was out there already, as you very well know.' He spoke with a well-bred, superior tone of voice, but his eyes twinkled merrily when he glanced at Charlotte. She watched him stroke his moustache and heard a low chuckle.

He's enjoying this, Charlotte thought. I wonder why?

Osbert was scowling at them both now. 'Nevertheless, you were out there when Father died and I was left to run this place on my own. At twenty.'

Euphemia laughed, a merry sound that was at once infectious. 'And you're trying to tell me you wanted it any other way? What could I have done? A mere *girl*?'

Charlotte caught her breath. So, she thought, her father's antagonism against girls went even further back. It sounded as if his attitude towards his sister had been the same as it was now towards his daughter. But at her aunt's next words, Charlotte realized that the feeling went back a generation further.

'Father always made it perfectly clear that I – as a daughter – would inherit nothing.'

'That's why he wanted you to marry well. So that you'd be provided for and not be a burden on me.' He glanced with a sneer at Percy, who was still smiling benevolently. Charlotte doubted the man could be offended, however hard one tried. And it seemed her father was trying to do just that.

Osbert sniffed. 'He didn't think a junior in the Foreign Office would ever amount to much.'

'Well, he was wrong,' Euphemia said tartly. 'Percy did amount to something. He rose to an important position, as a matter of fact. We've had a wonderful life and he's retired on a very nice pension which allows us to do just what we like. But I would have married him anyway. We, Osbert dear, married for love, but of course you wouldn't know anything about that, would you? When I think of poor, dear Alice–'

Osbert sprang to his feet with an agility that Charlotte had not seen for years. He thrust his face close to Euphemia's and spat out the words, his spittle showering her face. 'Her name – is – not – to be spoken – in – this – house. Do – you – hear – me?'

Euphemia blinked, but remarkably she kept her

composure. 'I can hardly fail to, Osbert,' she said calmly.

'No need for that, old boy,' Percy put in mildly.

Osbert turned his venom on his brother-in-law. 'I am not your "old boy". I believe I am a good ten years younger than you, if I remember rightly. And now I'd be obliged if you would leave my house. As I said, you are not welcome here.'

'But Father, surely–?' Charlotte took a step forwards, but her father flung out his hand towards her, pointing his forefinger threateningly. 'And you can hold your tongue, girl. This is no concern of yours.'

'Oh, but I think it is, Osbert. Surely even *you* would not stop me becoming acquainted with my own niece? Especially if, in view of Percy having done so very well in his career, I give you my word, brother dear, that I shall never become a burden on you or your daughter when she inherits. That's if I outlive you, of course.'

Osbert's eyes gleamed. 'There's no fear of that.' His voice was silky with malice.

Euphemia laughed. 'What? That I shall outlive you?'

Osbert shook his head. 'No, not that.' His eyes narrowed as he said, 'Of my daughter' – he said the word as if the very feel of it on his tongue was abhorrent to him – 'inheriting Buckthorn Farm.'

Euphemia gaped at him and Charlotte couldn't prevent a startled gasp.

'I don't understand–' Euphemia's glance went from one to the other.

'It's not for you *to* understand,' Osbert snapped. 'It's none of your business.'

206

'But she's your only child, isn't she? And she's not married, is she?' She turned to Charlotte. 'Are you?'

Wordlessly, Charlotte shook her head.

There was silence in the room. Everyone seemed like a statue, stunned into stillness. Osbert, having delivered the bombshell, calmly sat back down in his chair.

'You mean to tell me,' Euphemia said, her own temper rising now, 'that you are not going to leave the farm to your daughter? Your only child?'

'That's correct.'

Charlotte, her eyes wide, stared at her father and put out her hand to the nearest chair to steady herself. Her legs felt weak and her head was swimming. So it was true. She was hearing it now from his own mouth. He was not going to leave the farm to her. She knew only too well that her being a daughter had disappointed him deeply, but she'd never thought that his bitterness was quite so vindictive.

'My dear girl.' Percy moved solicitously towards her. 'Are you all right? You look as if you've had a shock. D'you mean to tell me that you'd no idea?'

'Not – not really.'

'Appalling,' the kindly man said. 'Absolutely appalling!' But whether he meant the fact that she was to be left penniless or that she hadn't known her fate was unclear. Probably he meant both, Charlotte thought.

Her aunt was still locked in a battle of wills with Osbert.

'You're quite right, as always, Percy dear,' she murmured, though her gaze was still on her brother. 'That is exactly the word for it.' She paused and, with her head on one side, added, 'Then who, if I might be so bold, is to inherit?'

'Philip Thornton.'

As her legs finally gave way beneath her, Charlotte sank into a chair.

'And who's he when he's at home?' Euphemia demanded.

'None of your business,' Osbert snapped again.

At last, summoning all her strength, Charlotte said quietly, 'The Thorntons have just come to live at the manor.'

Euphemia turned towards her. 'Where Jeremy Davenport lived?'

'That's right.'

'What happened to him? Oh, don't tell me he's dead.'

Her hand fluttered to her mouth and her eyes were wide.

Charlotte regarded her aunt. She must have known him, she thought. 'I'm afraid so,' she said gently. 'His heir was a second cousin once removed who lived abroad and didn't wish to take up occupancy. The manor and the whole estate were sold to Mr Thornton and – and–' her voice faded to a whisper, 'his three sons.'

Euphemia stared at her for a long moment, absorbing the news and beginning to realize what the arrival of the new family had meant for Charlotte.

Osbert leaned towards his sister. 'It was Davenport whom Father had lined up for you. So you see, if you'd been obedient and married him, you would now be a very wealthy woman.'

Pulled back to the present, Euphemia started and then, in a very unladylike manner, snorted with laughter. Despite the shocking confirmation that what Philip had told her was true, Charlotte smiled. She was beginning to like her new-found relative very much.

'Me! Marry Jeremy Davenport?' Euphemia almost squeaked. 'Don't be ridiculous, Osbert. He was a philanderer. A womanizer. No girl in her right mind would have *married* him.'

Osbert put his head on one side as he said slyly, 'Maybe it was Davenport who had the lucky escape. He did marry late in life – someone much younger than him – and had two sons. Sadly, they were both killed in the war and his wife – still young enough to have borne more children, mark you – died in 'eighteen of the influenza.' He paused and then smiled maliciously at Euphemia. '*You* haven't been able to give your husband any children at all, let alone sons.'

All through the exchange of heated words, Euphemia had remained in control, but now her brother had touched a raw nerve. Her hand fluttered to her mouth and tears filled her eyes. At once, Percy was at her side. 'There, there, old girl. Don't take on.' He turned towards Osbert. 'And you, sir, mind your tongue. Even if she is your sister, it doesn't give you the right to be so cruel.'

'Huh, we're in the same boat. I've no son, only a useless, good-for-nothing daughter, who can't even catch a husband. I tried to arrange a marriage with Miles Thornton, but even he won't have her. Not even to secure his son's inheritance.'

'Father!' Charlotte gasped. 'What are you saying? What d'you mean?' This she did not know.

He turned to her now. 'I intend to leave all my lands and possessions to Philip Thornton, but I tried to make provision for you. As a condition, I proposed that his father – Miles – should agree to marry you. But he refused.' His lip curled disdainfully. 'But who can blame him? Look at you. Just look at you! Drab, colourless and spineless. Who on earth would ever want you for a wife?'

Hurt and humiliated more than ever before, Charlotte pulled herself up and ran from the room. As she dragged herself up the stairs, the racking sobs built in her chest, but not until she reached the sanctuary of her own room, did she throw herself on her bed and give way to a storm of weeping.

Twenty-Five

She must have fallen asleep for it was dusk when she woke. Her face was blotchy, her eyes swollen. She splashed cold water from the ewer into the bowl and washed her face. Then she unwound her plait, brushed her long, shining black hair and replaited it. She looked at herself in the mirror. Her violet eyes stared back at her. She picked up the spectacles she had worn since the age of seven. She remembered her father taking her to Lincoln. It had been such a rare occasion that he took her anywhere that the day was still clear in her memory.

They'd gone to an optician where her father had insisted the man test her eyesight. When she'd done reading all the letters and he'd looked into her eyes, the man declared that she had perfect eyesight.

'She needs glasses,' her father had said abruptly. 'You will make her a pair of spectacles with round, plain steel frames.'

The man had spread his hands helplessly. 'But she doesn't need spectacles. She–'

Slowly and clearly, Osbert had repeated the words, 'You will make her a pair of spectacles to my specification with plain glass.'

The man had gaped in surprise. He'd tried to argue once more, but to no avail. Osbert had been adamant and the man, only an employee who dared not turn away a customer for fear of his superior's wrath, duly obliged. On completion, the spectacles were posted to Buckthorn Farm and from that day Charlotte had worn them. They had been replaced twice more, but still they were the same style of round, steel-framed glasses that she had worn as a child.

Staring at herself in the mirror, Charlotte felt an overwhelming rebellion. The spectacles slipped from her fingers to the floor and before she had scarcely stopped to think what she was doing, she had ground them into the worn linoleum with the heel of her sturdy shoe.

Then she left her room and went down to the hall. She paused a moment. There was no sound now from the sitting room, so she turned towards the door to the kitchen.

Mary and Edward were seated either side of the range. The remains of their meal still lay on the kitchen table and a plate of food, which had obviously been taken on a tray to her father, had been returned untouched.

At the sound of her entry, they both stood up and Mary came hurrying towards her, arms outstretched. 'Miss Charlotte – there you are. I came up, but you were sleeping, so I left you.'

Charlotte smiled weakly. 'Is there any tea? I could drink a horse trough.'

'Of course, of course. There's still some in the pot, but I'll make you a fresh one.'

'No need. That'll be fine.'

'Are you hungry?'

Charlotte shook her head. 'Not really.' She sat down at the table and, when Mary poured a cup of tea out, she drank it gratefully.

'So,' she began, 'have our visitors gone?'

A glance passed between husband and wife. 'They've gone, but they left you a message, miss,' Edward said. 'They're staying at the White Swan in Ravensfleet and they'd like you to contact them there.'

Charlotte placed her cup back in its saucer with deliberate care. 'D'you know them, Mary?'

Again Mary and Edward exchanged a swift look. When they didn't answer, Charlotte said, 'It was my aunt and uncle. It seems–' she paused with a wry smile – 'that my father has a sister I've never known about.'

Mary was twisting her apron between nervous fingers. Charlotte eyed her suspiciously. Softly, she said, 'You *do* know her, don't you?'

212

Mary's eyes filled with tears and she put her apron up to them, half covering her face.

Edward touched his wife's arm comfortingly and then turned to face Charlotte. 'Miss Charlotte, we saw her once or twice, years ago, before – before–' he gulped nervously, 'before your mother went. But since then – nothing. I swear, miss.'

'It's all right, Edward. Mary, please don't distress yourself,' Charlotte tried to reassure them both, though secretly she was puzzled over their reaction to what seemed to her a simple question.

'Euphemia!' She smiled, trying to lighten the tension. 'It seems my paternal grandparents had a penchant for ridiculous names for their children.' She chuckled and repeated, 'Euphemia.' Then she went on, 'From what I can gather, my father and his sister fell out some years ago and the feud has lasted all this time. So like my father, don't you think?' she added dryly. 'And they've been abroad for many years. Uncle was with the Foreign Office. Did you know that? But now he's retired and they've come back to England.' She shrugged. 'And I suppose my aunt wanted to see her only living relative – well, relatives, if you count me too.'

Mary nodded and whispered, 'Yes, miss.' Then she seemed to pull herself together. 'I must get on, Miss Charlotte. I've a lot of work to do. Peggy's not coming today. Joe came in to tell me. I think she's going down with the flu that Jackson's got.'

'Oh dear,' Charlotte said, at once concerned for the Warren family. 'Look, pack some food into a basket, Mary, and I'll take it over later. I want to see Jackson anyway.'

'Now don't you go running into infection, miss,' Edward warned. 'We don't want you going down with the flu. It's the very devil. Let's hope it doesn't get as bad as at the end of the war.'

'I'll be fine,' Charlotte said airily. She'd always been blessed with robust health and never feared catching anything. She'd had all the usual childish ailments, but wasn't a martyr to winter coughs and colds or even the dreaded influenza that everyone feared so. She rose. 'And I suppose I'd better get on as well. Now all the excitement's over.'

It wasn't until she was halfway along the passage leading to the farm office at the back of the house that she realized she hadn't asked Mary and Edward if they knew about the will her father intended to make.

Later that afternoon as the dusk of a winter's afternoon settled over the marsh, Charlotte took the basket of food and walked down the lane to the Warrens' cottage. She hadn't been able to concentrate properly on her paperwork today. Plans for spring planting had been pushed aside not only because of the sudden appearance of relatives she'd known nothing about, but also because, obliterating everything else, of the revelation about her father's intentions towards her.

She'd always known that she was a bitter disappointment to him, but it was only recently that she'd realized she was not treated as a daughter should be treated. She'd been naïve, ignorant, but she'd never known any different. How could she? The realization had come only very slowly. Subconsciously, she realized now, she'd seen the contrast between her own life and that of the Warrens. But she'd thought that their happy family life was because there was a mother in the household; a mother around whom the home and family life revolved.

She'd had no such good fortune.

But now that she'd seen Miles Thornton's affection for his sons and how he managed to make a happy home life for them even without his wife at his side, it had dawned on her that her father had not a scrap of paternal affection for her. Indeed, it could be said that he hated her and her very existence. This last callous act proved it.

The thought saddened her. She'd tried to be a good and dutiful daughter. She'd done everything he'd demanded of her. She'd dressed in the drab garments, worn the clear-glass spectacles. Tied her long, glossy hair into an unbecoming plait. All as he'd dictated. She'd taken over the day-to-day running of the farm – with Joe's help and advice, of course. She'd even hidden her one pleasure – her hobby of drawing and painting – because he ridiculed it.

She sighed as she reached the cottage and raised her hand to knock. John opened the door.

'Please don't come in, Miss Charlotte. Me ma's gone down with it now. Jackson's on the mend, but she's real bad.'

'Have you had the doctor?'

He shook his head and smiled wryly. 'No, miss. She fetched him for Jackson, but she won't have him for hersen. She sticks to all the old-fashioned

215

remedies. Swears by 'em.'

Charlotte smiled. 'She is very knowledgeable about such things, I know. But just promise me, John, that if you're worried about her, you'll call the doctor. You needn't worry about the bill. I'll see to that.'

'You're very kind, miss.'

'Mary's sent this. Just to help out.'

John took the basket and smiled his thanks.

'I really wanted to see Jackson, but–'

'He's on the mend and he'll be out and about in a day or so, I shouldn't wonder. Will it wait till then?'

Charlotte bit her lip. 'Of course,' she said, but was bitterly disappointed.

As she left the cottage, she took the path across the fields to the manor. She was shown at once into Miles's study. At once Duke lumbered towards her, wagging his tail and pushing his head into her skirt to be patted. 'Now then, boy,' she said softly.

'Miss Charlotte – what a lovely surprise. Please, sit down,' Miles invited, gesturing towards one of the leather winged chairs near the fire. 'Wilkins, would you bring us tea, please?'

The manservant gave a little bow and left the room.

Miles didn't return to his seat behind the desk, but sat down in the chair opposite. 'What brings you here?'

Charlotte took a deep breath. 'Several reasons. First, the Warren family has influenza. At least, Jackson and Peggy have and I wondered if you'd allow Lily to go home to help them. I know it's

216

an imposition of me to ask, especially as you have a guest coming and the dinner party on Friday evening–'

'Of course, she must go at once.' He made as if to stand up that instant to send for her, but Charlotte put up her hand to stop him.

'Would you mind if I told her myself? I want to impress upon her that they must call Dr Markham in.' She smiled. 'Peggy is just like most of the country folk – they try their own remedies first when they get sick, but sometimes...' She shrugged and spread her hands in a helpless gesture.

Miles nodded. 'I understand. Of course, you must see Lily yourself.' There was silence before he prompted, 'And what else?'

Putting off the real reason for her visit for as long as possible, she said, 'How is Philip getting along with Midnight?'

'Ah.' Miles smiled ruefully. 'Well, now – I hope you won't mind, but I've taken Midnight as my mount for the moment. Philip is still wary of him and the animal gets restless every time he goes near him. And as Philip is away at school for several weeks at a time, and Midnight is a big animal who needs his exercise, I'm riding him. He's too big and still a little difficult for Ben, and certainly for Georgie.' He laughed and suddenly his face seemed much younger. 'Though that little rascal would have a go, if I let him.'

Charlotte smiled at the thought of her daring 'golden boy'.

'But he's fine with me,' Miles went on. 'So, I hope you don't mind.'

'Of course I don't. He's your horse.'

'But you trained him for Philip.'

'I know.' Her eyes twinkled merrily as she added, 'But, to tell you the truth, I'm relieved.'

'Because it's not Philip riding him?'

'Well–' She hesitated to criticize his son yet again, but Miles only laughed.

'Perhaps you're right. I think my eldest son has some growing up to do, and learning the right way to treat animals – and people, if it comes to that – is part of it. Anyway, you need have no worries for the present whilst I'm riding him. We're getting along fine. He's a beautiful animal. Still a little wilful, but we respect each other, I think.'

'I'm glad.'

He waited a moment before saying softly, 'But there's something else, isn't there?'

Charlotte took a deep breath, but at that moment Wilkins returned with a tray of tea, freshly baked scones, jam and cream.

'Thank you, Wilkins. We'll see to it.'

As the butler left the room, Miles said, 'Will you pour?'

'Of course,' Charlotte said, but as she reached for the teapot she was trembling so noticeably that Miles touched her hand and said gently, 'Allow me...'

As he handed her a cup her hands were still shaking so that the cup rattled in its saucer.

'My dear girl, whatever's the matter?'

Charlotte set her teacup down. 'I scarcely know where to begin.'

He sat back in his chair, waiting patiently until she regained her composure sufficiently to explain. 'You can tell me whatever you like, you know. It will be in the strictest confidence, I promise.'

'I've had two shocks recently. One was that – out of the blue – an aunt and uncle I never knew existed arrived at Buckthorn Farm. She's my father's sister and they've – they've not seen each other for years. Some sort of family feud, it seems. She's trying to make it up, but my father...' Her voice trailed away.

'And the second surprise?'

Charlotte bit her lip, not wanting to tell tales on his son. Although it had been Philip who'd first told her, now she'd learned the same fact from another source. The horse's mouth.

'You probably know about it.' She took another deep breath. 'I'm sorry, I find this very embarrassing. It seems that my father wishes to make Philip his heir.'

Miles rubbed his hand across his eyes and groaned. 'Oh, that ridiculous nonsense. I'd hoped you'd never hear of that. We've refused, of course.'

Charlotte smiled a little sadly as she added quietly, 'Because of the condition he made? That you should marry me?'

'No – no–' Miles started forward, spilling his tea into the saucer. 'What he's suggesting is not right. *You* should inherit everything. The farm shouldn't go to a comparative stranger.'

'But what does Philip say? Doesn't he want it?'

'To my eternal shame – yes, he does. But as I say, he has some growing up to do.'

'Don't be too hard on him. It's not his fault. He's only young. And let's be honest, who wouldn't want to be left a thriving farm?'

'Well, we won't accept it. *He* won't accept it. I'll make sure of that.'

'I don't think he – or you – will have any choice. I think my father can will his estate and his possessions to whomsoever he pleases. Can't he?'

'No doubt,' Miles said curtly, 'but I'm taking legal advice from my solicitor. He's looking into the matter. There may be some way round it.'

'And if there isn't?' she asked softly.

'You will always have a home – I promise you. I would see that you were provided for.'

'I don't want charity,' she snapped and then added swiftly, 'I'm sorry. That came out all wrong. I know you meant it kindly, but–'

'Don't apologize. I'd feel exactly the same in your place.'

There was silence between them before he asked tentatively, 'Charlotte, is there anyone in your life – a young man? What I mean is, is there any possibility that you could get married?'

She pursed her lips and glanced down at her lap as she twisted her fingers together nervously. She shook her head and said huskily, 'No one. He – he's never let anyone get close. And if there's ever been the slightest sign – well, he gets rid of them.'

Miles knew that was true because of Cuthbert Iveson.

'It's strange,' she mused, thinking aloud. 'You'd think he'd be just the opposite, wouldn't you? That if he doesn't want me to inherit, he'd want to encourage suitors to get me off his hands.'

Miles laughed wryly. 'Huh! You're too useful to him. You run the farm, don't you?' He raised his hand as she began to refute the suggestion. 'Don't deny it. I have it from a good source. A very good source – but one which I'm not about to reveal.'

Charlotte smiled. 'Joe, I suppose.'

'Now, now.' He wagged his finger at her playfully.

She sighed. 'Yes, it's true. Father does very little nowadays. Even when I try to talk over any problems with him, he just waves me away and says, "Ask Joe."'

'This aunt and uncle of yours who have suddenly appeared – are they staying with you?'

Charlotte laughed. 'No. They got short shrift when they came to Buckthorn Farm. Father more or less ordered them out. They're staying at the White Swan in Ravensfleet, so I intend to go and see them.'

There was mischief in Miles's eyes as he said slowly, 'We-ell, invite them to dinner on Friday night.'

'Oh, I couldn't – I mean–' She blinked. 'Why on earth would you want to do that?'

'Because sometimes I find life a little – shall we say, quiet – in the countryside.' He chuckled, a deep, rumbling, infectious sound. 'It might liven things up a bit.'

Charlotte gaped at him and then started to laugh too. 'D'you know, I think you have a wicked streak in you. Now I know where Georgie gets his mischievous ways from.'

'Most certainly it's from me.' But there was

pride in his tone when speaking of his youngest son.

'Well then, I will. I will invite them,' she said, surprising herself with her sudden daring. She got up and held out her hand. 'Thank you for listening to me. And for being so understanding.'

He rose, too, and took her outstretched hand. Looking down into her eyes, he said, 'I hope you know you can always count on me as a friend, Charlotte.'

As she looked up into his kindly face and read the concern in his dark eyes, Charlotte felt a tremor run through her. She caught her breath and her heart began to race. Her hand trembled a little in his warm grasp, but she managed to say levelly, 'Thank you. You're very kind.'

Then she turned and walked out of the room in search of Lily, marvelling at the strange trembling in her legs that his touch had caused.

Twenty-Six

'She's in there, miss,' Mrs Beddows said, nodding towards the back scullery situated off the main kitchen. 'Though what you'll mek of her, I don't know. She's upset about summat, but I can't get a word of sense out of her.'

'Oh dear,' Charlotte said. 'Perhaps she already knows that her mother's ill.'

But Mrs Beddows shook her head. 'She might, but I dun't reckon it's that.' The woman cast an anxious glance at Charlotte. 'I'd be grateful if you could find out what's ailing her, miss. And that's the truth, 'cos she's neither use nor ornament to me like she is.'

Charlotte hid her smile. The words, spoken lightly by the cook, bore none of the malice they held when issuing from her father's mouth.

She went into the scullery to find Lily with her arms in the deep sink washing clothes. The girl was scrubbing vigorously at a shirt collar, sobbing as she worked, her tears falling on to the garment.

She jumped as Charlotte put her arm round the girl's shoulders. 'Lily dear, don't take on so. Your mam'll be all right and Mr Thornton's given permission for you to go home and take care of the family until she's better. And Jackson's on the mend now and–'

Lily turned red-rimmed eyes to face her. 'What – what are you talkin' about, miss?'

Charlotte stared at her. 'I – I thought that's why you were crying. Because your mam and Jackson have the flu.'

Lily shook her head and mumbled, 'I didn't know.'

'Oh.' For a moment, Charlotte was dumbfounded. 'I'm sorry – I thought that's what was upsetting you.'

Lily sniffed and dried her hands on a towel. She was still hiccuping miserably.

'What is the matter, then?'

Lily looked frightened and shook her head violently. 'Nothing, miss. Honest. Does Mrs Beddows know about me mam and about Mr

223

Thornton saying I can go home?'

'I don't think so, but I'll tell her.'

'How long can I go for?'

'You'd better talk to Mrs Beddows, but I'll wait for you and walk back with you, if you like.'

'No, no, miss. Don't wait.' Again the girl seemed fearful. 'I'll be a bit finishing up here and then getting me things together. I'll be home later tonight, though.'

'All right. Would you like me to call as I go home and tell them you'll be coming?'

'If – if you like, miss.'

Charlotte frowned. The girl seemed distracted and as she walked home, it was now thoughts of Lily that troubled Charlotte. There was something very wrong with the girl. Was she not happy working at the manor any more? Was Mrs Beddows too strict? Had someone been unkind to her? Perhaps she had a young man and they'd had a tiff. Yes, Charlotte thought, that would be it. Oh well, no doubt it would all come out in the wash, as Mary was fond of saying. Charlotte felt a pang of envy for Lily. Not because she was upset – of course not. But she doubted she would ever know the pangs of love and all its vicarious emotions. What was the phrase? 'Better to have loved and lost than never to have loved at all.' Well, right at this moment, Charlotte would give anything to love and be loved. Even if it all ended in heartache, she'd just like the opportunity to experience it.

But whilst her father still held sway over her life there was no chance of that.

'My dear child how wonderful to see you again.' Euphemia held out her arms in welcome. 'Do come up to our room. Percy has gone out for a stroll. He loves quaint old places like Ravensfleet. They say it was a Roman settlement. Is that true?' Without waiting for an answer, she linked her arm through Charlotte's. 'I'll get them to bring some coffee up.'

The bedroom was quite small, but there were two easy chairs set near the window.

'Now,' Euphemia said, sitting down, 'we can have a nice little chat.'

'Before I forget,' Charlotte said, 'you are both invited to a dinner party at the manor on Friday evening.'

Euphemia's eyes gleamed. 'How kind of Mr Thornton. I must send a note at once, thanking and telling him we'll be delighted.' She leaned forward as if sharing a confidence. 'Might one of his three sons be paying court to you, dear child?'

Charlotte almost laughed aloud at the innocent irony of her aunt's words.

'No. The eldest boy is only sixteen.' Then, in spite of the bitter pill she was being forced to swallow where Philip was concerned, her innate sense of humour reasserted itself when she thought of Georgie. 'Though the six-year-old is a little charmer.'

'What about the father, then? Do you like him? He's a widower, isn't he?'

Embarrassed now, Charlotte said, 'That's the man my father was trying to marry me off to.'

'Yes, I know, but do you like him?'

'He's a very nice, kind man, but–' Charlotte

smiled wistfully – 'I don't think he'd even look at someone like me. Not in that way.' She sighed inwardly, but smiled brightly at her aunt. 'If you accept his invitation, you'll see the portrait of his beautiful wife hanging over the fireplace in the dining room. He has another in his study. I – I think he's still in love with her. After all, it's only been six years since she died.'

'Six years! My dear girl, in my day a widower would be married again within six *months*. Especially if he had young children.' Euphemia put her head on one side and regarded her niece. 'You're not wearing your glasses today, my dear. You look so much better without them. You've got lovely eyes. Just like your mother's.'

Charlotte's heart leapt. 'You – you knew my mother?' Perhaps here was someone who'd be willing to talk to her about the shadowy figure from the past. Mary always seemed reluctant to talk about Alice Crawford. Charlotte believed it was because the woman was afraid that Osbert would find out that she'd been speaking about the forbidden subject.

Euphemia regarded her for a long moment before choosing her words very carefully. 'I – knew your mother. Not at first, of course. As I told you, we were abroad, and by the time your parents married, Osbert and I had fallen out – well, we'll talk about all that some other time.' It was obvious she was anxious to change the subject. Charlotte sighed inwardly. She'd so hoped her aunt would be willing to answer some of the questions that had troubled her for years. 'You know, my dear,' Euphemia had turned her attention back to Charlotte's appearance. 'You could be quite pretty if you had a new hairstyle, some fashionable clothes and, with a very discreet use of cosmetics–'

Now laughter bubbled up inside Charlotte. 'Cosmetics! Father would have a seizure at the mere thought.'

Euphemia's mouth tightened. 'Mm,' was all she said.

'So, you will accept Mr Thornton's invitation?'

'Just try and keep us away!'

Osbert was incensed when he heard. 'What on earth is the man thinking of? Inviting those two. You should have put a stop to it, girl. How did he know anything about them?'

Charlotte answered him calmly. 'I mentioned their arrival to him and he said he'd like to invite them.'

'You'd no right to mention private matters to strangers.'

Greatly daring, Charlotte snapped back, 'They're hardly strangers now, since you intend to leave Buckthorn Farm to Philip.'

He glared at her. 'Well, you'd better undo your meddling, miss. I won't have them anywhere near me.' His eyes narrowed. 'Have you seen them again? Answer me.' His tone was a whip crack.

Charlotte lifted her chin with a defiance she'd never realized she possessed. 'Yes, I went to the White Swan.'

He took a step towards her. 'You deliberately dis-obeyed me, girl. I won't have it.' He was shouting now, enough to bring Edward to the other side of the door, bending so that he could listen, and poised to enter if the row got any uglier than it already was.

'You keep away from them, do you hear me? I don't know what my sister's been telling you, but you're not to believe a word of it. It's all lies to discredit me. She wants to get her hands on my farm. Well, she won't. Not now. Not ever. And nor will you. And the sooner they go back abroad, the better. Out of my way.'

'They're not going abroad again. They're going to settle in England now.'

'Well, they needn't think they're going to stay around here. I won't have it.'

For the first time in her life, Charlotte retorted, 'I don't think you'll have any say in the matter.'

Osbert stepped close and, for a moment, Charlotte thought he was about to strike her. Instead, he shook his fist in her face. 'Don't you back-answer me, girl, else you, for one, won't be going to any dinner party. Or staying in this house for much longer. I'll throw you out, without a penny to your name or clothes on your back. You hear me?'

Charlotte turned away and headed for the sanctuary of the farm office. Her father's threats no longer frightened her. She'd heard them all before. He wouldn't throw her out. Not yet. He needed her to run the farm. But she did believe that he intended to leave Buckthorn Farm to Philip Thornton. Oh yes, that she did believe.

She sighed as she sat down at her desk and tried to concentrate on the paperwork in front of her. Joe would be calling in soon and she was anxious to know how the family fared.

But Joe didn't come and by mid-morning, Charlotte was worried. Perhaps he, too, had flu now. She went down to the kitchen. 'Edward, I'm very concerned about the Warrens. Joe hasn't arrived and he always comes in on Monday and Thursday mornings, as you know. I don't want to go down to the cottage again myself, however; it might look as if I'm – well, implying he shouldn't be off work. D'you think you could go there or maybe find John and ask him? If they've all fallen victim to the influenza, we must do something to help.'

'Of course, Miss Charlotte. I'll go at once.'

Edward was gone a long time and he returned with bad news. 'You were right, miss. Joe's got it now, and John too. Lily's looking after them all, but she looks very peaky. She's sickening for it an' all, I reckon.'

'We must call the doctor.'

'I've already done that, miss. That's why I've been a long time getting back. I went into Ravensfleet and left a message for Dr Markham to call to see them all. I thought it'd be what you'd want.'

'Shall I pack another basket of food, miss? Edward can take it down.'

'I think you'd better make it a hamper, Mary,' Charlotte said wryly. 'Poor Lily won't have much time for cooking and baking with all of them ill. And I'd better see if Matty's managed all the milking.'

Mary nodded and bustled into her pantry. 'Soup,' she murmured. 'That's what they all need. Nourishing soup. That'll not cause Lily too

229

much trouble just to heat it up.'

Later in the day, Edward brought more news. The doctor had called and pronounced Jackson and Peggy 'on the mend'. They'd soon be up and about again. Joe and John were still in bed.

'And Lily?' Charlotte asked. 'Is she coping?' She saw Edward and Mary exchange a glance.

'She'll be all right, miss,' Mary said, but Charlotte had the strange feeling that she was not just referring to caring for the rest of the family.

Charlotte frowned but asked no more questions. 'Let me know if there's anything else we can do. Anything they need.'

'We will, miss.'

Twenty-Seven

'I've a good mind not to go. And I certainly shouldn't be letting you go. You're not used to civilized company,' Osbert grumbled as he and Charlotte climbed into the motor car that Miles Thornton had sent to fetch them on New Year's Eve. 'And where are your glasses? You should be wearing your glasses. You're as blind as a bat without them.'

Charlotte said nothing. She'd known her father would not stay away from the dinner party – not when Philip was home from school. And he couldn't leave her at the farm; Miles had been adamant that his invitation included her. As for the remark about her spectacles, she chose to ignore that.

Euphemia and Percy were already there when Charlotte and her father arrived.

'Dear me,' Euphemia murmured in her ear as she kissed Charlotte's cheek. 'I really must take you in hand, child. That dress is like something out of the ragbag.'

Far from being insulted, Charlotte felt an overwhelming desire to giggle. It was a perfect description for her shabby, purple dress. Euphemia was dressed in a lovely silk, low-waisted pale-blue dress and dainty high-heeled satin shoes.

'Miss Charlotte, Miss Charlotte...' Georgie was at her side, taking her hand and dragging her across the room. 'Come and meet Uncle Felix. He's a friend of Papa's. They were in the war together. He's an artist. He painted the portraits of Mama.'

'I'd love to, Georgie dear, but first I must give Ben his birthday present.'

'Ooh, what have you got for him? Ben – Ben, come here. Charlotte's brought you a present.'

Shyly, Ben unwrapped the leather hunting whip with a staghorn handle and silver collar. 'It's wonderful,' he stammered, taken aback by her generous gift. 'Thank you.'

'You're most welcome.' Charlotte smiled. 'I know *you* will use it properly.'

There was the merest accent on the word 'you', but Ben met her steady gaze and, understanding, nodded. 'I will, Miss Charlotte, I promise you.'

Georgie was tugging at her hand. '*Now* come and meet Uncle Felix.'

The man held out his right hand, but Charlotte

231

noticed, with a shock, that the sleeve of his left arm was empty and tucked into the pocket of his jacket.

'Felix Kerr.' The man smiled at her.

'Charlotte Crawford,' she murmured.

He was small and thin, but his bearing was upright, his back straight. He had a small, goatee beard, once brown but now liberally flecked with grey. His hair was thinning a little, but his dark eyes looked boldly into hers as if he would read her very soul.

With a jolt, Charlotte realized. 'Felix Kerr. Not *the* Felix Kerr?'

The man laughed.

'I'm so sorry.' She blushed, feeling foolish. 'You must get inane remarks like that all the time.' Perhaps her father was right; she wasn't used to polite society. She shouldn't have come. She'd be embarrassing Miles and she'd no wish to do that. She tried desperately to repair the damage. 'I've read about your work, but I'm sorry, I've never been able to see any of it – except, of course, the portraits of Mrs Thornton.'

But his eyes were twinkling with amusement. 'Don't apologize. Of course, the last portrait I did of dear Louisa – the one with her two children that we'll see in a moment in the dining room – was done at the beginning of the war just before I volunteered.' He sighed. 'My style has changed a little since.'

'Oh? Why?' The direct question was out before she thought to stop it, and once more she found herself apologizing.

But Felix was happy to explain. 'Not because of

my injury. Luckily, I'm right-handed. It would have been devastating if I'd lost my right arm, I don't mind admitting. But no, it's because of what I went through – what all of us went through.'

Charlotte glanced across the room towards Miles. 'Mr Thornton too? Was he wounded?'

'Twice, I think, but fortunately not seriously, though the last injury ended the war early for him. I had to wait until the very last month of the war, would you believe, before I got myself a Blighty wound. Still, we should be grateful. We're both still here. So many of our fellow soldiers aren't.'

'It was a dreadful time,' Charlotte murmured. 'The papers were full of casualty lists every day and almost every family had someone involved. And waiting for the dreaded telegram...'

'I know. And then the influenza that swept the country at the end of 'eighteen. I lost my wife and child in that epidemic.'

'I'm sorry.'

He shrugged and sighed. 'I wasn't the only one who'd lost loved ones. All those mothers and wives losing their men in the war. And Miles, too, losing poor Louisa in childbirth.'

'What – what was she like?'

'Louisa? A lady in the very best sense of the word. Beautiful, charming, but with a deliciously wicked sense of humour. I can see a lot of her in Georgie. He's a charmer, isn't he, but in a nice way?'

Charlotte laughed. 'He most certainly is. He's adorable.'

She saw Felix glance down at her left hand.

'You're not married, Charlotte?' She was startled, but pleasantly surprised, at the use of her Christian name after such a short acquaintance, but perhaps, she thought, that's how things were done in the artistic world. She felt a sudden pang of longing; not, for once, to be married, but to be part of the exciting world of artists.

'No – no, I'm not.' She was stuck now for a topic of conversation and suddenly felt her in-adequacy in socializing. But, like the perfect host, Miles arrived at her shoulder. 'I'm so glad you and Felix are getting to know one another. I've heard a whisper that you are an artist too, Miss Charlotte.'

Now Charlotte blushed. 'No – oh no,' she pro-tested. 'Please – I don't deserve such a title.'

Miles chuckled. 'That's not what I've heard. You're being modest.'

'No, no, really I'm not. I love drawing and pain-ting – that's true. But I've no talent. It's just a hobby.' She glanced across at her father as she added, 'A *secret* hobby.'

'A secret?' Felix was scandalized. 'You should never keep a talent hidden, my dear. You should be proud of it.' He linked his arm through hers as dinner was announced and the guests moved through to the dining room. 'Now, I shall insist I see your work. *I* will tell you – truthfully – if you have any talent.'

Charlotte smiled, but said no more as Georgie appeared at her other side and took her hand. 'You're sitting by me, Miss Charlotte. I arranged all the places especially.'

'I see you have an admirer, my dear,' Felix

whispered. 'But I do hope I'm placed on your other side.'

Indeed he was, and by the end of the evening, Charlotte could not remember ever having enjoyed herself so much. She'd even managed to ignore her father's glowering looks from the other end of the table. She'd been monopolized by Felix and Georgie, so there'd been only a brief exchange of words between herself and Cuthbert Iveson. And she had the feeling that he was avoiding being seen talking to her. Besides, at the dinner table it was Euphemia who held sway, regaling them all with tales from their days of living abroad. As for Osbert, his attention was taken up by Philip sitting opposite him.

Miles sat at the head of the table, surveying his guests and making sure they were looked after and entertained. He watched Charlotte and Felix talking and was fascinated by how the girl's face came alive as she talked and listened to Felix. But she was attentive to Georgie, too, turning every so often to make sure he was not left out.

She's a kindly soul, he thought, who deserves a better life than the one she's got.

As the party broke up at about eleven, Felix squeezed her hand. 'I don't know when I last enjoyed myself so much.'

'Nor me,' Charlotte said with guileless honesty.

'And you must let me see your work. I'm staying the weekend with Miles. Perhaps you could come over tomorrow and bring some of your drawings and paintings. I—'

'What's that?' Her father was at her side. He

had his hat and coat on and was carrying his walking stick.

'I was just asking your daughter—'

'Oh please,' Charlotte whispered, suddenly frantic. 'Don't—'

'You're the artist fellow, aren't you?' Without waiting for a response, Osbert turned on Charlotte. 'What have you been saying? Making a fool of yourself again, I don't doubt.'

He grasped her arm and began to pull her towards the door. 'Get yourself home. You're a disgrace. I wish you'd never been born. I'd rather be childless than saddled with you.'

The other guests stood rooted to the spot, shocked to the core by the vicious words spilling from his mouth. Miles stepped forward, but Osbert was already pushing her down the steps and into the waiting motor car. Though Miles hurried after them, Osbert slammed the door and the vehicle moved off before he could reach it. He returned to his other guests, still standing where he'd left them.

Euphemia found her voice at last. 'I see my dear brother hasn't changed in all these years. That poor girl.'

It was a sentiment echoed by all of them, except one. Philip Thornton turned away with a smirk on his face.

When they arrived back at Buckthorn Farm, Osbert hustled her into the house through the door Edward was holding open.

'Stay here,' Osbert commanded. 'Morgan – see that she does, else it'll be the worse for you.'

White-faced, Charlotte watched her father mount the stairs.

'What's wrong? What's happened?' Edward whispered urgently as soon as Osbert was out of earshot.

'There was an artist there. Felix Kerr. And Miles – Mr Thornton' – she had begun to think of him as 'Miles' in her head – 'told him that – that I painted.'

'Oh dear!' Edward murmured.

'Yes,' Charlotte said flatly. 'Oh dear.'

Osbert had reached the top of the stairs, had turned to the left and disappeared. They both heard the door of Charlotte's room being flung open, crashing back against the wardrobe that stood behind it. Then the sound of crashing, things being swept off a table, pots and paints scattered and, finally, whilst Charlotte closed her eyes and cringed, the sound of tearing paper.

'Come on, love.' Edward put his arm about her shoulders. 'Let's go to the kitchen.'

Dumbly, she allowed him to lead her, stumbling, through the door and into the warm, comforting kitchen. She was shaking. Mary, knitting by the range, let her work fall to the floor as she got up. Her worried eyes went to her husband.

'It's him,' Edward said shortly. 'He's upstairs in her room, destroying everything, by the sounds of it.'

'Destroying?'

'Her paintings. Just because some chap at the dinner party – an artist – took an interest.'

'In her,' Mary asked shrewdly, 'or in her paintings?'

'Both, I expect.'

'Come on, lovey. Sit down. I'll make us some cocoa. Edward can go up in a bit and see if the coast's clear.'

Mary was pouring hot milk into a mug, when they all heard footsteps in the passage and the door was flung open. Osbert came in, brandishing his stick. Bravely, Edward leapt up and stood in front of Charlotte.

'Out of my way, man. This is between me and my hussy of a – *daughter.'* He spat out the last word with venom.

He raised his stick, but Edward stood firm. 'You'll not hit her again. Not ever, not whilst I'm in this house.'

'Then you can pack your bags and go. The pair of you. You and your good-for-nothing wife.'

'Gladly, but if we do,' Edward said with surprising calm, 'Miss Charlotte goes with us. We'll not leave her here to your tender mercies,' he added with sarcasm.

'And where d'you think you'll go, eh? The workhouse – the three of you.'

'Mebbe that'd be preferable to staying here. Aye, I reckon it would, an' all. But dun't you forget, *sir,'* Edward grabbed the stick and twisted it out of Osbert's hand, 'that me an' my missis know a few secrets, now, don't we? We've only stayed here all these years and kept silent for *her* sake. Not yourn. Never yourn.'

'You wouldn't.' Osbert's voice was a whisper now – a menacing, terrifying whisper. 'You wouldn't dare!'

'Oh we would. Believe me, we would. Because

she's old enough now to know the truth. And now that Miss Charlotte's aunt has come back, well, she's someone of her own flesh and blood to turn to, hasn't she?'

'My sister will keep her nose out of my affairs, if she knows what's good for her.'

'I doubt you have any hold over her now – that is, if you ever had.'

'Oh, I had. I still have, because I doubt she's ever told that milksop of a husband of hers the truth about herself. She was a whore, that's what my dear sister was. Still is, by the look of the way she dresses. I won't have her corrupting *her*.' He stabbed his finger towards Charlotte. Irrationally, at such a moment of drama, Charlotte realized that she couldn't remember when her father had ever called her by her name. She had always been 'girl', 'her', 'she' or even, on occasions, 'it'.

Seeing that he was not going to get beyond the stronger, fitter Edward, Osbert turned away. 'Go on, then. Get out. Do your worst. See if I care. There's plenty more to take your place. And you can take her with you – and welcome. I never wanted her in the first place.'

As the door swung to behind him, the three in the kitchen were left staring at it.

Twenty-Eight

The following morning Charlotte rose with bleary eyes and a heavy heart. Whilst she'd never been really overwhelmingly happy, she'd never been sad. She'd never realized that her life should, and could, be very different. But now the misery lay like a heavy weight on her chest.

I'll go and see Jackson, she thought. Maybe he's well enough to talk to me. But it was Peggy who opened the door of their cottage and when Charlotte saw her face, her own worries were forgotten.

'Whatever's the matter, Peggy?'

The woman's face was pale and drawn – no doubt from the illness. But the anguish it showed could have nothing to do with a bout of influenza. For a moment Peggy stared at her, almost as if she didn't recognize her. The older woman was locked in some private grief that obliterated everything else.

'Is it Joe?'

Mutely, Peggy shook her head.

'One of the others, then? Are they worse? Have you called the doctor again? You must–'

'No, miss.' Peggy's voice was husky with weariness following a sleepless night. Her eyes were dark hollows and her mouth quivered. She was close to tears. 'Please, miss. I can't say. Just leave us.'

'No, I won't. There's something obviously very wrong. And I want to help.'

'You can't help. Nobody can.' Peggy's voice was flat, drained of emotion. For some reason her world was in tatters.

'Don't shut me out, Peggy.' Charlotte touched her hand. 'You're like my family. You, Joe, the boys–' She forced a smile, trying to cheer Peggy somehow. 'Even that little rapscallion, Tommy. And Lily, too.'

At the mention of her daughter's name, Peggy's mouth trembled. Tears welled in her eyes and trickled down her cheeks. 'Oh, Miss Charlotte...' She covered her face with her hands and as Charlotte stepped forward to put her arms round her, Peggy wept against her shoulder.

'You can tell me,' Charlotte murmured against her ear. 'Whatever it is. You know it will go no further.'

Peggy sniffed, raised her head and scrubbed at her face with the corner of her apron. 'It'll get round eventually, miss. Bound to. You can't keep summat like this secret for long. Everyone'll know soon enough.'

'Then–?'

'But we're so ashamed, miss. We never thought summat like this'd happen to our little family. We've tried to bring the bairns up proper. To know right from wrong. But this – it's destroying my Joe. Lily was the apple of his eye and now she's brought shame on all the family.'

Realization began to dawn in Charlotte's mind. 'She's – she's not–'

Peggy nodded. 'She's got 'ersen into trouble.'

241

'Who's the – the father?'

'She won't say. We thought it might be Eddie Norton. You know, the stable lad at the manor. Seems he's always been sweet on our Lily. But Jackson went to see him. Gave him a bit of a leathering, I reckon, but the lad still denied it. When they'd both calmed down, Jackson says Eddie was genuinely shocked.'

'She really won't tell you? But – but surely – I mean, perhaps they could get married.'

'She's shut up like a clam and barricaded herself in her bedroom. Well, I say *her* bedroom. It's Tommy's room now, 'cept when she comes home for a night or two. Then he moves in with the boys. They've got Grandad's old room.' She sobbed afresh. 'All Joe can say is, "Thank God me poor ol' dad's not here to see this."'

Charlotte caught her breath. When Lily comes home, Peggy had said. Of course, the girl spent most of the time at the manor now as a live-in maid. A shudder ran through her as brief images flashed into her memory. Lily emerging from one of the outbuildings and Philip appearing moments later; Lily and Philip holding hands in the icy weather. Lily and Philip... Oh, surely not.

Charlotte hugged Peggy again, feeling tears stinging her own eyes too. Then she stood back and said briskly, 'Now, come along, let's see what we can do to sort this out. May I come in?'

'I don't know, miss, Joe won't–'

'Never mind Joe. I'll deal with him.'

With a sigh Peggy gave way. She was obviously troubled about her husband's reaction as she led Charlotte through the back scullery and into the kitchen, but Joe didn't even look up. He was sitting hunched in front of the range, as if the weight of the world rested on his shoulders. And, at this moment, Charlotte thought, no doubt it felt as if it did.

'Joe?' She sat down opposite him and reached across the hearth to touch his hand. 'Joe, don't be angry with Peggy. I want to help. What can I do?'

Slowly, he raised his head and stared at her for a moment. In a low, defeated tone, he said, 'There's nowt can be done, Miss Charlotte. If she won't even tell us who the – the bastard is, who's–' For a brief moment he was roused out of lethargy by the anger surging through him.

Peggy stood between them, wringing her hands. 'She – we ought to tell them at the manor. She – won't be going back.'

'Leave it!' Joe snapped and then said more calmly, 'leave it for now. They'll think she's still looking after us. It can wait a day or two. Till I've got me head round it.' He paused and added heavily, 'If I ever do.' He covered his face with his hands. 'Oh Lily. My Lily. My little girl,' he moaned, his shoulders shaking, whilst Peggy looked helplessly at Charlotte.

Charlotte waited patiently, until Joe became calmer. 'Joe, I promise I won't do anything behind your back – without your permission, but I really believe I could help you. Will you trust me?'

Slowly, he raised his head. 'Miss Charlotte, I'd trust you wi' me life. I know you'd never knowingly do anything to hurt me and mine. But, I beg you, don't tell anyone. Not yet.'

Charlotte bit her lip. 'I understand how you

243

feel, Joe, but I may not have much time.'

'I don't understand.'

Charlotte sighed. 'There's been trouble at home. My father's more or less told me to leave. Mary and Edward too. At the moment, I don't know if he was serious or whether it was just said in a fit of temper. All I know is my own future is uncertain.' She took a deep breath. 'It seems my father intends to leave all his worldly goods to someone else, leaving me penniless. Even I never thought his bitterness went quite so deep.'

She saw the glance that passed between husband and wife and a gasp of surprise escaped her lips. 'You – you *knew?*'

Joe looked guilty and Peggy wouldn't meet her eyes.

'I'm sorry, miss. Mr Thornton told us in confidence.'

'And did he tell you too,' Charlotte added bitterly, 'that my father tried to – to blackmail him into marrying me to ensure his son's future?'

Joe nodded and Charlotte felt the flush of embarrassed shame creep into her face. But then she sighed. It wasn't the fault of these good people. They'd been put in an invidious position. Again, she reached across and touched Joe's hand. 'It's all right. I understand and respect you keeping the man's confidence. But, Joe, I'm begging you to let me help you now. Lily's – condition – is bound to be obvious very soon. What difference would a few weeks make when we may be able to sort something out?'

Joe sighed and glanced up at his wife. Peggy gave a little nod.

'I suppose you're right, miss. Do whatever you think best. I know you'll have our best interests at heart. And Lily's.'

'You can be sure of that, Joe. Very sure.' There was a moment's silence before she asked gently, 'So, do you want to know what I intend to do?'

Joe shook his head. 'No, miss. I can't take any more. Not just now. Just – leave me be. Leave me be.' The last was said in a whisper as he buried his face in his hands again.

Twenty-Nine

It took all Charlotte's courage to saddle a horse and ride to the manor. Leaving her horse with the stable lad, she entered through the kitchen door. Mrs Beddows greeted her.

'Am I glad to see you, Miss Charlotte. D'you know when we can expect Lily back? We're run off our feet here. She's such a good little worker. I never realized just how much work that lass gets through until she's not here, if you know what I mean.'

Charlotte smiled weakly. 'It – it might be a little while yet, Mrs Beddows.'

The cook's face fell. 'I'm sorry to hear that. Mebbe I'd best get someone from the village in temporary, like. That's if the master doesn't mind.'

'Perhaps it would be best, Mrs Beddows.' She paused and then, trying to make her question sound casual, she asked, 'Is Mr Thornton in?'

'I think so. I'd get Lily to take you up if she was here, but—'

'Don't trouble, please. I can find my own way.'

'But Wilkins should announce you, miss.'

Charlotte hid her smile. Mrs Beddows liked things to be done properly. 'I'll see if I can find Wilkins,' she promised the cook.

But as she emerged from the door leading from the kitchens into the main hall, Charlotte saw Miles running down the stairs, heading for his study.

Hearing the sound of the door, he turned.

'Charlotte,' he said in surprise. Irrationally, her heart lifted as she noticed he'd dropped the 'miss' when addressing her. But her pleasure was lost in an instant as she thought about the reason for her unannounced visit. 'Come in, come in. Shall we go into the morning room? I'll ring for coffee.'

'No, no, your study will be fine. I – I like your study.'

Miles laughed. 'So do I. It's my favourite room in the house.'

When they were comfortably seated and Wilkins had been summoned and instructed to bring coffee, Miles said, 'I'm so relieved to see you. I was so worried after last night. We all were. Georgie couldn't sleep. He came into my room twice in the night because he was so worried about you. Your aunt too – she said she'd be going to Buckthorn Farm first thing this morning. And Felix – he felt responsible. *Are* you all right?' he ended, concern etched on his face.

Charlotte took a deep breath. 'Well, there was some trouble at home. I'm not quite sure what will happen yet, but that's not what I've come to see you about.' She bit her lip.

Wilkins brought the coffee in and they were obliged to wait whilst he poured them both a cup. As the door closed behind him, Miles said gently, 'You can tell me anything, you know.'

'It's – very difficult. It's about Lily.'

'Has she caught the flu too?'

Charlotte shook her head. 'No – it's worse than that.'

There was a pause but now Miles asked no more questions.

'She – she's in trouble.'

Miles frowned for a moment and then understood. 'Lily? *Lily?* She's pregnant?'

Charlotte nodded miserably.

'Bless my soul. I can hardly believe it. Lily – of all people. She seemed such a good, sensible girl.'

'She is – usually.'

'Poor Joe – and Peggy. They must be devastated.'

'They are.'

'Is there anything I can do?'

'Yes. Help me find the father of her child.'

'I don't understand.'

'Lily is refusing to name him.'

He eyed her shrewdly. 'But you think you have an idea who it might be?'

Charlotte set her cup down. This was where it got very difficult.

'Had she any–' she almost smiled at the use of the old-fashioned term, but it seemed to sum up the situation – 'any followers?'

'Not that I know of, but then, I'm afraid I don't know everything that goes on below stairs.' His face clouded for a moment as he murmured, 'Perhaps if Louisa was still here...'

'I understand,' Charlotte said gently. She paused a moment before adding, 'Would you give me your permission to talk to the staff? They might know something.'

Miles ran his hand across his face. 'Of course. Oh dear, I feel so responsible. She's been in my care, so to speak, and now – this.'

'It's not your fault. It happens. But I did think,' she added sadly, 'that Lily had more sense.'

'Do you think whoever is the father might marry her?'

Charlotte shrugged. 'That rather depends on who it is.' She avoided meeting his gaze. A suspicion had begun to grow and take root, but it was one which, until she knew more, she could not share with Miles. Especially not with Miles.

She finished her coffee, set the cup down and stood up. 'If you'll excuse me, the sooner I start, the sooner I can find out, and we might be able to – to arrange something.' She was praying silently that her misgivings were not true. What trouble it would cause if they were.

Miles rose too. He took her hands in his and looked down into her face. 'Promise me that you'll come to me if there's anything – anything at all – that I can do.'

Charlotte nodded, whilst hoping fervently that it had nothing at all to do with Miles Thornton and his family.

Moments later, she was back in the kitchen

talking to Mrs Beddows and the kitchen maid – a young girl of fourteen from the village who lived in too. For the moment, Charlotte confided in the cook, keeping her voice low so that Jane should not hear.

'Mrs Beddows – I'm so sorry, but I don't think Lily will be coming back. She's – she's in trouble.'

The woman's mouth dropped open, not because she didn't understand at once what Charlotte meant, but because she was shocked to hear such a thing about the girl she liked so much. *'Lily* is?' Her surprise was as great as Miles's had been.

'Do you know if she'd been walking out with anyone?'

Mrs Beddows pursed her lips. 'I don't encourage it, Miss Charlotte. Oh, I know you can't stop it like you could in the old days, but–' she sighed – 'look where it leads.'

Silently, Charlotte thought, Maybe it wouldn't have if you'd allowed her to meet her young man openly.

'It'll be that Eddie Norton,' Mrs Beddows said grimly, nodding her head as if agreeing with her own statement. 'He's always hanging about the kitchen when she's about. I've had to clear him off many a time.'

Charlotte sighed. 'Apparently not. Jackson's already spoken to him and he's denied it.'

'Well, he would, wouldn't he?' Mrs Beddows pursed her lips. 'That's what they all do. Have their fun and then leave the poor girl to cope. The silly, silly girl!'

'Is there anyone else who works here other than

Eddie who–?'

But the cook was shaking her head. 'No, not that I can think of. No one of her own age, certainly.' Then she nodded towards the girl washing dishes at the deep sink in the scullery. 'You'd better talk to Jane. She sleeps in the same bedroom. Mebbe she knows summat.'

'Thank you, Mrs Beddows.' As she went towards the scullery, she heard the woman muttering beneath her breath. 'Wretched girl! Now I've got to train another one to my ways.'

'Jane?'

The girl, singing softly to herself as she worked, gave a startled cry and almost dropped the wet plate she was holding. 'Oh, miss, you gave me a fright.'

'I'm sorry. Could you spare me a moment?'

'Of course, miss.' The girl dried her hands on a rough piece of towelling.

'Lily's in trouble. You – you know what I mean, don't you?'

The girl's eyes widened. 'You mean she's going to have a bairn?'

Charlotte nodded. 'But she won't tell us who the father of her child is. And if we could find out, then maybe we could help her. Help them both.'

Jane was biting her lip anxiously and looking away. Quietly, Charlotte said gently, 'I think you know, don't you?'

'I – I daresunt tell, miss. She'd never forgive me.'

'Your loyalty does you credit, Jane, but we all need to be able to help Lily, and the only way we

250

can do that is to find out whom she's been seeing.'

Now tears were running down the young girl's cheeks. She twisted her fingers together agitatedly.

'Is it one of the stable lads? Eddie – or someone else?' Jane shook her head.

'One of the farm workers, then?'

Again, a shake of the head.

Charlotte took a deep breath and plunged in, forced into voicing her own fears. 'Is it – is it someone who lives here? In this house?'

'Please don't ask me,' Jane wailed.

Charlotte took hold of the girl's shoulders and shook her gently. 'You must tell me. Is it?'

The girl's tears flowed freely and she pressed her lips together as if to stop the words bursting out. She closed her eyes, trying to shut out Charlotte and her troublesome questions.

'Is it – Philip?'

Jane's eyes flew open, staring and frightened. Then, slowly, she nodded.

Thirty

Charlotte now believed she knew the truth. What she couldn't decide was how best to deal with it. She didn't feel able to tell Miles until she was absolutely sure; until Lily had admitted it. So, the only thing to do, she decided, was to confront the girl herself.

She remounted her horse and rode slowly back towards the Warrens' cottage. The family were seated much as she'd left them, except that John had now got up out of his sick bed and was sitting huddled in a blanket near the range. He still looked pale and ill. Joe was sitting just as Charlotte had last seen him, but Jackson was pacing the floor of the small room.

'Peggy, could I speak to Lily, please? Alone?'

'If you can make her open her door, miss. She's put summat against it and none of us can open it from this side. Not even Jackson, an' he's as strong as an ox. Usually. Reckon the flu's taken more out of us all than we realized. And now this.'

Charlotte went up the dark, narrow staircase. How ironic, she thought, that only a few months ago she, too, had locked herself in her room and refused to come out. She sympathized with Lily; she knew just how she felt.

Only one bedroom door was closed. She knocked and called out softly, 'Lily, it's me – Charlotte. Please open the door. I need to talk to you. I want to help.'

Silence.

She tried again. 'Lily–' Her voice was firmer now and she was aware that Jackson was listening at the bottom of the stairs. 'You've got to come out some time, so why not now? Let's talk about it and see what can be done.'

Still – silence.

Charlotte sighed. There was nothing else for it except to be cruel to be kind. 'Lily – I believe I know who the father of your baby is and if you don't come out, then I'm going to tell your family

252

– and his father.'

There was a scrambling sound inside the room, the scraping of something heavy being pulled away from the door and then the door itself was flung open. Wild-eyed, her face swollen and ravaged by tears, Lily faced her. 'Don't you dare say anything, miss. It's nowt to do wi' you. Leave me alone. I'll sort it out mesen. I'll go away–'

'Now, now, don't be silly. There's no need for all this. Your family's shocked and hurt, but if I know them – and I think I do – they'll stand by you. *I'll* stand by you.' She wasn't sure how she was to do it when her own future was so precarious, but somehow she'd see the girl cared for.

Suddenly, the girl was crying heart-wrenching tears. She sobbed against Charlotte's shoulder. Charlotte put her arms round Lily and held her close. 'There, there,' she soothed. 'We'll see what's to be done. Come along downstairs now.'

She led the weeping girl to the head of the stairs to see both Peggy and Jackson staring up at them. Lily gave a sob and tried to flee back to the sanctuary of her bedroom, but Charlotte held her firm. 'It has to be faced, Lily.'

Downstairs in the crowded kitchen, the atmosphere was tense. Even Tommy, the only one to escape the influenza, had come indoors from playing outside and was staring wide-eyed at his sister, not understanding what was happening.

'Tommy, love, go out and play, there's a good lad,' Peggy said.

'But, Mam–' he began to protest but seeing the

253

look on his mother's face, his father hunched by the fire and Jackson looking like thunder, the boy went meekly, even closing the back door quietly behind him.

Lily flew into her mother's arms. 'Oh, Mam, I'm so sorry. I thought he really loved me. He said he knew how to – to be careful. He *promised* me...'

Seeing her genuine distress, the tension in the room eased. The Warren family came together in their love for this daughter, this sister, who'd been so hurt.

'Who is it, Lil?' Jackson demanded. 'Just tell us who it is? I'll bloody kill him.'

'Aye, well,' Peggy said, holding her daughter close. 'You're not the first lass to be taken in by promises, an' I don't expect you'll be the last.'

'Come here, love,' Joe said huskily, standing up and holding out his arms. 'Come to your ol' dad.'

As Lily went into his embrace, Charlotte couldn't help feeling tears prickle her eyes. How wonderful to have a father who loved his daughter enough to forgive her anything.

'Don't worry, Lily.' John spoke up too. 'If he can't or won't marry you, we'll take care of you and your bairn. Fancy,' he smiled round at the rest of the family, trying to lighten the tension even further, 'our Tommy is going to be an uncle. Whatever will he say?'

'Sit down, lass,' Joe urged at last. He pushed her gently into the chair and sat down opposite her, taking her hands in his. 'Now, you've got to tell us who it is.'

'I can't, Dad.'

'Why not, lass? Whoever he is, he ought to know.'

'Is he married?' Jackson asked bluntly.

Lily's head shot up. 'No – no. I'd never...' She began to deny it hotly, then subsided into fresh tears.

'Then tell us.'

Lily glanced at Charlotte, who asked, 'You want me to tell them?'

The girl bit her lip but nodded.

'Of course, if I'm wrong–'

'I'll say if you are, miss. I won't let someone else take the blame, I promise you that.'

All eyes turned upon Charlotte now, Lily's almost imploring her to be wrong, so that she could deny it. How desperately she wanted to keep her secret.

'I've seen you with him twice,' Charlotte said quietly. 'Once coming from one of the out-buildings at the back of the manor. The other time was in the icy weather on Christmas Eve. He was holding your hand, saying he was helping you...'

Lily gasped, her eyes wide, her hand flying to cover her open mouth and everyone in the room knew that Charlotte was right.

'It *is* Eddie Norton! The little liar,' Jackson shouted, thumping his fist into the palm of his other hand.

'No, Jackson,' Charlotte said softly. 'It isn't Eddie, though–' She stopped herself mid-sentence. She'd been going to say that if the father of Lily's baby had been Eddie, then she'd no doubt the lad would marry her willingly. Charlotte pulled

255

in a deep breath before she said, 'It's Philip, isn't it, Lily? Philip Thornton.'

There was a stunned silence in the room, but seeing Lily hang her head and make no denial, they all knew it was the truth.

'Philip Thornton!' Joe was incredulous. 'But – but he's only a boy. He's – he's still at school, for heaven's sake.'

'Huh!' Jackson spat through gritted teeth. 'Not such a *boy*.'

Lily clutched at her father. 'Please, Dad, don't make trouble for him. I'm as much to blame. I – I love him and he loves me. I'm sure he does.'

'Aw, lass,' Joe said heavily. 'But he'll never marry you. Not the likes of him with – with *us*.'

Now Peggy turned to Charlotte. 'Thank you for your help, miss. We appreciate it. At least we know the truth now. We know what we've got to deal with.'

Already Peggy was stronger. The whole family was rallying round, taking strength from their love for each other and determining to protect Lily. They'd be all right now, Charlotte was sure.

'If there's anything I can do to help, you let me know.' She looked straight at Joe. 'Promise me?'

Joe nodded. 'Aye, an' thank you again, miss.'

She left the cottage and walked her horse back up the lane towards Buckthorn Farm. They'd be all right. They'd come through this trouble, she knew. They'd pull together as a family.

As she neared her home, she lifted her head and let her glance roam over the house, the buildings and the surrounding fields.

But what about her? What was to become of her?

The only two people in the world who had any affection for her were no blood relation: Mary and Edward. And by nightfall, if her father had meant what he'd said, they could all find themselves homeless.

She smiled wryly to herself. Never mind trying to help others in trouble – who was going to help her?

Thirty-One

Charlotte entered the farmhouse by the back door to find the kitchen alive with chatter. Euphemia and Percy were sitting in the Windsor chairs on either side of the range whilst Mary was busy making tea and handing round her home-made biscuits. Edward stood to one side, listening as Euphemia held court.

As Charlotte opened the door, they all looked up.

Euphemia flung her arms wide. 'My dear child, we were so worried about you after last night. We just had to come and see if you're all right. Come here and kiss your old aunt.'

Charlotte was enfolded in a perfumed embrace. 'Now, sit down, dear girl. Your uncle and I want to talk to you.'

Edward placed a chair for Charlotte to sit beside her aunt, who didn't let go of the young woman's hand.

'We've seen your father – briefly – but he's made

257

it quite clear we're not wanted in this house, but' – she glanced up – 'we found a welcome with Mary and Edward. From what I can glean, it's these two good people who've been the mainstays in your life. Am I right?'

'You are, Aunt,' Charlotte said huskily, realizing just how very much she owed these loyal people. She couldn't and wouldn't call them servants. They were more than that. So much more.

'Well, now,' Euphemia went on, patting Charlotte's hand. 'We've come to ask you to come and live with us when we find a place and get settled. We're hoping to buy a house somewhere near Lincoln.' She looked up at the couple standing nearby, a question in her eyes. 'I don't know, though, what Mary and Edward want to do. I mean, we'll be needing a cook, so...'

Edward was shaking his head. ''Tis very kind of you, ma'am, but as long as Miss Charlotte's settled and cared for, then maybe it's time me an' Mary thought about retiring.' He smiled ruefully. 'We're not getting any younger, as the saying goes.'

There was silence as they all looked towards Charlotte. It was for her to make the momentous decision. She took a deep breath. 'Aunt Euphemia – Uncle Percy. I am touched by your kindness. Really I am. We've only just met and yet here you are offering me a home.' Tears filled her eyes. She'd rarely known such thoughtfulness. And from comparative strangers, too, even though they were blood relatives. She bit her lip, not quite knowing how to phrase her next words. 'At the moment, everything here is in turmoil. I really don't know what's going to happen. If my father didn't really mean what he said yesterday, then I must stay here and – and run the farm.'

'Run the farm?' Euphemia almost squeaked. '*You* run the farm?'

Charlotte lowered her gaze. It had been kept a secret for so many years that she found it hard even now to break her silence. But Edward had no such qualms – not now.

'Miss Charlotte has run things since she was about eighteen. When she was growing up, she helped around the farm all the time. The labourers and their families have been her friends, ma'am. As she got older, your brother passed more and more responsibility on to her shoulders. "You see to it, girl," he'd say, waving his hand and disappearing into the sitting room. D'you know, ma'am, except for church on a Sunday, he's spent the last few years shut away in that room. I mean, if he'd been off out to the city or going to shooting parties or to market, like he used to, I could've understood it. But no, he's done nothing 'cept sit in that room ever since–' he paused abruptly, cleared his throat and then went on, 'well, for years. He's had no life, ma'am, and, if you'll excuse me saying so, he's made sure his daughter hasn't had either.'

'Yes,' Euphemia said slowly. 'I can see that.' She turned back to Charlotte. 'But you still feel dutybound, I suppose – to stay here?'

Charlotte sighed. 'At least until things sort themselves out a little. Then I'll know. But I must see that Mary and Edward are all right.' She held out her hand and reached for Mary. 'But for them' – her voice was husky with emotion – 'I don't know what would have happened to me.'

'Oh, Miss Charlotte,' Mary wept.

'I do understand,' Euphemia said. 'We just want you to know that you'll always have a place to come to if ever you should need it.'

'Thank you, Aunt.'

'And now, I'll brave the lion in his den one last time. I still don't like being at loggerheads with my brother, but there you are. There's nothing more I can do. I've tried.'

In the sitting room Osbert was as truculent and determined as ever. 'I don't want to see you again, Euphemia. You're nothing to me. And if you think you've a right to the farm when I'm gone, then you can think again. I shall be making a will that cannot be broken. Philip Thornton will get everything.'

Euphemia, for once in her life lost for words, turned away and, with her husband, stalked from the house.

In the farmhouse kitchen, Charlotte, Mary and Edward sat around the table.

'There's something you'll have to know,' Charlotte began. 'I don't usually break confidences, but I know I can trust you both.' Quickly, she told them of the misfortune that had befallen the Warren family. To her surprise, they both took the news calmly and philosophically.

'We knew summat was wrong, but not what.' Mary sighed and shrugged. 'It happens, Miss Charlotte. I could tell you about one or two folks round here whose marriages were hastily arranged and then their bairns appeared less than six or seven months afterwards.' She smiled. 'But I won't.'

'The Warrens took it hard at first, but I think they're coming to terms with it now. They'll all stand by her.'

'Of course they will,' Mary said firmly. She wouldn't have expected anything less.

The two young men, crouching in the long grass near a copse to the south of Ravensfleet, watched as the rider on horseback approached.

'Is it him?' John whispered. 'We don't want to get the wrong one.'

'I don't much care as long as 'tis a Thornton,' Jackson muttered.

'It could be the master. Philip's horse is that big black one that Miss Charlotte brought home to break in. That's a grey.'

Jackson squinted through the grass. 'Aye, but it's him, right enough. It's Philip.'

'Are you sure he ain't gone back to school? All the kids round here have gone back.'

'Nah – his fancy school don't start back till next week. It's him, right enough. Look sharp – he's coming this way.'

'I'm not sure we ought to be doing this,' John murmured.

'He needs teaching a lesson. He's brought our sister down. He's going to pay.'

As the horse neared the shadow of the trees, its pace slowed. The brothers stretched a rope across the pathway – and waited.

Thirty-Two

In the afternoon, Charlotte went into Ravensfleet to do some shopping. Walking across the market place, she heard shouting coming from the direction of the school.

It was 'home time' and the cries of joy as the children were let out for the day always made her smile. But then her smile faded. The cries she was hearing today were not the joyful sounds of laughter she'd expected. She glanced down the side road leading out of the market place where the school was situated. A group of boys – and even a few girls – were standing in a circle on the pathway and spilling out on to the road. They were shouting and yelling encouragement to two boys fighting in the centre of the ring.

Charlotte hurried towards the mêlée, glancing around for a teacher who might put a stop to the trouble. But there was no one.

'Never someone in authority when you want them,' she muttered to herself and quickened her step. Placing her shopping basket on the ground, she waded in amongst the crowd of children.

'Stop it! Stop it at once,' she shouted. As she pushed her way through, she saw to her horror that the two boys fighting were Tommy Warren and Georgie Thornton. 'Not you two again,' she said, grasping them strongly, one in each hand. 'Stop it – the pair of you.' As she pulled the two boys apart, they stood glaring at each other, gasping for breath. Georgie had a bleeding nose and Tommy's eye was beginning to swell alarmingly. His lip was cut and bleeding too.

Still holding them, Charlotte turned back to the other children. 'Away home with you. The fight's over.'

'No, it ain't, miss. Not till I've knocked 'im flat.'

'Tommy! I thought you two were friends now.'

'Friends?' the boy spat. 'After what his precious brother's done to me sister?'

Charlotte gasped. 'Tommy! How – how d'you know about such things?'

'I heard,' the young boy muttered.

'And what good do you think fighting with little Georgie is going to do, eh?' She bent closer. 'Tommy, I shouldn't think he even understands what it's all about.'

'He does now.' With a sudden twist, Tommy pulled himself free of her grasp and, before she could stop him, landed another vicious punch to Geordie's tender chin. Then he turned and began to run, shouting as a parting shot, 'You wait, Georgie Thornton. I'll get you. You won't allus be able to hide behind Miss Charlotte's skirt.'

When Charlotte looked down at him, she saw that Georgie was crying, but she had the feeling that his tears were not so much for his injuries as for the broken friendship.

She bent down in front of him and gathered him into her arms. 'Don't cry, darling. Please don't cry. It's not your fault. Tommy is upset about something and he's taken it out on you,

I'm afraid.'

'I – I don't know what he meant, Miss Charlotte. What has Philip done to Lily? Has he hurt her? I thought he liked her. They're always laughing and talking. I've seen them.'

Charlotte straightened up and took his hand. She picked up her basket and began to lead him back towards the market place where she'd tethered the pony and trap. 'Come, you shall ride home with me.'

'But what's Philip done?' the boy persisted.

'It's not for me to explain, Georgie. You must ask your father.'

And now, she realized, as she helped the boy into the back of the pony and trap and prepared to take him home, she would have to be the one to break the news to Miles.

She pulled up in front of the manor and helped Georgie down, leading him by the hand up the front steps. She rang the bell. Miles himself flung the door open. He stared at them for a moment as if it didn't register who they were. But as he glanced down and saw the battered face of his son, he sighed heavily and pulled the door open wider. 'Now what?' he muttered, but he seemed preoccupied, almost irritated that there was yet another problem to deal with.

As she and Georgie stepped into the hall, Charlotte's heart missed a beat. He must know, she thought. His distracted air was shock.

'Take him through to Mrs Beddows. She'll clean him up.'

'I'll see to him,' Charlotte said softly. 'Come along, Georgie.' But as she tried to lead him away, Georgie looked up and asked, 'Papa, what has Philip done to Lily?'

Charlotte saw Miles blink and stare at his young son. 'What? What are you talking about, Georgie?'

'Tommy said Philip had hurt Lily.' He wiped the back of his hand across his nose and blood smeared his sleeve. 'He hit me, Papa.' Fresh tears welled in his eyes. 'He says he's not my friend any more because Philip's hurt Lily.'

'Come along, Georgie,' Charlotte urged, pushing him gently towards the door leading to the kitchen. 'You can talk to your papa when we've got something on those cuts and bruises.'

'But–'

'Come along,' she said firmly and, at last, he allowed her to lead him away. But with every step, Charlotte was aware of Miles watching them with a worried frown on his face.

Half an hour later, Charlotte prescribed a mug of hot milk and rest on the nursery couch.

'But I want to talk to Papa,' the little boy insisted, though his eyes were drooping. The long school day and then the distressing fight had taken its toll even on the stalwart Georgie.

'Can Jane take him up and stay with him, Mrs Beddows? I must speak to Mr Thornton.'

'She can, miss, but I don't think the master'll want to be bothered about a playground fight just at the moment. He's worried out of his mind.'

'So he does know?'

The cook stared at her. 'Know what, miss?'

Charlotte blinked. 'Er – I just thought – cr–'
She took a deep breath and asked, 'What is he
worried about?'

'Master Philip. He's missing. Been gone since
early morning when he went out riding.'

'Oh no!' Charlotte breathed, and she turned
and hurried back towards Miles's study. She
found him pacing the floor.

'Mrs Beddows has just told me that Philip's not
come home since early morning. Have you got
people out looking for him?'

'I sent two of my men out a couple of hours
ago, but there's been no word. I'm about to ring
the police.'

'Give me half an hour, Miles. I'll be back...'
Once more she turned and ran out of the room,
out of the house, climbed into her pony and trap,
and drove off at speed. It wasn't until she was
halfway down the long lane that she realized she'd
addressed the man to his face by his Christian
name – the name she always used in her own
thoughts.

Charlotte banged on the door of the Warrens'
cottage and then, without waiting for it to be
answered, opened it and went in.

The family was in the kitchen. Peggy was bending over Tommy, tending to his black eye. They
all looked round, startled, as she entered like a
whirlwind. Charlotte's glance sought Jackson.

'Where is he? What have you done to him?'

Jackson refused to meet her gaze but she saw
the glance that passed between him and John.
She took a step closer. 'Jackson – Mr Thornton is

266

about to call the police. If you value your freedom you'll tell me now what you've done. Where is Philip?'

'Philip?' Lily cried before anyone else could answer. 'What about Philip?' Her wild glance went to her brothers. 'Have you hurt him? If you have, I'll never forgive you. Never!'

Joe and Peggy looked anxious but mystified. Joe had had no part in whatever had happened, Charlotte could see that.

'Come on, you'll have to tell me. He's not been home since he went out early this morning. Mr Thornton has sent two men out, but he's about to take matters further.'

Again the brothers exchanged a mutinous glance, but it was John who said, 'We – we brought his horse down and then–'

'We gave him a bloody good hiding,' Jackson spat out. 'One he won't forget in a hurry.'

Charlotte turned from them. She'd have more to say to the pair of them later, but for now she must find Philip.

'Where is he? Where did you leave him?'

Reluctantly, Jackson muttered the answer. 'The copse south of the town.'

Charlotte turned to their father. 'Joe – you'd better come back with me.'

'But he ain't well enough yet–' Peggy began.

'He'll have to be. And as for you two–' she nodded towards the brothers, 'if you're fit enough to give a boy a hiding, you're fit enough to be back at your work. I'll expect you first thing in the morning. In fact, you can go and do the evening milking right now. It looks like I'm going to be too busy.'

With that she stalked out of the house, Joe following reluctantly in her wake.

Thirty-Three

Back at Buckthorn Farm, they saddled two horses and rode towards the town, then veered to the left. Neither spoke, each busy with their own thoughts and trying to keep an overwhelming fear in check.

They found him lying motionless in the long grass at the edge of the copse as if he'd been thrown there and callously abandoned.

'My God!' Joe breathed, as they both dismounted and ran towards him. 'What have they done to him?'

'He's alive,' Charlotte said, feeling for the boy's pulse. She took off her coat and laid it over Philip. 'You'll have to fetch something to carry him home on, and a farm cart. If he's been thrown from his horse and then set upon, there's no knowing what injuries he's suffered. Go to the manor, Joe, it's nearer.'

'Can't we–?'

'No,' she said firmly. 'We might cause more damage.' Beneath her breath she added, 'If that's possible.'

They both glanced across at Philip's horse. It was writhing in agony, trying to stand and falling again.

'Bring Eddie back with you and tell him to bring a gun. That poor creature's not going to make it.' She forbore to add the word 'either'.

It took a while longer than the half-hour she'd promised Miles, but at least Philip had been found and carried home and upstairs into his own bed. His father had not called the police. At least, not yet.

Now it was the doctor they called.

Whilst they waited, Miles said, 'If – if he lives, it will be thanks to you, Charlotte.' His glance rested upon her as he added quietly, 'But you seem to know what's happened. Will you tell me?'

'Of course. When the doctor's been, I'll tell you everything.'

'He'll have to go into hospital for observation. None of his limbs are broken, but he's concussed and I'm worried about his spine. I can't tell if there's damage there.'

'My God,' Miles muttered, running his hand through his hair.

Within an hour, Philip was on his way to the cottage hospital in Lynthorpe. When Miles returned from accompanying his son and seeing him admitted, Charlotte was still waiting anxiously.

'I need a drink,' Miles said, leading the way back to his study. 'And I don't mean coffee. Brandy, Charlotte?'

'I don't usually, but on this occasion,' she muttered grimly, knowing the task that lay before her, 'I need it too.'

They sat down and sipped the liquor but

Charlotte knew he was anxious to hear what she had to say.

'I'm so sorry to have to tell you this, but you have to know. I – I should have told you before, but' – she sighed, wishing she'd not delayed even the few days – 'Miles – Philip is the father of Lily's child.'

He sat forward in his chair, his hand shaking so suddenly he almost spilt what was still in the glass he held. 'Philip!' he said hoarsely. 'My son – my seventeen-year-old son has – has seduced a girl who was living in my house – under my *protection?*' He groaned, closed his eyes and fell back in the chair. The glass slipped from his hand and fell to the floor, spilling the brandy on to the carpet.

Charlotte bent and picked up the glass, mopping the spillage with her handkerchief. She glanced up at him anxiously, fearing she was going to have to send for the doctor yet again. He sat slumped in the chair with his hand covering his eyes. She poured another brandy and took it to him.

'Here – drink this.'

He pulled himself up like a man rousing himself from a nightmare. He took the glass, but his hand was still shaking. Charlotte remained standing close by. At last, he took in a deep, calming breath. 'Thank you,' he murmured.

She moved across the hearth and sat down again. 'I'm sorry.'

Slowly, he raised his head to look at her. 'Sorry? What have you got to be sorry about, my dear?' He smiled wryly. 'I'm not one to blame the bearer of bad news.' He sighed, groaned and swept his hand across his forehead again. 'What a mess!'

'Joe and Peggy were very shocked, of course, but they're standing by her.'

'They know about Philip?'

Charlotte nodded and bit her lip. 'Yes,' she admitted huskily, 'and I'm afraid that's my fault. At first she refused to name the father, but of course her family wanted to know. They thought there might be a chance of whoever it was marrying her. But they realize that's impossible now.'

Miles's head shot up. 'Why? Why do they think that's impossible?'

'Well – they wouldn't expect – I mean–'

Bitterly, he said, 'They wouldn't expect the squire's son to marry the maid he's seduced, eh? Well, that's not what happens in my family. At least–' he closed his eyes and groaned again. 'At least, I didn't think it was.'

'I have to tell you that Jackson and John went out looking for him. They brought him down off his horse and attacked him.'

For a long moment, Miles stared at her, a blank, unreadable expression on his face. Then, to her surprise, he muttered, 'It's no more than he deserves. If it'd been *my* daughter – if I'd been blessed with a daughter–' His voice broke with such an unexpected depth of longing, almost loss, that Charlotte was shocked. 'I would have done exactly the same. I – I hope Philip's not permanently injured, of course I do. But I can't blame those lads, even though I know I should.'

'You really are a most extraordinary man.'

271

She'd spoken the words aloud without meaning to, but now it was said, she went on, 'You're so kind and considerate of others' feelings. And *very* understanding.'

'I must go and see the Warrens at once,' he said.

'Do you want me to come with you?'

He shook his head. 'No. I must face the music myself.'

Charlotte smiled sadly. 'I think they'll be thinking they've "music to face" now too. But just one thing, Miles.' The name came naturally from her lips. She didn't even stop to think about it now. 'Just remember it's not *all* Philip's fault. It takes two, because I am sure of one thing. Philip didn't force himself upon her. She was a willing – a willing–' She couldn't think of an appropriate word, but Miles understood and nodded.

'And you,' he said huskily, 'are very generous to be so fair-minded. My eldest son hasn't exactly treated you with the courtesy and respect you deserve.'

'He's young.'

Miles's face clouded again. 'But not too young to sire a child, it seems.'

Charlotte returned to Buckthorn Farm to face her own particular music, whilst Miles saddled Midnight himself and rode over to the Warrens' cottage.

Joe, grey-faced, opened the door and held it silently for the man to enter. Miles removed his hat and bent his head as he passed through the door. As he went into the kitchen, he saw that the whole family were gathered there, even Lily, almost as if they were waiting for him. Young Tommy was standing in the corner, his eyes fearful.

Miles glanced round at them all and then spread his hands. 'I don't know what to say to you. I'm so very sorry.'

He saw glances pass between them. Surprise, shock and the beginning of relief. Joe spoke first. 'We expected the constable, sir.'

'The constable? Whatever for?'

Joe gestured towards his sons. 'We knew Miss Charlotte would tell you. Oh, she had to – don't get me wrong. But we thought – when you found out what my – my boys had done... Is he badly hurt, sir?'

'He's in hospital and his back may be damaged. I don't know yet.'

Lily let out a wail and buried her head against her mother's shoulder, sobbing and distraught.

'He shouldn't have brought our Lily down,' Jackson burst out. 'We didn't mean to injure him, sir. Not like that, not permanent like, but...'

'I know,' Miles said gently. 'Like I said to Miss Charlotte, in your place I'd've done the same. Maybe not brought him off his horse, perhaps, but I'd have given him a good thrashing. In fact,' he added grimly, 'if he wasn't lying in a hospital bed right now, I probably still would.'

'So – you're not bringing charges against them?' Joe still couldn't quite believe what he was hearing.

Miles shook his head and his glance went to Lily. 'No – it's Lily and her child we must think of now.'

Joe stuck out his hand awkwardly. 'You're very generous-spirited, sir. The lads shouldn't have done what they did, but I'm sorry to say I can understand *why* they did it. And they've lost you a valuable horse an' all.'

Miles shrugged. He was a kind man and the harm that had befallen the animal distressed him, but the welfare of his son was what mattered most.

Solemnly, he took Joe's outstretched hand. 'There is just one more thing...' As he released Joe's hand, his eyes sought Tommy, skulking in the corner. The young boy had been listening to every word, yet taking no part. Miles crooked his forefinger, beckoning the boy towards him. Tommy came, dragging his feet and hanging his head.

Miles put his hand gently on the boy's shoulder. 'It's all right. I'm not angry with you, but I just want your promise that you will not fight little Georgie again. At least, not over Lily. He's too young to understand what it was about and he's in tears at home – not because of his bloodied nose and black eye–' Miles heard Peggy's gasp, but he carried on, saying gently – 'but because you've fallen out with him. What's happened is not Georgie's fault. And he shouldn't have to bear any retaliation. Do you see that, Tommy?'

The boy nodded. 'I'm sorry, sir. It was just – it was just–'

Miles squeezed his shoulder. 'I know, I know. And sticking up for your sister does you credit. But–'

'What happened?' Joe interrupted sternly.

Tears streamed down the boy's face now. 'I'm sorry, Dad. I – I thumped Georgie because I heard you saying Philip had hurt our Lily.'

'Oh Tommy,' Peggy cried. 'You shouldn't have done that. Poor little boy. It's not *his* fault.'

'Miss Charlotte saw us and stopped us. She – she took Georgie home.'

Joe's face paled. He glanced round his family. 'Miss Charlotte knows it all. Everything you've done.' There was a veiled threat in his tone. His sons, all three of them, had brought more trouble on the family than Lily had caused. She might have brought shame upon them, but her trouble would not see them dismissed and turned out of their home. But the action of his sons might well do so when Osbert Crawford got to hear about all this. Even Charlotte would not be able to save them then.

Miles cleared his throat.

'I'll talk to Philip. We must arrange a marriage as soon as we can.'

Now the whole family was dumbstruck. They'd not expected this. Even Lily's sobs subsided and she looked up at him, her eyes swimming in tears.

'Marriage?' Peggy said. 'You – you'd *want* them to get married?'

'I presume they must love each other, else–' He waved his hand unable to find the words, though everyone knew what he meant.

'Oh we do, we do,' Lily burst out and, wrenching herself from her mother's arms, she went to Miles and caught hold of his arms. 'I do love him, sir, with all my heart and – and he loves me. I know he does.'

Miles put his arms round her. 'There, there, Lily. Don't cry, my dear. We'll sort it all out. Your parents and I. Everything will be all right, I promise.'

'Where's Warren? And those idle sons of his? They're not at their work.'

When Charlotte stepped back in through the front door of Buckthorn Farm, she was startled to find her father standing in the middle of the hall, thumping his stick on the floor. 'I want to see him. Good for nothing layabout.'

She sighed. Today of all days he would have to decide to take a sudden interest in the workings of the farm again.

'Joe and his sons have all had the influenza. The boys have done the evening milking and they'll all be back at work full time tomorrow.'

Osbert scowled at her. 'Mind they are. And you can stop their wages for the days they didn't work.'

Charlotte didn't reply. She'd no intention of doing any such thing. But he'd never know that. One thing he never did now was look at the paperwork in the farm office any more. That had become her domain.

He turned away, heading once more for his sanctum. She watched him go, biting her lip. It seemed he'd forgotten all about ordering her and the Morgans to leave his house. Or, more likely, he'd chosen to forget it.

But what would happen, she wondered, when he learned the latest news of his protégé, Philip Thornton? What then?

276

Thirty-Four

It was four days before Osbert found out. Four days in which Charlotte had learned that Philip had been moved to a hospital in the Midlands for tests on his spine.

'He – can't feel anything,' Miles had told her distractedly when they'd met accidentally whilst riding on the beach. 'They think his spine might be broken.'

'Oh, dear Lord,' Charlotte had breathed. 'No!'

'And there's another thing,' he said, his eyes dark with anxiety and something that Charlotte couldn't quite define. Disappointment? Shame? At his next words, she understood.

'I've talked to Philip about Lily. But he flatly refuses to marry her. He says she was only a bit of fun to him. Nothing more. Charlotte, I'm so ashamed of my own son.'

'I'm sure the Warrens hadn't expected you to suggest such a thing. Servant girls don't expect their masters to marry them. I'm sorry to say it, but Lily, being four years older than Philip, should have known the score.'

Miles sighed. 'I don't blame the girl. My son' – a note of bitterness crept into his tone – 'can be very charming and very persuasive when he wants to be.'

Miles was right, Charlotte thought, the young man had certainly charmed her own father.

277

When she returned to Buckthorn Farm, an agitated Edward met her at the door.

'Your father wants to see you in the sitting room, miss. He's in a high old dudgeon.'

Charlotte pulled a face. 'Now what?'

'He's found out about Master Philip being injured. Evidently, the boy was due to visit here before returning to school tomorrow and when he didn't arrive, the master made enquiries.'

'Who told him?' Charlotte asked sharply. She knew it wouldn't have been Edward.

'I believe he sent a note to the manor and word came back saying the boy was in hospital. That sent him into a panic, I can tell you. He had the pony and trap harnessed and he rode over to the manor. Mr Thornton was out, it seems–'

Charlotte nodded.

'One of the servants – Wilkins, I believe – told your father that the Jackson brothers had set upon Master Philip and injured him so badly that he'd been taken to hospital.' He paused, then added, 'But from what I can make out, miss, the man didn't tell the master the reason behind the lads' attack.'

'No,' Charlotte said grimly. 'I don't suppose he did. And even if he had, I doubt my father would have believed it. Not about Philip.'

She took off her riding jacket and hat, smoothed her hair back, and went towards the sitting room. Edward hovered in the hallway, and Charlotte was glad to know he was close by.

'What's this I hear?' Osbert demanded almost before she had stepped into the room.

There was no point in prevaricating, so

Charlotte said, 'Lily Warren is pregnant with Philip's child, that's what. And her brothers – well, they gave him a good hiding because of it. They didn't intend to cause such serious injury, but sadly, they have.'

Osbert stared at her. 'Don't talk ridiculous, girl. Philip's only a boy. No – no, I won't believe it. The little slut's laying it at his door to get money out of the family.'

'I've seen them together, Father, holding hands, and Philip had admitted it to his father. Mr Thornton is trying to persuade Philip to marry her, but he's refusing.'

'I should think so too. The very idea. My boy being forced to marry that little trollop.'

Charlotte stared at him. My boy, he'd said. My boy, as if he'd taken ownership of someone else's son. His disappointment and bitterness had coloured the whole of his life and now was turning his mind. Osbert thumped his stick on the floor, frowning angrily. 'The very idea,' he muttered again. And then he seemed lost in thought.

Quietly, Charlotte left the room.

'All right?' Edward whispered as she emerged.

She shrugged. 'I'm not sure, Edward. He refuses to believe that Philip is the father of Lily's child.' She smiled wryly as she added with heavy sarcasm, 'He can't believe such a thing of "his boy", as he called him.'

Edward made a noise in his throat that sounded suspiciously like a growl, before saying, 'Jackson's in the kitchen, miss, asking to see you.'

Charlotte sighed and followed him along the passageway.

Jackson was standing nervously by the table, turning his cap through agitated fingers. 'We're back at work, Miss Charlotte. All of us. That's if – that's if – you want us.'

'Of course I do, Jackson. This trouble has nothing to do with your work on Buckthorn Farm.'

Relief flooded across his face. He pulled on his cap, gave her a quick grin and almost ran from the house to prove his eagerness to resume his work. Charlotte watched him go, a heavy feeling in her heart.

She had no wish to dismiss any of the Warren family. But she wasn't so sure what was in her father's devious mind.

She didn't have long to wait to find out. The following morning, she rose to find that her father had already left to catch the train to the city where Philip was hospitalized. For the rest of the day, Charlotte was on edge and her anxiety was only lifted slightly by a letter addressed to her from her aunt:

We have found the loveliest little house near Lincoln, my dear. You must come and visit very soon. And don't forget, Charlotte, there is always a home with us should you ever need it.

Now Charlotte did not feel so alone.

Her father returned late that night, tired but jubilant. Even as Edward helped him remove his coat, he was saying, 'He's standing firm. He's not going to agree to marry the little slut.' And then he added the words that Charlotte had been

280

dreading. 'And as for those Warrens, they're to be dismissed and turned out of their cottage. Do you hear me, girl? They're to be given notice.' His pronouncement delivered, he glanced at Edward. 'You may serve my dinner now.'

Charlotte sat in the kitchen, her elbows resting on the table, her head in her hands.

'What am I to do, Mary? What *am* I to do?'

'Nothing – for the moment, love.' Mary placed her dinner in front of her. 'Now eat up.'

Charlotte pushed the plate away. 'I can't eat a thing.'

Edward and Mary sat down to their own meal.

'He'll not want to lose Joe Warren. Where would the farm be without him and his sons? That'd only leave old Matty and you'd be in a pretty pickle, miss.'

Charlotte sighed. 'He'll only say there's plenty of folks looking for work to take their place.'

'Aye, mebbe so, but not half as good.'

'But he'll do it. I know he will.'

Thirty-Five

For the first time in her life Charlotte stood up to her dictatorial father. She refused to issue the notices to the Warren family.

At church on the following Sunday morning, there was tension in the air. Everyone felt it. Miles and Ben were subdued. Even little Georgie's merry smile was gone. He walked down the aisle

281

behind his father and brother without even glancing to left or right as he usually did, greeting everyone in his cheery, high-pitched voice. Instead, he ignored everyone and especially Tommy Warren. Only when he reached the front of the church and was about to step into his family's pew, did he glance up to his left and give Charlotte a watery smile. She smiled down at him and touched his shoulder.

Cuthbert Iveson seemed even more nervous than usual. When it came to the part in the service where he made special prayers for any parishioner who was ill, he said in a halting voice, 'We pray for the recovery of Philip Thornton and for his family in their time of trouble. And we ask you to forgive those who perpetrated the – the attack upon his person. Lead them to repentance, Lord...' Cuthbert mumbled on but his words were lost to Charlotte. She glanced up to see that Miles had raised his head and was staring angrily at the vicar. Then suddenly, he stood up. 'Come,' he said to his sons. 'We're leaving. This is a mockery.'

A shocked gasp rippled through the congregation as, prayers forgotten, they watched Miles lead his two sons out. The door banged behind them and, as Charlotte turned back to face the front, she saw Cuthbert glance down at her father. Osbert was smiling and nodding.

He'd arranged that, she thought. Not Miles. Miles wouldn't do something like that.

But her father would. And his reaction to the vicar's words proved it.

When the service ended, the members of the

congregation trooped out, their faces solemn or puzzled. They stood in small groups, those who knew what had happened whispering the tale to those who did not.

Charlotte glanced around for Miles. He was pacing up and down the narrow path leading round the side of the church. Ben was standing close by amongst the gravestones, his hands pushed deep into his pockets. Georgie stood beside him, watching his father's agitated pacing with anxious eyes.

The Warren family, without Lily, stood together but a little apart from their neighbours and friends. No one, it seemed, knew quite how to deal with the news they were hearing. They didn't know what to say.

Charlotte plastered a smile on her face and walked across the long grass between the gravestones towards Peggy and her family. She stretched out her hands and took Peggy's.

'How are you? And how's Lily?'

'Oh you know, miss. Still crying. Still heartbroken. You know the young master has refused to marry her?'

Charlotte nodded.

Peggy went on in a flat, emotionless voice. 'We didn't expect it, but it was good of Mr Thornton to try. We – we appreciate that.'

'He's a good man,' Charlotte said softly. 'I'm sure–'

Charlotte was interrupted by her father's strident voice. 'Warren. You there, Warren.'

Charlotte turned to see him a few yards away, leaning on his stick and shouting so that all the world might hear. 'You're fired. The lot of you. And you're to leave the cottage at once, d'you hear me? At once. You'll be packed and gone by daybreak tomorrow.'

Charlotte turned and ran towards her father. 'No, Father, no. You can't do this. I won't let you.'

As she met his glare, she stopped, shocked by the vehement hatred in his eyes.

'You'll hold your tongue, girl, if you know what's good for you. Else you'll be gone an' all...' In a swift movement, he raised his stick and brought it down against her shoulder in a vicious blow. Charlotte reeled and fell to the ground. She heard everyone's cries of shock and alarm, but before anyone could reach her, Miles's strong arms were round her and he was lifting her up. Before he carried her away, he glanced just once at her father.

'You'll rue this day, Crawford. Mark you well. You'll rue this day.'

'You're coming home with us,' Miles said. 'And I won't hear any arguments. You're not staying with him a moment longer.'

Charlotte was too shocked to argue. She felt foolish, but her shoulder was hurting so much, and her legs felt so weak, that she had no choice but to allow him to carry her to his motor car and place her gently inside.

He straightened up and looked around for his sons.

'Ben,' he called. 'Come along. We're going home. Where's Georgie?'

Ben came running up. 'He's with the Warren

284

family. I think he and Tommy are making up.' He climbed into the front seat. 'They're all smiles, anyway. He didn't see what happened. How are you, Miss Charlotte?'

She touched her shoulder and winced. 'I'll be all right, I think. I don't think it's broken.' She glanced out of the window to see Edward wrenching her father's stick out of his hand and flinging it as far away as he could. Then he grasped the older man by the arm and hustled him towards the pony and trap. She didn't think she had ever seen Edward look so angry or stand up so defiantly to his master.

'Now he'll sack Edward and Mary for real. It won't be just one of his threats this time.' She leaned her head back against the leather seat and closed her eyes. 'Oh dear!'

Georgie came running across the grass to the car. He made no attempt to get in but, instead, stood near the driver's door, his face upturned towards his father. 'Me'n Tommy is friends again, Papa,' he said, the wide beam back on his face. 'Can I stay to Sunday school?'

'I don't think there'll be Sunday school today, Georgie. Come along, climb in.'

As he clambered in, he saw Charlotte. 'Oh! You're here! Are you coming to luncheon?'

'I—'

Ben turned round in the front seat. 'Didn't you see? Mr Crawford hit her and Father rescued her. We're taking her home with us, aren't we, Father?'

'Indeed we are, Ben.'

As Miles got out of the car again to crank the

285

starting handle, Georgie slipped his hand into Charlotte's.

'Wilkins, show Miss Charlotte to one of the spare bedrooms. See she has everything she needs. Then I need to see you and Mrs Beddows in my study. Boys, amuse yourselves until luncheon.'

A short while later, a rather nervous Wilkins and Mrs Beddows tapped on the study door.

'Wilkins – Mrs Beddows – please sit down.'

The servants glanced anxiously at each other. They were not used to being treated with such courtesy by an employer. But then Mr Thornton had already proved himself to be an unusual master. They sat down nervously on the edge of their seats.

'There may have to be some changes here and I want to – well – consult and include you in any decision I make. But let me make it quite clear from the outset that, although it might affect you, your employment with me is quite safe and your home is here for as long as you want it. Now, I'm not sure yet what is going to happen, but it may mean that Miss Charlotte and Mr and Mrs Morgan, too, will be coming to live at the manor...'

For the next half an hour, the two servants listened in amazement, nodding their ready agreement when Miles finished by saying, 'Can I rely on you both to keep everything I've said confidential for the moment?'

'Most certainly, sir, and thank you for your trust in us. I think Mrs Beddows would join me in saying that.'

Mrs Beddows smiled and bobbed a curtsy. As they left the room, it was Miles who was left with a small smile on his face. What good people there were in these parts. At least, some of them were. His face sobered as his thoughts returned to all the problems that faced him.

There was a small tap at the door and Wilkins entered again with a letter on a silver tray. 'This was delivered by hand, sir, whilst you were at church. I do apologize for not handing it to you sooner.'

'No matter, Wilkins,' Miles said mildly. 'I don't expect it's anything important.'

But he was wrong. It was important. Very important. He sat for a long time in his study, the single sheet of paper in his hand, thinking. It didn't alter any of the plans he'd discussed with both Wilkins and Mrs Beddows. But there were things it could alter.

As he rose to go to the dining room for luncheon, he was smiling. Despite his concern for Philip, the unexpected letter had brought news that could make his other problems easier to resolve.

Perhaps, after all, there was some truth in Cuthbert Iveson's sermons. For, at this very moment, it seemed as if some, if not quite all, his prayers had been answered.

But for now he must make his unexpected guest feel welcome in his home.

That evening Miles rode over to the Warrens' cottage once more.

'I'm sorry to disturb your evening,' he began,

but Joe held the door wide, inviting him in.

''Tis already disturbed, Mr Thornton. We're in the throes of packing up our belongings. Please excuse the chaos,' Joe said apologetically, adding, 'and don't mind the wife. She's been crying ever since we got home from church.'

'I do mind, Joe, I mind very much. About all of you.'

'Here's Mr Thornton, Peggy love. Boys, mek room for the master.'

Jackson leapt up at once and placed a chair near the fire.

'Please excuse me, Mr Thornton.' Peggy was still dabbing her eyes with the corner of her white apron. 'I must look a sight, but I just don't know where we're all goin' to go, and given a moment's notice like that. By daybreak, he said.'

'I know,' Miles said grimly. 'But I wouldn't take that too literally, if I were you. He can't turn you out physically.'

Joe and Peggy gaped at him. 'Can't he? I mean, won't he get the constable – the bailiffs – if we don't go?'

'I doubt it.'

Peggy sank into a chair. 'And then there's Miss Charlotte. I can't stop thinking about that poor girl.' Fresh tears welled in her eyes. 'How is she, Mr Thornton?'

'Well enough. The doctor's been this afternoon and there's nothing broken. She's just badly bruised and shocked.'

Joe snorted. 'Who wouldn't be? Her own father striking her like that. And it's not the first time, is it?'

'She's going to stay at the manor for a day or two until things calm down,' Miles told them. 'But she's insisting on going home. She says the farm won't run itself and she–' he paused, his final words coming out on a sigh – 'she still feels she has a duty to her father.'

'I wouldn't go back, if I was her,' Jackson muttered.

'What about Edward and Mary?' Peggy asked.

'I'm going to see them when I leave here.'

'Edward and Mary'll look out for her.' Joe tried to soothe his wife's worries.

'They won't be able to stop him hitting her, though, will they?'

Joe was silent, unable to argue the facts.

'Maybe when things have settled down a bit, Miss Charlotte will get the old man to change his mind. I mean, about sacking us and turning us out,' John put in. 'It was all done and said in a fit of temper. You could see that. Let's face it, Jackson. It's because of you an' me. Because of what we did to Master Philip.'

Miles waited, looking round at their anxious faces.

'Well, I'm not bothered about me job,' Jackson muttered stubbornly. 'I can get work anywhere.'

'I don't know that you can,' John said. 'The state the country's in at the moment, jobs are going to be hard to come by.'

'Then I'll emigrate,' Jackson muttered, but this only brought a wail of desolation and fresh tears from his mother.

'But the real worry is Dad getting a job.' John was still the one speaking what was on all their minds. 'And somewhere for them to live with Tommy and Lily and her bairn. We'd be all right, Jackson. We can go anywhere, but what about them?'

Miles cleared his throat and, from his pocket, brought out the letter he had received that morning.

'Perhaps there is something I can do to help in that respect. I had notice this morning from Mr and Mrs Bailey, who–' he smiled – 'as you probably know even better than I do, are my tenants in Purslane Farm, the other side of Ravensfleet.'

'Aye, we do, sir. Poor old Dan Bailey's not been well for some time and his farm – if you'll forgive me saying so – has not been run as well as it once was.'

Miles chuckled. 'If you say so, Joe, if you say so. But here's the thing. Mr and Mrs Bailey are moving down south to live near their married daughter, it seems.'

'That'd be Elsie, their eldest. She married – oh, must be ten years back – and moved away,' Peggy put in, always ready with a bit of family history. She perked up a little now her thoughts had been distracted for the moment from their problems.

Mr Thornton fingered the letter, turning it round and round. 'The thing is, I'll be needing new tenants, won't I?' Joe stared at him and Miles returned his gaze steadily. 'I'm not sure what acreage it is, but is it big enough to support you and all your family, Joe?'

Joe stared at him open mouthed. 'You mean – you mean...?' He was overcome and couldn't get the words out, but Jackson could.

'You're giving us first chance of the tenancy, Mr Thornton?'

'If you want it, yes.'

Jackson gave a whoop of delight, jumped to his feet and slapped first his father and then his brother on the back. 'Our own farm. Our very own farm.'

'Wait a bit, our Jackson. Just hold yar 'osses.' Joe faced Miles. 'Is this 'cos of our Lily?'

Miles nodded. 'Yes, Joe. I'll not deny that. I feel – very responsible. I'm ashamed to say that Philip is still refusing point-blank to marry Lily. But she is, after all, carrying my grandchild. But besides that, I like your whole family, Joe. You're good people. You don't deserve the way that bitter old man is treating you any more than his daughter does. I don't know if there's anything I can do to help her – not yet – but I *can* help you. And I want to – if you'll let me.' He held out his hand to Joe. Slowly, not quite knowing how this good fortune had befallen him, Joe took his hand and shook it firmly. After all the heartache and tragedy of the past few days, Joe felt humbled by this man's goodness.

'We'll not let you down, master,' he said huskily. 'We'll mek a go of it and turn that farm around, back to what it used to be.'

'I've no doubt of that, Joe. No doubt at all. The only thing that does worry me is, what's going to happen to Buckthorn Farm?'

But to that, no one had an answer.

Thirty-Six

'I have to go back, Miles,' Charlotte insisted two days later. 'You've been so kind – incredibly kind. And your offer to take in not only me but also Edward and Mary is so, so generous. But my duty is at Buckthorn Farm. Now Joe and the boys are leaving, I must seek more workers. And Edward and Mary – I must find out what is happening to them.'

'They're fine,' Miles insisted. 'I saw them yesterday and their only concern is for you. Your father seems to have conveniently ignored Edward's actions. I expect it suits him to do so,' he added wryly.

Charlotte smiled weakly. 'Father can be very perverse.' She leaned forward across the breakfast table. 'I don't want to go. You – and the boys – have made me so welcome. Despite your worries over Philip, this is still a happy household. I've loved being here, playing with Georgie' – she put her head on one side and her eyes twinkled mischievously – 'and with the dolls' house.'

But Miles didn't smile. His expression was wistful. 'I bought that when my wife was expecting Georgie. We so longed for a daughter, you see.'

She shook her head. "It's amazing,' she murmured.

'What is?'

292

'That you should have wanted a daughter so much, when my father...' She stopped, but there was no need for her to say more. She sighed. 'And talking of my father, I really must go home. You do see that, don't you, Miles?'

He sighed heavily. 'I suppose so, but I want you to promise me that you'll come back here at the very first sign of trouble.'

'I will. I can promise you that.'

'Very well, then. I'll drive you over this morning.'

'No need,' she said getting up from the table. 'The walk will do me good.'

He rose too and laughed wryly. 'There's just one thing – I think you're going to have a much harder job persuading Georgie to let you go.'

Laughing together, they left the breakfast room to go in search of the little boy.

Charlotte entered Buckthorn Farm by the front door. This is my home, she told herself. No skulking in by the back door any more. She went at once to the sitting room. Osbert looked up as she entered.

'Oh, it's you. Come to beg forgiveness, have you?'

'I most certainly have not,' Charlotte said quietly, but with a firmness that had never before been in her tone when addressing her father. Until this moment, she'd always felt downtrodden in his presence. But now she'd found a self-confidence she'd never thought she possessed or could possess.

'Where are your glasses, girl?'

293

'They're broken, Father.'

'Then you must get a new pair at once.'

'There's no need, Father. My eyesight is perfect.' Her mouth twitched with mischief as she added mildly, 'I don't know what optician it was who told you all those years ago that I needed spectacles, but he certainly conned you into buying something I do not need.'

Her father glared at her, but said nothing.

'And as for the Warrens, Father, they will be staying for another month. I don't know if you know or not, but the Baileys are moving out of Purslane Farm and Mr Thornton has offered Joe the tenancy.'

Osbert's face turned purple and, for a moment, Charlotte thought she had gone too far. She took a step towards him. 'Father?'

'Get out,' he spat. 'Get out of my sight.'

Charlotte turned on her heel and left the room, heading towards the farm office. Her hands were trembling, but there was a small smile of triumph on her lips.

Today, she thought, my new life begins. From today, things are going to be very different around here.

After Sunday school the following week, Georgie slipped his hand into hers. His mouth quivered and his eyes were full of tears.

She squatted down so that her face was on a level with his. 'What is it, darling? What's the matter? Has Tommy been nasty to you again?'

The boy shook his head. 'No, no. It's just – we miss you. Won't you come and live with us?'

'Oh Georgie–'

'And Philip has come home.'

'But that's wonderful! How is he?'

'Horrible. He's in bed all the time. He can't walk and he's bad tempered. He shouts at everyone and throws things.'

'Oh dear.'

'Papa is so upset. He doesn't know what to do.'

'I'll come over this afternoon and see you all.'

Georgie nodded and allowed her to lead him to where Brewster was waiting to drive him home.

That afternoon, Charlotte found Miles sitting in one of the deep leather wing chairs beside the fire in his study. He looked tired and defeated. She sat down opposite him and poured the tea Wilkins brought into the room without being asked.

Miles had greeted her perfunctorily when she'd come in, but now he sat slumped in the chair, his long legs outstretched, his gaze on the flames in the fireplace almost as if he was unaware of her presence.

'Here,' she said gently. 'Drink this and tell me what's the matter. Is it Philip?'

With a deep sigh, he roused himself, took the cup she held out to him and stirred the liquid. 'Yes,' he said heavily.

'It's – it's bad news?'

'The doctors say,' he said slowly, 'there's nothing wrong with his back. Nothing's broken – badly bruised, of course – but not broken.'

'But that's wonderful news–' she began, then stopped. From the look on Miles's face, it didn't seem to be. 'Isn't it?'

'You'd think so, wouldn't you? But Philip says he can't move – can't feel his legs. He's not even trying. He's just lying there letting everyone wait on him. And his behaviour's – well, there's no other word for it – it's disgraceful. He shouts and screams at the servants. He throws anything he can lay his hands on. He threw his dinner last night at poor Lucy – that's the new girl Mrs Beddows took on to replace Lily. She's from Ravensfleet. She's a good little thing, but I doubt she'll stay long if she's treated like that. And as for Georgie, he's in tears every time he comes out of Philip's room. Do you know what Philip said to him yesterday?'

Charlotte shook her head.

'He said, "It's your fault Mother died. She'd have looked after me. She'd have taken care of me, but she died because of you." It took me two hours to get the poor little chap to calm down and make him believe he was not to blame. And I'm not sure if I succeeded even then. He still seems – subdued.'

'He was tearful at Sunday school – that's why I'm here. He said Philip was home.' She omitted to tell him what else Georgie had said, but she felt that Miles probably guessed. 'Is there anything I can do?' she added.

'I don't know what anyone can do. I'm at my wit's end, Charlotte, I don't mind telling you. Ben seems to be the only one he'll tolerate.' He gave a wry laugh, 'Mind you, that's probably because Ben doesn't let Philip rile him.' He paused then added, 'I'm getting a second opinion. A doctor from London is coming on Wednesday. Perhaps we'll know more then.'

'Well, if there's anything I can do, let me know. And after Wednesday perhaps we'll have a better idea as to how to handle it. If he really has nothing physically wrong, then it sounds to me rather like a case of very bad temper.' She chuckled, trying to raise Miles's spirits. 'Rather like Midnight was when you first bought him. Bad tempered and stubborn.'

He gazed across the hearth at her as he murmured, 'Maybe you're right.'

When he heard that Philip was home, Osbert insisted that Edward harness the pony and trap and drive him to the manor. On arrival, Edward told Charlotte later, Osbert demanded to be allowed to see the boy. What passed behind the closed door, no one knew, only that Osbert emerged with a satisfied smirk on his face and – for a while – Philip was more amenable.

But that all changed once more after the visit of the specialist on the Wednesday. He was a bluff, no-nonsense man. He was clever and knowledgeable and Miles had no need to doubt his opinion.

'He confirms what the other doctors said,' he told Charlotte when he drove to Buckthorn Farm to see her. 'There's nothing physically wrong. It's more – now what was the word he used? – psychological. It's all in his mind. But he did ask me if there was anything troubling the boy. Was there any reason why staying put was more attractive than getting up?'

'Is he worried Jackson and John might attack him again? Is that it, d'you think?'

'Possibly.'

'Well, he can be reassured on that point.'

'Yes, but...'

'But – what?'

'Surely he doesn't think that's going to happen again. I would call the police then. I can forgive – and understand – the first time, but I wouldn't tolerate any more attacks.'

'It's not going to happen. The Warren family have every reason to be grateful to you for what you've tried to do to make amends.'

'Short of Philip marrying Lily, you mean?'

Charlotte regarded him with her head on one side. 'Are you still pressing him to "do the decent thing"?'

Miles sighed. 'It's not been mentioned since he was injured, but I think he still knows that's what I think he *should* do.'

'Then I think that's the problem. It may not even be a conscious thought, but if he lies there, a helpless cripple, he can't be made to walk up the aisle with a girl he doesn't want to marry.'

'Do you think so?'

'It's possible.' She paused then asked, 'Would you let me see him?'

'Of course, but I doubt he'll want to see you. And I wouldn't like him to be rude to you.'

Charlotte laughed. 'He won't be able to throw me out physically, will he? And if he did,' she chuckled again, 'problem solved.'

Miles spread his hands. 'You can but try.'

She stood up. 'And have I your permission to tell him he's not going to be forced into marriage?'

Miles sighed once more. 'Sick or well, he's never going to agree to it. I rather gather that's what your father was telling him when he visited the other day – that he had no need to marry the–' He glanced at her. 'Well, I won't use the words he did.'

'I can guess,' Charlotte said wryly. 'Did he tell you what had been said?'

Now Miles chuckled. 'No, but Georgie – the little imp – was listening at the keyhole.'

'Good for him!' Charlotte smiled delightedly.

'What do you want? Come to gloat, have you? Think Buckthorn Farm will be yours if I'm a cripple? Well, it won't. Your father has been here and he's promised he'll draw up a watertight will. There'll be nothing you can do.'

'I don't think I particularly want to. Not now.'

'What d'you mean, "Not now"? My father's not been stupid enough to propose to you, has he?'

Charlotte threw back her head and laughed. 'No. What I mean is I have plans.'

'Plans?' he sneered. 'What plans can you have? You've no money. Nowhere to go. And who in their right mind is ever going to marry a drab, plain creature like you?'

'Very true.' To his utter surprise, Charlotte agreed. 'But you're wrong about one thing. I do have somewhere to go. My aunt has offered me a home with her. And I may well take her up on it.'

'Typical. You'd sponge off relatives for the rest of your life. I expect you hope they'll leave you all their money now your father's cut you out of his will?'

'No. I shall train to be a teacher. Women can go to college now, get proper qualifications.'

Without thinking what he was doing, Philip pressed his fists into the bed to lever himself upright. Charlotte noticed, but made no comment. 'And who's going to look after Buckthorn Farm if you go?'

Charlotte shrugged and turned towards the door. 'Buckthorn Farm? Why should I care about Buckthorn Farm?'

'Because it's my inheritance, that's why.'

'Really? Then you'd better get out of that bed and start learning how to run a farm, hadn't you?'

As she reached for the doorknob, she saw, out of the corner of her eye, the teacup come sailing through the air towards her. She ducked just in time and it smashed against the door panel.

She wagged her forefinger at him as she opened the door to leave the room. 'Temper, temper!'

Thirty-Seven

'Did you tell him about Lily?'

'Not this time,' Charlotte told Miles. He was waiting for her in the hallway when she came down the stairs. She smiled. 'We got on to other things. He sat up to throw a cup at me, so that's a start.'

'Charlotte—' Miles began to apologize, but she held up her hand to stop him.

'It roused him – made him move. It's a good sign. He's still in a filthy temper. though. Anyway, I'll come again tomorrow.'

'Well,' Miles was still doubtful, but felt obliged to say, 'the specialist from London did say we're not to pamper him.'

'We won't do that, I promise you. He needs breaking in – just like Midnight. And, sometimes, you have to be cruel to be kind. You have to let them know just who's the boss.'

'I thought you trained your horses with gentleness and kindness?' He couldn't hide the surprise and the amusement in his voice.

'Sometimes. It depends on the nature of the animal you're dealing with. If it's a nervous creature, it needs soft handling, but a bad-tempered, brutish beast needs taming. Anyway, I must go. Joe's coming to see me this afternoon. He has someone in mind to take over as farm foreman when he leaves.'

'I'm sorry if my offering Joe the tenancy of Purslane Farm will cause you problems.'

'I shall miss them all, but I'm happy for them.' She looked at him, her violet eyes softening. 'I expect you're doing it for your future grandchild, aren't you?'

He nodded. 'That more than anything, I suppose. But Joe – and his sons – deserve a chance. Besides, they made it quite clear that if you were likely to leave, they didn't want to stay at Buckthorn Farm anyway.'

'Really?' Charlotte was startled.

He regarded her thoughtfully. 'You know, my dear, I don't think you know how loved you are

301

by the people around here.'

At that Charlotte blushed and turned away. 'It's time I went,' she said over her shoulder but he heard the catch in her throat and knew his words had touched her.

As she walked home, Charlotte thought, *But there's only one person around here that I want to love me, Miles Thornton, really love me, but I don't suppose you ever will.*

Charlotte was quite happy to hire the new farm foreman and two young lads whom Joe had recommended to take the place of the departing Warrens. But before she made her final decision, she felt obliged to consult Miles once more.

Any excuse to see him, she castigated herself as she went again to the manor.

'It's Eddie Norton, Miles. Joe says he's the makings of a good foreman. He'll need some guidance for a while but Joe is sure he's the right one. But I'd be taking one of your best workers from here on Home Farm.'

Miles waved aside her doubts. 'No matter, Charlotte. Like John Warren rightly said, there are a lot of young men looking for work in these difficult times. There'll be dozens after the vacancy here, I've no doubt. No, no, you take Eddie.'

Eddie Norton had worked on the Ravensfleet Estate since leaving school. And, better still, he was the son of Peggy's cousin. Charlotte felt she would still have a member of the Warren family on Buckthorn Farm. And she felt he deserved a piece of good luck after being suspected of bringing Lily down.

'You'll be wanting to move into their old cottage, I take it?'

The young man stood nervously in front of her desk in the farm office.

'Oh no, miss. I'll still live with me ma near Ravensfleet, if that's all right with you.'

'I'm surprised you're not married,' she said candidly. He was a good-looking young man and he'd already told her he was twenty-six years old. The same age as she was and just the right age to train up as a foreman, she'd thought.

At her question, Eddie's face fell. 'No, miss. I was walking out with a lass from Ravensfleet way but she caught the influenza, when it was so bad, miss, if you remember. Just at the end of the war. We was only eighteen, but we was both serious, if you get my meaning. We'd talked about marrying, but then she got ill and – and she died, miss.'

'I'm so sorry, Eddie. I wouldn't have asked you if...'

''S'all right, miss. I suppose one day I might meet someone else. Me mam's allus on at me to find a nice girl and get wed. I had thought that me and Lily might–' He shrugged his strong shoulders and sighed, 'but you know all about that.'

'So, you won't be needing the Warrens' cottage, then?'

Eddie shook his head. 'Me mam's settled where she is. She moved in there as a young bride and she dun't want to leave all her memories. She – she still feels me dad's close.' He smiled, embarrassed. 'You know how some folks are, miss.'

'Of course,' Charlotte hastened to reassure him. 'I wouldn't dream of asking your mother to leave her home.'

'I'll mek sure it dun't interfere with me work here, miss. I mean, I know I won't be as close at hand as Joe's been, but–'

Charlotte raised her hand. 'It's not that. I just thought you might need a home of your own, that's all.'

At the end of the month the Warren family moved into Purslane Farm.

'It's the end of an era, Joe,' Charlotte said as she stood watching them load all their belongings on to the farm cart. There'd be one or two more trips before everything was moved.

'Eddie's here helping. His ma and Peggy have never been what you'd call close, but they're making up for lost time now. Edith and Eddie live just down the lane from Purslane Farm, so we'll be seeing more of them. It'll be nice for Peg. She's going to miss you – and Mary.'

'She's welcome here any time. She should know that.'

'She does, miss, but' – he puffed his chest out proudly – 'she'll not have much time, I'm thinking. She's a farmer's wife now.'

'She is, Joe, and you're a farmer.' She handed him the brown paper parcel she carried. 'And I've brought you a present to start you off.'

'That's very kind of you.'

Charlotte laughed. 'You might not think so when you see what it is. It's a set of ledgers to keep your accounts.'

Joe's face was a picture. 'Ah, but I'm not so good with the paperwork side of it, miss. I'm a hands-on type of a chap.'

'I know that, Joe, but I think your John is the ideal man to keep the books for you. And tell him not to be too proud to come and ask for a bit of help if he needs it.'

'I will, miss. And thank you.'

She stood watching as the cart swayed down the lane, Jackson driving with Lily sitting beside him. Walking behind and keeping an eye on the precariously balanced belongings were Joe, Peggy, John, young Tommy and Eddie. Charlotte felt a lump in her throat. She was so glad for them; they deserved this chance, but she was going to miss them dreadfully.

And there was someone else who was going to miss Peggy, too. Charlotte retraced her steps back to the kitchen of Buckthorn Farm. As she stepped through the door, she said, 'A cup of tea and a little chat, I think, Mary.'

With the departure of the Warren family and the removal of Lily from the immediate vicinity, Charlotte fully expected that Philip would make a miraculous recovery. Both she and his father had told him – more than once – that he was not going to be pressed into marrying the girl.

But still, he languished in bed, insisting that those louts had irreparably damaged his spine and that he'd never walk again. He'd not be able to return to school or go on to university as he'd hoped and his dreams of a career as a lawyer lay in tatters.

'Nonsense,' Charlotte had told him briskly. 'You could still be a lawyer from a wheelchair, if needs be.'

'Get out! I don't know why you keep visiting. Nobody wants you here, least of all me.'

Things might have continued thus if it hadn't been for another visit from Aunt Euphemia and her husband. She swept into Buckthorn Farm kitchen dressed in furs and in a cloud of expensive perfume.

'I want you to come on a little holiday with us, Charlotte dear,' Euphemia announced in a tone that brooked no argument. 'We're going to Derbyshire for a week at the end of February. Bakewell. It's a charming little place and so quiet at this time of year. You'll love it, I'm sure. Your father can manage without you for a week or two.'

Charlotte chewed her bottom lip thoughtfully.

'You go, miss,' Mary encouraged. 'You deserve it. You've never had the chance before. We'll look after your father and the farm'll be all right. Eddie can always go over and ask Joe if he's worried about anything.'

'D'you know, Mary,' Charlotte said slowly, her eyes sparkling with sudden excitement. 'I'll go.' She turned to her aunt. 'Thank you, Aunt Euphemia, I'd love to come. But – not a word to Father, mind, until everything is settled.'

Euphemia wriggled her plump shoulders. 'Oh, I do love a secret.'

Charlotte and Mary did not dare to catch each other's glance. They didn't think the loquacious Euphemia would be very good at keeping secrets.

Everything was ready; her suitcase packed with the meagre few pieces of clothing she possessed. Edward had the pony and trap waiting in the yard as Charlotte, in her best hat and coat, went into the sitting room to tell her father that she was going away for a week or so with his sister.

'You're what?'

For a moment, Charlotte felt a shaft of fear. Her father's face drained of its colour and then flushed a fiery red. His hands shook and when he tried to rise out of his chair, he fell back, panting. His eyes glazed over and Charlotte thought he was suffering a seizure.

'Father...' She stepped towards him, her hand outstretched.

'Get away,' he spat. 'You – you Jezebel! Leave me too, would you? Go, then, go and never come back. I never want to set eyes on you again.'

Seeing that he was not ill, Charlotte fled, but she was trembling and distressed when she returned to the kitchen. 'He – he was so angry, Mary. He said, "Leave me too, would you?" I don't know what he meant.'

She was so preoccupied that she didn't notice Mary turn pale and cast frightened eyes towards Edward, standing near the open door with Charlotte's suitcase in his hand.

But Charlotte, thinking aloud, answered her own question. 'I expect he meant the Warrens going. Perhaps he feels everyone's deserting him. But he dismissed them – he was going to turn them out. And who can blame them for taking the chance Mr Thornton offered? Anyone would have done the same, wouldn't they, Mary?'

Mary swallowed her panic and said shakily, 'Yes, of course, miss. That's what he does. He makes people leave. He–'

'Mary...' There was a warning note in Edward's voice, but Charlotte thought no more of it when he added, ''Tis time Miss Charlotte was leaving, if she's not to miss the train.'

Charlotte hugged her quickly and followed Edward out of the door. She was unaware of Mary, her hand to her throat and something akin to terror in her eyes, watching her go.

Thirty-Eight

'We shall have the most marvellous time and I have a lovely surprise for you when we get to Derbyshire,' Euphemia burbled, clapping her hands like a small child at the thought of a special treat.

'Now, now, Euphemia,' Percy said, smiling benignly. 'You promised.'

'I know I did, but I can hardly keep it to myself. But I must – I must. I mustn't spoil it. She'd be so cross with me if I did.'

'She?' Charlotte asked. 'Who, Aunt? Who are we going to meet?'

Euphemia pressed her lips together to stop the words escaping. 'My lips are sealed. In fact, I'll get Percy to put sticking plaster across them if I don't keep quiet.'

Charlotte laughed. She couldn't imagine what the great secret was or what wonderful surprise was in store for her. But she was content to wait. There were so many other things to interest and delight her.

For a start, her aunt insisted on a trip to Lincoln, where she swept her into one of the main department stores in the city. There she bought dresses, coats, hats, shoes and even two handbags.

'Now, you really should have your hair cut into an Eton crop. It's the very latest fashion for the young. And you have such a well-shaped head, it would suit you to perfection.'

But here Charlotte stood firm. 'Aunt, it's very kind of you, but I really don't want my hair cut short.' Not to seem ungrateful, she added, 'But what I would like is for a hairdresser to show me how to put my hair up into an elegant style.'

'If that's what you want, my dear, then that's what we'll do.'

The hairdresser was delighted. 'It's a while since I had the chance to put up long hair. And yours is lovely, Miss Crawford. You've kept it in wonderful condition. Now...'

For the next hour or so, Charlotte's hair was washed, trimmed and styled into the most elegant chignon she had ever seen and the hairdresser was kind enough to give her tips as to how she could achieve it for herself.

'My dear, you look wonderful,' Euphemia enthused.

'Whatever will Father say?' Charlotte murmured as she regarded her new self in the mirror. But Euphemia brushed her fears aside and led her eagerly to the next department. 'And now you must learn to use cosmetics. Discreetly, of course, my dear. Ah, now, here's the lovely April, who's going to show you what to do. April, this is my niece – the one I was telling you about.'

So, Charlotte thought, amused but not offended. This has all been planned.

When, at last, Charlotte emerged from the store, she didn't recognize the reflection of herself in the plate-glass window. The fashionable, pretty young woman, who stared back at her, was a stranger.

'My dear girl, you look adorable. Doesn't she, Percy?'

Her uncle nodded and smiled benignly. 'Adorable, my dear. Absolutely adorable. She'll have young men queueing at the door of Buckthorn Farm now.'

Charlotte laughed and pulled a face. 'I hope not. Father would have a seizure.' Her expression sobered. She knew he was going to be very angry with her for what she'd already done. She had no wish to make her father ill, but at almost twenty-seven, it was high time she stood on her own two feet.

'And tonight we're staying in a hotel here in the city and going to the theatre,' Euphemia went on. 'Then tomorrow, we must go home and pack all these lovely new clothes for our trip to Derbyshire.'

'You have been so generous, Aunt, but I can't let you pay for all this. You must let me–'

Euphemia flapped her hands. 'Nonsense, my dear. Besides, if I'm not mistaken, it's your birthday next week, isn't it? Just call it an early birthday present. It's wonderful to have someone to spoil, isn't it, Percy?' Her face clouded as she added sorrowfully, 'We've never had the chance before, have we?'

Percy shook his head. 'Sadly, no, my dear. We were not blessed with children, you see. And my darling Euphemia would have loved a daughter to spoil.'

'A daughter? You'd've liked a daughter?' Charlotte couldn't keep the surprise from her tone.

'Most certainly,' Percy said.

'But – but wouldn't *you* have wanted a son?' she asked him.

He wrinkled his forehead as he considered the question. 'Not particularly. You know the old saying, "A son is a son till he takes him a wife; a daughter is a daughter all of her life."'

'I – I've never heard that.'

'Har-humph,' Percy said, stroking his moustache. 'Haven't you, my dear? But more to the point, neither has your father, I suspect. More's the pity.' He turned to his wife. 'And now, let's book into the hotel and then I'll leave you two ladies to try on all these fripperies.' But his eyes were twinkling as he said it. 'I shall go for a walk up the hill to have a look at that magnificent cathedral.'

Charlotte had never been to the theatre, had never seen people acting out a story on stage. She'd read all her life; it had always been one of her greatest pleasures to lose herself in another world and escape from the loneliness of her own life shut away from all society at Buckthorn Farm except for Mary and Edward. But now, a whole new world was opening up to her. But with it came the bitter knowledge of just how deep her father's cruelty had been.

The following morning they returned home to pack for their trip to Derbyshire, which began the following day.

They stayed at a hotel in the centre of Bakewell. Charlotte sat at the window of her room looking out on the streets below. At this time of the year, the town was quiet, but she imagined it would be a popular place for visitors during the summer months.

At dinner that evening, Euphemia seemed unsettled. But it was a kind of scarcely suppressed excitement. She toyed with her food and kept glancing at the long-case clock standing in the corner, solemnly ticking away the hours. After a while her glances were directed towards the door, as if she was expecting someone.

As they left the dining room, she linked her arm through Charlotte's. 'My dear, do you remember that when I proposed this visit to Derbyshire, I promised a surprise for you? A nice surprise, of course.'

'I do, Aunt. But I thought that it was perhaps all the beautiful clothes you've bought for me. I can't begin to thank you—'

'No, no, child, that wasn't it.' Euphemia chafed her bottom lip nervously.

'Then – what?' Charlotte asked.

'Let's go into the lounge and then I'll explain.'

There were one or two other guests there, but

they found a quiet corner where they wouldn't be overheard. Percy hovered in the hallway, pretending, Charlotte was sure, to find a painting hanging there fascinating.

'Now, I must have your solemn promise that you will never, ever, tell your father.'

Charlotte stared at her. 'What about? The – the clothes, you mean?'

'No – no, not all that. That's not it at all.' Euphemia flapped her hands and glanced nervously at the door leading into the hall.

Charlotte followed her gaze and saw Percy greeting a woman who'd just come into the hotel by the main entrance. He was kissing her on both cheeks. A tall, dark-haired woman, dressed fashionably, with a lovely face and... As the woman turned and began to walk towards the lounge, Charlotte felt the room spin. She reached out and clutched at Euphemia for support.

No, no, it couldn't be...

But the woman was coming towards her, her arms outstretched, tears in her fine violet eyes. 'My darling girl...'

Charlotte stared at her, her head whirling and then everything went black.

Thirty-Nine

She thought she was in her own bed, at home at Buckthorn Farm, yet there were people bending over her, someone was cradling her head and trying to get her to drink something. She groaned and heard a strange voice say, 'She's coming round. Oh, thank goodness! We shouldn't have sprung such a surprise on her, Euphemia.'

'She'll be all right. She'll be fine and so happy to see you. She must have so longed all these years to find you.' Euphemia patted Charlotte's hand. 'Now, come along my dear.'

Charlotte opened her eyes and slowly pulled herself up. The stranger was still holding her, her arm about Charlotte's shoulders. Slowly, Charlotte turned to look into the woman's face and found it was like looking into an older version of her own. But this woman was beautiful; she was skilfully made up, wore lovely clothes, and had her hair professionally cut and styled.

'But – but you're dead!' Charlotte blurted out. She was still not thinking rationally. 'I must be dreaming.' She closed her eyes momentarily and then opened them again, but the woman – her mother – was still there, in the flesh, smiling at her.

'No, my love, I'm here. I'm really here.' Her eyes clouded with concern. 'Are you all right? I'm so sorry, we shouldn't have done that. Euphemia

314

should have told you gently before I arrived.'

'You know me, Alice.' Euphemia flapped her hands. 'I would have blurted it out and it would have been just as much of a shock for the poor girl. I'm like a bull at a gate – Percy always says so.' She peered at Charlotte. 'The colour's coming back to her cheeks. She'll be all right in a moment.' She turned and summoned a hovering waiter. 'Another brandy, if you please?'

'No – no, Aunt, I'll be all right now.'

'Oh, it's not for you. It's for me!' Euphemia said comically and patted her chest dramatically.

Charlotte turned towards her mother. 'I – can't believe it. Is it really you? All these years, I thought you were dead.'

'Dead!' Euphemia and Alice spoke together and Percy, standing close by, frowned. Charlotte's earlier words had not registered with any of them.

'Your – your grave's in the churchyard at Ravensfleet. I put flowers on it every week. But father doesn't know,' she added swiftly.

'Well, I don't know whose grave you've been tending all these years, but it isn't mine, my darling.'

Slowly, Charlotte shook her head, completely mystified. 'I don't understand.'

Euphemia and Alice exchanged a glance. 'No,' the latter murmured. 'And neither do we.'

When Charlotte was feeling quite well again, though her mind was still reeling from the shock, they began to talk.

'What happened?' she asked. 'I want to know. Tell me everything. Right from the beginning.'

'The beginning? You mean, how I met your

315

father and married him?'

'Yes, everything.'

Alice's eyes darkened as she was forced to relive her memories, memories that perhaps she would rather forget. 'I – I don't know how much you know already.'

'I know nothing. My only memories of you are fleeting, just vague pictures and – and then the day of your funeral.' Charlotte shook her head in total bewilderment. 'I still can't believe all this. I mean – I know I was only five, but I watched the funeral procession leave the house – my father and all the men walking behind the horse-drawn hearse. I was watching from an upstairs window with Mary–'

'Mary,' Alice cried, 'is she still with you? She promised she would always take care of you. She and Edward – oh my dear, what is it?'

'Mary,' Charlotte whispered. 'Mary – and Edward? They *knew* that you were still alive?'

Alice took hold of her cold hands and held them tightly, chafing them to warm them. 'Darling, you must believe me, I know nothing of what happened after I left.'

'Left? You left Father and – and me?'

At this, Alice's face crumpled. 'My darling, you don't know how difficult it was. It was the hardest thing I've ever had to do in my whole life. To leave you – my precious daughter, but I–' She closed her eyes and swayed slightly. When she opened them again, they were brimming with tears.

'Your father,' Euphemia stepped in, 'my dear brother,' her tone was hard and bitter, suddenly

316

totally unlike the gregarious, generous-spirited and jolly person Charlotte had come to know, 'was cruelty personified. Alice had no choice but to leave him. He'd probably have killed her if she'd stayed.'

Charlotte drew in a sharp breath. 'He – he hit you?'

Alice bit her lip and nodded. 'Has he ever hit you?'

Charlotte nodded. 'A few times, but Mary or Edward stepped in whenever they could. When he got in a temper, I'd lock myself in my bedroom until he'd calmed down. I learned to see when one of his black moods was coming.' She didn't tell them about the recent whacks with his stick that, to her shame, everyone knew about.

Alice groaned. 'I'm so sorry. I never thought he'd beat you. I – I thought it was just me. Because – because I couldn't bear him a son.'

Charlotte smiled wryly. 'I expect it was because I'm the daughter he never wanted,' she said matter-of-factly without self-pity.

Alice was still shaking her head in disbelief, guilt etched on her face.

'But why?' Euphemia couldn't believe what she was hearing either, even though she thought she knew her brother better than anyone. 'Even I didn't think he'd stoop so low. I mean, how's he kept it secret all these years?'

'Easily,' Alice said flatly. 'When I left, he threatened me that if I ever tried to contact Charlotte he'd kill me. I was frightened enough of him by that time to believe him. And besides, I thought it was perhaps best for you, darling, if I went out

317

of your life for good. I thought the dreadful rows would stop and that perhaps he'd be kind to you.'

Euphemia snorted but it was Charlotte who said thoughtfully, 'To be honest, until recently, I never questioned my life. There were times, of course, when I wondered why I was never allowed to have friends, never allowed to attend school. I had a governess until I was fifteen. The only people I knew were on the farm, but even then I was never allowed to mix socially with them.' She gave a wry laugh. 'I only attended my first harvest supper last year because–' She paused. She couldn't explain all that now, so she ended with the words, 'And *that* caused a lot of trouble.'

Charlotte looked into her mother's troubled face and said softly, 'Don't look like that. I just want to know what happened. I'm not *blaming* you, I promise.'

'Perhaps you should,' Alice said quietly. 'I should have been braver, stood up for myself more, but his cruelty had worn me down. I'd had three miscarriages – all boys. And when I lost the last one, when you were two, it just seemed to tip him over the edge. The mental cruelty was worse – far worse – than the physical abuse. I stayed for three more years, but I could bear no more. I was ill and desperate, but I should have taken you with me. I see that now. I should have run away in the night without him knowing, but I always thought he'd hunt me down and snatch you back.'

'I'm sure he would have done,' Charlotte agreed. 'Not because he wanted me, but out of spite.' She paused then asked, 'So where did you go?'

Alice took a deep breath. 'Let me tell you it all from the beginning. I met your father Osbert through our fathers. We lived in Boston – my father was a potato merchant. He came into contact with the Crawford family through business and I suppose it was what you would call an arranged marriage. My father was very strict – a real Victorian father – and he chose Osbert for me.'

Euphemia snorted and said dryly, 'Just like my father tried to do for me, only it didn't work.' She reached out and took Percy's hand, glancing up at him. He smiled benignly and patted her hand. Then he sat down beside her, making himself comfortable.

'Osbert was charming when he was paying court to me, generous and attentive. And – if I'm to be fair and I do want to be – in the first years of our marriage, everything was fine. But after the miscarriages, when I couldn't give him a boy, he changed. He blamed me and became obsessed with wanting a son.' Her voice quavered as she gripped Charlotte's hand tightly. 'He hardly took any notice of you. He resented you, I could see that. I suggested to him that he should divorce me and marry someone who could give him a son. I promised we – you and I – would live quietly and be no trouble to him. But he was vitriolic. "But you'll want keeping," he said. "You'll want my money. You'll drain all my future son's inheritance."' Tears ran down Alice's face and gently Charlotte wiped them away with her handkerchief.

'Don't cry, Mama.' The name she had called her mother in childhood came back to her and, hearing it, Alice cried all the more. She held out her arms and after so many years of separation mother and daughter hugged each other. After a few moments, Alice continued her tale.

'So – I thought that if I left him, he'd have grounds for divorce and he'd know that I'd make no demands on him, except that he should look after you. I always made sure his solicitor had my address, but no word ever came.' She looked questioningly at Charlotte, who shrugged and said, 'As far as I know, there's never been anyone else. For the first few years, he ran the farm but as soon as I was old enough, I had to work outside. Then as I got older, gradually he handed over more and more of the day-to-day running of the farm to me. Now I do everything.'

'You run the farm?' Alice was surprised but then, suddenly, she smiled. 'So, he's training you up to take it over one day. He does intend–' She stopped abruptly as she saw Charlotte shaking her head.

'Oh no, I'm not to inherit Buckthorn Farm. He's going to make a will and name Philip Thornton as his heir. He intends to leave me penniless.'

Forty

'Who is Philip Thornton?'

Swiftly, Charlotte explained.

'Your father intends to leave everything to complete strangers?' Percy asked. 'The man's lost his reason.'

'And all because I couldn't give him a son,' Alice said tremulously.

There was silence between them until Charlotte asked her mother, 'But where have you been all these years? Did you go home to your family? Your parents?'

Alice smiled wryly and shook her head. 'My father would have sent me back. No.' She glanced at Euphemia and Percy. 'Strange as it may seem, I went to my sister-in-law for help.'

'She's been with us ever since. She's been everywhere with us. My dear, dear friend and confidante all these years.' Euphemia smiled at Alice. 'Percy was very ill a few years ago and I don't think we'd have got through it without your mother's help.'

'Strange, isn't it?' Alice said. 'You'd think the one person in the world who wouldn't want to know me would be the sister of the man I was leaving.'

'Huh! I knew my brother. I knew what he's capable of. At least,' Euphemia hesitated, 'I thought I did, but this last – leaving Buckthorn

321

Farm to strangers, out of the Crawford family, just because you're a *girl* … well, that shocks even me.'

'Indeed it does, my dear,' murmured Percy. 'And if only we'd known how your father was treating you, well, we'd have come for you too. We'd have taken care of both of you.' He chuckled. 'We could have shared in your daughter, Alice.'

Charlotte smiled at the dear man. She believed him. Then she turned back to her mother. 'I still can't believe that he would deceive everyone into thinking you were dead. Hold a mock funeral–' Then she remembered what her mother had said earlier. She looked into Alice's eyes as she said softly, still not quite able to believe it, 'You – you said Mary knew that you hadn't died.'

Alice nodded. 'We worked it all out between us. She and Edward would stay and look after you, but even I never thought for one moment that Osbert would stoop so low. I expect poor Mary felt trapped. She and Edward would have to obey him or be turned out. And she'd given her promise to me. Besides, she loved you dearly. They both did.'

'But she's deceived me all these years,' Charlotte murmured. 'She could have told me when I was old enough to understand.'

'She was probably too frightened of Osbert,' Euphemia said tartly. 'It takes a lot of courage to stand up to him. He's like our father. A bully. Your poor mother endured years of misery before she dared to walk away. Her only regret is leaving you. But you must understand, my dear, that, at the time, she thought she was doing the right thing for you.' The two women exchanged a glance. 'She wasn't to know,' Euphemia went on softly, 'that the old tyrant would wreak his bitterness on an innocent child.'

With a supreme effort, Charlotte summoned a smile. Whilst she truly understood the nightmare her mother's life must have been, whilst, rationally, she couldn't blame her for going, there was still a tiny corner of her heart that questioned it. Why didn't she take her daughter with her? Why did she leave her?

But she buried her thoughts and said gently, 'Well, we've found each other now. That's all that matters.' Then she turned to Euphemia, 'But, Aunt, there's just one thing. I have to break my promise to you. I intend to have this out with my father.'

Euphemia laughed. 'Well, after what you've just told us, Charlotte dear, I release you from that promise with the greatest of pleasure. My word, Alice, what a girl to be proud of. What spirit she has.'

Now Charlotte threw back her head and laughed. 'And if the folks who know me back home heard you say that, Aunt, they'd laugh. They think I'm this downtrodden, good little daughter. But they're all about to find out that the worm has turned.'

At the end of the week – a week in which she had got to know her mother and her aunt and uncle so much better – Charlotte returned home. Her uncle had been generous in the extreme. He insisted on opening a bank account for her and pressed more cash upon her than she'd ever had for her personal use in her life before this moment.

'My dear girl, you'll be coming to live with us soon, now, won't you?'

'Uncle Percy, you're a dear and you don't know what it means for me to know I have somewhere to run to. But–'

He patted her hand understandingly. 'You still have responsibilities at home and I can see that you're not the sort of person to walk away from them. Not that I blame your poor mother,' he added swiftly, lest it should sound as if he was criticizing Alice. 'The poor woman had no choice. Things are very different now for women than they were in '05. Very soon, all women will have the vote. You can have careers and – thank God – you can marry whomsoever you choose. It's a very different world now compared with then. And in most ways, a better one.'

Charlotte smiled as she said softly, 'I certainly mean to change my world. Whether or not it means leaving home, I don't know yet. But I thank you from the bottom of my heart, Uncle, for your generosity, because it means I can decide for myself exactly what I do. You have given me my freedom.' She kissed him on both cheeks and then boarded the train. Her goodbyes to her mother and her aunt had been said at the hotel. Only her uncle had come with her to the station to wave her off. She could have stayed with them longer, but she needed – and wanted – to go home.

There was so much she must do. And there was one person she wanted to see and to talk to before anyone else.

Miles Thornton.

'Miss Charlotte, Miss–' Georgie was running down the drive to meet her, but he stopped suddenly and stood quite still, staring at her. 'Oh – I thought it was Miss Charlotte.' Then he squealed with delight. 'It *is* you.'

He ran towards her and took her hand, skipping beside her the rest of the way to the front door.

'You've got your hair so different, and you look so pretty. Papa – Papa – come and see,' he called as he bounded up the steps and in through the front door. 'Miss Charlotte's home and just *look* at her.'

Miles appeared from his study and Ben, halfway up the stairs, paused and turned to look down at her, his mouth gaping open.

Blushing a little, Charlotte submitted herself to their scrutiny. Dressed now in a fashionable coat and hat, she knew she looked very different from the drab creature they had known before.

'My dear, you look wonderful. What a transformation! Oh, I'm so sorry,' Miles added at once. 'That's sounds dreadfully rude.'

Charlotte threw back her head and laughed out loud. 'But true. You can't offend me, Miles. I'm too busy basking in your compliments.'

'Where've you been?' Georgie was tugging at her hand. 'We've missed you, haven't we, Papa? Even Philip. He says he's no one who'll answer him back now.'

Charlotte sobered and her glance went to Miles.

325

'How is he?'

Miles shrugged. 'No improvement, I'm afraid. Physically – or in his temper. I've had to ban Georgie from going in to see him. The little chap comes out crying.' He ruffled the boy's curls affectionately. 'And Ben only pokes his head in now and again. He tried to read to him, but Philip only snatched the book out of his hands and flung it across the room.'

'I'm sorry to hear that. I'll see what I can do later, but first, could I talk to you, Miles? I – I need your advice.'

Miles blinked. 'My advice? It's usually me coming to see you for advice about farming matters.'

'This has nothing to do with farming.'

'Ah well, in that case, please come into the study. Georgie – run and play, there's a good boy.'

'Please may I ask Brewster to drive me to see Tommy?'

'After luncheon.'

The little boy beamed and looked up at Charlotte. 'And will you come and play with me in the playroom after you've finished talking to Papa?' Artfully, he added, 'You can play with the dolls' house.'

'Maybe I'll come tomorrow, Georgie. I've only just come back from my holiday. I haven't even been home yet. But I'll come and see you and Philip tomorrow.'

Releasing herself from his hold, she waved her hand at both Georgie and Ben, who was still standing on the stairs gazing at her, and followed Miles into his study.

'So,' he said as they both sat down either side of the fireplace. 'How can I help you, Charlotte?' Just like his son, he was still gazing at her as if he couldn't quite believe his eyes.

She took a deep breath and relayed to him all that she'd learned. 'I still can't believe that my father could be quite so devious. And how he managed to arrange a funeral without a body, I just don't know.'

Miles's mind was working fast. He was remembering his conversations with the Warren family, how they had been mystified as to why old Harry had insisted on seeing the vicar before he died and how he'd been buried next to Alice Crawford's grave. A woman, who, Miles now learned, was not dead at all.

'Leave it with me, Charlotte. I have a suspicion as to how it was done, but will you trust me to find out for you?'

She nodded. 'Of course,' she said simply. 'I can hardly ask my father, can I?'

'What do you plan to do?'

She sighed. 'I really don't know. I have Mary and Edward to think of. They've devoted their lives to me, even though they've hidden this secret all that time.'

'Don't blame them. I expect your father put an intolerable pressure on them.'

'No, I don't.'

'But?'

'But I don't know if I want to go on living at Buckthorn Farm, running the place when it isn't even going to be mine eventually. I'm sorry,' she added swiftly, 'to sound so blunt.'

327

Miles grimaced. 'It's the truth, and I think you know I don't like it any more than you do.'

'If I could find a position for Mary and Edward, then I would leave.' She'd already told him that her aunt and uncle had offered her a home.

'They could come here and they would be welcome,' Miles said at once and then asked gently, 'but what of your father? I know you're angry with him and you have every right to be, but would you really leave him?'

She shrugged. 'He can employ people to do everything I do.'

'But they wouldn't be a daughter to him.'

Charlotte looked him straight in the eyes and her words broke his heart.

'He'll not miss me. He's never wanted me. All he's ever wanted was a son.'

Forty-One

It was getting late when she entered Buckthorn Farm and went straight to the kitchen. Mary and Edward, seated at the table eating their evening meal, looked up. Mary's spoon clattered on to her plate and she threw up her hands, giving a little scream. 'Oh, Miss Charlotte, whatever will he say? You look lovely, but – but whatever will the master say?'

Charlotte peeled off her new gloves and smiled at Mary. These two people were very dear to her.

They'd been like parents to her – better than either of her own. For she had to face the reality that, whatever her reasons and however good those reasons were, her own mother had abandoned her. She hoped that she could persuade Mary and Edward that she didn't blame either of them, even though they'd kept such a dreadful secret for over twenty years.

Mary bustled about the kitchen, spooning food on to a plate.

'I'm not hungry, Mary, truly, though I'd love a cup of tea. Then, please, sit down. I want to talk to you both.'

Husband and wife exchanged a glance but neither of them could foresee the bombshell that Charlotte was about to drop.

She told them everything that had happened over the past week. When she got to the part about meeting her mother, finding out at last that she was still alive, Mary's eyes widened and she burst into noisy tears. Edward hung his head and refused to look at her.

Charlotte clasped Mary's hands across the table. 'I don't blame you – either of you. You've always cared for me. You're the only people in this house who've shown me any love.'

'The master made us promise never to tell you,' Mary sobbed. 'He'd've sent us packing if we hadn't agreed. And I'd promised your mama that we'd look after you. Besides,' she added, as if it explained everything – and it did – 'we do love you, miss, like you was our own. We always have.'

'And do you know how he managed to arrange

329

that travesty of a funeral? Because that's what it was.'

Again, Mary and Edward exchanged a glance.

'No, we don't, miss,' Edward said. 'We never did know. That I promise you. When we got to the church gates that day, he sent us all packing. Said he wanted to be on his own. Just him and the vicar. None of us knew what happened after that.' He glanced at his wife. 'Of course, me an' Mary knew it wasn't really your mama in the coffin.'

'Then who was it? Or was it empty? Was it all just a charade?'

'I don't know, miss,' Edward said, looking harassed. 'Truly I don't.'

Slowly, Charlotte rose. Mary looked up at her nervously. 'What are you going to do?'

'I'm not sure yet.' Charlotte grinned impishly. 'Maybe the shock at the sight of the new me is going to be quite enough for the moment, don't you think?'

'You Jezebel! You whore! You – you wicked, ungrateful girl. When I think of all I've done for you and this is how you repay me.'

'All you've done for me, Father?' Charlotte repeated. 'Tell me – exactly what have you done for your *daughter*?'

'I've fed you and clothed you – kept a roof over your head. What more do you want? To be pampered and cosseted and spoiled, I suppose.'

'There's been no fear of that,' she retorted.

His eyes narrowed to spiteful slits as he looked at her. 'You're getting very cheeky, miss. I can see

Euphemia has been a bad influence on you. I might have known. She always was a flighty piece. Ran off to marry that good-for-nothing against our father's wishes. Thought herself better than the rest of us. We Crawfords have always worked for our living and worked hard.'

'And you think I haven't?' Charlotte said, deceptively softly.

He gave a low growl and his disdainful glance raked her from head to toe. 'You've been useful, I'll grant you that.' It was the closest he'd come – or was ever likely to – to giving her praise. 'So, you can take off those fripperies and get back to your work.'

'You told me to leave, not so long ago.'

'You'll do as you're told, miss.'

'Why should I work to keep this farm going for someone else?'

His lip curled. 'You'll be taken care of. D'you think his father won't make an offer soon? His son's a cripple now. He'll never walk again. His fancy notions of a career in the law are gone. And Thornton – if he's any sense, which I sometimes doubt – will want to secure his son's future. It's too good an offer to turn down.'

'And your will is made, is it? In favour of Philip Thornton.'

'It will be. I'll see to that.'

'I see,' she said quietly. For a long moment she was silent. She'd entered this room determined to face him with the news that she'd found out his dreadful secret; that, despite all his efforts to hide from her the fact that her mother was alive, she'd met her and talked to her. Moreover, she had the offer of a home with her aunt and uncle – and her mother.

But something held back the words. She saw him hunched before the fire, an old man before his time, his shoulders rounded, his back bent, his face lined with bitterness and his eyes joyless, and the words would not come. She had the uncomfortable feeling that such news would cause a seizure – one from which he might not recover. Oh, she would tell him – eventually. One day she would demand an explanation, but perhaps the sight of her transformation from the drab, docile creature he'd always demanded she be, was enough for one day.

'Get out of those clothes,' he said again. 'Burn them, d'you hear me? And find another pair of spectacles to wear. You must have an old pair somewhere. You look like a woman of the streets, dressed like that.'

As she turned to leave the room, devilment made her deliver her last remark. 'Well, if you're turning me out, that's what I may have to become.'

'I couldn't do it, Mary,' Charlotte laughed ruefully. 'There I was coming home dressed in all my finery, thinking I was this changed woman who would stand up to my bully of a father and, at the last minute, I couldn't do it.'

'Maybe now's not the right time, Miss Charlotte.' Mary's relief was obvious. 'I mean, do you really need to tell him at all? Isn't it enough that you know? That you can keep in touch with your mother in secret? Maybe see her from time to time?'

Charlotte took the older woman's hands into hers. 'Mary – darling Mary – what are you so frightened of?'

'Him. I've always been frightened of him.' Tears spilled down her face again. 'The times I've had to stop Edward from squaring up to him. And, sometimes, I haven't been able to stop him and I thought we'd be thrown out on the spot. But – but I think the master knows that he'd be hard pressed to find anyone to take our place.'

Charlotte laughed wryly. 'It would be impossible, I'd say.'

'He's hopping mad that the Warrens have left.'

'But he gave them notice. He said it in front of half the village.'

'I know, I know. But your father says these things and he doesn't mean them. They're all threats to keep people under his thumb.' She smiled wistfully. 'But he threatened your mama once too often – and she went.'

'Leaving me,' Charlotte whispered.

'That was the last thing she wanted,' Mary cried at once. 'It broke her heart. But she knew that if she took you, he'd hunt her down.'

'I don't know why, when he obviously didn't want me anyway. Because I'm a girl. Why didn't he just let me go – let us both go?'

Mary bit her lip, knowing what she was going to say was going to be painful for Charlotte. 'Because – because you were better than – than–'

'Than what?'

'Than nothing,' Mary whispered. 'And besides, you don't take anything from Osbert Crawford whether he really wants it or not. He's a vicious,

333

cruel, self-centred man, who doesn't know the meaning of the word "love". I doubt he ever loved your mother. He just wanted someone to bear him a son. There now, I've said it – even though he's your father.'

Charlotte shrugged. 'My mother said as much herself. She said it was a marriage arranged by their fathers.' She gave a wry smile. 'My two grandfathers, weren't they?'

'I never knew anything about all that,' Mary said. 'I only came to work here when your mother and father were married, and Edward only a few months before me. But I loved your mother. She was a sweet, innocent creature – and very young – who was cruelly used. I never blamed her for running away. She suffered cruelly.' Mary paused and looked at Charlotte. 'I hope you can find it in your heart to understand and forgive her.'

Charlotte nodded, but at the moment could not make that promise wholeheartedly – not yet.

'What happened to her when she left here?' Mary wanted to know. 'Did she tell you? Has she been all right all these years?'

Charlotte stared at her, realizing for the first time that Mary had never known what had become of Alice from the moment she'd 'died'. She began to smile and shook her head slowly. 'You're not going to believe this, Mary, but she went to my Aunt Euphemia for help. My father's own sister. They – Euphemia and Percy – took her in and cared for her – even took her abroad with them.'

Mary's mouth dropped open and then they both began to laugh.

Forty-Two

'So,' Charlotte said brightly, entering Philip's bedroom the following afternoon, 'isn't it time you made an effort to get up out of that bed and stop playing the fool?'

He glared at her. 'So you're back, are you? I was hoping you'd gone for good. But I suppose,' he sneered, 'you can't let go of what you consider to be your rightful inheritance.' Suddenly, he became aware of her changed appearance and he laughed. 'Ugly duckling turned into swan, is it? Well, allow me to tell you, it hasn't worked. Father still won't propose. He'll never forget my mother. Never.'

Quietly, she said, 'I don't expect your father to propose to me, Philip. My father was being vile in even suggesting such a thing.'

'Georgie'd love it. He'd like you as a stepmother. Ben too, probably. But not me.' Philip pulled himself up off the pillows. He was scowling at her and, in his anger, he was completely unaware of what he was doing. 'I'll never see the day you ensnare my father.'

But Charlotte was not looking at his face; she was staring at the bedclothes covering his legs. Slowly, she raised her eyes to look at him. 'Philip, how long are you going to go on with this charade?'

He lay back, as if exhausted. Covering his eyes with his arm, he muttered, 'I don't know what

335

you're talking about.'

She moved closer to the bed and leaned over him. 'Just now, when you were shouting at me, your legs moved. Are you, for some devious reason, *pretending* to be crippled?'

Slowly, he lowered his arm and she could see there were tears in his eyes. His mouth quivered as he said, 'No, I'm not. How could you even think that?'

'I don't *like* to think it of you, but you're not making any effort to help your recovery.'

'Those bastards broke my back. I'll – I'll never walk again.'

'No, they didn't,' she countered softly, but firmly. 'The doctors say your back was badly bruised and, yes, for a time maybe you couldn't move. But now they say there's no reason at all why you can't get up out of that bed.'

'What do they know? They're fools – all of them. They're not the ones lying here with their life in ruins.'

She stared down at him, chewing her lip thoughtfully. He was like a young, stubborn horse who needed firmness and gentleness in equal measure. And just like a horse needing to be broken, he had to know who was boss. 'Philip, please be truthful with me. Can you really not walk?'

His eyes were haunted and hopeless and tears shimmered in them.

'I – can't.'

She believed him.

Softly, she said, 'Will you trust me to help you?'

'You can't. No one can.'

'I think I can, but I need you to believe in me.'

'Why should you bother with me?' he whispered. 'When I'm the one taking everything that should rightfully be yours?'

'I don't blame you for that. What young man of seventeen would turn his back on such a gift?'

'My father thinks I should be "man enough" to do just that.'

'Is that what he said?'

Philip nodded and she saw fresh tears well in his eyes. She sat down on the edge of the bed, but she made no attempt to take his hand as she would have done with Georgie or perhaps even with Ben.

'What else is worrying you?'

Again, he covered his eyes with his arm. 'Nothing,' he muttered at last.

'I think there is,' she said softly and this time he was silent. After a pause, she murmured, 'Is it Lily?'

When he still didn't answer, she went on softly. 'You don't have to marry Lily.'

Now he burst out, 'Father thinks I should. I should take responsibility for my – my–'

'The Warrens don't expect you to marry her. They never did. Philip, unless you raped her–'

'I didn't,' he shouted, raising himself off the pillows again. 'I swear I didn't.'

'No – I know that. Just listen to me. Lily was as much to blame as you. More so, in a way. She's older than you and should have known better. She's not ignorant of the facts of life. How could she be, brought up on a farm? But she is, perhaps, a naïve country lass, who believed the

337

words of a charmer. Oh yes, I've no doubt you whispered many a sweet nothing into her willing ears. She would believe everything you said to her. Did you say you'd marry her?'

There was a long pause before he muttered, 'I – might have done.'

'But you didn't mean it?'

He shook his head.

'Then that's what you've done wrong. Making a promise that you had no intention of keeping.'

'I know.' His whispered admission touched her heart and for the first time, since she'd known him, she felt a stab of affection for him. He was, after all, little more than a boy. A boy who'd acted like a man and was having to live with the consequences. And now, for the first time she could see that, deep down, he felt shame. A shame and anxiety that was keeping him from making the effort to get up out of his bed and face the world. Shut away in his room, he was safe. And he'd turned any blame on to his attackers. Crippled for the rest of his life, he would provoke sympathy, not censure.

Now Charlotte dared to touch his hand. 'I'll talk to your father and then we're going to get you well again.'

Philip stared at her saying nothing. But she was worried to see the fear in his eyes.

'I need to talk to you.'

She found Miles in his study where he seemed to spend most of his time. He smiled and laid aside the book he was reading. But the deep sadness in his eyes was still there.

'More trouble?' he asked gently, seeing her anxious face.

'I hope not.'

She told him of her conversation with Philip and ended by saying, 'I expect there's some fancy medical name for his condition. All I can say is, he's not getting up out of that bed because he doesn't want to.'

'Doesn't want to?' Miles was scandalized and disbelieving. 'Surely not.'

'Miles, he needs your reassurance and support. He needs to hear it from you that you are not going to try to force him to marry Lily. I know you've already told him time and again,' she added swiftly as he opened his mouth to protest. 'But you've got to make him believe it. Also, you must tell him that you'll allow him to accept Buckthorn Farm and–' she hesitated over the final words, for her heart contracted as she spoke them – 'and that you are not going to propose to me.'

'Propose to you? Why should he think that?'

'He thinks you'll comply with my father's demands to secure his inheritance.'

Miles spread his hands. 'But that's contra-dictory. He knows I don't want him to accept your father's preposterous idea. So, how can he think I'd marry you to bring it about?'

Charlotte shrugged. 'I don't know. But that's what seems to be in his mind. One of the things, anyway.'

'I'll talk to him. If you – and the doctors – are right and there's nothing physically wrong with him, then we must get him back on his feet.'

'It'll take time. His muscles must be wasted with all these weeks in bed. And he'll have missed so much schooling. What'll happen about that?'

'I've been in touch with his headmaster. His place is still there for him, though he may have to drop back a year, start the Lower Sixth Form again. But that won't matter. He did well in his recent examinations and the headmaster said all the staff expect him to be a certain candidate for university.'

'Then you should tell him that, Miles. No more talk of marrying Lily. Or becoming a farmer. My father will probably live for years anyway – just to spite everybody. Philip should get on with his life – the life *he* wants.'

He sat gazing at her before asking softly, 'But what about you? Do you intend to carry on as before – running Buckthorn Farm just to hand it over to someone else?'

She shrugged. 'Perhaps Philip would let me see out my days there. Run it for him or even become his tenant.'

'That would be very unfair. What if you should marry and have children? What about their in-heritance, never mind yours?'

Charlotte laughed wryly. 'I don't think that's likely, do you?'

The conversation was getting too personal for comfort, so she got up quickly, saying, 'And now I must find Georgie. He's promised I may see the dolls' house.'

As she reached the door, Miles said, 'By the way, it's Georgie's birthday tomorrow. He's seven.' He sighed. 'He says he doesn't want a party, not whilst

340

Philip–' he gestured helplessly.

But Charlotte smiled. 'Perfect,' she said. 'We'll have a party in Philip's room.'

Philip's recovery took many weeks, but, with encouragement from his father and brothers and firmness from Charlotte, he made progress, albeit slowly. Charlotte was the one he shouted and raved at. It was she who could answer him back and fire him to anger. But it was intentional. She knew that was the only way to make him try. Tempered with understanding and gentleness when it was needed, she roused him back to a life worth living.

The day, in early June, when Philip walked outside on to the terrace at the side of the house caused great rejoicing. Georgie hopped up and down, whilst Ben walked beside him, giving Philip his shoulder to lean on. Miles watched with quiet thankfulness, and as for Charlotte, she turned away with tears in her eyes. Her job here was done and she could make a decision about her own future. But she was devastated that she now had no excuse to come to the manor most days. No more excuse to see and be near Miles.

Life at Buckthorn Farm had settled down into its old routine. In some ways little had changed, but in others nothing was the same. She still had Mary and Edward, as before, and her father had slipped back into his domineering ways. For the moment, she went along with it, but she missed the Warren family. Eddie Norton was a good worker and willing, but he hadn't got Joe's knowledge or devotion to Buckthorn Farm. And she missed Jackson's teasing and John's solid, dependable presence. She went often to Purslane Farm to see them, but it was not the same as seeing them every day, working with them and laughing with them.

And now she missed the Thorntons. All of them, but especially Miles.

'But nothing will ever come of it,' she murmured as she sat alone in the corner of her bedroom where she did her watercolour painting. 'I'd do better to resign myself to spinsterhood than waste my life yearning for something that will never be.'

Letters came frequently from her mother, but were always addressed to Mary. Her father would not open those addressed to their servants but he'd always opened any with his daughter's name on the envelope.

'And who's writing to you?' he'd say. 'That curate or some other schemer who has his eyes on my fortune?' Euphemia wrote too, reminding Charlotte that there was always a home with them. But something held her here and it was not just her desire to see Philip well again. No, Miles filled her mind and her heart and that, more than anything else, kept her at Buckthorn Farm. Even though she now had a gateway to freedom and a new life, she no longer wanted it.

Forty-Three

'Could I have a word with you, Miss Charlotte?' Eddie was standing before her desk in the farm office, twisting his cap round and round between nervous fingers.

'Of course, Eddie. What is it? Something wrong?'

'Not – not really, miss. At least, I hope you won't think so.' He paused, bit his lip and then burst out. 'Me an' Lily want to get wed, miss, and quick, like, afore the babby comes. 'Tis due at the end of June.'

'Eddie, that's wonderful news. But you'll have to be quick.' She laughed. 'Lily's the size of an elephant now.' Then her face sobered. 'Are you sure – both of you? It's a big step and – and to take on another man's child...'

'I'm sure, miss. Lily took a bit of persuading, like. And her mam and dad, but they're all happy about it. Even me ma. She dun't mind. Ses she'll like havin' a little 'un to spoil and she's not the sort to mek a difference because it's not mine. She loves kids.'

'I think that's wonderful news. So what's the problem?'

'There's a couple, really. One is that although Lily's mam and dad say there's plenty of room at Purslane Farm for us to live with them–' He paused and twisted the cap faster and faster. Taking pity on him, Charlotte said, 'You'd like to

343

start married life as you mean to go on? In a place of your own?'

'That's about the size of it, miss, yes.'

'That's easily solved. Since you're employed on Buckthorn Farm, you can have the Warrens' cottage. I did offer it to you before and it's still empty.'

Eddie beamed. 'And would you mind me mam living with us?'

'Of course not. But I thought she wanted to stay in the house where she's always lived?'

The young man shrugged. 'She ses she'll not know what to do wi' 'ersen. Never lived on her own, see. But she'd be willing to do jobs around Buckthorn Farm and here – in the farmhouse – if Mrs Morgan ever wanted any help.'

'I'm sure Mary'd be delighted. I know she's missed Peggy's help. So, that's settled then. You can move in whenever you like. So, what was the other problem?'

Eddie's face sobered again. 'Telling Mr Thornton, miss. After all, Lily's bairn *is* his grandchild.'

Charlotte stared at him, unsure where this conversation was leading. 'You mean – you expect him to help support the child?'

'Oh no, miss.' Eddie looked hurt. 'I wouldn't want anyone to think that of us. We don't want money. We want nothing from them except – approval, I suppose. And I'd like to know what they want us to tell the little 'un as it grows up, like. Mesen, I'd believe in being honest and telling it the truth, but mebbe the Thorntons wouldn't like that. I want the kiddie to have my name, an' all. Just so it doesn't get called horrible names as it's growin' up.' He shrugged. 'See, folks round here have got long memories. If we're not honest with it, poor little thing'll likely be told in the playground, don't you think?'

'Eddie Norton, you are a remarkable young man,' Charlotte said. 'And I'm sorry if you think I thought badly of you. I didn't and I don't. The reason I said what I did was because Miles Thornton himself said he'd always see that Lily and her child were provided for.'

'I see, miss. Well, there's no need. I'll look after it as if it were me own. I promise you – an' him – that, and mebbe, if we'm blessed,' the young man twisted his cap even faster in embarrassment, 'we'll have some little brothers and sisters for him or her one day.'

'I hope you will, Eddie.'

Charlotte pondered for a couple of days on how best to broach the subject with Miles, but she knew she couldn't put it off for long. The quiet marriage ceremony was to take place at eight o'clock the following Saturday, for Lily's baby was due any time and Eddie was determined that the child, in the eyes of the world at least, should not be born illegitimate. Not many folks knew the identity of the natural father and Eddie was more than happy to take the responsibility. To outsiders, he'd be seen to be 'doing the right thing' by the girl he'd got pregnant.

They met by accident on an early morning ride on the beach. Charlotte's heart turned over as she saw the familiar figures of Miles and Midnight cantering along the firm sand at the water's edge.

He saw her and rode towards her. After greeting each other, they rode for a while in companionable silence.

It was Miles who opened the subject she was finding difficult to broach by asking, 'What's this I hear about Lily and Eddie Norton getting married? Is it true?'

She glanced at him, trying to read his expression. Was he pleased or angry? But his face told her nothing.

'Yes, it's true. On Saturday at eight in the morning.'

He nodded. 'I suppose it's just family, is it?'

'Mm.' There was a pause before she said, 'Actually, I wanted to come and talk to you about it, but I've been putting it off.'

'Oh? Why?'

'Well – I wasn't sure how you'd feel.'

He sighed. 'I'm pleased for her.' His voice hardened a little. 'Since my own son refused to do the honourable thing.'

Charlotte smiled weakly, anxious not to get into that particular discussion again. 'Eddie wants the child to have his name but he wants to know if you'd have any objection to it being told the truth, when it's old enough of course. He promises he'll bring the child up as his own and no difference will ever be made between it and any more children they might have together. It's just that he doesn't want the child to hear playground gossip when it's older. He believes in honesty from the start.'

Miles was thoughtful for so long that she began to grow agitated, thinking that he disapproved in some way.

'He's a remarkable young man,' he murmured at last.

'Yes – I told him that. But he wanted your approval. That's what he said. Your approval.'

'Charlotte, would you ask him to come and see me? I'd like to talk to him, but reassure him, he has my blessing on everything he is planning.'

'There's just one thing I ought to mention. He's not looking for financial help. In fact, when I half suggested it, he was most indignant.'

'Then my admiration for him is growing by the minute. I'll tread carefully, Charlotte, I promise. I'll not offend him. But it *is* still my grandchild and I'd like to see if he would let me do something. Set up a trust fund, perhaps, for when the child comes of age.'

'Perhaps. But he might see that as being unfair on any other children, as he said, if they're blessed.'

'If they're blessed,' Miles repeated the words softly and then sighed. 'My grandchild...' And then he added words which brought a lump to Charlotte's throat and a twinge of envy. 'I hope it's a girl. Oh, I do hope it's a girl.'

Forty-Four

Miles's hopes were not realized. Lily's baby, born on the last day in June only five days after her marriage to Eddie, was a boy. He was named Alfred Joseph, but would always be known as Alfie.

Osbert almost danced with glee. 'There, my boy has proved he can sire a son. Now he only has to find someone worthy to bear him an heir. Someone better than that little trollop. Still–' his eyes gleamed with excitement – 'a young feller has to sow a few wild oats. But now he should choose more carefully, and next time–'

'I don't think Master Philip will be siring any more children – boys or girls – for a while yet,' Charlotte reminded him tartly. 'He's seventeen and is to return to school and his studies now he's recovering so well.'

'Yes, yes, but one day – one day he will marry well and have a family. I wonder,' the devious man mused aloud, 'if he would change his surname by deed poll to Crawford.'

'Father!' Charlotte was appalled. 'That would be grossly unfair on his own father. Think what you're saying.'

He regarded her through narrowed eyes. 'I know *exactly* what I'm saying.' He was thoughtful for a moment. 'Mm, yes, that's a good idea. Now, why didn't I think of that before? If the father won't marry you,' he looked her up and down, sniffed and then muttered, 'and I can't say I blame him – then the boy could take my name. He reckons he's going to be a lawyer, so he'll know how to go about it.'

Charlotte was so angry – not for herself, but for Miles Thornton – that she almost spilled out the news that she'd found her mother alive and well and had met her. But something held back the words. Was it still fear of this man? No – she didn't believe that. Not now. At least, not for herself. But perhaps she was afraid, deep down, of what he might try to do to her mother if he knew where to find her. Or was it pity? She looked at the man, wizened by bitterness and grown old before his time because of it. He looked seventy or even older – so much older than his fifty-seven years. She'd not had much of a life – but she still had a chance to make something of it. He'd wasted his. Of his own choice, he whiled away the years sitting wrapped in discontent and resentment, manipulating the lives of others for his own insidious schemes. And he was still trying to do it. No, she wouldn't tell him about her mother, but her decision was more to protect Alice than for any other reason.

Life settled back into a routine. The weeks passed – another haymaking and another harvest were over. Philip went back to boarding school at the start of the autumn term and, this time, Ben went too, so there was only Georgie left at home in the great rambling house to keep his father company. The little boy – though growing rapidly

349

now – still attended the village school, continued to play with Tommy Warren and the other boys, and never ceased to charm the locals with his cheeky grin.

'Perhaps he ought to go to boarding school soon too,' Miles confided in Charlotte. 'But I can't bring myself to let him go.'

'I can understand that,' she said quietly. She didn't add that she wouldn't be able to let her children out of her sight – if she were fortunate enough to have any. But she kept silent. Things were different for boys. They had to have the best education that could be found – or afforded. She'd have given her eye teeth to have been sent to boarding school, she mused, but that would have meant her father loosening his domination over her. And he'd never have done that. She sighed. Despite his threats, she knew he'd never let her go, even now. If she were ever to escape, the decision would have to be hers.

But something still held her here at Buckthorn Farm amidst the bleak, windswept marshland. Was it loyalty and duty to her father? Or was it the presence of the handsome man on the big black horse riding beside her along the beach? They met often and Charlotte no longer rode one of the shire horses now. At the August horse fair that year, she'd bought herself a more suitable horse for her outings to the beach where she hoped to encounter Miles.

One morning in October, when Charlotte took a well-earned break from work, they met on the beach. It was the first time in several days she'd had the chance to slip away, for she and all her workers had been fully occupied with the lifting of their first harvest of sugar beet. The crop had been good – better than they'd dared to hope for. But now it was safely on its way to Bardney, Charlotte allowed herself a brief respite. She'd also given Eddie and the other workers on Buckthorn Farm the day off. 'As long as the milking gets done and the animals are fed,' she'd warned.

After greeting each other, Miles asked, 'Have you ever told your father that you've met your mother?'

Charlotte shook her head. 'No,' she said hoarsely. 'I – I couldn't.'

'Mm. So,' he added slowly, 'you've never solved the mystery of the grave in the churchyard, then?'

She shook her head and murmured, 'I'm not sure I want to.'

'Ah,' was all Miles said and they rode on in silence. They parted in the lane, he to canter towards the manor, Charlotte to ride slowly back to Buckthorn Farm, her gaze holding sight of him until the very last moment when he disappeared from her view.

'Miss Charlotte–' Cuthbert Iveson had visited the Sunday school class as usual, but today he lingered until all the children had gone. This was the first time he'd deliberately sought her out since her father's threats to have him removed from his living.

She looked up at him and smiled, but her smile faded when she noticed how thin and pale he'd become. His hands were shaking and he chewed nervously on his bottom lip.

'Miss Charlotte – I have to tell you – I'm leaving.'

'Oh, Mr Iveson – no!' She paused and then asked, 'Has this anything to do with my father?'

'Well – in a way, but–'

'But I thought Mr Thornton wrote to the bishop and explained–'

'He did, he did,' Cuthbert said quickly. 'And I was grateful – most grateful. No, I'm leaving of my own free will.'

But his eyes were haunted and she was sure that this was not the truth – or at least, not the whole truth. 'Why?' she asked candidly.

'I am no longer comfortable here.'

'But I don't understand. Your services are well attended. The church is almost full – well, most of the time. And always on special occasions like Harvest and Christmas and Easter. So why?'

He avoided meeting her gaze. In anyone else, she would have described his manner as shifty. But in a vicar– Heaven forbid! she thought.

'There are things I can't tell you about. Confidences, you know.'

'Like confessions, you mean?'

'Well – sort of. Look, I'm sorry. I just have to go. Make a fresh start. I had hoped...' He looked at her now, meeting her gaze. 'There was a time I'd hoped that you and I...'

She touched his hand and said gently, 'I know.' But there was no regret, at least, not on her part. Now she knew how it felt to fall in love, she knew she could never have felt about Cuthbert the way she felt about Miles. 'When do you go?'

'The bishop has found me another living. My

352

last services here will be next Sunday.'

'So soon? Who will take the services until a replacement has been found?'

'Mr Knoakes from Lynthorpe will take one service a day here. Matins, I think.'

'And the Sunday school?'

Now he actually smiled. 'I hope that will continue as it always has – under your expert tuition.'

Charlotte laughed. 'I don't know about the expert bit, but I'll certainly do my best.'

'I'm hoping the next person to come here will be older. And a married man. I said as much to the bishop. I – I think he understood.'

Charlotte nodded and said quietly, 'I think it would be for the best. But I'm so sorry if it's my father who's caused you to leave.'

Cuthbert became agitated again. 'It wasn't because of you and me. It was something else.'

'Oh? What?'

He pressed his lips together. 'That's what I can't tell you. I'm sorry. It – it was a deathbed confession and must remain so. But it troubles my conscience.'

'Have you discussed this with the bishop?'

'Yes.'

'And?'

'He advised me to move away. It – it was none of my making, you understand. Something that happened years ago, but I'm finding it hard to cope with the knowledge.'

'I – see,' she said slowly, but of course she didn't understand at all. And yet, as they parted company, there was something nagging at the back of her mind, but she couldn't quite think what it was.

As she walked back towards the farm, she was deep in thought. Then suddenly, in the middle of the lane, she stopped and said aloud, 'A deathbed confession? Why, that'd be old Harry Warren. It must be.' She remembered suddenly that Peggy had told her of old Harry's agitation shortly before he died. And – he'd asked to see the vicar.

During the eighteen months since Harry had died, there'd been only two deaths of people Charlotte knew, which had also involved Cuthbert's church. One, Flora Brown, had been a non-believer ever since she'd lost her husband and two sons in the Great War. She'd raged at a God who could let that happen – and not only to her. Another had been a young man killed in a horrific accident with a traction engine. There'd been two or three old people in Ravensfleet who'd died, and whom Charlotte had known slightly, but she'd understood that they'd been chapel-goers and if they'd called for anyone on their deathbeds, it would have been the Methodist minister.

Miles, she decided as she reached the gate of Buckthorn Farm, *I'll ask Miles*. She remembered that he'd hinted at something. She would ask him.

Her heart lifted at the thought of an excuse to see him.

Forty-Five

He was standing on the terrace when she walked to the manor later that week. He was looking out over the flat land, most of which he owned, apart from Buckthorn Farm's acres. But, she thought, even those would one day belong to his family.

He turned and saw her walking towards him. 'Charlotte – how lovely. Just in time for afternoon tea when Georgie gets home from school. Brewster has just gone to fetch him.' He laughed. 'I think Georgie is the most popular boy in the school when my motor car turns up. Brewster says he can hardly drive sometimes for the number of excitable boys squashed into the vehicle. I'm not sure it's entirely safe, but there you are. Thank goodness for quiet country roads!'

Charlotte laughed. 'I think your motor car is one of the few round here, so I shouldn't worry.'

'Can you stay for tea?'

'I'd love to, but first, before Georgie gets home, there's something I want to ask you. Did you know that the Reverend Iveson is leaving?'

Miles raised his eyebrows. 'No, I didn't. Why? I thought that business with your father was all sorted out after I wrote to the bishop.'

She nodded. 'I don't think it's because of that particular letter my father sent to the bishop.' She frowned. 'There's something else troubling the vicar, but I think it has something to do with my

355

father. Indirectly. He said it was a deathbed confession that is troubling him. He wouldn't – couldn't – tell me more, of course, and I respect that, but I've been thinking...'

'And?'

'The only person I can think of who's died in the last year or so and who I know asked to see Mr Iveson and who also had a connection with my father is old Harry Warren.'

'Aaah.' Miles let out a deep breath as if, suddenly, everything had become clear. 'Charlotte, my dear...' He put his arm about her shoulders and led her down the stone steps towards a garden seat set in the rose garden just below the terrace.

She trembled at his nearness. They sat down side by side and he took her hands in his. 'My dear, I began to suspect some – shall we say, skulduggery – when you came home and confided in me that you'd met your mother whom you'd been led to believe was dead all these years.' His tone hardened at the cruelty of such an act. Cruelty, not only to the child Charlotte had been then, but to the mother, too. 'The mystery of your mother's supposed grave in the churchyard and why Harry Warren demanded to be buried beside her. Why he'd bought the plot next to her in – in readiness?'

Charlotte bit her lip and lowered her gaze. 'I wondered about that myself. I – I thought perhaps there'd been something between them. Between my mother and Harry. An affair, perhaps. And that was why my father was so bitter. My mother's never said anything, but then, perhaps she wouldn't confess to such a thing. Not even to me. That's why – for a while – I didn't want to know.

But now...'

Miles squeezed her hands gently. 'I don't think it was anything like that at all. What I think happened – and I don't believe even Joe knows this – was that your mother did leave your father, just as she told you, because of his cruelty to her. But her leaving happened at the same time – by sheer happy coincidence from your father's point of view – as Harry's wife died.'

Charlotte gasped and stared at him, her mind working feverishly. 'You – you mean it's old Mrs Warren who's buried in that grave?'

'I think so, yes.'

'But – but how could they do that? I mean, the vicar would know. And the undertakers. They'd all have known. They must have done.'

'I expect so. But your father has always got his own way, hasn't he? By fair means or foul, he manipulates people. Bribes them, threatens them. Who was the vicar here then?'

Charlotte frowned. 'I can hardly remember. An old man, I think. I can't remember his name now. He – he left soon afterwards...' Her voice faded away as she began to realize that the incredible picture Miles was painting was perhaps possible. Even probable. It all seemed to fit.

'So, you think Harry was – was *involved* – and that's what he wanted to confide in the vicar before he died so that Mr Iveson would understand why he insisted on being buried next to my mother's – well, what we thought was my mother's – grave?'

Miles nodded. 'And that knowledge is hanging heavily on poor Mr Iveson's conscience, so much so that he can't bear to stay here with the daily reminder. The grave isn't far from the path he treads every day from the vicarage to the church. Poor fellow, he can't betray the confidences of a dying man. And apart from that, I'm sure he wouldn't want to upset Joe and his family.'

'They know nothing, I'm sure, because when Harry died they couldn't understand why he'd bought that particular plot and–'

'Father – Father! Oh, Miss Charlotte!'

They both turned to see Georgie scampering down the steps. Miles released her and Charlotte felt a sense of loss. Her hands – and her heart – were suddenly chilled.

'By the way,' Miles whispered with a chuckle, 'now that both his brothers are away, Georgie feels himself "second in command", so he's calling me "Father" now, and no longer the childish name of "Papa".'

'What a shame,' Charlotte murmured, before she had stopped to think. 'They grow up so quickly, don't they?'

'Yes,' Miles said with a wistful tone. 'That's just what I feel, too.'

But they could say no more, for the young boy was hopping up and down in front of them. 'Come and play, Miss Charlotte. Tommy has come to tea. And Sammy Barker too. We'll have a party.'

And indeed they did. It was a merry, impromptu tea party, all the more enjoyable because it was unexpected. Almost, Charlotte thought, letting her imagination and her longing run riot, like a proper family; a mother, father and three little boys.

Afterwards, they played a noisy game of football on the lawn and when it was time for the boys to leave, Miles walked down the lane with her towards Buckthorn Farm.

'What do you think we should do?' she asked, coming back to the topic of their earlier conversation.

'I think Joe should know. He thinks his poor mother is buried in Lincoln.'

'Yes,' Charlotte agreed. 'And that's another thing. Joe told me that when their mother died, his father wouldn't let any of the family go to Lincoln with him to see her buried – ostensibly with her family.'

'I expect that was all a charade. I don't think there ever was a burial in Lincoln. The funeral director must have been in on the secret, provided an empty coffin and, well, just acted as if they were going to the city. For one thing,' Miles went on, 'I doubt someone like Harry Warren could have afforded to pay for his wife to be buried so far away. Think of the cost. Don't you have to pay something to each parish the coffin passes through or something?'

'I've no idea.'

They walked in silence for a while until Charlotte said, 'Yes, I think you're right. We should tell Joe.'

'Want me to come with you?'

'Please,' she said without hesitation. She didn't really need him there. She knew the family so well that she could talk to them about anything. But it was another excuse to be with him again.

'We'll go tomorrow afternoon. I'll pick you up in the motor car. About two?'

'Well, that certainly solves a mystery, Mr Thornton,' Joe said, running his hand through his hair. 'Dun't it, Peg?'

They were sitting in the huge kitchen at Purslane Farm, surrounded by an appetizing smell of freshly baked bread. Teacakes, scones and a sponge cake were laid out on the dresser top to cool. Peggy set out half a dozen scones, jam and fresh cream on the table and bade them help themselves as she poured out cups of tea and then sat down to join them.

'It does, Joe. We always wondered why he'd bought the plot next to your mother, Miss Charlotte.'

Charlotte had confided in Peggy and Joe that she'd met her mother. They'd been genuinely shocked and Peggy shook her head, saying yet again, 'I can't believe she's been alive all this time. And that wicked old man has kept you apart. Oh, begging your pardon, miss, I know he's your father, but...'

'Don't apologize, Peggy,' Charlotte said grimly.

'And you say Mary and Edward knew?'

Charlotte nodded.

'I reckon that shocks me more than anything else. That Mary's kept quiet all these years. Never told you...'

'Don't blame her, Peggy. He's threatened them. She did what she thought was right to protect me. In a way, I'm glad I didn't know, because if he'd found out she'd told me, he would have dismissed them both and then where would I have been?'

'I suppose so,' Peggy agreed reluctantly. 'But I don't think I could have carried such a burden all these years.'

'You,' Joe teased, 'keep secrets? That'd be a first.'

He was rewarded by a playful slap from his wife, but everyone smiled.

Joe was thoughtful. 'Do you reckon if we tell the vicar – unburden him, like – he'd stay?'

'I think it's better to let him go,' Miles said. 'Like we said, it's a constant reminder for the poor chap whilst he's here. And you knowing might embarrass him even further.'

Joe was looking straight at Charlotte. 'But do *you* mind him going, miss?'

'Me?' Charlotte was startled.

Miles frowned. 'Why should Miss Charlotte mind?'

Joe and Peggy exchanged a smile.

'Because,' Peggy said softly, 'we always thought Mr Iveson was sweet on our Miss Charlotte. And she'd make a lovely vicar's wife.'

'Did you indeed?' Miles murmured, so softly that only Charlotte, seated next to him heard.

On the way home Miles was quiet and withdrawn. As she alighted from the car, he gave her a cursory nod and drove away at once. Heavy hearted, Charlotte went into the house to find Mary in a state of panic and wringing her hands.

'Miss Charlotte, thank goodness you're home. Your aunt and uncle are here. And there's such a row going on. Your father's so angry. He's shouting–'

'Oh no! She – she hasn't told him, has she?'

Forty-Six

Flinging open the door of the sitting room, Charlotte stopped to take in the scene before her.

Her father was standing behind his chair, but hanging on to it for support. Euphemia stood before him, her head thrown back, her bosom heaving with righteous indignation. Percy, meanwhile, had withdrawn as far as the front window, keeping out of the argument as much as he was allowed.

'Aunt Euphemia...' Charlotte moved forward, trying to ignore the raging row, but her father, purple in the face, shook his free fist at her. 'Keep out of this, girl. Go to your room. This minute.'

She ignored his order and went to his side. Gently, she said, 'Father, sit down. You're distressing yourself.'

His whole body was shaking, his eyes bulging, his face puce.

'Please, do sit down,' she urged him again. As his handhold slipped, he fell against her and she manoeuvred him into his chair. Then she turned to face her aunt.

'Please, Aunt, this is not good for him...' She stopped, appalled as she saw the expression on her aunt's face. It was no longer the kindly, smiling face of the generous woman. Euphemia's face was twisted in fury with an expression so like her brother's that Charlotte was deeply shocked. She moved towards her to beg her, too, 'Please, Aunt, don't distress yourself. I don't know what this is about, but–'

'It's about you, my dear. You – and your *mother*.'

Startled, Charlotte gasped. 'Please – don't. I beg you–' She lowered her voice to an urgent whisper. 'You haven't told him, have you? You haven't told him that–'

Behind them, Charlotte heard a strange gurgling sound and turned to see her father slumped in the chair, his eyes staring, his mouth gagging open.

'Now look what you've done.'

'Me? I had nothing to do with it. He's an evil, deceitful man, who turned our father against Percy and me. He doesn't like to see anyone happy. Not even his own daughter.'

Charlotte was bending over him. 'Father – Father–' She was hardly listening to what her aunt was saying. But instinctively, she turned to Percy for help. 'Uncle, please fetch Edward.'

'Where will I find him?'

'In the kitchen.'

'Where's that?'

'You stay here. I'll go.'

But she'd hardly turned towards the door before it opened and Edward hurried into the room. He must have been hovering in the hall, listening to the quarrel.

'The doctor, Edward. We need the doctor. At once. Get Eddie to go for him. And ask Mary to come.'

After Edward had gone, she said, 'Do you think we should move him? Get him upstairs into bed?'

Euphemia's mouth twisted. 'No, leave him be.

Let him die where he is. It's no more than he deserves.'

'Euphemia...' At this, even the taciturn Percy protested. 'That's rather harsh, my dear.'

Charlotte's mouth hardened. 'I think you'd better leave, Aunt, if you please.'

'Oh, I'm going.' Euphemia was smiling now, but it was a hard, embittered smile. Beckoning imperiously to Percy, she flounced out of the room, her parting words shocking Charlotte. 'I've done what I came to do.'

'He's had a stroke,' the doctor pronounced. 'A bad one. The next few days will be critical.'

'Should he go to hospital?'

'Moving him might do more damage than letting him stay here.' He looked at her sharply. 'Can you afford a private nurse to live in for a week or so?'

'Of course. Anything.'

Dr Markham touched her cheek gently. 'You're a good girl, Charlotte,' he murmured. 'Not many daughters would be so caring after the way you've been treated.'

'He's still my father,' she said softly.

'And you,' the doctor insisted, 'are a remarkable young woman.' He cleared his throat and said more briskly, 'I'll make arrangements. She'll arrive by tonight.'

'She'll have to have my bed, Mary. I'll sleep on the truckle bed. We can screen off one end of the room.'

For the rest of the day, until early evening when the nurse arrived, Charlotte sat by her father's bedside. There was little she could do for him. She had no nursing knowledge and was afraid of doing more harm than good. She didn't even sit holding his hand. He was asleep or unconscious – she wasn't sure which. But her touch was not what her father would have wanted, she thought wryly.

Whilst she sat in the stillness of the sick room, her thoughts wandered over the years and all the events that had occurred in her life. Some, she'd learned so recently, were not what she'd thought they'd been at the time. Like the death of her mother. How could her father have been so vindictive, so vengeful? And how on earth had he managed to get others to join in his deception? Bribery, she thought, or threats. In the case of Harry Warren, she supposed, it had probably been a mixture of the two. A threat that he'd be dismissed if he didn't carry out Osbert's wishes and, at the same time, a promise that he and his family would always have work and a home if he went along with his employer's devious schemes. But, even so, Charlotte could not comprehend Harry agreeing to his wife being buried in someone else's grave, with no stone to mark her final resting place and nowhere for his family to visit and cherish her memory.

And the vicar? How could any man of the cloth agree to such a terrible deception? The vicar at that time had been an old man. Charlotte remembered him vaguely. Perhaps her father had had some hold over him, too, or he'd promised him a comfortable old age in return for his complicity. She sighed. Osbert Crawford was a difficult and

365

complex man with a streak of cruelty. But at this moment she felt desperately sorry for him. Despite his treatment of her, his lack of love, his hatred almost, because she'd been born a girl and not the son he craved, she felt only pity for him. He'd wasted his whole life yearning for something that could not be – was never going to be after he'd treated his young wife so abominably that she'd been forced to flee for her life.

She didn't blame her mother. Not any more. She wanted – needed – to believe in her. To believe that the reason she'd abandoned her small daughter had been forced upon her. Staying would have endangered her sanity, perhaps even her life. But the last few hours, Charlotte realized, had sadly disillusioned her about her aunt.

Euphemia was little better than her brother. Charlotte suspected that her actions – on the surface, kind and caring – had been for one reason and one reason only. To wreak revenge on the brother who had tried to rule her life and had succeeded in turning their father against her. Deep down, she was as embittered and vengeful as he was. Now Charlotte was sure this was the reason Euphemia had come back to Buckthorn Farm, had pretended affection for her niece, and had reunited her with her mother. It had all been for her own ends. Had she taken Alice in all those years earlier just to spite Osbert? Charlotte wondered, but realized she would probably never know the answer to that. She sighed. At least, her mother had seemed contented. She hoped it was the truth.

Nurse Montgomery – soon nicknamed 'Monty'

– was in her early thirties. She was round-faced with a jollity that belied a fearsome, protective attitude towards her patient. Charlotte was relieved to hand over the responsibility to the capable woman, remarking only, 'Please let me know if there's anything you want.'

'I most certainly will, Miss Crawford, of that you can be sure.'

Thankfully, Charlotte escaped back to her office.

Nurse Monty took charge, requesting that the truckle bed be moved into Osbert's large bedroom.

'I need to be able to listen for him in the night,' she explained.

'I'm so sorry we haven't another proper bed; perhaps–' Charlotte began, but the nurse waved aside her apologies. 'I've slept on worse, believe you me.'

On the fourth day after his stroke, Osbert was roused out of unconsciousness. There was some paralysis, one side of his face was dragged down and he could not speak, but he could make angry signs that he wanted to write. Nurse Montgomery called for Charlotte to bring a pad and a pen to his bedside and with his unaffected hand he wrote in shaky, but quite legible handwriting, two words: Philip Baxter.

Deciphering it, the nurse asked, 'Philip Baxter? Who's he?'

'It's two people,' Charlotte explained. 'Mr Baxter is his solicitor and Philip is Philip Thornton.'

The nurse eyed her patient, lying back against the pillows, quite exhausted by the effort. 'Then I think,' she said quietly, 'you'd better send for them both.'

'I'll send for the solicitor, but Philip's away at school—'

Her father waved his good arm angrily and made gurgling noises.

'I think he wants you to send for him,' the nurse interpreted.

Charlotte shrugged. 'I can only ask his father.'

She left the room with Osbert shaking his fist at her.

'I'll send Brewster to fetch him.' Miles glanced at Charlotte, trying to read her expression. 'If that's what you want me to do?'

When she nodded, he said, 'Then I'll write a note to the headmaster explaining the situation.'

The solicitor arrived that same afternoon and Philip was home by nightfall. The following morning the solicitor visited again, bringing Philip with him. They were closeted with Osbert for over an hour and a half, before summoning the nurse and Edward into the room.

When they all emerged, Mr Baxter looked grim and somewhat shell-shocked, Charlotte fancied, whilst Philip was smiling smugly.

'Mr Baxter...?' Charlotte began, but the man merely rammed his hat on to his head, gave her a curt nod, and hurried out of the front door. Meanwhile, Philip stood in the centre of the hall looking around him.

'There'll have to be some changes made,' he

muttered before he followed the solicitor from the house, leaving Charlotte staring after them.

'He's really done it, hasn't he? He's made his will and – and he's left Buckthorn Farm to Philip Thornton. Just like he threatened he would do.'

Forty-Seven

Charlotte was devastated. Until it was actually in writing, signed, sealed and witnessed, a tiny part of her had still clung to the hope that leaving Buckthorn Farm to Philip had been just another of her father's threats. He enjoyed playing with people's lives, manipulating them.

But now it was done. After her father's death, Buckthorn Farm would no longer belong to a member of the Crawford family.

Contrary to everyone's expectations – including his own – Osbert did not die. Slowly, he began to recover. He would never regain the full use of one arm but his speech returned, though he slurred his words and became angry and frustrated if people couldn't understand him.

'I really thought we were getting rid of the old bugger at last,' Edward muttered to his wife.

'Huh! Him? He'll live to be a hundred and twenty – just to spite us all. It's that lass I feel sorry for. She's trapped now for good an' all. And for what? To hand over the farm to that – that good for nothing when the old man does die.'

Life settled back into much the same routine

that had existed before Euphemia's arrival. Just as before, Osbert never mentioned her and whether or not he'd known that Charlotte had learned the truth about her mother, it wasn't spoken of between them. But just now and again Charlotte caught a wary look in her father's eyes. Whenever that happened, he would turn his head away, avoiding her gaze.

At the end of six weeks, just before Christmas, Nurse Montgomery declared that she was no longer needed and Dr Markham agreed. 'Edward and Mary can manage him between them. He's regained enough use in his limbs not to be helpless. He just needs a little assistance now and again.' Then the kindly doctor turned to Charlotte and asked, 'But what about you, my dear? I – er–' He cleared his throat in embarrassment. 'I understand your father has not left you provided for in his will.'

Charlotte sighed. 'So it would seem.'

'Then it's high time you got on with the rest of *your* life, whatever you want that to be.'

She smiled thinly and promised, 'I'll think about it.'

But what could she do? Whilst she would keep in touch with them – and especially with her mother – she had no desire now to live with her aunt. She'd seen another side to the woman and life under her roof, Charlotte was sure, would be little different to the one she had now. Euphemia would be every bit as domineering as her brother. She wondered why her mother had stayed with them all these years? But perhaps the answer was very simple. She had nowhere else to go.

370

So Charlotte made her decision. However bleak and dismal her future seemed, she would stay with her father. She would do her duty and continue to run Buckthorn Farm.

She wrote carefully worded letters to her mother and to her aunt, making no direct reference to Euphemia's recent visit and the catastrophe it had caused. She merely thanked her aunt for her kind offer of a home, but stated that her duty lay with her father. She hoped that they would allow her to visit them, maybe staying a few days so that she might get to know her mother. To her mother, whom she didn't blame in any way for Euphemia's outburst, she expressed affection and a hope that they might meet often. She posted the letters and bravely faced her bleak future; a future devoted to caring for a man who didn't deserve her sacrifice. Her decision had not been made out of fear of him – she was no longer afraid of his anger – but because of her own sense of duty and loyalty.

'Honour thy father and thy mother,' was her faith's teaching. The good book said nothing about 'only if they should deserve it'.

So Charlotte settled her mind to the future, taking delight in her work. She loved Buckthorn Farm and – for the time being at least – it was still hers in all but name. She revelled in her continuing involvement with the Sunday school, for she loved the children. All of them – even the naughty ones!

And she counted the hours till she might see Miles again.

'So, another Christmas is upon us,' Miles said as they walked along the sand, leading their horses.

Their 'chance' encounters were not so much by accident now. At least, not on Charlotte's side. She knew when Miles was likely to be riding Midnight along the beach.

'I do hope you'll be able to join us at some time over the festive period. Philip and Ben will be home and–' he paused and smiled, 'Felix is coming to stay with us over Christmas. As you might remember, he has no immediate family and life, even in the hustle and bustle of London, can be very lonely at such times.'

'How lovely!' she said and her pleasure was genuine. She'd liked the flamboyant artist.

She felt Miles's glance upon her as he added quietly, 'And he's asked specifically if you will be with us.'

'Has he?' She looked at him. 'How kind.'

'I don't think it's kindness, my dear. He likes your company.' Very softly, so quietly that she wasn't sure whether she had heard aright, he added, 'As do we all.'

Charlotte was invited to the manor to dine with the family and Felix on Boxing Day.

'Come and see all my presents,' Georgie greeted her excitedly, dragging her up the stairs to the playroom. 'I've got a train set. A Hornby clockwork one. Ben's setting it all up for me. It's got enough track to run all the way round the room. And carriages and even little people.' He flung open the door with a flourish. 'Look!'

For the next hour Charlotte knelt on the floor, playing happily with the two boys. Philip poked his head round the door once, sneered at the childish games and disappeared – much to Charlotte's relief.

At dinner, she was seated next to Felix, who kept them all entranced with his tales of the artistic world in the city. 'I'm opening a gallery soon. It's something I've always wanted to do.' He smiled archly at Charlotte. 'And whilst most of the paintings displayed will be my own,' he laughed heartily, 'that's the whole idea, of course, I shall also be on the lookout for other artists, especially unknown ones whom I can nurture.' He turned to Charlotte. 'Now, my dear, can I persuade you to show me some of your work?'

Charlotte blushed and shook her head. 'It's only a – a hobby with me. I'm not very good.' She hesitated, remembering her father's cruel destruction of nearly all her work. 'And besides, there aren't many paintings to see.'

'I'd like the chance to judge that for myself,' Felix said softly as he touched her hand.

At the end of the table Miles cleared his throat. 'Shall we adjourn to the drawing room, if everyone's ready? And Georgie – I think it's time you went to bed.'

The boy climbed down from his seat. 'Please, may Charlotte read me a story?'

'Well...' Miles glanced at her, a question in his eyes. 'If she doesn't mind.'

'Of course I don't mind.' She rose at once, glad to escape from Philip's sneering face.

'Now, don't be away too long,' Felix said, catching hold of her hand and raising it to his lips. 'Don't let that adorable little scamp monopolize you. There are others who want to enjoy your company, you know.'

To her relief when she returned downstairs, having tucked Georgie into his bed and kissed him 'goodnight', Philip had disappeared. Soon Ben excused himself and went to bed leaving only Miles, Felix and Charlotte in front of the blazing log fire. The rest of the evening was spent pleasantly enough, with Miles in the armchair beside the fire and Felix sitting beside her on the sofa. Charlotte couldn't remember a time when she had enjoyed herself so much and when at last she said she really must go home, Felix rose and gallantly kissed her on both cheeks.

'I hope we meet again very soon. I can't stay for New Year this time, though Miles has asked me; I must get back. My gallery has its grand opening in two weeks' time and there's so much to do.' His eyes sparkled suddenly. 'Now, why don't you come down to London for the opening? You could stay with me.' He turned to Miles, but almost as an afterthought. 'And you too, my dear friend.'

'Well...' Miles began hesitantly, but Charlotte said at once, 'I'd love to, but I'm sorry, it's really not possible. Though thank you for the kind invitation.'

Felix gave an exaggerated sigh and kissed her hand again.

'I'll see you to the motor,' Miles said abruptly. 'Brewster will drive you home.'

'There's no need,' Charlotte protested. 'I can easily–'

'I wouldn't dream of allowing you to walk

374

anywhere so late at night and in the dark,' he said stiffly as he opened the front door and ushered her down the steps to the waiting vehicle.

He held out his hand to help her climb in and then he closed the door. 'Good night, Charlotte.' He turned away abruptly and as the motor car drew away, Charlotte was left staring at his back as he ran lightly back up the steps and into the house.

'Now,' she murmured to herself, 'what on earth has got into him?'

She wrinkled her forehead, trying to think whether she had said anything untoward, but for the life of her she couldn't think that she had said or done anything which could have offended Miles.

Forty-Eight

On the morning after New Year's Day 1928, Charlotte was surprised to see Miles ride into the yard at Buckthorn Farm, dismount, and stride to the back door.

'A happy new year to you all,' he said, removing his hat and ducking his head as he stepped into the kitchen. His gaze sought Charlotte. 'Ah, I was wondering if you would come for a ride on the beach – that is, if you're not too busy?'

'You go, Miss Charlotte,' Mary said at once before Charlotte had time to reply. 'The fresh air will do you good.' Mary turned to Miles. 'Her father was troublesome in the night, sir. Restless and – demanding. She's not had much sleep herself.'

'Oh – well...' Miles hesitated.

'No – no – a gallop on the beach'll blow all the cobwebs away. She can rest this afternoon.'

'It seems your question's been answered for me.' Charlotte laughed. 'Give me five minutes.' She turned and ran from the room to change into her riding habit.

'A cup of tea while you're waiting, sir?' Mary said.

They reached the beach and rode to the water's edge where the receding tide had left the sand firm enough for them to urge their mounts into a gallop. When they slowed again they dismounted and walked side by side, leading their horses.

'Charlotte – there's something I want to say to you, but – but it's difficult.'

'Then the best way is just to say it outright.' She smiled up at him, completely unaware of the bombshell that was about to fall.

'Very well, then.' He paused and seemed to be gathering his courage. 'I would like to offer you my hand in marriage. I have been thinking about it for some time and–'

He got no further. Charlotte whirled round to face him, her temper roused by what she saw as an offer out of humiliating pity. 'Offer me your hand in marriage? How dare you? Is this still to do with Philip and his inheritance? Are you afraid that I will somehow find a way to contest my father's will when the time comes?'

He was staring at her, open-mouthed, shocked and – if she'd stopped for a moment to see – hurt.

'Charlotte, how can you even think–? Oh dear, I haven't expressed myself very well. I–'

'You most certainly have not,' she snapped. She turned away from him and, gathering the reins in her hands, flung herself up on to her horse.

Looking down at him, she said sarcastically, 'I thank you for the great honour you have bestowed upon me, but I regret I must decline your offer.'

She turned and rode away. When she realized that he was making no attempt to follow her, she allowed the tears to flow. Tears of frustration and humiliation, but, above all, heartbreak. More than anything else in the world, she wanted to marry Miles Thornton for now she knew she loved him with all her heart.

But not like that; not because he felt sorry for her or because he wanted to further safeguard his son's inheritance. Even though Osbert had made a will in the boy's favour, he was perfectly capable of making another that nullified the first. By marrying her, Miles would ensure that Buckthorn Farm came into the Thornton family one way or another. But Charlotte was not going to allow herself to be used.

Oh no, not like that.

It wasn't until the following Sunday that she saw any of the Thornton family again. Since her father's illness, Charlotte attended Matins with just Mary. Her father was not well enough to go to church and Edward stayed with him. Now she and Mary sat together in the front pew.

She heard the Thorntons, all four of them, enter the church and felt them take their places in the pew on the opposite side of the aisle. She heard Georgie whispering. Then, suddenly, he was squeezing into the pew beside her, his hand creeping into hers.

'Father says will you come back to luncheon with me after Sunday school? He says to tell you he's sorry and he wants to talk to you again.'

She glanced down to see the young boy looking up at her with such an appeal in his blue eyes that her heart melted. She might be angry with his father, but there was no reason to take it out on Georgie. Miles had certainly chosen his ambassador well. She could not refuse 'her golden boy'.

'What is Papa – I mean, Father' – for a brief moment, George's new-found 'grown up' status deserted him – 'sorry about?'

She smiled down at him. 'Oh, something and nothing. Grown-up silliness. Don't you worry about it, darling.'

'But will you come? He's been grumpy all week. Ever since the day after New Year. Like "a bear with a sore head", Ben says.'

Charlotte stifled the laughter that bubbled up inside her. 'Yes,' she managed to say as the vicar appeared from the vestry to begin the service. 'I'll come.'

She sighed inwardly. Of course, she should have refused the invitation, but she wasn't strong enough to fight the overwhelming desire to be with him.

Luncheon at the manor was difficult. Charlotte wished that the ebullient Felix was still there to lighten the tension and take command of the stilted conversation. Even Georgie seemed unusually quiet. Philip excused himself from the table as soon as he could and as the meal came to an end, Miles said, 'Ben, will you amuse Georgie for a while? I want to talk to Charlotte.'

'But, Father–' Georgie began to protest, but Miles held up his hand to silence the boy. Then he rose and led the way to his study, Charlotte following in his wake, her heart thumping.

As the door closed, they both began to speak at once. 'Miles – I'm sorry–'

'Charlotte – I'm such a fool–'

She was standing on the hearthrug and he came to her and took her trembling hands in his. He looked down into her upturned face and said softly, 'Charlotte, I have grown fond of you. Very fond. Will you please – please consider becoming my wife?'

She gasped aloud – searching his face for any sign that this was all an act. She wanted to believe him, yearned to believe him, but could she really trust him? She was so afraid of being hurt. Was her heart – which so longed to be loved by him – ruling her head? She fought for her reason to win. She half turned away from him so that they were both facing the portrait of his wife above the mantelpiece. She allowed her hands to stay resting in his, revelling in the strength and the warmth of his touch, as she looked up at the beautiful face of the woman in the painting.

'How – how can you say you want to marry me

after loving someone as lovely as Louisa?'

She heard him sigh. 'You want me to be truthful?'

Turning to meet his gaze, she whispered, 'Always.'

Heavily, he said, 'I don't know.' Swiftly, he added, 'Oh, that sounds awful, insulting almost.'

'But it's the truth,' she said flatly. 'And it's the truth I want.'

He squeezed her hands. 'I know. And I understand, too, how difficult it must be for you to believe me. You've been held down for so long, belittled constantly by your father. Never allowed to – to meet anyone, so how are you to know when a man makes a declaration–' he laughed wryly, 'and certainly such a clumsy one as I made the other day, that it's the truth? In addition to which Louisa's memory is still revered in this house. There are pictures of her everywhere. Philip remembers her well and will never entertain the idea of anyone taking her place. Ben has vague recollections of her and he's no doubt swayed by his elder brother. As for Georgie, well, of all of us, he's the only one who has no recollection of her. But he has been raised to know her.'

'And he carries the burden of thinking he caused her death.'

'I hope not. I've fought hard to explain that to him. No child should carry such guilt.'

'So – why?'

'I miss you when you're not here. I've gone down to the beach every morning, hoping to meet you – accidentally.'

She began to laugh, resting her head briefly against his shoulder.

'What?' he asked. 'Why are you laughing?'

'I have, too.'

'Have you? Have you really?' Now it was he who was uncertain, unable to believe what he hoped might be true. That she felt something for him too. He turned her to face him once more, his hands resting lightly on her shoulders.

'It's not the same feeling I had for Louisa, it's only fair to tell you that.'

Charlotte felt a coldness creep through her. But Miles was continuing, trying to be utterly honest with her so that there should be no secrets between them, no misunderstanding and, most of all, no misapprehension.

'You bring love and warmth and fun into the house when you're here. Georgie adores you and Ben, too, has started to talk about you and ask when you're to visit again.'

'And Philip?' she asked softly. 'How would Philip react to such news?'

Miles shrugged. 'Who's to know what my eldest son will do next? He's soon to go to university. He won't be here very much. And besides, it's my happiness and the two younger boys I'm thinking about. We're good friends, too, aren't we?'

'Yes, we are,' she said wistfully, 'but is that a strong enough basis for marriage? One day the younger boys will be gone as well. What then?'

'It's not just for them. I get lonely. I want – and need – someone to share the rest of *my* life with. I care deeply about you, Charlotte. I want to look after you and make you happy. Do you think I

381

could do that?'

Despite the fact that he had not once used the word 'love' when explaining his feelings for her, she could not lie to him. Her love for him, regardless of what he truly felt for her, would have to be enough. She loved him with every part of her being. If she were to refuse him now, she knew that there would never be another man whom she could love like she loved Miles. He'd said he was fond of her, he cared about her. He had become a good friend. It would have to be enough. She would put aside all foolish notions of a romantic, passionate lover. She knew that to be near him was all she ever wanted. All she would ever want.

'Yes – you could,' she whispered, but even now she had to be honest. 'But – but could I make you happy?'

'Of *course* you could. Oh my dear, we'll build such a happy home for the boys and our children – if we're blessed with any of our own; a daughter, perhaps, to make our family perfect.'

She didn't know whether to laugh out loud or allow the tears that were so close to fall unchecked. She was filled with a strange mixture of emotions. She loved Miles so much that she was willing to devote the rest of her life to him, but she was still unsure just why he wanted to marry her.

Was it, she couldn't help thinking, because he yearned for a daughter, just as, ironically, her father had craved a son? She could not, would not, ask him. She was honest enough to acknowledge that she might not like the answer.

'So, Miss Charlotte Crawford, will you marry me?'

'Yes, Mr Thornton, I will.'

Suddenly, he picked her up and swung her round. 'You've made me the happiest man alive.' Then, lowering her to the ground, he enfolded her in his arms and kissed her.

Forty-Nine

'Come, let's go and find the boys. We must tell them at once.'

'No – wait. This is going too fast.'

He laughed down at her. 'Not changing your mind already, are you?'

'Of course not, but – but there's so much to discuss. My father, Buckthorn Farm...'

'My dear, Mary and Edward will continue to care for your father. You can ride over every day, if you wish, to see him – run the farm, whatever you want to do. But at night–' he touched her face with a gentle finger – 'you will come home to me.'

'But I should be here all the time, helping you. Running this house – being a dutiful wife.'

Now Miles threw back his head and laughed aloud. 'I don't want a "dutiful" wife. I want a soulmate, a friend and' – he kissed her again – 'a lover.'

Now Charlotte blushed and dipped her head.

'But you're right,' he went on. 'I should speak

383

to your father first – ask his permission.'

Now it was Charlotte who laughed. 'His permission? I am twenty-seven. We don't need his permission.'

'No – but I'd like to ask him anyway. I want to see his face when he realizes that at long last his *daughter* is going to lead her own life.'

'Yes,' she said slowly. 'D'you know, I'd quite like to see that myself.'

'Then shall we go, hand in hand, like underage young lovers to seek his approval?'

Charlotte began to laugh and when Miles joined in, the sound carried out through the door and into the rest of the house. Hearing it, Georgie could contain his curiosity no longer and ran downstairs and into the study without pausing to knock, to find his father and Miss Charlotte in each other's arms.

A wide grin spread across his face. 'Are you two friends again, then?' he asked innocently.

They turned to look at him, then at each other as Miles said softly, 'You could say that, Georgie. We're definitely friends again.'

'Tell him,' Charlotte whispered. 'It's only fair.'

'Are you sure?'

When she nodded, he held out his hand to the boy, drawing him to them. 'Georgie, how would you like Charlotte to be your new mama?'

He gaped up at them for a moment and then he gave a whoop of delight and capered about the room, ending up with his arms round Charlotte, his head pressed into her waist. 'How wonderful! Oh, I must tell the others.'

'No – Georgie, let me...' Miles began, but the

384

boy was gone, running from the room and shouting at the top of his voice. 'Ben – Philip – Father's going to marry Charlotte.'

'Oh dear,' Miles said.

'"Oh dear" indeed,' Charlotte murmured. 'I don't think that's the best way Philip should hear the news, do you?'

'Brace yourself, my dear,' Miles said, taking her hand as they heard the clatter of footsteps coming down the stairs and heading across the hall towards the study.

Georgie arrived back in the room first, dragging Ben by the hand.

'Is it true?' Ben asked.

'Yes,' Miles said and Charlotte was overcome when Ben smiled, moved towards them to shake his father's hand. Then, blushing a little, he kissed Charlotte on both cheeks. 'I'm so pleased for both of you.'

'You – you don't mind?' she asked tentatively.

'Lord, no,' Ben said. 'I don't know why he didn't ask you months ago. We all love you–'

'You speak for yourself,' an angry voice interrupted and they all looked round to see Philip standing in the doorway, leaning nonchalantly against the doorframe, his arms folded. 'There's no need to marry her now, Father. The old man's made his will and everything will be mine when he dies – which can't be long now. And there'll be nothing she can do about it. I was there when he signed it. So, you don't have to marry her, you see. My inheritance is quite safe now.'

Miles took a step towards him. 'How dare you

speak to me like that?' he raged. 'And in front of Charlotte, too. I've asked her to marry me because I want to. I *want* her to be my wife. There's no other reason. It has nothing to do with your blasted inheritance.'

As he took in his father's words, Philip's twisted spitefully. 'So,' he snarled, 'you wouldn't agree to marry her to protect my inheritance, but now you're going to put that all at risk. Don't you see, Father—' suddenly, his tone was pleading, 'if you have a child – a son – he'll change his will again. He'll want his *grandson* to inherit, now, won't he?'

'So? What if he did?' He turned briefly to Charlotte to say, 'Forgive me, my dear...' Then back again to his son. 'What's so special about Buckthorn Farm? A few acres, a house, that's all?'

'But it'll be mine.' Philip thumped his own chest. 'All mine. And something I won't have to *share*.' He swept out his arm towards his two brothers and then turned about and stalked away.

Mildly, Ben, the quiet one of the brothers, said, 'You know, he never was very good at sharing his toys.'

'I suppose two out of three isn't too bad,' Miles said as he drove Charlotte to Buckthorn Farm. 'But how do you think your father's going to take the news?'

'Goodness knows,' she answered dryly. 'Or anyone else, for that matter.' She glanced at him. 'There are going to be a lot of raised eyebrows, you know.'

Miles chuckled. 'How delightful!' He took his hand from the steering wheel and reached across to grip hers. 'But everyone will be so pleased for you, my dear. Everyone loves you.'

She smiled weakly. Everyone except you, she thought.

They entered by the front door of Buckthorn Farm and went straight to the sitting room.

'Mr – Thornton,' Osbert slurred. 'How – nice. Fetch some tea, girl.'

'That would be nice, Mr Crawford, but first I have something to ask you. I'd like to ask you for the hand of your daughter in marriage.'

Slowly, Osbert raised his head, squinting up at the tall man standing in front of him. Charlotte found she was holding her breath. Not that his answer mattered. She was of age and she was going to marry Miles anyway, whatever her father said. She'd already decided that. Whatever Miles's real feelings for her were, it didn't matter. Not to her. She wanted to marry the man *she* loved, no matter what. No, the reason she was apprehensive was because she'd no wish to distress her father and bring on another stroke.

'And you'll give – me a – grandson?'

Miles looked aghast for a second, but then he nodded. 'If we're blessed,' he murmured. 'A grandson – or a grand*daughter*.'

'Huh!' Osbert growled. 'Don't want any more girls in this family.' He frowned now at Charlotte. 'Aye, you can take her, and you're welcome. And you, girl, do something useful for once. Give me a grandson.'

As they left the room, Miles heaved a sigh of

relief. 'Well, that was easier than I thought. I'd assumed he'd be reluctant to let you go.'

Charlotte laughed. 'Let me go? He can't wait to get rid of me. I wouldn't be surprised if he doesn't suggest Philip coming to live here with him.' She bit back the words she'd been about to blurt out; that her father had once suggested that Philip should change his surname to 'Crawford'.

'They'd be welcome to each other.'

'You don't mean that?'

'No – no, I don't suppose I do. But, just sometimes, my eldest son irritates me almost beyond endurance.'

'Well, as long as it's only "almost",' she teased. 'Now, let's go and tell Mary.'

The devoted Mary burst into noisy tears, but they were tears of joy. 'Oh Miss Charlotte – Mr Thornton, sir. What wonderful news! Edward – Edward, d'you hear? Our little Charlotte's going to be married.'

Edward nodded and smiled and shook Miles's hand. And there were tears in his eyes, too. ''Tis the best news ever, miss.'

'There's just one thing – will you stay here with Father? I mean, if you'd rather not–' She paused and glanced up at Miles for support.

'If you'd rather leave,' he said, 'then we'll employ someone else to take care of him.'

Husband and wife glanced at each other. 'No, no,' Edward said. 'We know his little ways. We'll stay.'

'"Better the devil you know",' Mary said and then added hurriedly, 'begging your pardon, miss.'

'I'll see that you both get a rise in your wages,' Charlotte promised. 'You'll be taking on more responsibility.'

'That'd be very kind of you, miss. We'll need to put a little by for our old age,' Mary said.

'You see,' Edward said tentatively, 'we'd always believed we'd have a home here with you, miss, when you inherited the farm. But since we know that Master Philip will one day be the new owner, well, our future's a bit uncertain.'

'I think I can speak for my future wife,' Miles smiled, 'as well as for myself when I tell you that you need have no fears on that score. We shall find a home for you somewhere on the Ravensfleet Estate, you can be sure of that. Though I hope that won't be for many years yet.'

'Thank you, sir.' Mary, overcome with gratitude, kissed a startled Miles on both cheeks.

As they left the house again, Miles murmured, 'What good people they are.'

'I don't know what would have become of me if it hadn't been for them.'

He squeezed her hand. 'Then I have every reason to be grateful to them. And now, my dear, we have a wedding to plan.'

Fifty

Charlotte wrote to her mother and her aunt with the news. She didn't want an estrangement between herself and her aunt, but she was now a little wary of her. She was careful what she said or wrote. Despite her outward display of affection, Euphemia had the same vengeful streak in her that her brother had. It was in their genes. Charlotte fervently hoped she hadn't inherited that same flaw. She felt she must be more like her gentle mother, who'd run away from the cruelty. And yet Charlotte was now finding that there was a spark of defiance in her that surprised her. Until recently she'd never questioned her life, never compared it to the lives of others and found her own lacking. But now she did. She'd been treated abominably by her father and she owed him nothing. Yet her innate goodness demanded that she should still see that he was cared for and comfortable.

She received an enthusiastic letter back from Euphemia:

You must come and stay a few days with us. We'd love to have you. And we can go shopping in Lincoln for your wedding finery. Your uncle is insisting that he should pay for your dress and accessories. And your mother would so love to help you choose. Don't deny her that little pleasure, Charlotte, I beg you…

'Shall you go?' Miles asked when she showed him the letter.

'Yes, I think I will.'

'I'm thinking of asking Felix to be my best man.'

Charlotte looked at him in surprise. 'I thought you would ask Philip.'

'I did,' Miles said shortly. 'And he refused.'

'Ah.'

'In fact – I'm sorry to say it – he's refusing to attend the wedding.'

'Miles,' Charlotte cried, 'I don't want to be the cause of trouble in your family.'

'You're not, my dear. If anything's causing a rift it's your father's ridiculous actions. Philip's getting above himself. At eighteen he sees himself as a future landowner.'

Charlotte shrugged. 'Well, he will be. You can't deny that.'

'No – but it's not good for a boy of his age to know it.'

She was silent for a moment before she suggested, 'What about Ben being your best man?'

Miles stared at her for a moment. 'I – I hadn't thought of Ben. I'd considered him too young.'

Charlotte smiled. 'Your quiet son has more maturity than some young men twice his age. If you'd like one of your sons by your side, then I think you should ask Ben. Of course, Georgie...' She broke off as they both began to smile at the mere thought of the boy. That was what Georgie did to people; he made them smile just thinking about him.

'Georgie would do it like a shot, but I *do* think he is a little young at seven, don't you?'

'I suppose so,' she said fondly. 'But he'd certainly liven up the proceedings as your best man.'

'Mind you, I'd forget to be nervous if I had him to worry about.'

'Nervous? You're not going to be nervous, are you?'

Miles laughed. 'I don't think so. I shall just worry you might have changed your mind and won't turn up.'

'Oh, I'll not change my mind,' she said firmly and then asked softly, 'Will you?'

'Never!' he said and gently raised her hand to his lips and kissed her fingers.

The wedding was fixed for the Saturday after Easter, so that Miles's sons would be still at home for the holidays.

Charlotte enjoyed a few days in Lincoln with her aunt and uncle and – more importantly – with her mother. Euphemia was nothing if not generous with Percy's money but he only smiled benignly and admired all their purchases. Euphemia swept Charlotte and her mother into the city's largest store, leading them from department to department and demanding the attention of the head saleswoman in each. Her aunt suggested the very latest fashion for the wedding dress, but Charlotte was adamant.

'I don't like the modern shorter dresses, Aunt. I'd like a traditional Edwardian style and a hat trimmed with yards of tulle rather than a veil.'

Euphemia beamed. 'Of course, my dear, you

392

shall have exactly what you want. And have you decided on a bridesmaid?'

'Ah, now, that caused me a bit of a problem. I don't have any close friends of my own age.' Euphemia and Alice glanced at each other, realizing what a lonely life Charlotte had led. 'Mary and Peggy felt they were too old, so I've asked Lily to be my matron of honour.' She smiled. 'She was thrilled and our local dressmaker is making her a dress in pastel blue.'

Euphemia gave an exaggerated sigh but, for once, said nothing.

Once the wedding dress, hat, shoes, gloves and underwear had been bought, Euphemia led the way to the hairdresser. 'And this time, my dear, I really think you should have your hair cut into a fashionable bob.'

'No, Aunt.' Once again, Charlotte gently stood up to her aunt. 'I think my hairstyle should match the style of my dress. I've become quite adept at putting my hair up now, though I would like the hairdresser to show me a style befitting a bride.'

'I agree,' Alice put in quietly.

This time Euphemia capitulated gracefully. 'I'm no match for both of you.'

But when the hairdresser had shown Charlotte how to put her long dark hair up in a profusion of curls and waves, even Euphemia had to admit that it suited her to perfection.

'Darling, you look absolutely beautiful,' Alice said with joyful tears. 'Do you think you'll be able to do it on your wedding day?'

'I'll get Peggy to help me. We can have a few practice sessions beforehand.'

They returned home tired but elated. 'I can't thank you enough, Uncle...' Charlotte began, but Percy waved her aside, smiling benevolently. 'Think nothing of it, dear girl. It's our pleasure. And to see you mother so happy too...'

'Ah, now, that's another thing,' her aunt said. 'We intend to come to your wedding, Charlotte. *All* of us.'

'Euphemia, dear, I don't think–' Alice began, but her sister-in-law was adamant. 'You have been denied access to your only child all these years, Alice. But you are going to be there on her wedding day.'

'Everyone thinks she's – she's dead. Just like I did. I told you, there's a grave in the churchyard with her name on the headstone.'

'Well, we're coming and, whatever happens, your father will deserve whatever's coming to him.'

'I would love to go,' Alice said, and suddenly there was a surprising note of firmness in her tone, 'but I will only go if I can be incognito. I will wear a hat with a veil and no one will know who I am. Now you're to promise me, Euphemia.'

Euphemia wriggled her shoulders but, for once, was obliged to say, 'Oh very well, then.'

'Miles, I don't know what to do. It could cause my father another serious stroke. If my mother turns up the whole village will know of his deception. I fully intend to put matters right about the gravestone once he's – he's gone. It won't matter then. It can't hurt him, but for her to come back now...'

Miles chewed his lip thoughtfully. 'It is a bit of a dilemma. But you say your mother's going to wear a veil. Will anyone recognize her?'

'I don't know,' Charlotte wailed. Her joy in her wedding day was already being spoiled.

Miles put his arms round her. 'Have you told your mother and aunt about the gravestone?'

She nodded and told him of Euphemia's response.

'Your aunt's certainly vicious towards your father, isn't she?'

'Yes – it goes back to their youth. Her father was against her marrying Percy and I think my father fuelled the quarrel. My grandfather evidently cast her off when she defied him. But my father's as bad – worse, if anything, than she is. He – he calls her the most dreadful names.' Colour rose in her cheeks as she recalled the distressing scenes she'd witnessed between her father and his sister.

'Do you want your mother to be at your wedding?'

'Oh yes, yes. She's the innocent in all this. She's gentle and doesn't want to cause trouble. It's Aunt Euphemia who's so vitriolic against my father.'

He put his arms round her and she leaned against his shoulder, revelling in his strength and his support. No longer was she so alone. She'd always had Mary and Edward, of course, and they'd been wonderful, but they'd never been able to help her with important decisions. Even if she'd asked their advice, they'd always said primly, 'It's not our place to say, Miss Charlotte.'

But now she had Miles.

'Why don't you sound your father out on his plans for the day? Is he to give you away?'

She raised her head to look up at him. 'I don't know. I'd never really thought about it. I'd just presumed he would.'

'Talk to him.'

'I will.'

Charlotte was trembling as she stood before Osbert.

'Father – you will give me away on my wedding day, won't you?'

He frowned. 'It depends,' he growled.

'On what?'

'On how you're going to be dressed. If you're going to deck yourself out like some trollop, then I have no intention of being disgraced. I shall not be there.'

Charlotte lifted her chin defiantly. 'I've already bought my wedding dress.'

He glowered at her. 'And I suppose *she* went with you? Helped you choose?'

'If you mean my aunt, then yes. She did.'

He glared at her, and she could read the question in his eyes. Did he guess that her mother had been there too? But the words remained unspoken.

'So,' she said at last. 'What am I to do? Do you wish me to show you what I shall be wearing and then you can make up your mind?'

His eyes narrowed. 'You're getting very uppity, miss. Just because Thornton's come to his senses and decided to protect his son's inheritance, there's no need to forget your duty to your father.'

'I won't. I'll always make sure you're cared for. I promise you that.' Then, boldly she added, 'Philip's afraid that if I do have a child – a boy – you will change your will.'

Osbert's eyes gleamed. 'I might. We'll have to see about that, won't we?' He gave a humourless laugh. 'So – he doesn't want you to have a son – and I do. What about Thornton? Does he want another boy?'

'Oh no,' Charlotte threw back over her shoulder as she left the room with, for probably the first time in the whole of her life, the last word. 'He wants a daughter.'

Fifty-One

'You are not wearing *that!*'

Her father thumped his stick on the floor with his good hand. Then he lunged out at the dress she was holding up for his inspection, trying to hook it out of her grasp and throw it towards the fire. Charlotte stepped backwards just in time.

'You hussy – you whore! Just like your – your aunt.'

For a moment she thought he'd been going to say 'mother'. With an outward calm she was not feeling inside, she said, 'This is the dress I shall be wearing on my wedding day, Father. So – do I take it that you will not be attending?'

He glared at her. 'You dishonour me. You bring shame to my name.'

'I'm sorry you feel that way,' she said with a quiet dignity. 'But very soon I'll no longer bear the name of Crawford, will I?'

He glared at her and was silent for several moments whilst she waited, her heart pounding nervously. Then he raised his head and said slowly, 'But I'll be there. I won't let folks say *I* didn't do my duty. But you'll make a laughing stock of yourself.'

'So, he's coming to the wedding, is he?' Miles said when she told him what had passed between her and her father.

'He says so. But I wouldn't put it past him to cry off at the last minute. And then who would I get to give me away?'

'There's your uncle or Edward – or even Felix. He'd step in if he was needed, I know, now that Ben's agreed to be my best man.' He paused and then, smiling mischievously, added, 'So – what is so dreadful about this dress?'

Charlotte laughed and tapped him playfully on the nose. 'Now, now, you know I'm not going to tell you anything about my dress. It's unlucky.'

'What does Mary think of it?'

Charlotte's eyes were suddenly dreamy. 'She thinks it's lovely.'

'And your aunt and mother helped you choose it – so what are you worrying about?' He put his arms round her. 'I'm sure it'll be wonderful.'

'I'll have to write and tell them that Father's going to be at the wedding.'

'By all means warn them, but let your mother make up her own mind. From what you've told me about her, I'm sure she'll do nothing that would embarrass you or spoil your day.'

Charlotte looked up at him with troubled eyes. 'Yes – but what might my aunt do?'

Charlotte's wedding day dawned fine and sunny, with a light breeze. She was incredibly nervous and Mary could do nothing to calm her anxieties. But it had nothing to do with her future husband or even his family. For once, not even Philip's spite could overshadow her happiness. Her only anxiety was her own relatives and what they might – or might not – do.

Mary went ahead, whilst Edward drove Charlotte and her father to the church in a flower-bedecked carriage that Miles had hired especially.

'Such nonsense,' Osbert growled as Edward almost lifted him into the vehicle. 'A waste of money. I hope you're not expecting me to pay for all this.'

'No, Father. Miles is paying for everything. The reception is in a marquee in the garden at the manor.'

'And your fripperies?' he sneered. 'Am I expected to pay for you to dress like a whore? And where are your spectacles?'

'No, Father. You're not paying for anything.' She bit back the words to tell him that her uncle had paid for her wedding finery and her going-away outfit; indeed, all her trousseau, even down to the half-dozen fine lace handkerchiefs. As for the question about her spectacles, she chose to ignore it.

As the carriage jerked and they set off towards the church, he grumbled, 'And I suppose you are going away on *honeymoon* for weeks on end.'

'Just one week, Father. We're only going to London.'

'That den of iniquity. What is the man thinking of? I'm beginning to have doubts about letting you marry him. It's not too late, we can still turn back.' He raised his voice. 'Edward–'

'I have no intention of turning back, Father. Drive on, Edward,' she commanded and her heart was singing as Edward slapped the reins to quicken the pace towards a new beginning with the love of her life.

The church was full to overflowing. Several people couldn't even get into the body of the church and crowded into the porch, jostling each other to hear the couple make their vows. Smiling and nodding, they made way for the bride, her father and Edward.

A gasp rippled amongst them as Charlotte lifted her head and smiled at them.

'Miss Charlotte, you look lovely,' someone called out.

The same surprise ran through the whole of the congregation, when Charlotte and her father made their slow progress up the aisle.

She caught some of the whispers. 'Why, she's lovely.'

'Just look at her.'

'Who'd have thought it?'

And when Miles turned to watch his bride

coming towards him, she saw a brief look of amazement in his eyes, which he was unable to hide. He held out his hand and she took it, in that moment placing all her trust and her future happiness in his hands.

'Doesn't she look pretty?' Georgie's voice piped up from the second pew. Laughter rippled through the congregation and someone – she was sure it was Jackson Warren – called, 'More than that, Master Georgie. She's beautiful.'

Miles, his gaze never leaving her face, raised her hand to his lips and whispered, 'Indeed you are, my dear.'

She turned briefly to glance at Georgie and to her surprise saw both Ben and Felix sitting beside him. Then who–? She leaned forward a little to look beyond Miles and saw, for the first time, that it was Philip standing next to him. The young man was staring straight ahead, stony faced, and Charlotte knew he was only there because he hadn't wanted his younger brother to usurp his rightful place. But at least, she thought, his presence will have made Miles happy.

She smiled up at Miles as they both turned towards the vicar who'd replaced Cuthbert Iveson. He was a much older man, with a benign smile and twinkling eyes. Her father would not be able to manipulate this man, Charlotte thought, as he began to speak in a deep resonant voice that carried down the church and even out through the door so that all might hear.

The service went ahead without any interruptions or hitches and at last they were walking back down the aisle between row upon row of

401

beaming faces accompanied not only by the 'Wedding March', but also by a storm of clapping and cheering and shouts of 'Good luck' and 'God bless you'.

'See how everyone loves you?' Miles murmured.

She smiled up at him but the one question she longed to ask remained unspoken. But do *you* love me?

Just as they were about to step out of the church, Charlotte noticed a woman sitting in the far corner, half hidden behind a pillar and wearing a wide-brimmed hat with a veil over her face.

Alice Crawford had come to her daughter's wedding.

'Of course you're coming to the reception.' Euphemia's raised voice could be heard ringing through the churchyard as the guests and onlookers watched the couple emerge from the porch. Miles and Charlotte paused for photographs to be taken by the man who kept disappearing beneath the black cloth covering the huge box camera set up on a tripod between the graves.

'Smile,' he burbled.

'No one's recognized you,' Euphemia said. 'Just keep away from *him*.'

Mary hurried up to Charlotte. 'Your aunt's talking to – to the woman who was sitting at the back of the church. Is it – is it who I think it is?'

Charlotte nodded and glanced anxiously across to where her aunt and uncle were standing talking to the heavily veiled woman. She was about to turn towards Miles to seek his help, when another voice rose above the rest. 'Are we going to stand about here all day, taking ridiculous photographs?' Osbert rasped. 'Philip, my boy, your arm, if you please.'

Philip moved to his side. 'It seems,' Osbert said, his tone heavy with sarcasm, 'that I shall no longer have my daughter to rely on.' He sniffed. 'Not that she ever was much use. Now, shall you and I go back to Buckthorn Farm? Mary will make us a meal.'

Before Philip could answer, Miles cut in, 'Philip will be coming back to the manor for the reception. He agreed to be my best man, so he must fulfil his duties for the rest of the day. And Mary and Edward are our guests.' Mildly, he added, 'And I'd have thought you'd wish to be there – as father of the bride.'

Osbert glowered. He could not return to the farm on his own and Mary was busy throwing confetti and enjoying a rare day of freedom.

'Seems I have no choice,' Osbert grumbled 'That girl! Such a lot of fuss. I hope your father is going to keep her in line, Philip. She'll get above herself, given half a chance.'

'Mm,' Philip said, his eyes narrowing. 'Well, we'll just have to see that doesn't happen, won't we?'

And then a rare thing happened; Osbert Crawford actually smiled.

Miles had let it be known that anyone and everyone was welcome at the manor. Mrs Beddows had been baking for weeks and extra help had been employed from Ravensfleet so that there was enough food to feed an army. The guests mingled freely and happily on the sunlit lawn, but one woman kept herself in the shadow of the trees at the end of the garden. Only Mary approached her, taking her a drink and some food on a plate.

Charlotte watched from a distance, but did not dare go to her mother for fear Osbert's eagle eyes would see and guess just who the stranger was. She spent the afternoon on tenterhooks, not enjoying her wedding day as she should have done.

It was almost over and Charlotte began to breathe more easily. A few guests were already drifting away and the afternoon was growing cooler.

Euphemia was standing before her. 'Well, my dear, it's time we were making our way home. We have a car waiting and your mother flatly refuses to come indoors. It's getting chilly now, so—'

'What's that?'

So intent had she been on saying goodbye to her guests that Charlotte hadn't seen her father standing close behind her. Her heart missed a beat as she saw Euphemia's eyes widen as if in surprise, but Charlotte had the uncomfortable feeling that her aunt had known all along that Osbert was in earshot. Maybe she'd even engineered it.

'Oh, Osbert, my dear brother. I didn't see you there. We're just about to leave. Now how about a kiss for your sister? Isn't it time we let bygones be bygones?'

But Osbert held himself aloof, glaring at her with hatred in his eyes. Through clenched teeth, his eyes boring into hers, he asked his sister, 'Who is that woman?'

Euphemia, her eyes sparkling for a fight, stepped closer, but Charlotte caught her arm, 'Please, Aunt, no...'

But Euphemia was not to be outdone. She shook off Charlotte's hand, her eyes narrowing as she said slowly, 'Don't you recognize your own wife?'

Osbert reeled and might have fallen had it not been for his arm still through Philip's. The young man steadied him, but glanced, mystified, at Charlotte for an explanation.

Charlotte looked around her wildly. Miles – where was Miles? She saw him talking to Joe and Peggy Warren. She hurried across the grass. 'Miles – oh please, Miles, come quickly. My aunt...'

'My dear, whatever's the matter?'

She caught hold of his hand. 'The woman down there – under the trees – is my mother, and Aunt Euphemia has just told my father...'

Leaving Joe and Peggy staring open-mouthed after them, Miles hurried back with Charlotte towards her father and aunt, still locked in a battle of wills. 'Leave it to me, my dear.' Raising his voice, Miles greeted them heartily, as if knowing nothing of the contretemps. 'Mrs Bell – just leaving. And you, Mr Crawford. Philip, would you please accompany Mr Crawford to Buckthorn Farm? Brewster will drive you and I'll see that Mary and Edward know you've gone home.'

With a smooth, but authoritative air, Miles shook hands with them both and also with Percy, who'd ambled across the grass. 'I'm so glad you could come. Let me see you to your car?'

'But—' Euphemia began.

'Come along, my dear.' Percy, catching on very quickly, took hold of his wife's arm and, with surprising determination, led her away.

But Euphemia was not to be outdone. As Percy led her to the driveway at the side of the lawn and towards their waiting car, she called out in a loud, imperious voice, deliberately so that everyone would hear.

'Alice – come, my dear, we are ordered home.'

As the last guest departed down the driveway, Charlotte said, 'Thank you, Miles. Your diplomacy avoided an ugly scene.'

'I think I missed my vocation,' he chuckled, putting his arm round her. 'Now, forget all about it, my dear. No harm done.'

But Charlotte wasn't so sure. Soon, the whole district would hear the gossip and would be speculating on how Alice Crawford came to be still alive when she was supposed to be buried in the churchyard.

'Before we leave, there's just something I want to show you,' Miles said.

Charlotte had changed from her wedding gown into her going-away outfit. Their suitcases were packed and loaded into the car and Miles was to drive them as far as Grantham where they would stay the night in a hotel. The following day, leaving the car there, they would travel to London by train.

Taking her hand, he led her upstairs to the top

floor and along the landing to a room at the far corner of the house.

'I've never been up here before,' Charlotte said.

'It's where the servants sleep but there's one room unoccupied and I just thought it would be ideal. It's a north-facing room, so there should be plenty of light from the big window. I've had it enlarged especially.'

Oh dear, she thought, he's decked out a nursery in pink. Oh dear...

But when he flung open the door, Charlotte gasped aloud. The whole room was fitted out as an artist's studio. There was everything there that she could possibly want and more; desk and chair, easels, drawing boards, canvases stacked against the wall, tubes of oil paints, watercolours, brushes of every size and shape, pencils, pens and inks, pastels, paper of all types and sizes in abundance and all manner of accessories that, at the moment, Charlotte had no idea exactly what they were for. She gazed around, her mouth open in wonder.

'It's my wedding gift to you, my dear. Felix had free rein. I don't think he's enjoyed himself so much in a long time. We didn't know what was your favourite medium to work in, so we just got everything we could think of. But if there's anything we've forgotten, just say the word.'

'Miles, I don't know what to say. This is wonderful.'

'I want you to be happy, my dear. And I know you love to paint. There's just one thing – Felix is demanding to see some of your work and now there's no excuse.'

'But I'm not very good...' she began.

'That's not what I've heard. Jackson Warren told me you'd painted some lovely pictures.'

Charlotte's face clouded as she remembered her father's cruel destruction of her work. But here she would be safe. Here she could paint and draw to her heart's content. They'd thought of everything. In one corner of the light, airy room there was a sofa and, close by, a small bookcase which Felix had filled with books on drawing and painting and the lives of some of the great painters.

There were tears in her eyes as she kissed him. 'It's the most wonderful wedding present. I never dreamed...'

He chuckled as he pulled her close. 'I do, of course, have an ulterior motive.'

'What?'

'Whenever you're missing, I'll know exactly where to find you.'

Fifty-Two

Charlotte was happy – happier than she'd ever been in her life or ever dared hope to be. Ben and Georgie accepted and welcomed her whole-heartedly. Only Philip was still prickly, but even he seemed to mellow a little after the incident over Louisa's portrait.

On the afternoon of their return home from honeymoon, Georgie flew across the hall, slipping and sliding on the polished floor as he ran to greet them.

'Papa, Charlotte...' He threw himself against them in turn, forgetting in the excitement of the moment that he was supposed to be quite grown up now. Ben smiled quietly from the staircase.

Philip appeared on the landing. He leaned over the banister. 'And what,' his voice rang out, 'do you mean by leaving instructions for Mother's portraits to be removed from the dining room and even from your study, Father? I suppose *she*'s demanded it, has she?'

Charlotte gasped and turned wide eyes on her new husband. 'You shouldn't have done that, Miles. I'd never ask such a thing.'

Miles ignored her. Instead, he raised angry eyes to Philip. 'We'll talk about it later.'

'No,' Charlotte said sharply. 'We'll talk about it now. Philip, please come down.'

Sulkily, the young man descended the stairs.

'Now,' she said, more gently, 'what is all this about?'

Georgie said nothing, but she felt his hand creep into hers.

'Philip?' Charlotte prompted. 'Please tell me.'

'Father left instructions that whilst you were on – whilst you were away, Wilkins should remove the paintings of our mother from view.' His lip curled. 'I suppose he thought it would upset you being constantly reminded of how beautiful his first wife was and how much he loved her.'

'Philip!' Miles thundered, but Charlotte put her hand on his arm and said softly, 'It's all right, Miles.' Turning back to Philip and including Ben and Georgie too, she said gently, 'I wouldn't dream of allowing the portraits of your mother to be removed. They will be put back at once and there they will stay.'

Philip blinked, wrong-footed for a moment. But then he smiled sarcastically. 'Another of your little schemes to ingratiate yourself into the family, is it? Making out you're not trying to take her place?'

Charlotte shook her head. 'I'm not.' But she could see he did not believe her. 'No one can take another's place. We're all individuals and loved, in different ways, perhaps, for ourselves, for who we are.'

Philip laughed, but without humour. 'And you really think my father loves you like he loved my mother?'

'Philip!' Miles began again and took a step towards his son, but Charlotte held him back and answered the boy quietly, 'No, Philip, I expect no such thing. Your father has been very honest with me about his reasons for asking me to marry him.' Her tone was firmer as she added, 'But those reasons, my dear, are private between us and no concern of yours.'

Philip laughed again. 'Oh, but I think they are. I think they have everything to do with me. *And my inheritance.*'

Now Miles shook himself free of Charlotte's restraining hand and stepped towards his son. Through gritted teeth, he demanded an apology.

Philip stood his ground. 'See what she's done, Father? For the first time in my life, I'm going to disobey you. Already, she's coming between us.

She'll break up our family. You'll see.' He glanced towards Charlotte now. 'I will not apologize, but I will say one thing. Whatever your ulterior motive is – and I'm sure you have one – I'm grateful for you allowing the portraits to be put back where they belong. I do thank you for that. And now I'm going back to school.'

As he turned to go upstairs, he passed Ben standing on the bottom step.

'You know, Phil, I never thought I'd say it because – until recently – I've always admired you and looked up to you. But you're an idiot – you have been ever since Mr Crawford promised to make you his heir. It's gone to your head and turned you into someone I don't like very much. Charlotte is a good person. I like her and so does Georgie and if she makes Father happy, then you should be glad. Glad for them both.'

It was the longest speech any of them had ever heard the quiet Ben make and they all stared at him. Georgie clapped his hands and began to skip around the hall, chanting, 'Philip's an idiot! Phil-ip's an id-i-ot.'

'Stop that, Georgie,' Charlotte said sharply and held out her hand to him. 'That's not nice.'

The little boy stopped and came meekly back to her. 'Sorry, Charlotte.'

She stroked his hair and smiled down at him and he knew himself forgiven. As for Philip, he stared at Ben for a long moment and then turned and ran up the stairs, two at a time.

It had spoiled their homecoming, but Ben and Georgie made her so welcome, that Philip's cruel jibes, if not forgotten, were soothed. And once both Philip and Ben had gone back to school, Charlotte had her little golden boy all to herself.

Over the following weeks and months, life at the manor slipped into a routine that seemed to suit them all. Philip was away at school and, when he was at home, Charlotte took refuge in her studio. She studied the instructional books that Felix had left her and her work improved – even to her own critical eye. She experimented with all the different mediums that Miles had so generously bought for her. But watercolour and oils were her favourites. She grew bolder and painted larger pictures, stacking them against the walls or on the top shelf.

But she was still too shy to show her work to anyone and certainly not brave enough to hang her pictures on a wall.

At Christmas Felix visited them and now he was adamant.

'You mean to say, my darling Charlotte,' he said throwing out his arm in his usual flamboyant gesture, 'that I am to be denied seeing the fruits of all my labour? I, who designed and equipped your studio?' His eyes were twinkling merrily at her. He wanted to see her work, wanted to know if it was just a daubing of colours on to paper or canvas or whether this adorable creature had real talent.

He traced a finger down her cheek. 'My dear girl, you have blossomed. Marriage suits you so and if your paintings are half as beautiful as their creator, then they should be hanging in every gallery in the land.'

'Oh, Felix.' Charlotte laughed, loving his teasing but never taking it seriously. 'Very well, then, but on two conditions.'

'Name them,' he said kissing her hand.

'Firstly, Miles must come too.'

'At last,' Miles said, joining in the fun and throwing his hands in the air in delight.

'And me,' Georgie piped up. 'I want to see your paintings too.' He beamed. 'You can paint me, Charlotte.'

She laughed. 'Do you think you could sit still for long enough?' And they all laughed, even Georgie.

It had been agreed that the boys should not call her Mama or Mother after Philip's outburst on their arrival home. 'I could never replace your mother,' she'd told them gently.

'You certainly could not,' Philip had muttered, but she'd chosen to ignore him.

'And I'd never want to try, so, I'd like you to call me Charlotte. All right?'

Georgie had flung his arms about her waist and Ben had nodded shyly. Only Philip had given a sniff that sounded suspiciously like disapproval. But then, she supposed, Philip would disapprove of anything she did. She was glad, at this moment, when they were insisting on seeing her work, that he was out riding.

'And the second condition?' Felix prompted.

'That you are entirely honest with me. Give me constructive criticism. I've studied all the books you've given me, but I could use some practical advice.'

'I promise I will tell you truthfully what I think,'

413

Felix said solemnly. He linked his arm through hers as they mounted the stairs side by side, Miles, Ben and Georgie following.

Her heart was racing as she opened the door and ushered them inside. It was the first time anyone had been into her studio. They all, even Georgie, respected her privacy.

'I've had a go at everything,' she began shyly, 'but I find I still like watercolour the best, though oil painting is now a close second. I can't seem to get to grips with pastels.' She laughed. 'I always seem to end up smudging my picture. I like pencil drawing, but I find pen and ink difficult and too – too–' She paused, searching for the word.

'Tedious?' Felix offered. 'I do, too.' He began to wander around the room, pausing in front of the canvases leaning against the wall to complete their drying process. A process that with oils took some time.

'That's the street in Ravensfleet,' Georgie cried. 'That's my school.'

'And that's the manor,' Ben pointed.

'And the beach where we go riding with the town's pier in the background,' Miles put in.

Felix was silent and Charlotte waited anxiously, surprised how much his approval meant to her. Still he said nothing, standing before each one, considering it, and then moving on to the next.

'And your watercolours?' Felix asked when he'd pondered over each and every one of her oil paintings.

She reached the stack of paintings from the top shelf of the bookcase and, standing a sensible distance from him, she held up each one, the paper trembling a little in her nervous fingers. Now no one made any comment, copying Felix's way of perusal. Laying the last one down, she looked at him, her heart thumping. 'Well?' she whispered, unable to wait a moment longer. 'Tell me the worst. I've wasted your time and all Miles's money.'

Felix stared at her for a long moment, his face expressionless. Then suddenly, he beamed and held out his arm to her. 'My darling girl, your paintings are wonderful – magnificent. They are good enough to hang in a gallery.'

'Felix,' she said, somewhere between laughing and crying, 'I asked you to be honest.'

'I am – I am. Would I' – he smote his chest with his fist – 'lie about *art?*'

'I–' she hesitated, searching his face, trying to see if he was teasing her, being kind to her feeble efforts.

Miles moved to her side and put his arm round her shoulders, then Georgie ran to her and hugged her waist. Ben was smiling and nodding.

'Your paintings are amazing, my dear,' Miles said. 'I'd never imagined how good you really are. To think that all this time...' He stopped, realizing that he was in danger of criticizing her father – something he'd vowed to himself he would never do.

'All this time,' Felix declared happily, 'she has been learning and practising and improving. My dear, there are one or two things I could help you with, but these paintings – almost all of them – are good enough to sell now. If you wanted to sell them, that is?'

'She can't sell them,' Georgie said. 'We'll hang them up here. We've plenty of room. Charlotte,' he looked up at her, 'may I have the one with my school on in my bedroom? Please?'

'Of course you can,' Charlotte laughed nervously, still overcome by Felix's praise.

'You must advise us on mounts and frames,' Miles said, giving her shoulders a quick squeeze and then moving away to discuss how best to show off Charlotte's work.

'It depends on the pictures themselves, of course, but also where you want to hang them,' Felix advised. 'Not everyone would agree with me, but my taste is that, if you're hanging say four or five together on a wall, they should all have the same mounts and frames. And the subjects should complement each other – perhaps have some sort of theme.'

'Yes, I see...'

Their conversation went on whilst Georgie dashed from one to another of the paintings, choosing his favourites.

Ben came to stand beside her.

'I don't quite believe this,' she murmured.

'Well, you'd better,' Ben said quietly. 'Old Felix wouldn't lie to you. And even we non-experts can see how good they are.' He paused and then asked, 'Have you ever tried portraits?'

She turned to meet his gaze. 'Why do you ask?'

He shrugged. 'Well, even though photography's all the rage these days, people still like their portraits painted. It's a status thing. I bet you could make a lot of money, like Felix says. If you

416

wanted. Felix is a portrait painter.' It was a long speech for Ben, but he still hadn't quite finished. 'And – and I was thinking – it would be nice if you could do a portrait of Father. We've been on at him for years to have one done. We wanted him to commission Felix, but he said because he'd become a friend since then he didn't want to put Felix in a difficult position as regards a fee.'

Softly, she said, 'As a companion to one of your mother's?'

'Well–' He hesitated, anxious not to hurt her feelings. 'Felix did the ones of mother. That's how we met him. I think he was going to do one of Father too, at that time, but then – but then Mother died and – and Father lost heart.'

She squeezed his hand and whispered, 'I'll show you something.' She led him to the far side of the room where, from behind a stack of new canvases, she pulled out a picture. With her back to the others, she showed him the painting she had done of Miles.

Ben gasped aloud. He glanced up at her and then back to the picture. 'Oh Charlotte, it's brilliant. Your others are good – very good – but this – this is fantastic.' Now, reluctantly, he dragged his gaze from the picture. Shaking his head slowly, not understanding, he said, 'Why have you hidden it?'

'I didn't know whether your father...'

'You mean he doesn't *know*? He didn't sit for you to do this?'

She shook her head.

He touched her hand. 'Please show it to the others. You *must*.'

'Well, if you think...'

'I don't think – I know. It's truly wonderful. Let me show them – please.'

'All right.'

'Sure?' Ben was gentle. He was not one to persuade someone into something they really didn't want to do.

She laughed nervously, 'No, I'm not, but if you think so, then–'

She thrust the portrait towards him and he took it, carrying it carefully to the centre of the room.

'I say, chaps, just look at this.'

They turned with one accord and Charlotte, still standing in the far corner, almost as if she was hiding, watched their reactions.

Georgie clapped his hands in glee. 'You *can* do people. Oh paint me, Charlotte. Please, please, please paint me.'

Felix threw out his arms. 'Ah, the masterpiece. *Magnifique!* Such care has gone into it. A work of love.'

But Charlotte was watching Miles's face. And then, slowly, he looked up and smiled. 'It's marvellous, my dear.'

And her happiness was complete.

Well, almost. There was one more thing she would dearly love to do for this man she loved so very much. And that was to give him what he desired most: a daughter.

Fifty-Three

But it seemed it was not to be.

As time passed and the family settled down into their new routine, there was no sign of Charlotte becoming pregnant and eventually they ceased to speak about it, but it lay between them like an unanswered prayer.

Apart from that one sadness, they were content. Miles was happy to play the country squire and to leave the running of the estate to his foreman, though more and more he sought Charlotte's opinion. She still ran Buckthorn Farm and saw that her father was well cared for and that Mary and Edward had all they needed. Osbert had improved sufficiently for Nurse Montgomery finally to depart, but she had promised to come back if there were any problems.

The community seemed shielded from the economic devastation that troubled the rest of the country during the early years of the nineteen thirties. Joe and Peggy flourished at Purslane Farm and whilst Jackson continued to enjoy his bachelor state and had a string of girlfriends all eager to lead him to the altar, he resolutely resisted. John, meanwhile, quietly married his long-time sweetheart. They rented a small cottage in Ravensfleet, and John continued to help his father and brother run the farm. Eddie and Lily, having moved into the Warrens' old cottage on Buckthorn Farm with Alfie, added to their family with another son and a daughter.

'They can breed like rabbits, but it seems you're barren, girl,' Osbert goaded Charlotte crudely. 'I hope you're doing your duty by your husband. I want a grandson.'

At such times, Charlotte would silently turn her back on him and walk out of Buckthorn Farm to her home, where there were no recriminations. Miles never once broached the subject, though secretly Charlotte consulted the doctor to see if it was her fault. Dr Markham declared her fit and healthy and told her not to worry.

'Sometimes conception doesn't happen, my dear, because you want it too much. You're too tense. Just relax and enjoy your life. You're happy, aren't you?'

'Very. I've never known such happiness,' she confided. 'But I know Miles so wants a daughter.'

'A daughter, eh? Well, well,' he murmured, knowing full well the humiliations that had been heaped on Charlotte's head all her life for being a girl. 'Life's strange, my dear, isn't it?'

In time, Philip gained a place at university to study law and after qualifying found work in London. Ben attended agricultural college and at the end of the course he came home to help run the estate. His career was mapped out for him and it seemed he was happy to follow it, gaining a quiet confidence in his own abilities and his future.

As for Georgie, all he wanted to do was to learn to fly aeroplanes and the RAF seemed to be the best place he could do that.

'Cranwell, Father,' he said as he neared his eighteenth birthday. 'That's where I want to be.'

But Miles had frowned. 'I'm not so sure, Georgie. There are storm clouds gathering in Europe, I fear. And if there's a war, the RAF would be in the front line.'

Georgie only grinned. 'Then I'll be a fighter pilot.'

He'd not altered at all. Of course, he'd grown and was now tall and handsome with fair, curling hair and a strong, lithe body, and seemed always to have a permanent grin on his face. But he was still the same mischievous, lovable scamp he'd always been.

'Georgie's never-failing good humour can get a little wearing,' Philip would remark loftily on his rare visits home. 'Is he ever going to grow up?'

Privately, Charlotte hoped Georgie would never change. She couldn't help him being her favourite, though she would never have voiced such a thing. She treated all three boys fairly and only Miles was aware that her eyes lit up and her mouth curved into a smile when Georgie entered the room or even when his name was mentioned.

Nothing could dissuade the young man from applying to join the RAF and though they did nothing to try to stop him, both Miles and Charlotte felt their hearts sinking with fear when he waved the letter of acceptance, dancing a jig around the breakfast table.

Miles reached across the corner of the table and covered Charlotte's hand where it trembled on the white cloth. 'He'll not be far away.

Cranwell's still in Lincolnshire. And Ben's home now.'

He did not mention Philip, sensitive as ever to the fact that his eldest son and his young wife had an uneasy relationship. Though it was never talked about, it was sometimes like watching two fighting cocks, skirting each other warily. He dreaded the day when one might push the other too far and there would be a flurry of feathers.

Charlotte continued her painting and Felix would visit every so often and bear away several canvases and watercolours, sending her what she regarded as a ridiculously large cheque when he sold them in his London gallery.

The only thing that she remained adamant about was refusing all attempts to encourage her to advertise her talents as a portrait painter. Those she confined to the people around her whom she loved, presenting them, rather shyly, with a work of art they would cherish.

She visited her mother, aunt and uncle in Lincoln regularly, often taking Miles with her, but her mother steadfastly refused to come to Ravensfleet.

'As long as I can see you from time to time and hear from you by letter, that is all I ask,' Alice declared. And for once, even Euphemia could not move her.

'They've quite a stubborn streak,' Miles laughingly commiserated with Charlotte's aunt. 'For such seemingly docile creatures, they can dig their heels in at times. I cannot get Charlotte to paint portraits by commission. She'd be in great demand, I know she would.'

422

Euphemia had smiled at him archly. 'The only thing she wants to do is to make you happy, dear boy.'

He'd smiled readily, even though there was the longing for a daughter that never left him. 'Oh, she does.'

'And you make her supremely happy,' she'd patted his arm, 'I never thought to see the dear girl so contented.'

Euphemia had not alluded to the 'patter of tiny feet' making their idyll complete. Her own childlessness made her sensitive to the feelings of both Miles and Charlotte.

Fifty-Four

At a few minutes past eleven on the morning of Sunday, 3 September 1939, the whole family at the manor sat in Miles's study, clustered around the wireless set listening to Mr Chamberlain's solemn pronouncement that the country was now at war with Germany. Electricity and even the telephone had come to the manor in recent years, though not to Buckthorn Farm. Osbert Crawford resolutely refused to have 'such newfangled nonsense' installed.

Miles switched off the set and sighed heavily. Charlotte's eyes widened with fear, but Georgie, having driven over from Cranwell for the day, rubbed his hands together gleefully. 'Now we can get at 'em. Hitler's been allowed to get away with

423

far too much already.'

Philip, home from London, paced the floor. 'I suppose I shall have to enlist.' He glanced at his father. 'Do my bit.'

'You needn't. You could wait until you're called up. And even then, with your job, you might be able to apply for a dispensation.'

Philip gave a wry laugh. 'I doubt it, Father. Everyone's going to be too busy to be needing lawyers.'

Miles glanced at Ben. 'You'll be all right, son. The list of reserved occupations includes farmers.'

Ben stared back at him and seemed to straighten his shoulders. With quiet determination, he said, 'But I don't want to do that, Father. I shall volunteer for the army.'

Georgie clapped him on the back. 'Good for you, old boy.' He grinned at Philip. 'Now, Phil, you just need to join the navy and we'll have all three services covered.'

Charlotte moved to stand beside Miles's chair and rest her hand on his shoulder. Softly, she whispered, 'You won't have to go, will you?'

'No, my love, not this time. Though...'

Fear clutched her heart. 'What?' she demanded swiftly.

'I think we should do something to help the war effort.'

'What?' she asked again.

Miles twisted his head to look up at her. 'Take in evacuees. They're coming in droves from the big cities. It started three days ago.'

For a moment, she stared at him, then smiled. 'Of course. What a brilliant idea, Miles. We've 'heaps of room here.'

'Right,' Miles heaved himself to his feet, 'no time like the present. I'll go and see the billeting officer in Ravensfleet this very minute.' He turned briefly and touched Charlotte's cheek. 'Do us good,' he smiled, though the smile did not quite reach his eyes. 'To have something else to think about other than these three reprobates.'

The house felt very empty with only Ben still at home. Philip had returned to his law firm in London and Georgie, fairly bouncing with excitement, had headed straight back to camp leaving only Ben to carry on the work of Home Farm and the estate.

'What about the Warren boys?' Charlotte asked Miles. 'Do you think they'll go?'

'Shouldn't think so for a minute. They'll be in a reserved occupation for sure. Besides–' he chuckled – 'I think you're forgetting just how old those "boys" are now?'

Charlotte thought for a moment, then smiled. 'Heavens, yes, I suppose I am. And I'm forgetting how old I am, too.' For a moment, her eyes were bleak. There was still no sign of a baby and the clock was ticking.

Breaking into her thoughts, Miles added, 'Apart from Thomas. How old is he now?'

'Twenty,' Charlotte whispered.

Of all the Warren family, Thomas was the only one who'd decided he didn't want to work on Purslane Farm. He'd turned out to be the brightest one in the family and was in the middle of a university degree studying medicine.

425

'I'd've thought he'd be a good bet to be granted a dispensation, if he applies. But I don't really know, Charlotte,' Miles said. Then his face brightened. 'Mr Tomkins – he's the billeting officer for Ravensfleet – telephoned this morning. He has an evacuee for us.' His smile broadened. 'A little girl.'

Charlotte forced her thoughts back to the present moment. 'How lovely. How old is she? Where is she from? When is she coming?'

'Whoa, whoa there.' He took her hands in his. 'She arrived three days ago with the party of children from London.'

'Three days!' Charlotte was puzzled. 'So why hasn't she been found a billet – a home with someone – before now?'

'Er – well,' Miles was hesitant. 'She did. In a way.'

'Then why–?'

'She was sent back because she's – she's – difficult.'

'Difficult? How d'you mean?'

'She had head lice when she arrived. A lot of the children did, but this little girl was unlucky enough to be placed with two spinster sisters in Ravensfleet who just threw up their hands in horror and dispatched her back into Mr Tomkins's care. He and his wife have done their best, but he says she's very wilful and has tantrums. They can't get her to wash and they certainly haven't been able to deal with the lice.'

Charlotte's eyes softened. 'Poor little scrap. Sent away from her home. She must be so lonely and afraid. Oh Miles, let's fetch her. Now. Let's

426

go this minute.'

Miles hugged her swiftly. 'I knew you'd say that. I'll get the car.

As they walked up the front path of Mr Tomkins's neat cottage, they could already hear the high-pitched screaming from inside. Charlotte and Miles glanced at each other.

'Poor mite,' Charlotte murmured. 'She only needs a little love and care, I'm sure...'

As Mr Tomkins opened the front door to their third loud knock, Charlotte thought she'd never seen the usually calm, mild-mannered man look so harassed.

'Thank goodness you've come, but I'm not sure I'm doing you any favours...'

He was interrupted by a whirlwind of blond hair, wiry limbs and a face like thunder, pushing past him and then between Miles and Charlotte. The child ran down the path, flung open the gate and started off along the road.

'I ain't stayin' here no longer,' she shouted over her shoulder. 'I'm going 'ome. I'd sooner face old 'Itler's bombs than stay here anuvver minute.'

'I'll go after her,' Miles said grinning from ear to ear, completely unfazed by the child's tantrum. 'You talk to Mr Tomkins, dear.'

He set off after the girl, his long strides soon shortening the distance between them, for the child had slowed to a walking pace, though she still marched towards the railway station with a grim, determined set to her jaw.

Mr Tomkins smoothed his hand through his thinning hair and ran his forefinger round the inside of his collar as if it was restricting his neck. 'Do come in, Mrs Thornton. Mabel's just clearing up the mess. The child threw her breakfast on the floor. Dear me, I've never seen such a temper in a child. Perhaps we'd better let her go back.'

'No,' Charlotte said swiftly. 'We can't do that. We can't send her back into danger, if it's going to be as bad as they say.'

'Mm,' Mr Tomkins murmured. 'I suppose you're right, but the expected onslaught doesn't seem to be happening.'

'Not yet,' Charlotte said quietly, her thoughts drifting to Georgie. Resolutely, she turned them back to the little waif, sent far away from her home to strangers. 'But we can't take that risk.'

'Charlotte.' Mrs Tomkins came into the room. She and Charlotte were a similar age and had known each other from childhood even though Charlotte had never been allowed to make friends.

'Mabel.' Charlotte greeted her warmly and held out both her hands. 'Don't worry. We'll take her home. Do our best.'

Mabel grimaced. 'I wish you luck, because I think you're going to need it.'

'Where do you think they've gone?' Charlotte said, stepping to the front window and peering out through the lace curtains.

'She said she was going home, but she's not taken her belongings.' Mabel sniffed. 'Mind you, they're hardly worth taking. She's only got the clothes she's wearing and they've seen better days. Poor little lass. The only other thing she brought besides her gas mask was a moth-eaten old teddy.'

'And she's gone without it?'

Mabel nodded.

Charlotte's eyes gleamed as an idea formed in her mind. 'What's his name?'

'Her name, you mean? Jenny Mercer.'

Charlotte laughed. 'No – I meant the teddy bear's, actually.'

Mabel shrugged. 'I've no idea.'

'No matter,' Charlotte murmured, heading for the front door. Leaving the cottage, she headed down the path and out into the road. In the distance she could see that Miles had caught up with the wilful little girl. They were at the corner and were standing facing each other. Or rather, Miles was squatting so as to bring his face level with Jenny's.

Charlotte bit her lip, hesitating, unsure whether she should interfere. Perhaps Miles was doing a better job on his own. She walked slowly towards them. Then she saw Jenny turn swiftly away and begin to cross the road. Miles caught hold of the child's arm and a high-pitched scream rent the air. Charlotte quickened her pace.

The girl was wriggling and kicking out at Miles's shins, but he held her fast. 'You'll get run over, love. Calm down. I'm not going to hurt you. But you must look where you're going.'

He glanced helplessly at Charlotte but still kept a firm grip on the squirming little body.

'Jenny,' Charlotte began. 'If you're going back to London, haven't you forgotten a couple of things?'

For a moment, Jenny's efforts to break free

429

stopped and she stared up at Charlotte.

'What?'

'For one thing, you must take your gas mask and for another – what about Teddy? You surely weren't going to leave him, were you?'

The young girl became perfectly still.

'If you promise me not to run into the road without looking both ways,' Miles said, 'I'll let go.'

Jenny nodded and Miles released his grip, though he remained standing close by – just in case.

'His name's Bert,' Jenny muttered and took a step – albeit a reluctant one – back towards the cottage. 'I'd better get him. And me gas mask.'

'And what about the train fare? Have you any money?'

As the child blinked and looked up at her, Charlotte saw that she had the bluest eyes she had ever seen.

'Don't need no money. We come on the train an' didn't 'ave ter pay.'

'I think that was special, because the train was bringing you all to the country. But if you choose to go back without the others, you'll have to pay.'

The girl looked suddenly even smaller, lost and afraid. Her lower lip trembled and she ducked her head, but not before Charlotte had seen the tears welling in her lovely eyes. Now Charlotte squatted down in front of her. 'Tell you what, how about you come home with us for a day or two? If you really don't like it, then we'll pay for your train fare back home.'

The girl's head jerked up. 'Promise?'

430

'Well, I don't think your mum'll want you to go back to the city when she's sent you here to be safe, but if you're really so unhappy, then—'

'Don't think mi mum'd be bothered. She's got a fancy man an' I was in the way.'

'Oh – oh, I see,' Charlotte murmured, but she didn't really. She knew nothing about this child's background but it sounded as if she'd been sent to the country with the other evacuees more to get her out of the way than for her safety.

Charlotte stood up, smiled down at Jenny and held out her hand. 'You come with us, Jenny. Give us a try, eh? Maybe you'd like to stay with us for a little while and then we'll see, eh?'

The child looked up at her, staring straight into Charlotte's eyes. Then she nodded. 'All right, missis. I'll give it a go, but if I don't like it...'

'Then I promise we'll take you back to London ourselves and talk to your mum. All right?'

Again the little girl nodded and put her grubby paw into Charlotte's outstretched hand.

Above her head Charlotte and Miles exchanged a smile.

Fifty-Five

Georgie arrived home on a seventy-two-hour pass. The first sounds he heard on entering the front door were high-pitched screams and a great deal of splashing water emanating from the first-floor bathroom.

'What on earth's going on?' he laughed, dumping his kit bag in the hall and greeting his father, who emerged from the sanctuary of his study.

Miles smiled wryly. 'It's our new houseguest. An evacuee from London. She's got nits or head lice or something. She's not taking kindly to the treatment Charlotte is meting out. I'm keeping out of the way.' He chuckled. 'Playing the good guy when all the screaming's over.'

'You might be waiting a while, by the sound of it.' Georgie began to take the stairs, two at a time with his long athletic legs. Miles called after him, 'I'd change out of your uniform first, Georgie. It might be rather wet in there.'

'I will.'

Minutes later, Georgie was knocking on the bathroom door and opening it to a wall of noise and a wave of water sloshing across the linoleum towards him. 'Need any help, Charlotte?' he shouted above the din.

'Georgie! What a lovely surprise.'

At the sound of the man's voice, the child, fighting Charlotte's every attempt to wash her hair, was suddenly still and quiet. The silence was as deafening as the noise had been a moment before.

Georgie stepped through the water and squatted down in front of the girl and held out his hand. 'Hello, I'm Georgie. I'm very pleased to meet you.'

The child stared at him with her brilliant blue eyes. 'Would you like me to dry your hair for you, while Charlotte clears up all this mess?'

Jenny considered for a long moment, her face tear-streaked and sullen. Then, suddenly, she smiled and it was like the sun coming out from behind the darkest storm cloud. She nodded.

Charlotte wrapped the huge white towel round her skinny wet body and handed her over to Georgie with an inward sigh of relief.

'Take her to the nursery. Kitty's been busy all morning cleaning it and lighting a fire in there. It should be cosy by now.'

Georgie lifted the little girl up into his arms and carried her from the bathroom, leaving Charlotte to mop up the tidal wave and set the bathroom to rights. Not for the first time, Charlotte marvelled at how Georgie's charm worked such wonders.

A little later, when order had been restored to a still rather damp bathroom, Charlotte went along to the nursery. Miles was hovering on the landing.

'Do you think they're all right? I can't hear anything. The silence is almost worse than the noise.'

'Oh Miles, you should have seen her smile at Georgie.' She laughed and shook her head in wonderment. 'That boy never ceases to amaze me. He can charm the birds out of the trees.'

Miles chuckled. 'He always could.'

Charlotte smiled fondly. 'I remember.'

They listened outside the door for a moment before opening it quietly and peering round it. Georgie was sitting on the hearthrug, with the child curled against him, her head on his chest, whilst he read to her one of his own favourite books from childhood – *The Wind in the Willows*.

'Just look at her hair,' Miles whispered. 'What pretty blond curls she's got, now it's clean.'

Charlotte glanced at him but his gaze was fastened on Jenny.

'Blond hair and blue eyes – what a little stunner,' he murmured.

'And she has the prettiest dimples in her cheeks when she smiles,' Charlotte whispered back.

He turned to her, dragging his gaze reluctantly away from the little girl for a moment. 'She smiled? She actually smiled?'

Charlotte chuckled softly. 'Oh yes – but only at Georgie.'

'That figures!'

They watched for a few moments longer before Georgie became aware of their presence. He grinned and beckoned them in.

'We're reading,' he informed them unnecessarily.

'So we see,' Miles murmured, his eyes still drinking in the sight of the clean, sweet-smelling child, leaning against Georgie and sucking her thumb. Her eyes drooped with tiredness.

'I think it's time she went to bed,' Charlotte said quietly, torn between not wanting to spoil the tranquillity, but conscious of her duty as a surrogate mother.

'Right, little one,' Georgie said, moving her gently from his lap and standing up. 'Time for beddibyes.'

Charlotte held her breath, expecting an outburst, but none came. When he picked her up, Jenny wound her arms round Georgie's neck and laid her head against his shoulder. She was almost asleep already.

'Poor little scrap,' Miles murmured, touching her curls gently as Georgie carried her out of the nursery and into the bedroom next door to it. He tucked her into bed, promising, 'Charlotte and Miles are right next door and I'm just down the corridor. If you want anything, you only have to shout and we'll come running. All right?'

'Mm.' There was a pause before she murmured, 'Bert?'

Georgie looked round at Charlotte and Miles standing in the doorway. 'What'd she say?'

'Of course. It's her teddy. Now where–?' Charlotte hurried into the room and towards the bundle of Jenny's few belongings, fishing out the shabby teddy bear.

'Here he is – hiding amongst your clothes.' She tucked him in beside the child and then bent to kiss her forehead. 'Night, night, sleep tight, mind the–' Then she stopped.

Any reference to bugs was not the most appropriate thing to say to the little girl, she realized just in time. She bit her lip and exchanged a rueful smile with Miles.

They left a night light burning on the mantelpiece in case Jenny should wake in the darkness and be frightened. And then, sure that she was already sound asleep, the three crept out of the room, leaving the door ajar.

Georgie led the way downstairs and into the dining room, where Wilkins hovered anxiously. Dinner had already been held back almost an hour.

'Now,' Georgie demanded. 'I want to hear all about her and how she comes to be here.'

Over the three days Georgie was at home, Jenny

435

never left his side. She followed him about the house like a little shadow, her teddy clutched in her arms, her thumb in her mouth. But there was one thing that even Georgie could not persuade her to do, which was to go outside.

'Wouldn't you like to see the animals? We've got pigs and chickens and one or two horses in the stables,' Georgie coaxed her. 'Maybe, my dad would get you a little pony and you could learn to ride.'

Jenny shook her curls vehemently. 'Don't like it.'

'What? A pony?'

'No, outside.'

'What do you mean?'

'It's too big.'

Georgie glanced helplessly at Charlotte and Miles, who shrugged, completely at a loss, too.

'What's too big, darling?' Now Charlotte knelt in front of her. 'A horse, d'you mean? We won't make you go on one if you don't want to.'

The girl blinked up at her. 'It's too big,' she repeated.

'What's too big, Jenny?' Miles asked gently. 'Try to tell us.'

'Outside. The sky. It's – frightening. There's no houses an' buildings.'

The three adults exchanged mystified glances, then suddenly Georgie's face cleared. 'I think I understand. She's used to living in the city with buildings all around her. The open flat land and the skies here must look huge to her, when you think about it. Is that it, Jenny love?'

The girl nodded, her shining curls bobbing.

'It's too big.'

'We understand, but there's nothing to be afraid of. Come.' Miles held out his hand, realizing that somehow he and Charlotte must prise her away from Georgie. He had to return to camp the following day. Miles foresaw trouble when the young man had to leave Jenny. 'We'll take it in easy stages. Come to the window and look out. Georgie, you go outside and wave to her. In fact, get one of the lads to bring one of the smaller horses on to the lawn so she can see it.'

The rest of the morning was spent gently coaxing the child outside and by lunchtime she was happily kicking a football backwards and forwards to Georgie on the front lawn.

'I bet she'd love the beach. Digging sandcastles and paddling.'

'Oh, one step at a time, I think, Miles. Besides, aren't they putting rolls and rolls of barbed wire along the beach now and building concrete pill boxes all along the coast?'

'Yes,' Miles said grimly. 'Soon we won't be able to go to the beach. What a shame!'

'Perhaps they'll leave a little space for holidaymakers in Lynthorpe. We could take her there.'

'Holidaymakers?' Miles's tone was doubtful. 'Do you think we'll get any next summer?'

But that was a question Charlotte could not answer.

Fifty-Six

'I'm not going without saying a proper goodbye to her.' Georgie was adamant.

'She'll likely scream the place down,' Charlotte warned.

'That'd be better than me sneaking off without her knowing. I'll explain it carefully. Tell her I'll get home again as soon as I can and that she's to let you or Miles carry on reading *The Wind in the Willows.*'

'He's right, darling.' Miles put his arm round her shoulder. 'We've got to be honest with her. I bet half these poor kids weren't told what was happening to them. They were just shoved on a train and waved off by tearful mothers, not even knowing where they were going or how long for. Georgie's right. We've got to be truthful with her.'

But Charlotte was right about one thing. There were tears – and plenty. A proper tantrum, where Jenny lay on the floor of the hall, screaming and kicking out at anyone who tried to get near her.

At last, the only thing Georgie could do was to say firmly above all the noise, 'I've got to go now, Jen. Won't you come and wave me off?'

But the screams only increased.

Georgie stood up, looking harassed. He hated leaving the child like this, but he'd no option. He had to go.

'I'll try to get home again as soon as I can, even if it's only for a few hours. In the meantime – good luck!'

Shaking his father's hand and kissing Charlotte's cheek, he ran down the front steps to the waiting pony and trap which they were already making more use of in an effort to save petrol.

'There are going to be shortages,' Miles had warned her. 'Just like in the last lot.'

Now, as they stood helplessly watching the writhing little body on their hall floor, shortages, rationing and all the coming privations they were sure they were going to feel, were nothing in comparison to this sad little girl so far from home.

Eventually, the sobs subsided and Miles, instead of being cross, merely held out his hand and said, 'Shall we go and see if we can find Ben and help feed the chickens? It's about time they were having their tea. Perhaps we could help feed the pigs too.'

Jenny stood up, scrubbed away her tears with the back of her hand, and marched towards the front door, Bert's legs dangling from her arms. Miles winked at Charlotte and followed the child.

The following weeks were not easy, but gradually Jenny seemed to be settling down. The first time they took her to morning service, Osbert Crawford descended from the pony and trap and stood looking down at the child standing between Miles and Charlotte.

'What on earth have you got there?'

'Father – this is Jenny Mercer. She's come to

stay with us for a while.'

'An evacuee?' Osbert snorted. 'A *girl?* Couldn't you have got a boy? At least a boy would have been useful about the farm.'

'We wanted a little girl,' Miles said firmly, putting his hand on Jenny's shoulder.

'Huh! What use is a girl?' Osbert eyed the child and sniffed.

The little girl returned his frown steadily and then, to Charlotte's secret delight, Jenny stuck out her tongue at Osbert, turned and marched ahead of them all into the church.

'The cheeky little urchin,' Osbert growled. 'I'd horsewhip her if she was mine.'

'Then thank goodness she isn't,' Miles said sharply and followed Jenny inside.

Osbert hobbled after them, but Charlotte was obliged to wait outside for a few moments longer – until she had controlled a fit of the giggles.

There were still tantrums, tears and a stubborn, scowling face when something didn't suit her, and Jenny flatly refused to go to the local school.

'I don't like the other kids. The ones what live 'ere, I mean. They call us "vaccies".'

'Do they, indeed?' Miles said grimly. 'Then I shall have a word with the teacher.'

'Nah, don't do that, mister. It'd only make it worse. Kids don't like telltale-tits.'

Miles couldn't bring himself to make her go, but the child's non-attendance bothered Mr Tomkins.

'It's our responsibility,' he told Miles anxiously on one of his weekly visits to check on Jenny's

440

progress. 'She must go. Unless, of course...' He hesitated.

'Unless what, Mr Tomkins?' Miles prompted.

'Er, well, I wouldn't dream of suggesting such a thing in normal circumstances. Funds won't run to it...'

'Out with it, man.'

Diffidently, as if he expected to be sent packing with the proverbial flea in his ear, Mr Tomkins said, 'Unless you could arrange for her to receive her schooling at home.'

But Miles's face brightened. 'Of course. What a good idea. And perhaps there's more we could do here. I've heard tell that the school is so over-crowded with the influx of all the evacuee children that some of the pupils are only going for half a day. Is that true?'

'I – believe so.'

Miles beamed.

'We've plenty of rooms here not being used. We could – with the help and approval of the Education Authority – set up classes here. That way, Jenny would have some playmates and all the children would get their proper schooling.'

'It *sounds* like a good idea,' the man agreed. He was thoughtful for a few moments before saying, with a degree of increased interest, 'Let me make some enquiries and I'll get back to you.'

Events moved swiftly; the authorities were only too pleased to accept any help they could get, especially if it came from a reliable and well-organized source.

'There'll be inspectors calling. You understand

that?' Mr Tomkins said earnestly, trying to make sure that Miles and Charlotte knew just what they were taking on.

'I wouldn't want it any other way,' Miles reassured him. 'And we'll do everything in our power to comply with whatever they want.'

So before long, the manor was overrun with noisy children running riot in the grounds and clattering through the hall to the dining room, which had been turned into a schoolroom. Mrs Beddows was in her element, cooking nourishing meals – only Wilkins wore a perpetually worried expression, but even he at last began to feel that he was 'doing his bit' to help the war effort and stopped feeling so guilty that he was too old to volunteer.

As for Miles and Charlotte – they revelled in every minute of it. Miles couldn't wait for lessons to end when he could round up all the children – about a dozen of them, locals and evacuees, plus Jenny of course. Then he'd lead them out on to the front lawn to referee a rowdy game of football. Charlotte timed her visits to Buckthorn Farm when the children were at their lessons so that she could be on hand to bathe a grazed knee or to play with those who wanted a quieter pastime, or just read a story aloud to a group.

Jenny seemed to settle in a little better. The tantrums grew less frequent and she began to smile more than she frowned. But her most often asked question was not, as they might have expected, 'When am I going home?', but 'When's Georgie coming home again?'

Christmas that year was strange – as if everyone, was waiting for something to happen. Several of the evacuees who'd arrived at the beginning of September returned home when the expected air raids did not happen.

But no one sent for Jenny.

The whole family was home for the festivities, but it was Georgie whom Jenny monopolized.

'She doesn't give him a minute's peace,' Philip muttered, adamantly refusing to join in a game of charades.

'Oh come on, Phil, old chap. Lighten up.' Georgie laughed. 'The poor little scrap's miles from her home – her family. Come down off that high horse, just for once, eh?'

'Mm.' Philip frowned and regarded the little girl for a moment, before giving an exaggerated sigh and throwing down his newspaper. 'Very well, but only because it's you asking, Georgie. This family's never been able to refuse its golden-headed little cherub anything, now, has it?'

It was a merry Christmas, despite the thought at the back of everyone's mind that the waiting for the war to begin in earnest could not last for ever. Early in April the 'phoney war' came to an abrupt end when Hitler invaded Denmark and Norway. Then, at the beginning of June, news filtered through of the evacuation of the British Expeditionary Force from Dunkirk.

Now, it seemed, Britain stood alone and only the RAF could protect its shores and its people.

Charlotte felt a cold terror creep around her heart.

One Saturday morning in June when there were no lessons and no other children came to play, Jenny went missing.

Miles was beside himself. 'Where can she be? Oh Charlotte, she wouldn't try to go to the beach, would she?'

'She doesn't know the way, does she?'

'I've taken her a few times. She might.'

Charlotte thought for a moment and then shook her head. 'I don't think she'd go on her own. She's still a little nervous of the great outdoors and you said she found the vastness of the sea scary at first.'

'But Georgie takes her every time he comes home. She's not so frightened now. She just might have thought she'd go on her own. We must get everyone searching. And I mean everyone. Wilkins, Brewster, Cook, Kitty and all the men on the farm. Let's send word to Eddie, too–'

'Calm down, Miles. Let's not panic. We haven't even searched the whole house yet.'

'D'you think she'd go into the town? Try to get on a train home?'

Charlotte shook her head then gave a thin smile. She was as worried as Miles, but she was trying not to show it. 'If she has gone there, it's more likely she's looking for Georgie coming home.'

Miles's face brightened. 'Maybe she has. I'll get Brewster to drive into–'

'Wait a minute, Miles. Let's search here first. She'll come to no harm. Not in Ravensfleet.'

'You're right. Of course you are. But, Charlotte, I couldn't bear it if something's happened to her.'

Charlotte touched his arm and said softly, 'I know, I know.'

The child had wound her way into both their hearts, but Miles was besotted with her. Little Jenny was fast becoming the daughter he'd always longed for. But Charlotte was fearful for this man she loved so very much. Jenny wasn't theirs. Never could be theirs. She had a mother back in London who, one day, would want her daughter home again.

Despite Jenny's offhand remarks about her mother's 'fancy man' and feeling that she was in the way, Charlotte could not understand any mother not wanting her child close by.

And yet, a niggling little voice reminded her, didn't your own mother run away and leave you? Not all mothers are the kind Charlotte knew she would be, she told herself.

She dragged her thoughts back to the present anxiety. With greater calmness than she was feeling inside, she said, 'Let's do this in an organized way. Not running around in circles like headless chickens.'

'You're right. I know you're right, but...' Miles ran his hand through his hair again.

'We'll search the house first, from top to bottom. Everywhere – every nook and cranny and then, if we haven't found her, we'll extend the search outside and rope everybody in.'

Miles nodded. 'Where shall we start?'

'Down here and work our way upstairs.'

'I've already looked in her bedroom and the playroom. She's not there.'

At that moment, Wilkins appeared in the

hallway carrying a tray and Miles dispatched him at once to ask Mrs Beddows and the housemaid to join in searching the house.

After only a few minutes, whilst they were still searching the first floor bedrooms, they heard the maid, Kitty, calling from the top landing.

'Sir – madam, she's up here.'

Miles galloped up the stairs with the agility of a man half his age, with Charlotte running up behind him as fast as she could.

Kitty was waiting for them at the top, her eyes anxious.

'Is she all right?' Miles asked urgently. 'Where is she?'

'She's fine, sir, but – but it's madam's studio. Such a mess she's made. There's paint everywhere.'

'Oh no,' Miles breathed as he turned to Charlotte. 'Please, my dear, don't be angry. Whatever she's done, I'll get it all cleaned up, I promise.'

Charlotte linked her arm through her husband's and smiled up at him. 'Let's go and see, shall we?'

The sight that met their eyes took their breath away and they both stood in the doorway, their eyes roaming round the scene of devastation. Charlotte had not had time to paint recently, with all the extra work the children brought, and she hadn't been into her studio for almost a fortnight. The damage that Jenny had wrought had not been done in one day, nor even two or three. She must have been creeping up here for quite a while. The linoleum floor was splattered with paint and there were splashes on the white wall. She'd even used one of the walls to paint a

446

childish picture on, when she'd run out of paper.

Pieces of paper, all covered with daubs of paint, littered the floor and Charlotte's precious canvases had been used, too. Open tubes of oil paints and watercolours oozed on to the desk and the table by the window and dirty brushes, caked with dried paint, were strewn around.

'Oh Jenny,' Miles began, sadly, but Charlotte squeezed his arm quickly and whispered, 'Don't, Miles, don't chastise her.'

The girl was standing in front of Charlotte's easel, wearing the white smock which Charlotte herself used to protect her clothes.

That's why we've never seen paint on her clothes, Charlotte thought. I'd never have guessed. There've been no telltale signs. But there were plenty now. The child's fingers were sticky with blue oil paint and she had a streak of the same colour down her cheek. With a loaded brush poised in front of a canvas on the easel, she glanced up at them standing by the door and grinned.

'Hello, I'm painting a picture for Georgie.'

Charlotte took a deep breath and, leaving Miles standing by the door gazing helplessly at the carnage, she crossed the room. Smiling, she said, 'How nice, darling. May I see?'

She stood beside the child and together they scrutinized the canvas. Cerulean blue streaked the top part of the picture with the darker cobalt blue below it. Beneath that was yellow ochre.

'Why, it's the beach,' Charlotte said, and was rewarded by a beaming smile from the artist.

'I want some green for that spiky grass, but I

447

can't remember what to mix.'

'Blue and yellow. Here, let me show you.'

Charlotte reached for her palette and, heads bent together over the board, she showed Jenny how to mix the different greens to represent the grasses and bushes that grew on the sandhills.

'I'll – er – um – leave you to it, then, shall I?' Miles said uncertainly.

Charlotte glanced up and winked broadly. 'We'll be fine.'

As he closed the door softly behind him, he heard Jenny's high-pitched voice say, 'I'm sorry if I've made a mess, Charlotte, but it is such fun, isn't it?'

And at once, he knew what he would buy the little girl for Christmas. Perhaps he could turn a corner of the playroom into her own little studio so that she wouldn't invade Charlotte's domain again.

He would talk to Charlotte later, he promised himself.

Fifty-Seven

A week later, Georgie managed to get home on a short leave. Charlotte met him in the hall before Jenny could reach him.

'She's painted you a picture,' she warned him, forbearing to tell of the disastrous consequences of the child's efforts. 'Miles got it framed. It's of the beach, so be sure to recognize what it is.

Actually,' Charlotte put her head on one side and smiled, 'for her age, it's really quite good.'

Georgie hugged her close, holding her for what seemed like a long moment. Charlotte pulled back and looked up into his eyes. His smile was still there, but to her sharp, observant eye it looked forced. The brightness, the sparkle of mischief that had always been in his blue eyes, was gone.

'My dear – what is it?' she whispered.

He smiled ruefully. 'There's no hiding anything from you, is there?'

'Nor your father. Not where his boys are concerned.' She linked her arm through his and led him towards the stairs. 'Come up to my studio. No one will bother us there. We can snatch a few minutes alone. The children are still at their lessons. But keep your voice down. If Jenny hears you...' As they began to mount the stairs, she asked, 'Are you hungry? I could ask Wilkins to bring a tray up.'

'A whisky would be nice.'

Whisky, she thought, suddenly very concerned. It was two in the afternoon. But she made no comment, except to say, 'You go on up. I'll just find Wilkins.'

She joined him in her studio; he was sitting on the wide window seat staring down at the garden below.

'How's it all going, then?' he wanted to know. 'With all these kids?'

She had the distinct feeling that he was leaping in first, before she could ask him awkward questions.

Charlotte crossed the room which was once

449

more neat and reasonably tidy for an artist's studio. Little trace of Jenny's first experiments remained, but one corner of the room had now been set out for the child. A little table with paints, brushes and paper of her own, kept her confined to her 'painting room' as she called it. When Miles had suggested setting something up for her in the playroom, Charlotte herself had said she could share her studio. 'Keep all the mess in one place,' she'd said smiling.

'Fine,' Charlotte said now in answer to Georgie's question as she took a seat beside him. 'We have a nice teacher who comes in every day. A young woman whose fiancé is in the army. They have lessons and then play out in the garden, if it's fine, before going home. Miles loves those sessions. He never misses them. And then he takes some of the ones who live the farthest away home in the farm cart. And *they* love that!'

'It sounds idyllic,' Georgie murmured wistfully.

'Not really. A lot of the evacuees are still homesick. But we're doing our best.'

'And Jenny? What about her?'

'She's settling in better now, though it's taken a while. We still get the odd tantrum, but Miles spends a lot of time with her.'

Georgie smiled pensively. 'The daughter he never had, eh?'

Charlotte couldn't answer. Her throat was too full of tears. Though it was never spoken of, never referred to, except by her father almost every time he saw her, Charlotte still lamented the lack of their own child in their lives.

She turned her thoughts away from her own

sadness and said softly, 'So, my darling, how are things with you?'

He took a moment to answer. 'You'll have been following the news.' It was a statement rather than a question. 'You know all about Dunkirk. And I expect you have heard about Mr Churchill's speech that the Battle of France is over and – and the Battle of Britain is about to begin. Everyone's getting jittery about a possible invasion. We're not – we're not exactly at our strongest at the moment, Charlotte. It has to be said. Though I wouldn't say it to just anyone.' He looked across at her and held her gaze. Softly, he said, 'The RAF chaps are in for a pretty tough time. We're the only ones to defend our shores at the moment. You – you understand what I'm saying, don't you?'

Wordlessly, she nodded.

'If – if anything happens to me, look after Dad, won't you?'

Huskily, she murmured, 'Of course. You know I will.' But silently she thought, *But who will look after me if I lose my golden boy?*

Georgie forced a smile, held out his hand to her and, with his glass of whisky in the other, said, 'And now, let's go and find that little scamp.'

Jenny positively glowed at Georgie's unstinting praise of the picture she had painted just for him. 'I must hang it up in my room at once, alongside Charlotte's.'

Later that day, the four of them stood back to admire Jenny's painting of the beach hanging beside the painting Charlotte had done years earlier of the village school. It had hung on

Georgie's bedroom wall ever since.

Miles put his arm round Charlotte's shoulder and, glancing down at her, winked. 'Do you know, my dear, I think you have a rival for your talent. You'll have to watch out. Felix will be coming to take Jenny's pictures back to London.'

Solemnly – and quite seriously – Charlotte said, 'There's real talent there, if only it can be nurtured.'

'Then we must make sure it is,' Miles said softly.

Their words passed over the child's head. She was still basking in Georgie's approval.

There was a tap on the bedroom door and Wilkins's face appeared.

'Excuse me, sir – madam. Master Philip has arrived home.'

'How lovely,' Charlotte said, injecting what she hoped was as much pleasure as she had genuinely felt at Georgie's arrival. But Jenny made no such effort. Her smile disappeared to be replaced by a glower.

Noticing, Georgie took her hand. 'Come along, let's go and greet him. And Ben will be home soon too. Then we can all have a lovely family dinner, because you're part of our family now, aren't you, Jen?'

The child looked up at him, smiling, and with adoration in her eyes.

Watching them, Miles felt his heart turn over.

Ben was later arriving home from his work than normal. Charlotte had to hold dinner back by half an hour, much to Mrs Beddows's consternation.

He came into the room solemn faced and avoiding his father's eyes.

Charlotte's heart leapt in her breast. Something was wrong – she could see it in his manner and written on his face.

And so could Miles. 'What is it, son? Bad news?'

Several young men from the district – though no one close as yet – had been reported killed or missing since Dunkirk. Miles feared the worst.

'Let's have dinner.' Ben smiled thinly. 'I'm sure Mrs Beddows is in a flap already.'

'Tell us now,' Charlotte said. 'Another few minutes won't matter.'

Ben sighed. 'I'm sorry – I know you think I shouldn't, but – but I've volunteered for the army.' Now he met his father's gaze. 'I know I could probably get out of it, but I can't sit around here whilst others are – are going. My conscience won't let me.'

Charlotte gasped and sat down suddenly, her hand to her breast, her eyes wide and fearful. 'Oh, Ben, no.'

She felt Philip's eyes on her, his mouth twisting in a sardonic smile. He moved and put his arm about his brother's shoulders, but his gaze was on Charlotte's face.

No one else in the room had spoken. Miles and Georgie seemed to have been turned to stone by Ben's announcement. Jenny, wide-eyed, stood watching them all.

'I wonder,' Philip drawled, 'if I shall get the same reaction. As it happens, I've volunteered too. The army. That's what I've come home to tell you all.' Now he smacked Ben on the back. 'You've rather stolen my thunder, old boy.'

With a supreme effort, Charlotte jumped to her feet and clasped her hands, staring at them both. 'Why? Why? How could you do this to us? Isn't it enough that Georgie–?' she stopped, realizing that she was in danger of betraying the very emotions she fought so hard to keep hidden.

'Ah yes,' Philip said softly. 'Georgie.'

That was all he said, but no one in the room, except perhaps Jenny, misunderstood the meaning behind his words.

It was Georgie who broke the tension. He crossed the room in a few strides to slap his brothers on the back. 'Congratulations. Old Hitler doesn't stand a snowball in hell's chance with all three Thornton boys after him.'

Charlotte moved to Miles's side. She looked up into his face. He was grey with sadness and his strong shoulders seemed to sag. It seemed to her that he had aged ten years in a matter of seconds. But, true to his nature, he said no word of censure. He merely stretched out his hand – a hand that trembled a little – to congratulate his boys. And to wish them well.

But only Charlotte knew the dreadful fear that was in his heart, for it took root in her own and she knew she'd never know another moment's peace until this war was over.

Fifty-Eight

Osbert had plenty to say about Philip's foolish action.

'What on earth is he thinking of?' He thumped his stick angrily. 'Send him to see me,' he demanded imperiously. 'I'll talk some sense into him.'

'It's done now, Father,' Charlotte said heavily. 'And I don't think it can be undone.'

'We'll see about that,' Osbert growled.

But even Osbert Crawford was no match for His Majesty's Services and so now there was only Jenny left at home to brighten their day and take their minds off their boys. But thoughts of them were never very far away.

'How many more are going to go?' Charlotte worried.

'Too many.' Miles paused then, trying to turn their thoughts to other matters, although everything they discussed seemed to be connected to the war in one way or another. 'Tommy Warren has gone. Had you heard? The army, I think.'

'How's he managed that?' Charlotte asked in surprise. 'Surely he's classed as being in a reserved occupation, isn't he?'

Miles shrugged. 'Well, Ben was, too, but he managed it. I don't quite know what they've done.' Then he asked, 'What about the workers on Buckthorn Farm? Are you coping?'

455

Charlotte sighed. 'At the moment, yes, but I think Eddie is beginning to feel frustrated that he can't go.'

'Tell him there are countless soldiers who would give their eye teeth to swap places with him. He's doing a valuable job and shouldn't feel guilty.'

Charlotte nodded. 'I will.'

'It's a pity Ben and Tommy couldn't see it that way,' he muttered, frowning. Then he sighed, trying to bring his thoughts back to the hole in the workforce that Ben's departure would leave. 'We've got land army girls coming to Home Farm. I'll see if Joe needs anyone. What about one or two for Buckthorn Farm?'

'Mm, I'll talk it over with Eddie.'

Georgie made the most of his leave. No one else except Charlotte seemed to notice the haunted look deep in his eyes. If they did, they said nothing. Like Georgie himself, everyone put on a brave face and laughed and joked as if all was right with the world instead of acknowledging that perhaps their country was facing its darkest hour.

Georgie spent most of his time with Jenny, teaching her to ride the second-hand bicycle that Miles had bought for her, even sitting her in the saddle on a docile pony and leading her along the quiet lanes. He took her to the seashore to see if the samphire was ready for picking.

'We'll take some home,' he told her, 'and Mrs Beddows will show you how to cook it.' He laughed. 'She's quite the expert since Charlotte first showed me where to pick it and...' There was a catch in his voice as he remembered his happy childhood. As Georgie had no memories of his own mother, Charlotte had filled that void for him at least. And he knew she looked upon him as her own son, her special boy. He realized now, how desperately worried both she and his father must be about him. And now his two brothers had joined up too.

He stood up suddenly and glanced around. 'Come on, Jen,' he said, holding out his hand. 'Time to go home, the tide's coming in.'

When they arrived back at the manor, it was to find that an urgent message awaited him. All leave had been cancelled and Georgie had to return to camp immediately.

As he bade everyone farewell in the hallway, he shook his father's hand, clapped his two brothers on the back and picked Jenny up and swung her round. But he saved his special bear hug for Charlotte, whispering close to her ear, 'Look after yourself, dearest Charlotte.'

And then he was gone, running down the steps, his kit bag bumping against his legs, out to where Brewster waited to drive him to the station.

Over the following weeks, the war news was no better. Britain now fought on alone and, as Mr Churchill had called it, the Battle of Britain was being fought by the RAF over the south of England. And whilst Georgie was in the thick of the fighting, Philip and Ben completed their basic training and awaited a posting.

They both came home on a week's leave and

Charlotte tried to make their time at home very special. She planned their favourite meals – as far as rations would allow – and made a determined effort to heal the rift between herself and Philip. But she couldn't prevent Georgie being never far from her thoughts. Ben went back to the life he loved – working on Home Farm – whilst he waited, but Philip didn't want to involve himself in anything. He whiled away the days reading or just sitting staring into space, preferring to be alone rather than in company.

Jenny stood in front of him as he sat on the terrace one sunny August morning reading the newspaper. She regarded him solemnly for several moments before Philip became aware of her silent presence. He frowned over the top of the paper. 'What d'you want?'

'Georgie's not here.'

'No-o,' Philip said carefully. The child was stating the obvious, he thought, so why–?

'And Charlotte's gone to see that grumpy old man.'

'Ye-es.'

'And the mister's busy, so–'

'So?'

'Will you read to me?' She held out the book. 'It's the one Georgie gived me.'

'Did he now?' He could see the battered copy of *The Wind in the Willows* in the child's hands. It had always been a favourite – one he remembered his mother reading to him...

Before he knew quite how it was happening, Jenny had tweaked the newspaper from his grasp and dropped it on the floor. Then she handed him the book and clambered on to his knee.

'We've got to Chapter Eight where Mr Toad's just been put in a dinjun.'

'A dungeon,' Philip said mildly.

'That's what I said – a dinjun.' With Bert clutched under one arm, she put her thumb in her mouth, curled up on his lap and, resting her head against his shoulder, waited for him to begin.

Half an hour later, that was how Charlotte, returning from Buckthorn Farm, found them.

'He was reading to her,' she told an incredulous Miles. 'There she was, sitting on his knee, and he was reading to her. *And* doing all the funny voices just like Georgie does.'

'Well, I never,' Miles murmured. 'You know, Philip hasn't always had this – this prickly side to his nature. When he was young–' He stopped, afraid he would cause Charlotte pain, but she finished his sentence for him.

'When his mother was alive, you mean?'

Slowly, Miles nodded.

For the remaining days of his leave, Jenny monopolized Philip.

'Georgie's not here,' she told him candidly, 'so you'll have to do.'

Hearing it, Charlotte held her breath, expecting a bad-tempered outburst from her stepson. But to her amazement, Philip only laughed. 'Well, I suppose it's no bad thing to be second-in-command. So, Jenny, what do you want to do today?'

Charlotte turned away, shaking her head in wonderment. I must be dreaming, she thought.

Charlotte's thoughts were never far away from her beloved Georgie in his Hurricane. And though they tried not to speak of it too often, Miles's preoccupied air told her that his thoughts, too, were often in the skies over the Channel. Philip and Ben had both gone and there was only Jenny to take their minds off their worries.

Charlotte went as often as she could to Lincoln to see her mother, aunt and uncle, but still there was no evading the talk of war that seemed to dominate everyone's thoughts. As she arrived home from one such visit in early September, Miles greeted her. He was distraught.

Seeing his ravaged face, Charlotte's knew in an instant that it was the news she'd dreaded the most.

Georgie.

He held opened the front door as she climbed the steps on trembling legs. She reached out to him. 'What is it?'

'The worst possible.' His voice was deep and thick with emotion. 'Georgie's missing. One of his pals telephoned. He was seen going down over the coast of France. There is a chance – a slim one – but...'

Charlotte was dying inside. Her 'golden boy' lost. Missing – presumed killed. That was the heartbreaking official wording they would receive in a day or so.

'Perhaps...' she began, clinging to any vestige of hope, but the bleak, defeated look in Miles's eyes told her she was clutching at straws.

'Don't tell Jenny,' he pleaded hoarsely. 'It'll break her heart. She idolizes him.'

Her throat too full of tears to speak, Charlotte nodded as Miles turned away towards his study. She let him go, aware that he needed some time alone. Slowly she climbed the stairs towards her studio to seek her own solitary consolation. But it was not to be found; Jenny sat in her own little corner daubing a piece of paper with yellow ochre and dots of green.

'I'm painting another picture for Georgie,' she said brightly. 'He'll be home again soon. That's samphire, that is. We picked it together – me an' Georgie.'

Charlotte had never known what it felt like to have her heart broken.

But in that moment, she knew.

'Where is she? I can't find her.'

Miles burst into the morning room where Charlotte was patiently darning a sock. Make do and mend was the order of the day now.

She raised her eyes, pausing in her work but not flying into a panic straight away. 'Isn't she outside with the others?'

'No. They're clamouring to be taken home. Miss Parker too.'

Miss Parker was the teacher who came every day to the manor.

Charlotte rose with an outward calm she wasn't feeling inside. 'You take them all home and I'll mount a search party.'

'Easier said than done,' he muttered, but turned away to do as she suggested.

'Be careful,' she called after him, knowing he would drive like the wind, taking the corners in the narrows lanes far too fast in his haste to get back.

This time Jenny was not in the studio, nor in any other part of the house.

'Where can she be?' Charlotte worried, biting the edge of her thumb as she hovered in the hall, uncertain what to do next. 'Where might she go?'

But she couldn't answer her own question. Jenny was still a little afraid of the great outdoors unless there was someone else with her.

'If only you were here, Georgie,' she murmured sadly, 'she wouldn't have gone missing. She'd be stuck to your side like a limpet.'

Miles burst in through the front door.

'They've told her,' he blurted out. 'Those little buggers have told her. About Georgie. That's why she's run off.'

Charlotte gasped and her eyes widened. 'Oh, how could they?'

He ran his hand through his hair and took a deep breath. 'I suppose we shouldn't blame them. The whole village knows. The kids are bound to pick it up and – and they don't understand...'

'But where's she *gone?* I've looked everywhere I can think of.'

'Where did Georgie take her? Where did they go together?'

'The shore!' Charlotte gasped. 'Last time he was home, he took her to the seashore.'

Fifty-Nine

Within minutes they were both on horseback riding towards the sea, neither of them daring to voice their fears. Jenny didn't understand the ways of the sea, its tides and treacherous currents and creeks. She wouldn't know what to do if the water came swirling in around her...

They galloped down the long lane towards the sea bank. Pausing at the top of the rise, they scanned the beach.

'The tide's coming in,' Charlotte cried.

'Samphire? Where's the samphire.'

'Yes, yes. They collected samphire. She was painting a picture. This way.'

Leaving their horses, Charlotte led the way carefully across the marshy ground to where the samphire grew.

'There – over there. I thought I saw something...' Miles pointed. 'No – I'm imagining it.'

They walked on, scanning the marsh and the creeks around them. And with every second the incoming tide was coming closer and closer. After a few moments Miles shouted again. 'There! There, Charlotte. I did see something.'

Charlotte too had caught a movement a short distance in front of them – something white and fluttering in the breeze.

'Look!' She pointed excitedly. 'She *is* here. There's a peg with a piece of white rag tied to it.'

Miles frowned, then he remembered. 'You – you think Georgie told her what you told us all those years ago? So she could find her way back?'

'I'm sure of it.'

They quickened their pace towards the peg and its makeshift flag.

'There's another – and another,' Charlotte cried.

Just then, a figure bobbed up, stretching up to glance around her, watching the tide and the encroaching water. 'There she is,' Miles breathed. 'Thank God.'

'Don't be angry with her, Miles. Please. If she's just been told about Georgie...'

Jenny had seen them and was standing perfectly still watching them approach, a look of fear on her face. She knew she was in trouble.

'My, you've collected a lot. Mrs Beddows will be pleased.' Miles smiled down at her, reining in his instinct to either shake her roundly or clutch her to him in a thankful embrace. Instead, keeping his tone level and calm, he went on, 'But the tide's coming in now, love. Time we were heading back. Come on. We've got the horses on the sea bank. You can ride in front of me.'

They walked back the way they had come, collecting the pegs and pieces of cloth as they went. Miles hoisted her up on to the horse's saddle and then swung himself up behind her. She was still clutching the bag of wet samphire she'd collected.

'I was all right, mister. Honest. Georgie told me to watch out for the water comin' an' how to set the pegs. I wouldn't have drownded. Georgie...'

Her voice broke and her head dropped. Miles held her close feeling the thin little body racked with sobs.

Beside them, Charlotte rode in silence, her throat full of tears, remembering how she'd taught Georgie about the tides and how to mark the path back across the marsh.

And he'd passed the knowledge on to little Jenny. Georgie had kept her safe even though he'd not survived.

Late one afternoon in October, when Charlotte and Miles were having tea in the morning room, the door was flung open with a crash and Jenny leapt on to the end of the sofa.

'There's an 'orrible noise an' banging,' Jenny wailed. 'I don't like it.'

Miles got up and went to the window, whilst Jenny scrambled along the sofa and snuggled up to Charlotte. 'I don't like it,' she muttered again and put her thumb in her mouth.

'It's only the sirens,' Charlotte said, thankful that they were far enough away from Lynthorpe for them to be no louder than they already were.

'And planes,' she heard Miles mutter. 'There are planes almost overhead.'

Jenny gave a scream and buried her head against Charlotte as more dull thuds sounded in the distance. 'It's 'Itler. He's comin'.'

Intrigued rather than frightened, Charlotte tried to untangle herself from the child, but Jenny held on tightly.

'What's happening?' Charlotte asked.

In a low voice, Miles said, 'They're dropping

bombs. On Lynthorpe.'

'Don't like it,' came Jenny's muffled voice. 'And Bert don't like it neither.'

The banging ceased and soon the 'All Clear' sounded.

'There, there, it's all over now,' Charlotte comforted Jenny.

It was over for that day but, a month later, several incendiaries fell in a field belonging to one of Miles's tenant farmers. No one was hurt but the incident was to bring Miles and Charlotte more heartache than they could ever have imagined.

'I want 'er back 'ome with me, where she belongs, an' there ain't nuffin' you can do to stop me.'

Miles and Charlotte stood on the driveway facing the stranger, helpless in the face of her anger. Jenny clung to Miles's hand and made no move towards the woman, whom Charlotte presumed to be her mother.

'I ain't coming,' Jenny blurted out and pointed a trembling finger at the tall, thin man lounging against the motor car, smoking a cigarette. He was thin faced and handsome, Charlotte supposed, in a flash kind of way. She fought back a rising bubble of laughter. The man reminded her of Max Miller, the outrageous comedian, whom they'd seen once at the theatre and heard often on the radio. This man sported a thin, neatly trimmed moustache and was dressed in a flamboyant check suit. Loud, Miles would have called it. 'Not if *he's* still there.' Jenny spat out the final words.

Charlotte saw the flash of anger in the man's face and he pushed himself upright, jabbing towards Jenny with his cigarette.

'Now look here, young 'un, I've been good to you, I have.' The man smirked. 'And even better to yer ma, so don't you go bad-mouthing me to these nice people.'

Jenny cowered behind Miles, her boldness deserting her suddenly.

'Mrs Mercer...' Miles released himself from Jenny's grasp and strode towards the woman, holding out his hand in welcome. 'Shall we go inside and have a cup of tea and maybe something to eat? I'm sure you must be–'

'We gotta get goin' if we've to be back before the blackout,' the woman said. 'It's a long way to London.'

Keeping the smile firmly fixed on his face, Miles glanced towards the man and spread out his hands. 'You could both stay here tonight. You're more than welcome.'

'Nah thanks, guv'nor,' the man answered again. 'Like the little lady ses, we've got to get back. I've got mi business to think of.' He winked broadly at Miles. 'Know what I mean.'

Miles didn't, but he could make a shrewd guess: black market 'business'.

'I'm staying here,' Jenny's shrill voice piped up. 'I ain't going back wiv 'em.' She turned to Miles. 'I'm all right here, ain't I?'

'Of course you are, Jenny.' He held out his hand to her. 'But let's go inside and talk it over.'

'Well–' the woman hesitated and glanced at the

man. 'Just a cuppa while she gets her things together.'

They turned towards the house, all except Jenny. She tore her hand from Miles's grasp and began to run across the grass towards the little gate leading to the lane to Buckthorn Farm.

''Ere, come back, our Jen. Don't you want to come home with your ma?' the woman called after her, but Jenny kept on running.

Inwardly, Charlotte smiled. She guessed exactly where the child was heading. Buckthorn Farm. But she wasn't worried. Mary would look after her. And, later, when the couple had gone, Charlotte would fetch her back. But meanwhile, she would play the perfect hostess.

When they'd had tea, Charlotte offered, 'Would you like to see Jenny's bedroom? To see for yourself how well we're looking after her? Won't you leave her with us a while longer, Mrs Mercer? She'll be so much safer here.'

'No, I want her home. She's been away a whole year now, an' I don't want no one sayin' I'm a bad mother, sending my child to live wiv strangers.'

'I'm sure no one would think that,' Miles said smoothly, carefully avoiding Charlotte's glance lest his face should give him away. 'In fact, quite the contrary. You've shown remarkable unselfishness in sending your daughter to safety. You are to be commended.'

The woman stared at him, clearly not understanding if she was being insulted or complimented. She sniffed. 'Well, that's as may be, but we want her home now, don't we, Arfer?'

Arthur shrugged. 'Whatever you say, Dot.' Again he winked at Miles. 'Just like to keep the little ladies happy, don't we, guv'nor?'

Miles beamed at him, recognizing an ally, albeit for very different reasons. The man didn't want Jenny back with them any more than Miles wanted to let her go.

But Dot was the little girl's mother and she was adamant. 'All the other kids is back now. Jen's the only one in our street not back home and folks is talking.' She nodded towards Arthur. ''Specially now Arfer's moved in. But we're getting married, ain't we, Arfer? And we want her back. We want to be a family.' She smiled archly. 'You never know, there might be a little brother or sister for 'er one day.'

Miles was amused by the flash of sheer terror which flitted across the man's face, but Arthur hid it manfully and forced a thin smile. 'Yer never know yer luck,' he murmured.

'So,' Dot said, standing up, 'if you can let me have her things, missis, we'll be on our way. Arfer, go an' call 'er. She can't be far away.' She shuddered dramatically. 'She'll not like all them open spaces we drove through to get here, I know.'

'I don't know where she'll be. Look, Dot, she don't want to come home. It's obvious. Why don't you–?'

'Shut up, Arfer. She's comin' back with us and that's final.' She turned back to Miles. 'You'd best find her, mister, 'cos I ain't going back without her.' Dot sat down again, a stubborn look on her face.

'She could be anywhere–'

'Then you aren't looking after 'er very well if you let her run wild like this.'

'We don't– I mean–' Miles was floundering and Charlotte stepped in.

'Jenny will be quite safe,' she said calmly, pushing aside the memory of their own panic when the girl had gone missing. 'She knows the area well now, and–'

'Well, you'd best find 'er, missis,' Dot said again. ''Cos I'm staying here till you do.'

Charlotte caught sight of Miles's face and her heart turned over with love for him. They were going to lose Jenny and he was devastated. They were no match for this determined woman, who was, after all, the girl's mother. Miles sighed heavily and turned away. 'I'll send out a search party,' he murmured.

'I'll go,' Charlotte said at once and hurried out of the room before anyone could stop her. 'I'll organize it.'

The November afternoon was turning to dusk and there was still no sign of Jenny.

'Dot, we'll have to go,' Arthur insisted at last. 'We'll be all night getting home now. Have to go slow, y'know,' he winked at Miles, 'in the blackout.'

Miles nodded absently. He rather thought the man would break the blackout regulations, put his car lights on full beam, and drive like the wind.

'Oh, all right. Have it your way.' Dot stood up and wagged her finger at both Miles and

470

Charlotte. 'But I want her home. I'm going to the authorities when I get back.'

Miles's face was bleak. But, at least, for the moment, Jenny would be staying.

Sixty

Charlotte found Jenny in the place that had been her own childhood hideaway; the hayloft at Buckthorn Farm. The girl had fallen asleep, nestled in the dry hay. Charlotte sat beside her, gazing out of the small, square window until Jenny roused herself, rubbed her eyes and sat up.

'Have they gone?'

'Yes – for the moment. But your mother wants you home, darling.'

Jenny's lower lip trembled. 'But I don't want to go. I like it here. Don't you want me any more?'

Charlotte put her arm round Jenny's shoulders. Her voice was husky and not quite steady as she said, 'Miles and I would like you to stay for ever, and that's the truth, but your mum loves you. She wants you to go home.'

The girl was silent for a long time before she said in a small voice, 'Are they coming back to get me, then?'

Charlotte sighed. 'Your mother said she would be going to the authorities when she got home. Darling – if she does – there'll be nothing we can do.'

'I could hide here again. They wouldn't find me.'

Charlotte was silent. She didn't tell her that she'd told the searchers not to go into the hayloft at Buckthorn Farm. She'd guessed that was where the girl would be. She'd deliberately prevented them from finding Jenny. She sighed inwardly. She knew the girl would have to go back to London sooner or later, but at least she'd won them a little time. Time in which they could all get used to the idea.

Especially Miles, though she doubted he would ever come to terms with letting Jenny go.

Christmas was always going to be difficult. It was their first since the awful news that Georgie had been posted missing and now it was likely that very soon Jenny would have to leave them. There'd been no word yet from Dot, but they all knew it was only a matter of time. Even if she'd changed her mind and decided to let her daughter stay in the country, once the war ended the little girl would have to go home.

'I don't suppose,' Miles murmured one night as they lay in each other's arms, 'that they'd let us adopt her?'

Charlotte sighed. 'I don't think so. The mother seemed – well – possessive. It didn't seem like real affection to me, more like a status symbol. That she wanted to appear a good mother in front of her neighbours. I got the impression that was why she wanted Jenny home. Because all the other children in the street were back.'

'Mm. She said as much, didn't she?'

There was a pause before Charlotte said, 'Maybe Dot latched on to what you said and has gone back lording it over everyone about how she

472

had been selfless in allowing Jenny to stay with us.'

'Perhaps,' he murmured, sounding doubtful.

Philip arrived home on Christmas Eve. 'I'm one of the lucky ones,' he told them, dropping his kit bag and a pile of gifts on to the floor of the hall. 'I've got five whole days.' His face sobered as he took a deep breath, 'But it's likely I'll be posted abroad soon after Christmas, so...'

He forced a bright smile and, before either Miles or Charlotte could make any comment, added, 'We're going to make it a good one, especially for little Jen.' Seeing their subdued faces, he glanced from one to the other. 'What? What is it?'

Charlotte sighed and moved to kiss his cheek, whilst Miles held out his hand to shake his son's. Drawing Philip into the morning room whilst Charlotte sent for tea, he told Philip about Dot Mercer's visit.

'I doubt we'll be able to hold out for ever. She was very determined and–' he sighed heavily – 'she's the girl's mother.'

'Then let's do our best to make it a memorable Christmas for her.' Philip glanced at Charlotte as he added softly, 'It's what Georgie would have wanted us to do.'

To everyone's amazement, Philip was the 'life and soul' of Christmas. Ben hadn't been able to get leave, so it was Philip who took Jenny out that afternoon to collect holly and ivy to decorate the house. Then in the evening he commandeered everyone into helping with the decorating of the

473

Christmas tree in the hall. And just before Jenny's bedtime, he suggested she should ask Mrs Beddows for a mince pie for Father Christmas and a carrot for his reindeers.

'We'll put them near the tree in the hall. He'll be sure to find them there.'

'Whatever made you think of doing that?' Charlotte asked. 'What a lovely idea.'

'One of the lads at camp was talking about his kids and it's what they do.' For a brief moment, his eyes were haunted. 'Poor feller. He was posted abroad last week. He'll not get home for Christmas.'

Just after midnight, Philip dressed up in a red dressing gown and cotton wool beard and crept into Jenny's bedroom with an armful of presents to fill the pillowcase that the excited little girl had hung on the end of her bed. And he was up at six o'clock the following morning, grinning from ear to ear as Jenny woke the whole household with her cries of 'He's been! He's been! *And* 'ee's eaten the mince pie.'

'Who'd have thought it?' Miles murmured as they watched Philip kneeling on the bedroom floor helping Jenny open her presents. 'It's as if–'

He stopped, not wanting to bring sadness to the moment, but Charlotte added softly, 'Yes, it's as if Georgie's here, isn't it? That's just what he'd've been doing.'

Christmas Day and Boxing Day passed all too quickly with noisy games and such a wonderful array of food that Charlotte wondered if Mrs Beddows had links to the black market.

Miles threw back his head and laughed. 'I don't

think so, my dear, though I wouldn't put it past Brewster. No, Charlotte, she's been holding secret meetings with Mary and Peggy for weeks.' He chuckled as he added, 'She's become a real country woman and revels in learning your ways.'

Charlotte was about to ask him if he had any regrets about moving to the country all those years ago, but at that moment, Jenny grabbed his hand and pulled him into a game of hide and seek through the rambling house.

'You too, Charlotte,' she insisted. And neither of them could refuse – even if they'd wanted to.

As he left on the morning after Boxing Day, Philip put his arms round Charlotte's waist. 'Charlotte, thank you for a lovely Christmas.'

'Thank *you*, Philip. You – you've been wonderful.' She kissed him and then, drawing back a little, murmured, 'Please, take care of yourself.'

For a brief moment, the same haunted look she had seen in Georgie's eyes was in Philip's. 'I'll try,' he said huskily and turned away abruptly.

He swung Jenny high into the air, making her squeal with delight, before setting her down again and shaking his father's hand.

And then he, too, was gone.

There were two serious air raids over Lynthorpe during January and February 1941, killing at least two residents. Soon after news of this had spread, the moment they'd all dreaded came when they saw Mr Tomkins riding up the drive on his bicycle.

Jenny ran and, for once, Miles and Charlotte let her go, preparing to face Mr Tomkins together.

475

He dismounted from his bicycle, leaned it against the pillar at the foot of the steps, and climbed to the front door. Miles opened it.

'I'm sorry,' Mr Tomkins said at once as he stepped inside. 'The girl's mother's demanding we send Jenny back. She heard about the air raids here. One of the other evacuee children who comes from the same neighbourhood as Jenny wrote home and Dot got to hear about it. She's saying the girl's no safer here now than she would be in London. Her argument is that at least they've got the Underground to shelter in.' He sighed. 'And – in a way – you've got to agree with her. We've nothing like that here. Even an Anderson isn't quite the same, is it?'

Grim faced, Miles nodded. 'Then I shall take her home myself.'

'Oh, I don't know–' Mr Tomkins began, but whatever he'd been going to say was cut short by Miles saying firmly, 'That's the only way I'll let her go. I want to know she's going to be all right. If she isn't,' he glared at the inoffensive man who was only trying to do the duty that had been imposed upon him, 'then I shall bring her back here and no one – no one – will be able to stop me.'

This time, even Jenny was helpless in the face of her mother's demands. Backed by the authorities now, Dot held the trump card. She was the child's mother.

'She's better off back where she belongs,' was Osbert's only comment, but he was alone in his thinking. Everyone else in the district had taken the little girl to their hearts and they were all sorry to see her go.

Miles and Charlotte organized a farewell party for her. Since many of the children had returned home, lessons at the manor had ceased. The school now had room for the few evacuees still left, Jenny amongst them. But Charlotte invited all the children who'd had lessons at the manor, together with those in Jenny's class at school. Miss Parker, the Warrens and Mary and Edward came too, but Osbert refused to attend. 'Such a fuss over a grubby little city urchin.'

Mary and Mrs Beddows had combined their resources and made as many treats as rations would allow for the children. All the guests played rowdy games on the lawn, led by Miles and, at the end of the afternoon, as they waved everyone 'goodbye', Jenny slipped her hand into his.

'That was a lovely party. I just wish Georgie'd been here.'

Charlotte felt a lump in her throat and tears prickle her eyes. When Miles did not answer the child, she knew he was feeling just the same as she was.

How she missed Georgie every minute of every day. And now they were to lose the child who'd brought sunshine into their lives and helped to ease the pain of their loss.

'Do you want me to come too?' Charlotte asked the following morning – the day that Jenny had to return home. By poignant coincidence, the date was 1 March and would have been Georgie's twenty-first birthday.

Miles shook his head and Charlotte felt hurt.

He didn't want her with him, she thought. Didn't want – or need – her support. But his next words lessened her pain, though only a little.

'I want to spare you having to leave her with – with *them*,' he said bitterly. 'I'm not even sure I'm going to be able to do it.'

'Then let me–'

'No, Charlotte,' he snapped. 'I have to do this.'

He turned away from her and Charlotte watched him go with tears in her eyes, feeling rejected yet again.

Jenny clung to her when the time for parting came and sobbed noisily. Charlotte could no longer hold back the tears that flooded down her face. Perhaps, after all, Miles was right. She wasn't able to hide her distress now and leaving the girl in London would be even worse.

'Promise you'll write to us, Jenny.'

Against Charlotte's shoulder, which was already wet with her tears, the girl nodded.

Charlotte watched them go until they were out of sight, then she turned and headed for her studio, but even here she could find no comfort. Not today. Jenny's childish paintings littered the floor and Charlotte couldn't bring herself to tidy them away. As for painting herself, which usually gave her such solace, she hadn't even the heart for that.

She retraced her steps downstairs and, putting on a warm coat and sturdy boots, she went out for a walk. She headed towards the sea bank, where she sat down and allowed the tears to flow for Georgie, for Jenny and even for herself because she couldn't give her beloved Miles what

478

he most desired, a daughter. And now he'd lost the closest thing he'd ever had to that.

He'd lost the little girl who'd found her way into both their hearts.

Miles telephoned that evening to say that he couldn't get home that night and would stay in the city.

'Was it – bad?' she asked tentatively, not wanting to rub salt in the raw wound, but needing to know.

'Worse than you could possibly imagine,' he said tartly and rang off quickly.

The following day Charlotte waited restlessly for Miles's return, watching the driveway from the window of his study. She wanted to greet him the moment he returned. Her heart leapt as she saw movement at the end of the driveway. But it was not Miles returning.

It was a telegraph boy riding solemnly towards the house.

Sixty-One

The telegram was addressed to Miles. Charlotte bit her lip, fingering it, not knowing what to do. She was frightened to open it and yet afraid not to do so.

At her elbow, Wilkins said, 'The master would want you to open it, madam, I'm sure.'

Charlotte took a deep breath and slit open the

thin, folded sheet. She read the words with growing dread.

'*...Regret to inform you Philip Thornton seriously wounded...*' There followed a telephone number for further information.

'It's Master Philip. He – he's been wounded.'

'Do you wish me to obtain the number for you, madam?' Wilkins prompted gently.

Charlotte bit her lip. 'No – no. I'll wait for Mr Thornton. He – he should be the one to telephone.'

'Of course, madam. Would you like me to get Brewster to drive you to the station? Perhaps you'd like to meet the train?'

But again Charlotte shook her head. She couldn't bear to give Miles yet more bad news in such a public place. 'No – no. It'd be best for him to get home first.'

'Very good, madam.'

She had to wait another two hours before she saw Miles walking up the driveway. She went to the front door and waited for him to reach her. She had the telegram in her hand and he knew at once that it bore bad news.

He gained the top step and leaned wearily against the door jamb. 'Which one is it this time?'

'It's Philip – he's been badly wounded. There's a number to ring.'

With a supreme effort, Miles pushed himself upright and walked, shoulders hunched, towards the study. Charlotte followed him, watching him with worried eyes as he sank into the chair behind the desk, reached for the telephone and motioned to her to hand him the telegram.

Wilkins entered the study quietly and set down a tray with sandwiches and tea. Charlotte nodded her thanks and the manservant left the room, closing the door discreetly behind him.

When, after what seemed an age, Miles replaced the receiver, he sat a moment with his head in his hands. At last he raised his eyes, bloodshot with weariness, to look up at her.

'He's in hospital, but there's nothing they can do for him except try to alleviate the pain as much as they can. He's very badly shot up and–' He buried his face in his hands and his huge shoulders shook.

Charlotte hurried round the desk and put her arms about him. He turned and buried his face in her neck, weeping unashamedly.

A little later, when he was calmer, they drank the tea though the sandwiches lay untouched. 'I'll hire a special ambulance, and a nurse – that one you had for your father, if she can come. We'll bring him home. He – he'd want to be here, I know.'

Charlotte wasn't so sure, but she said nothing as Miles went on. 'I'll get the best doctors, the best surgeons. Surely, there's something that can be done'

Still Charlotte remained silent. She doubted the medical people would allow Philip to be moved if he was so seriously injured. But she was wrong. Desperate for beds, the hospital was only too glad to release Philip into his father's care.

On the afternoon that he was carried into the manor and up the stairs to his bedroom, the sight of the young man's ashen face shocked Charlotte. Later, when Nurse Monty gave her permission and they were allowed to see him, some colour had returned to his cheeks, but he was thin and obviously in dreadful pain in spite of the morphine the nurse had administered. He reached out his arms to them both and they each took one of his hands and sat on either side of the bed.

'I'm – so – sorry.' It was an effort to speak and at once Charlotte shushed him and bade him rest. 'You'll soon be stronger. Now you're home.'

He smiled thinly. 'Dear Charlotte,' he whispered, 'ever the optimist, but I'm sorry to say that this time' – he managed a wry smile – 'I'm not pretending.'

Tears filled her eyes as she squeezed his hand gently, but she could find no words.

Philip closed his eyes and slept, but they remained sitting beside him until the nurse shooed them away. They left him reluctantly, knowing that every moment with him was precious.

'I suppose,' Miles said carefully as they sat together in the growing dusk, the first time they had found a little peace in the flurry of the last few days, 'we should let your father come to see him. Does he know yet?'

Charlotte shook her head. 'I haven't told him. What with Jenny going and – and then hearing about Philip...' Her voice trailed away. There was silence between them until at last she said tentatively, 'You – you've never told me about Jenny and – and how things were.'

Miles sighed and ran his hand through his hair.

482

'It was awful. They live in a dirty, dilapidated back street. Kids were playing in the roadway, kicking a tin can about. Oh Charlotte, I wanted to gather them *all* up and bring them home – every last one of them.'

'And Jenny? Was she – all right when you left?'

Miles shrugged. 'I suppose so. Her mother certainly seemed to have made an effort. She'd got her some clothes – not new, but I wouldn't blame the woman for that. Times are really tough for them down there, what with all the Blitz damage and the rationing. But even Arthur had bought her some toys. And, surprisingly, a few books, too. Mind you,' Miles allowed himself a wry grin, '"bought" might not be quite the right word for how he came by them.'

'I hope they'll let her draw and paint. I let her take a set of paints and brushes with her. And some of my paper, though she insisted on leaving her paintings here, all except one of the beach – like the one she – she did for Georgie.' Charlotte stopped. The tears were choking her. So much sadness. First losing Georgie and then Jenny being forced to leave them and now Philip, for whom there was little hope. They would have to stand helplessly by and watch him die. The best they could do was try to keep him out of pain and to be beside him until...

Breaking the long silence at last, Miles said, 'I think you should ask Philip if he wants to see your father and then let Osbert know. After all, he – might want to change his will.'

'I don't want him to do that,' Charlotte said at once. 'It would seem very cruel to Philip. No –

483

no, I don't want that.'

Miles touched her face gently. 'My dear, dear Charlotte. Always putting others before yourself.'

If only, she thought, I really was his 'dear, dear Charlotte'.

Miraculously, over the next few days, Philip seemed to grow a little stronger. His appetite improved though he still ate like a bird. He was drowsy, yet his nights were restless and filled with nightmares.

'That's the side effect of the morphine,' Nurse Monty told them. 'But without it...'

Miles asked Dr Bennet, the young doctor who had replaced Dr Markham, to arrange for a specialist to visit. 'Surely there's something they could do?'

Dr Bennet eyed Miles shrewdly. 'You're right to want to explore every avenue. It's only natural, and I will see that we get the very best to give their opinion, but I should warn you against holding out much hope. Philip himself knows the score. I've talked to him. His injuries are such that his organs are failing, Mr Thornton. With your love and care he'll live a few weeks – maybe even months – but they can't give him new kidneys, liver and a whole string of intestines. My dear fellow, I'm being blunt, but I'm not one to give out false hope to anyone. If folk can't take the truth from me, then they'd better find themselves another doctor.' He paused and then said soberly, 'To be honest, Mr Thornton, I don't know how he's survived this long. Sheer willpower, I shouldn't wonder. I think he just wanted to get home – to be with you all for the short time he has left. Anyway, I'll get in touch with my colleagues. You shall have a second opinion. A third and fourth, if you wish.'

The young doctor was certainly from the same mould as his predecessor and well liked by his patients for it. He had a similar bluff, no-nonsense manner, yet he was kindly and caring, too. And he was as good as his word; two consultants came to the manor to examine Philip, a week after each other, but could not give any better a diagnosis than Dr Bennet had done.

'No more, Father. I've accepted the inevitable and so should you. And now,' Philip grinned weakly, 'you'd better let Mr Crawford come. I've a few things I want to say to him.'

Charlotte rode alone to Buckthorn Farm to break the news of Philip's dreadful injuries to her father.

At first Osbert ranted and raved and accused Miles of not trying hard enough to find medical attention for the boy. 'There must be someone somewhere who could do something.'

'Dr Bennet–'

'Bah – what does he know? He's still wet behind the ears.'

'We could ask Dr Markham, if you–'

'That country yokel. I never did like him.'

Charlotte sighed. 'We've had the best – the very best – specialists visit, but sadly they all say the same. There's nothing that can be done.'

'I'll see the boy myself. I'll rouse him. He'll make the effort for me.'

'You'll do no such thing, Father,' Charlotte

snapped. 'I won't allow you to upset him.'

Osbert glared at her. '*You* won't allow it. Who do you think *you* are, all of a sudden? Just because Thornton married you, you think you're someone now, don't you? Well, you're nobody, miss, let me tell you.' He shook his fist in her face. 'You can't even give me a grandson!'

It was a cruel jibe, but Charlotte stood her ground. Her father no longer had the power to rule her life or to hurt her with his barbs. Life was dealing her the bitterest of blows: Georgie was lost, Jenny was gone, and Philip was facing death. Osbert's cruelty in the face of all that was nothing.

Of Ben, she dared not even think. If anything were to happen to Ben, too, then... She blocked the thought and dragged her mind back to the present. Taking a deep breath, she said, 'You'll come on condition you don't upset him – or not at all.'

Of course her father came to the manor, as Charlotte had known he would. She'd no wish to stay in the room with them, but she asked the nurse to stay within earshot. 'If you hear anything you're not happy with, please send him packing. And if you have any trouble, Mr Thornton is in his study. He'll be there until he knows my father has left. Just in case. If you need me, I'll be in my studio.'

Monty nodded and smiled. 'I think I can handle Mr Crawford. I've had plenty of practice, remember?'

The two women smiled at each other before

Charlotte gave the nurse a brief nod and went upstairs to shut herself away at the top of the house. She was no longer frightened of her father as she had once been, but she was wary of him.

But the visit passed off peacefully and Charlotte was not even aware that Osbert had left until Kitty came to fetch her. 'Mr Crawford's gone, ma'am, and Master Philip is asking for you.'

'Oh dear, is he-?'

'Nothing's wrong, ma'am. He's fine – well, as fine as the poor man can be, but he says he wants to talk to you.'

As soon as she sat down at the side of Philip's bed, he said, 'I'm sorry, Charlotte, I tried my damnedest, but he's a stubborn old goat, isn't he? I tried to get him to agree to change his will leaving Buckthorn Farm to you, but he refused.'

'Philip, I don't need the farm. Not now. You should write a letter making *your* wishes clear.'

'Once I'm gone,' he murmured, seeming to ignore her remark, 'he might reconsider.'

Charlotte said nothing. She believed her father would bequeath his farm to anyone he could think of, just so long as it wasn't his daughter. But she said nothing.

'I wanted you to have it, Charlotte. I owe you such a lot.'

She was startled. 'Me?'

'Yes, you. It was thanks to you I ever got up out of this bed and walked again. But for you, I might have been here all this time.'

Charlotte's tears flowed. 'Perhaps it'd have been better if you had been. At least, you'd have

487

been safe.'

'But I'd've had no life. No life at all. Thanks to you, I qualified, had a few years as a lawyer, which I loved...' Then he grinned cheekily. 'Had a few girls, and I've fought for my country. No, Charlotte,' he squeezed her hand, 'I don't regret a moment. In fact, I'm grateful you gave me that chance. That I'm to die now, well, I'm not the only one. There are thousands of families mourning their sons. I just hope old Ben keeps himself safe...'

With those last words, he drifted into sleep.

It seemed that Philip's prayers for his brother were answered. News came in a long letter from Ben himself the very next morning that he'd been awarded the George Cross and was also being promoted:

I've been with a bomb disposal unit for some time now. I didn't tell you, because I knew you'd both worry. Anyway, I was wounded in the leg as the result of an incident. It's not serious, but it means I can't continue in bomb disposal. I'm being allowed to stay in the army. They seem to think I'll be useful training new recruits!

'What did he do?' Charlotte asked.

Miles continued to scan the thin sheets of paper. 'He doesn't say. That's typical of Ben, isn't it? But it must have been something incredibly courageous.'

'If he's to train recruits, will he be safe?' Charlotte hardly dared to voice the question.

Miles nodded cautiously. 'Relatively safe, I hope.' They stared at each other, appalled to think of the danger Ben had been in every day and they hadn't even known.

When they told Philip the news, he smiled. 'Good old Ben. Who'd've thought that the quiet one of the three of us would be decorated? Rather appropriate, don't you think, the *George* Cross? Old Georgie would have been tickled pink.'

The thought brought tears to Charlotte's eyes; a mixture of pride and heartache.

She sat beside Philip's bedside talking when he woke or keeping silent whilst he slept. But as long as he clutched her hand and, quite literally, held her there, she stayed.

'Charlotte?' He woke suddenly, his eyes wide.

'Yes, dear. I'm here.'

He let out a long sigh and she felt him squeeze her hand. 'Can I ask you something?'

'Of course.'

'I don't want to hurt your feelings, but...' He stopped and Charlotte leaned closer, finishing his sentence softly. 'You'd like the portrait of your mother to hang on the wall opposite your bed, so you can see her?'

Slowly, he turned his head to look at her. 'How – how did you know?'

'I just felt that you'd like it.'

'And – and you don't mind?'

'Of course I don't.' She bit her lip and then added hesitantly, 'And would – would you like one of Georgie beside it?'

'You've painted one?'

Charlotte nodded. 'After that first one of your father, I've painted you all as you've grown.'

'Ben?'

'Yes, Ben too.'

'And – and me? Surely you haven't painted me?'

Now she laughed aloud. 'Of course I have. Why wouldn't I?'

'Because – oh, just because...'

Now it was Charlotte who squeezed his hand gently.

Sixty-Two

'Will you pose for me in your uniform and your medal?' Charlotte asked Ben when he came home on compassionate leave to visit Philip.

'I couldn't. I'd be far too embarrassed.'

'Then may I at least see your uniform and the medal and will you tell me how you'd wear it? Please, Ben.' Her voice dropped. 'It's for Philip.'

Ben smiled sadly. 'You're a crafty little minx, Charlotte Thornton. You know I can't refuse if you put it like that.'

Charlotte widened her gaze innocently. 'But it's the truth. He wants one of all of us. Even me.' She pulled a face. 'Though I'm not very happy about doing a self-portrait.'

'Then get Father to ask Felix to do one of you. I bet he would.'

Charlotte stared at him, not sure if he meant

Felix would paint one or his father would ask his friend.

'Er – well – yes,' she murmured.

Ben agreed to sit for her and they spent a few companionable hours in her studio, talking when the mood was right or in comfortable silence whilst she worked. When the portrait was finished, they all assembled in Philip's room to hang the new picture beside those of Louisa, Miles and Georgie.

Philip pulled himself up in the bed, wincing as he did so. 'That's wonderful, Charlotte. What a handsome fellow you are, Ben. I'm proud of you, old boy.' His voice shook a little. Then he cleared his throat and said with greater firmness, 'But there are still at least two people missing. You, Charlotte. I must have all of you. And Jenny? What about little Jenny? She was part of this family for a while.'

'I've got one of her – in fact, two or three. You could have a look at them and choose which you like best. And,' Charlotte added shyly, 'I've done another of your father recently. Would you like to see that too?'

'Aha, an updated version with my grey hair and wrinkles, I expect.' Miles laughed.

Half an hour later, two more pictures had been hung on the wall opposite the end of Philip's bed.

'There still isn't one of you, Charlotte,' Philip said.

She turned to him, forcing a teasing laughter into her voice. 'Now, what would you want a picture of me for? I'm here every day. All the time. In fact, you hardly get a minute's peace from me.'

Philip closed his eyes with a sigh, but there was a smile on his lips as he said, 'Father, talk to her, will you? I want all of you there. And can you fix a light so that it shines on them. You see, in the night, when I'm awake...' He drifted off to sleep, but they knew what he meant. He spent many long, wakeful and uncomfortable hours in the night. He'd insisted – no, demanded – that none of the family should sit with him and lose their sleep, so only the nurse ever kept him company during the lonely hours of darkness. But if he could see his family, feel them close by, especially Georgie and even Jenny, then it would bring him comfort.

'Have you really never done a self-portrait?' Ben asked Charlotte softly.

As Charlotte shook her head, Miles put his arm about her shoulders. 'She's far too modest, and I doubt she'd do herself justice if she did. I'll get in touch with old Felix. Perhaps he'd come for a weekend and do one of you. He could use your studio. I'm sure he'd do it as a special favour.'

'There's someone else...'

They all turned towards the bed as Philip, rousing himself momentarily, murmured, 'Alfie. I want to see Alfie.'

'What do you think he meant?' Charlotte asked as the three of them went back downstairs, leaving Philip to rest. 'Does he want us to fetch Alfie here – in person – or does he mean he wants me to do a painting of him?' Since the birth of his son, Philip had had little to do with either Alfie or Lily.

'I don't know,' Miles said. 'Could you do one? A painting of Alfie?'

'Yes.' Charlotte was confident. 'I see him often enough and besides, I can always make an excuse to visit their cottage if I need to.' Eddie, Lily and their growing family still lived in the Warrens' former home.

'I think he meant both,' Ben put in quietly. 'I think he wants a painting, yes, but I also think he wants to see Alfie in person.' He paused and then asked, 'Do you think they've told the boy the truth? How old is he now, by the way?'

Charlotte shook her head slowly. 'He'll be fourteen at the end of June and, no, I don't know they have told him. Lily told me not so long ago they keep putting it off because they find it difficult. But still, there might be a way.'

'*Now* what is that pretty head of yours scheming?' Miles smiled.

Charlotte tapped him on the nose. 'Never you mind.' She turned to Ben. 'Could you find out from Philip if you're right? It might be better coming from you.'

Ben nodded. 'I'll go back up. Sit with him until he wakes and bring the conversation round.' He looked at his father. 'May I tell him you'll get in touch with Felix? That would be a way to open up the topic again.'

'Of course. I'll telephone him at once.'

A little later, Miles sought out Charlotte. 'He's coming at the weekend. He'll be glad to get away, he says. London had a dreadful bombing raid last night and his gallery was badly damaged. I was lucky to get through on the telephone...' Fear

493

haunted his eyes. 'Oh Charlotte, I do hope little Jenny is all right.'

Felix came the very next weekend, arriving in a flurry and throwing his arm round each one of them in turn, his beaming smile only sobering when he stood beside Philip's bed and looked down upon the broken body of the fine young man he'd known. Then he turned to the paintings on the wall, studying each one.

'Ah, she has such talent, your stepmother,' he murmured. 'Such a waste.'

Philip lifted his head. 'A waste? What d'you mean?'

'All those years when she was young she was denied the chance to learn and flourish. It's a miracle she paints as well as she does. But then, no amount of learning replaces genuine inborn talent. But if only she could have studied with the best...'

'Could she still?'

Felix gave a hearty laugh and turned to look at him.

'My dear, dear boy, Charlotte would never leave your father to go to study in London or anywhere else. She's devoted to him. "Besotted" might be a better word.'

'You mean – you mean she really loves him?'

'Oh my goodness, yes. Haven't you seen it in her eyes? At the mere mention of his name, her eyes light up and when they're together, her gaze follows him around the room.'

'Really.' He lay back as Felix came and sat down beside the bed. 'And my father? Does he love her?'

'Ah,' Felix sighed. 'Now that is a little more difficult to say. He loves her, yes, but I'm not sure it's in quite the same way.' His glance turned slowly to rest on the portrait of Louisa Thornton. 'There's always the memory of your mother, you see.'

'Poor Charlotte,' Philip murmured, and as he drifted into sleep once more, he heard Felix say, 'Poor Charlotte indeed. The only thing she wants out of life is to make your father happy and to give him his heart's desire. And even that is denied her.'

Sixty-Three

Felix promised to stay until the paintings were completed, working each day with Charlotte in her studio.

'At last,' he cried as he entered the room on the first morning. 'I am to be allowed to work in the room I created. What joy!'

Smiling, Charlotte sat at her own easel to work on the portrait she'd already begun of Alfie.

Ben, with his usual gentle tact, had found out that Philip did want Alfie to visit. Going to the cottage, Charlotte had learned that, no, Alfie had still not yet been told the truth as to the identity of his biological father. Instead, both Eddie and Lily, who'd no wish to keep a dying man from seeing his son, generously agreed that Alfie should visit the manor on the pretext of sitting for Mrs Thornton.

'I'm running out of subjects,' she told the boy, crossing her fingers behind her back at the half-lie.

'Thought you'd prefer to do our Lizzie. She's much prettier.'

'Well, maybe I will, when she's older, but I want to start with you.'

The boy visited the manor each day for a week and whilst he posed for Charlotte, she, in turn, was being painted by Felix. Though Alfie was a little in awe of the artist from London at the start, Felix soon charmed the boy and the sessions in the studio were full of laughter and teasing.

On the fourth day, Felix played his part in the scheme. Late in the afternoon when the natural light was fading, he threw down his brush and cried, 'Enough! Work is over for the day. Come, Charlotte, you must stop, too, and let this poor boy ease his aching muscles.'

Charlotte set aside her brushes and stood up, stretching her back.

'But before you go, dear boy,' Felix said, putting his arm about Alfie's shoulder, 'I want to show you just how good the portrait of you is going to be. She's painted pictures of all the family. They're hanging in Philip's room.'

The boy stopped. 'I can't go in there, mister. Me mam said he's very ill.'

'He'll be pleased to see you,' Felix insisted. 'He gets few visitors and a new face will brighten his day. You're a big lad now,' Felix added softly. 'Living on a farm, you understand about life and death. And you understand about the war too, don't you?'

'Well, I know what's happening, but I don't understand *why*.'

'Nor do a lot of us, dear boy, but we must all try to do our bit. And if your bit is to brave seeing an injured soldier and to bring him what comfort you can, then you'll do it, now won't you?'

Alfie was thoughtful for a moment, as if plucking up courage. When he nodded, Charlotte let out a sigh of relief and smiled at Felix, thanking him with her eyes.

'Come along, then, dear boy, you really must see these magnificent portraits and afterwards, well, perhaps you could have a word with Philip.'

So it became a routine that each day when work on their pictures was over, Alfie would go to Philip's room and spend half an hour with him.

'Me mam's sent her best wishes,' Charlotte heard Alfie say as she closed the door quietly and left them alone. To her joy, the boy continued to visit Philip even after he was no longer required to sit for Charlotte.

'Charlotte! Charlotte! Come quickly!' Miles's voice resounded from the hallway, reaching to every corner of the house. Even in the studio, they heard him.

Charlotte's heart skipped a beat and then began to thud painfully. Her eyes wide, she exchanged a frightened glance with Felix. Oh no, not more bad news.

She ran downstairs, whilst Felix hovered anxiously on the landing. At the foot of the stairs,

Miles was waving a piece of paper and smiling jubilantly. 'He's alive! Georgie's alive!'

Charlotte cried out with joy and launched herself from the third step into his outstretched arms. He swung her round, laughing and shouting, 'He's alive. Georgie's alive.'

The household staff, hearing the commotion came running. Mrs Beddows and Kitty from the kitchen and even Wilkins, always sedate and controlled, was flustered momentarily, beaming his relief and delight at the news. On the landing, Felix closed his eyes in thankfulness. How good it was to see his dear friends receive good news for once.

'Champagne, Wilkins. For everyone. And bring a bottle to Philip's room. We must tell him at once.'

They mounted the stairs, hand in hand. At the top, Felix tried awkwardly to embrace them both at once, his eyes shining with tears.

Philip was sleeping fitfully. His face was flushed and his eyes dark with pain.

'Do you think we should tell him?' Charlotte whispered as the three of them tiptoed into his room.

'I–'

'Tell me what?' Philip asked, his eyes fluttering open.

Miles couldn't contain his excitement, his relief, any longer. He moved to the side of the bed and put his hand gently on Philip's shoulder. His voice husky with emotion, he said, 'Georgie is alive.'

Philip closed his eyes on a long sigh and

whispered a heartfelt, 'Thank God.'

There was a gentle tap on the door and Wilkins entered the room carrying a tray and beaming. 'The staff send their congratulations, sir. This is wonderful news.'

Philip opened his eyes and, wincing a little, pulled himself up in the bed. 'Tell everyone to come to my room, Wilkins. Let's have a real celebration.'

A while later, everyone gathered in Philip's bedroom to drink champagne. Mrs Beddows and Kitty giggled at the unexpected treat and the bubbles tickling their noses. When things had calmed down a little and the staff had returned to their duties, leaving the four of them alone again, Charlotte asked, 'Where is he? Is he coming home?'

Miles's face sobered suddenly. He shook his head. 'Maybe we shouldn't be celebrating so soon, but I was so overjoyed to hear he's alive when – when...'

Charlotte moved to his side and linked her arm through his. 'Of course we should celebrate. It's wonderful news. The very best. But – where is he?'

'In a prisoner of war camp.'

Charlotte stared at him. 'But – but is he all right? I mean, is he safe?'

Miles pulled a face. 'I don't expect conditions will be ideal, but he's probably safer there than flying a fighter plane.'

Charlotte was thoughtful. 'Can we write to him? Send food parcels?'

'I don't know. I'll get in touch with the authoriies. The Red Cross, perhaps.'

'Is it a German POW camp?' Philip asked.

'I believe it's a place called Colditz.'

Philip raised his head, stared at his father for a moment, and then began to laugh.

Mystified, Miles and Charlotte glanced at each other and then looked at Philip questioningly.

'Dad, that's the safest place in Germany at the moment. It's a castle where they send unruly prisoners. All the escapees end up in Colditz Castle. Good old Georgie, he must have been giving the Germans a right run-around to end up there.'

'You mean, he's been trying to escape, Phil?' Miles asked.

'Several times, probably. It's the place they send POWs who *keep* trying to escape. Good old Georgie.' Philip raised his glass again. 'Give 'em hell, little brother.'

'I must go to London,' Miles said suddenly the following morning at breakfast.

Felix and Charlotte exchanged a puzzled glance.

'To see the authorities, you mean? About Georgie?'

'Well, perhaps, but I want to tell Jenny myself. She adored Georgie. I want her to know that he's alive.'

'Of course.' Charlotte smiled. 'Would you like me to come with you?'

'If you'd like to. But what about old Felix here? He's our guest...'

'Goodness, don't worry about me, my dears. I

still have a lot of work to do on my painting. I shall be quite happy. And I'll keep Philip company too, when he's feeling up to it. No, no, you two go. And take my key. You can stay at my flat overnight, if you have to. Travelling is abominable just now.'

'We must take some food for Jenny's family,' Charlotte said, getting up from the table. 'I'll go and see Mrs Beddows.'

As Felix had predicted, their journey was fraught with delays and the carriages were packed with troops. But everyone was good-humoured and the soldiers readily gave up a seat for Charlotte.

At last they arrived in the city and it was already mid-afternoon by the time the taxi cab dropped them off at the end of the street where Miles knew Jenny lived.

'Bombing's not so bad now, mate,' the friendly taxi driver told them as he handed Miles his change. 'But you'll see for yourself how bad we had it in the Blitz. Let's hope it don't all start up again. It's like this all over the city.'

He nodded down the street where Jenny lived. 'You can see for yourself. That happened earlier this month. They reckon there was a hundred thousand bombs dropped on poor ol' London in one night. Poor devils down this street got it bad. Direct hit on those houses in the middle of the street.'

'What?' Miles's face paled and he turned around to look. 'Oh no – no!'

The taxi driver was pulling away from the kerb, leaving them standing on the uneven pavement.

Sensing Miles's anxiety, Charlotte linked her arm through his. 'Let's go and see before we start to panic.'

'But – but their house is in the centre of the row. Oh Charlotte...' His voice was hoarse with unshed tears.

They walked down the rubble-strewn street, appalled to see huge piles of debris where once a house – someone's home – had been.

Suddenly Miles stopped in front of a mound of bricks and shattered glass. A door lay drunkenly on its side and amongst the rubbish they could see torn curtains, a table, a broken chair, and even shattered pots and dented pans.

'Is it – is it *their* house?' Charlotte whispered.

'I – I don't know. I can't quite get my bearings. I only came that one time and Jenny led me here, so... There were children playing in the street.'

But today there were no children anywhere.

'It's number fifteen,' Charlotte ventured. 'That's where we've been writing.'

'Ah, yes, of course, then...?' He glanced around and saw a woman climbing over the rubble further down the street. 'Let's ask her. She might know.'

They picked their way carefully towards the stranger, who was bending over, picking up bricks and discarding them, obviously trying to uncover some of her precious possessions – anything that she could salvage.

'Excuse me...'

The woman looked up at the sound of Miles's voice. She didn't smile and Charlotte was shocked by the look of defeat and hopelessness in her eyes.

'I'm sorry to intrude,' Miles said gently, 'but we're looking for number fifteen.'

The woman's face was grim as she pointed to the ground beneath her feet. 'This is it. I lived at number seventeen – right next door.' She scrambled over the rubble towards them. Miles held out his hand to help her step down on to the pavement.

'Ta, mister.' On firm ground, she glanced from one to the other. 'You want to know what happened?'

Charlotte nodded.

'Took a direct hit, our houses did. Mine and Dot's. Well, what was Dot's. Rest of the street–' she glanced behind her and waved her arm – 'damaged, o' course, but most of 'em's still standing. Still, we was lucky in a way. No one was killed in this street.'

Charlotte's heart lifted. 'So – where are they? Where's Jenny and her mother?'

The woman shrugged. 'Gawd knows. Done a moonlight weeks back. Just after Jenny came back from the country.' She glanced at them, searching their faces keenly. 'Are you the folks the little lass stayed wiv?'

When Charlotte nodded, the woman actually smiled, though it was a sad, wistful smile. 'Eh, fancy that. She never stopped talking about you. About the fields and the beach and how you let her paint pretty pictures. She loved it up there wiv you, she did.' Her face clouded. 'But Dot got a bee in her bonnet that we were thinking she was a bad mother 'cos all the other kids'd come home and hers hadn't. Silly cow,' she added with feeling. 'If my lads'd had a nice place with you, I'd've left 'em there till all this bloody lot's over. Hadn't got the sense she was born with, Dot 'adn't. And then she buggers off without a word of goodbye, an' we've lived next door to one another for ten years or more.' She shook her head. 'I blame that feller she took up with. A right spiv, if you ask me. I reckon the law was on his tail and that's why they 'opped it.'

'I should have fought harder to keep Jenny,' Miles murmured heavily. 'But Dot was the girl's mother and–'

'I know,' the woman said with feeling. 'More's the pity. Oh dear – there I go again. Dot was all right in her way, but she was a selfish cow. Everything always had to be what *she* wanted. Even that Arfer had to dance to 'er tune. She should've left the little lass with you. Jen was happy wiv you.'

Miles smiled feebly and said huskily, 'Thank you for that.'

'Have – have you any idea where they've gone?' Charlotte asked.

Again, the woman shook her head. 'Nah, an' if she's still with that Arfer, then I don't want to know. Tried to get my son involved with 'is black market racket, he did. I gave him a clip round the ear.' She laughed and her whole face was suddenly younger and free of worry for a brief moment. 'My son, I mean. Not Arfer, though for two pins I'd have given him a fourpenny one, an' all.'

Charlotte held out the basket of food they'd brought. 'We brought this for Jenny and her

504

mother, but please, we'd like you to have it.'

'That's very kind of you, an' I ain't too proud to say "yes". Not just now, I ain't.'

'Come,' Charlotte said softly to Miles. 'We'd better go.'

'I'm sorry I can't offer you a cup of tea. I would, but...' The woman gestured towards her flattened house.

Miles roused himself. 'Have you somewhere to go? I mean, you and your family could come to us if–'

'Now that's real generous of you, mister. I 'preciate that, I really do. But we'll be all right. We'll tough it out now. Can't last much longer. 'Sides, I need to be here when my old man comes home on leave. An' we've got a good shelter to go to. The Underground. We have a sing-song down there most nights. An' to be honest wiv you, the bombing's not been so bad just lately. Mebbe ol' 'Itler's realized he can't beat us Londoners.'

On that note, they said goodbye and made their way back to the station.

'Do you want to stay at Felix's flat, Miles?' Charlotte asked as they walked, clinging to each other for comfort and support.

'No. It was good of him to offer it, but I just want to get home. If there's a train, I want to get home. Oh Charlotte, where can she be? How can we find her?'

Sixty-Four

'You look a little pale this morning, my dear,' Felix said as they sat together working on the final stages of their two paintings. 'Is the strain getting too much for you?'

It had been a week since they'd returned from London and since then, Miles had shut himself away in his study, hardly eating, hardly speaking and not sleeping well, either. He'd spent hours on the telephone and written countless letters to anyone who might be able to help them locate Jenny. Charlotte often woke in the night to find the place beside her in bed empty. When she crept downstairs, she would find him sitting at his desk, staring at one of the pictures Charlotte had painted of the little girl and which Miles had insisted should hang in his study.

'Will we ever see her again?' he asked repeatedly, but Charlotte was unable to give him a hopeful answer. All she could say was, 'Perhaps we should be grateful they'd left that street. If not...' She left the words unsaid, but even the thought that Jenny was still alive somewhere in the world didn't seem to bring Miles any comfort. He wanted the little girl who'd become like the longed-for daughter here at the manor, safe and well with him. 'I'll never stop looking for her, Charlotte,' he vowed. 'Never.'

Nightly, as she said her prayers as she always

had, Charlotte asked, 'Please, Dear Lord, bring him comfort. He has borne so much sadness, please – if there's any way – let me help him.'

Now, in answer to Felix's question, Charlotte laid aside her brush and sighed. 'Maybe. I've been feeling unwell for a few days, but please, don't say anything to Miles, will you? I'm so worried about him. First, the wonderful news about Georgie, and then finding Jenny had gone and we can't find out where she is. It's too much of a see-saw of emotions for anyone to bear. Even for someone as strong as Miles. He's just devastated. And, of course, poor Philip...'

'My dear girl, Miles has a right to know if you're feeling under the weather. He'd want you to see the doctor.'

'I'm sure it's nothing. I don't want to cause him more worry.'

'I know, I know,' Felix said gently. 'But you should look after yourself, too. Please, go and see the doctor. For me, eh? If it's nothing, then you needn't even tell Miles, but you should go.'

Charlotte smiled at him, trying to quell the queasiness in her stomach. 'I will.'

'Then I'll make sure you do.' He winked broadly at her. 'We'll take a little ride in the pony and trap tomorrow morning by way of the surgery in Ravensfleet.'

When she walked out of Dr Bennet's surgery, Charlotte was in a daze.

Felix could not read the expression on her face. There was something, he could tell, but wisely he asked no questions. Whatever it was, Miles should be the first person she told. They drove home in unaccustomed silence. Even the ebullient Felix could think of nothing to say except the question uppermost in his mind. And that he could not ask.

When she climbed carefully down from the trap, she smiled her thanks and walked slowly up the steps into the house. Felix watched her go with a heavy heart. Sighing, he took the pony and trap round the side of the house to the stable yard, where he whiled away the time petting the horses and talking to the stable lads.

'You know, I've never painted a horse. Perhaps I should try,' he murmured, trying to keep his thoughts away from what was happening in Miles's study at that very moment.

Charlotte opened the door to her husband's study very quietly and, for a few moments, stood watching him seated at his desk. His head was bent over the papers he was reading, his brow creased in concentration. She was pleased to see that at least he was starting to take an interest in something again other than his letters about Jenny. But she wasn't sure just how he would take her news.

Becoming aware of her presence he looked up and began to smile. But then his smile faded. He rose slowly.

'What is it, my dear? Is something wrong? Is it Philip?'

He came swiftly round the end of the desk towards her, holding out his hands.

Charlotte shook her head and said huskily, 'No, no. He was fine when I left.'

She closed the door quietly and then put her hands into his. She stood looking up at him, drinking in every detail of his face – the face that had become so very dear to her.

'Left?' Miles frowned. 'I didn't know you'd gone out. Where've you been?'

'I – I've been into Ravensfleet to see Dr Bennet.'

'Dr–? My dear, are you ill?'

Tears welled in her eyes and spilled down her cheeks, but she was laughing. 'No – no. I'm gloriously, wonderfully well. Oh Miles, I'm – we're – going to have a baby!'

He stared at her, dumbstruck for a moment. Then he whispered hoarsely, 'Pregnant? You're – you're pregnant?'

'Yes – isn't it wonderful?'

But it didn't look as if he shared her joy. She felt his hands holding hers begin to tremble and he was biting down hard on his lower lip.

'Aren't you pleased? It's what we've wanted.' She paused and added uncertainly, 'Isn't it?'

It was certainly what she'd always wanted but now, watching the fleeting emotions on his face, she wasn't so sure about Miles. 'Yes – yes – of course it is, but–'

Her heart seemed to turn over in her breast. 'But – what?'

He drew her into his arms and buried his face against her neck. 'Oh, Charlotte – I'm so afraid. I couldn't bear it if anything happened to you, my love.'

She nestled against him, revelling in his tender

509

words, words and emotions she'd never dared to hope to hear from his lips. She understood why he was afraid for her. He'd lost Louisa through childbirth and he was fearful of it happening again.

'I'll be all right,' she said softly. 'I'm fit and healthy and strong.'

He drew back a little and traced the line of her cheek with a gentle finger. 'But – but you're too old to be having a baby.'

Charlotte chuckled and her eyes sparkled. 'Evidently Mother Nature thinks otherwise.'

'But it could be – dangerous.'

She hugged him. 'Please don't worry so. Don't spoil it, Miles.'

'That's the last thing I want to do, but I'm afraid I can't promise to stop worrying.'

She took his hand. 'Let's go and tell Philip – and Felix. He took me into Ravensfleet but of course I said nothing on the way home. The poor man was bursting to ask questions, I could see. But he didn't.'

Miles began to smile. 'That's not like Felix.'

'No.' Charlotte laughed. 'He showed remarkable restraint.'

They began to climb the stairs, hand in hand, but halfway up Charlotte stopped and turned to face Miles. 'You do think we should tell Philip, don't you? I mean, he – he won't mind, will he?'

Miles reassured her. 'Philip has changed from the resentful young man he was, though I'm sad that it has taken a war and the prospect of death to do it.'

They entered the room together to find him

sitting up in bed reading, looking the best he had done since arriving home. He looked up and smiled. 'What's this? A state visit?'

'You could say that,' Miles said as they sat down on either side of the bed. 'Charlotte has some news for you.'

'The portraits are finished? When can I see them? How long will they take to dry enough to hang?'

'They're nearly ready, but drying thoroughly will take a while, though Felix thinks we can frame them and hang them, if we're very careful.'

'But that's not what she wanted to tell you,' Miles chipped in.

Philip turned enquiring eyes towards Charlotte, who blushed. 'I – we're going to have a baby.'

She held her breath whilst Philip stared at her and then, to her enormous relief, his face broke into a wide grin. 'That's the best possible news I've heard since we heard Georgie was alive. But there's just one thing, Charlotte.'

'What's that?'

'It's got to be a girl!'

The three of them burst out laughing.

Sixty-Five

Over the next few weeks, Philip joked, 'I'm hanging on until your baby's born, Charlotte, and maybe even until old Georgie gives the enemy the slip and comes home.'

'I do hope he won't do anything silly.'

'He might try to escape again – if you call that "silly". Perhaps he'll just turn up on the doorstep one morning.' He chuckled at the thought.

Charlotte sighed. 'I just want him to be safe. It's all I wanted for all of you.'

'I know, I know,' he said softly. 'If he'd just hang on a while longer, I don't think the end will be long coming now.'

Charlotte glanced at him. She knew he was referring to the end of the war, but no doubt he was also thinking of his own end, too. Could he do as he wished and hang on until Georgie came home or until her child was born in six months' time?

The weeks passed and to her infinite sadness, Charlotte began to see a steady decline in Philip's condition. The doctor visited every other day and at Miles's insistence, he kept an eye on Charlotte too.

'She's fit and healthy and remarkably strong,' she heard Dr Bennet say as she showed the doctor into Miles's study after his visit to Philip's room and after having had a chat with her. 'I wish I was as happy about all my mothers-to-be as I am about Charlotte. All that farm work when she was a young lass, I expect,' he added dryly as Charlotte smiled and turned to leave the room. A newcomer to the district, he'd learned about Mrs Thornton's early life at Buckthorn Farm.

She was pulling the door to, when she caught Miles's words. 'I wanted a word with you in private, Doctor. About Charlotte's confinement.'

Outside the door, Charlotte bent closer, hold. her breath and feeling guilty at eavesdroppin. and yet...

'I want you to know my feelings now, whilst I'm rational and not faced with – with an unbearable decision.'

'I understand,' she heard Dr Bennet's calm tones. 'If there should be complications, you mean?' He'd heard that the cause of Miles's first wife's death had been childbirth and he could understand the man's natural anxiety. Especially, given Charlotte's age.

'I want you to know that if there's a choice to be made, then Charlotte's life is to be saved. I – she means everything to me. Everything. I couldn't bear to lose her.'

Charlotte almost gasped aloud and clapped her hand over her mouth to stifle the sound. She'd never thought to hear such words of love and devotion and sacrifice, yes sacrifice. For at their next words she knew for sure.

'You'd forfeit the life of the child in favour of the mother?'

'Yes, I would.'

Softly, the doctor asked, 'Even if it's a girl?' He seemed to know everything and Charlotte realized that Dr Markham must have told the young doctor all about the patients he was taking on.

There was not the slightest hesitation before Miles replied firmly, 'Even if it's a girl.'

Her heart soared. Now she could believe that Miles loved her, truly loved her, as she'd longed for him to do.

'Madam...' Kitty's face appeared round the door of the sitting room one November morning.

Charlotte laid aside the tiny white coat she was knitting, giving it one last, fond touch before she looked up with a smile to say, 'Yes, Kitty, what is it?'

Before she had finished forming the question she could see from the girl's face, that something was wrong.

'It's Mr Philip, ma'am. He – he's asking for you – and the master.'

Charlotte rose at once and hurried as fast as her bulk would allow her to out of the room. As she began to pull herself up the stairs, she asked, 'Where is the master?'

'Out riding, ma'am. He's been gone about half an hour.'

'Send someone to find him. Tell them to go to the beach at Lynthorpe. That's his favourite ride.' She paused at the top of the stairs. 'Is he bad, Kitty?'

The girl nodded. 'Nurse is with him. She's telephoned for the doctor, ma'am.'

Charlotte nodded, unable to speak for the tears stinging her eyes. She blinked and pulled in a deep breath. She mustn't cry, she told herself firmly. She must be strong for Philip – and for Miles.

When she entered the bedroom, the sight of him shocked her. He was obviously in great pain. His face was grey, his cheeks hollow and the suffering in his eyes was unbearable. Sweat glistened on his forehead. Nurse Monty stood at the side of the bed, gently wiping his face. She looked up as Charlotte came into the room. Her solemn expression and her dark eyes told Charlotte that the end was very near.

Philip tried to smile and he held out a trembling hand. 'Sit beside me, Charlotte,' he gasped, his breathing laboured. 'Hold my hand.'

Discreetly, the nurse moved to the other side of the room, where she could not overhear their whispered words, but was still near enough if she was needed.

'Try to rest, my dear,' Charlotte said gently, wiping his forehead with the flannel Nurse Monty had passed to her. 'Save your strength.'

Philip closed his eyes but he opened them again to say, 'No – no. There's no time. There are things I need to say to you. Especially to you, Charlotte.' He paused, summoning up the strength to carry on. 'I haven't always been kind to you and I'm so sorry.'

'Don't, Philip. None of that matters. It never did.'

'It – matters to me. I was a conceited oaf and I'm ashamed. Say you forgive me?'

'Philip – there's nothing to–'

'Please – say it. I need you to say it.'

'Of course, I forgive you with all my heart.'

'I wasn't lovable like Georgie or even our quiet Ben. I was prickly and difficult and – and openly hostile to you, wasn't I?'

'I understood. You were the one who could remember your mother the best. It hurt you to see someone else in what you thought was her place. But I never presumed to do that, Philip.

No one could ever replace Louisa in your father's heart or in yours. Certainly not me.'

'You've done a damned good job,' he rasped with some of his old spirit. 'You've come close. We all adore you, Charlotte, you must know that.' She felt him squeeze her hand. 'Even me – in the end.'

She felt the tears welling again and fought to hide them. Behind her, the door opened and Miles came into the room, still in his riding habit. He strode to the other side of the bed, pulled up a chair, and sat down.

'Hello – Papa.' Philip's use of the name the boys had used in their childhood threatened to be Miles's undoing. But, like Charlotte, he took a deep breath and managed to say gently, 'Son.'

'This is it, then,' Philip whispered. 'I'm so sorry I can't wait to see my little sister and – and to see old Georgie come home.'

'The doctor's on his way. He'll–'

'Papa – he can't work miracles. Let's face it – I need you both to help me face it.'

Miles and Charlotte exchanged a grief-stricken glance.

'Charlotte,' Philip said, 'I want to ask you something. Will you – if your baby's a girl – will you call her Louisa?'

'Philip, you can't ask–' Miles began, but Charlotte held up her hand.

'Of course I will,' she promised. 'I'd be proud to.'

Philip let out a deep sigh and closed his eyes. For a moment, they both thought he'd slipped away, but then his eyes fluttered open again. 'I've

516

written a letter to your father asking him to mak
my son, Alfie, his heir. I don't know if he will, bu
I hope you don't mind, Charlotte. By rights, of
course, he should leave the farm to you.'

'No – no – you did the right thing.'

'But–'

'No "buts", Philip.' She stroked his forehead. 'If
it is left to me, I'll see Alfie gets it.'

'You will?'

'Of course I will.'

'But it should come to you and then, one day,
to your daughter.'

'You're so sure it's going to be a girl, then?'

'Oh yes. It – it has to be – for – for Papa...'

They were to be the last words he ever said. His
voice faded away and he slept. Though they sat
beside him for the remainder of the day, he did
not wake again and as darkness fell, Philip died
peacefully in his own bed with his father and
Charlotte beside him.

Ben came home for the funeral, resplendent in
his uniform and wearing the George Cross on his
chest. Philip was laid to rest in the village churchyard beneath the shade of a beech tree.

'He's free of pain now,' Miles said, trying to
comfort them all. As they turned to leave they
saw Eddie, Lily and Alfie standing a respectful
distance away. Miles went across to them. 'Thank
you for coming. It would have meant a lot to
Philip.'

Lily bobbed a little curtsy and said, 'I've told
him, sir. Alfie knows the truth now.'

Miles nodded and smiled at the boy who was

y-eyed but solemn-faced. He looked up into
Miles's face and said, 'Eddie's me dad, sir, but
I'm glad I got to know Mr Philip.'

Eddie put his arm round the boy's shoulder.
'I'll always look after him, sir. You can be sure of
that. I've never made no difference between him
and me own bairns, an' I never will.'

'I know that, Eddie. But if you – any of you –
need help at any time, you only have to ask.' He
smiled and held out his hand to shake the boy's
hand. 'After all, I am your grandfather.'

For a moment the boy looked startled and then
he grinned. 'By heck, Dad, I've got a toff for a
grandad.'

They all laughed and it didn't seem at all
irreverent or unfeeling, Charlotte thought. It was
the way Philip – the Philip of the last few months
– would have wanted it.

That night, Miles drew Charlotte into his study.

'There's something I want to show you.'

He settled her in a chair beside his own at the
desk and reached down a large old-fashioned bible
from the bookshelf. He laid it reverently on the
desk and opened it up at the flyleaf. On the page
that should have been blank was a handwritten list
of the births, marriages and deaths of the
Thornton family going back several generations.

'Oh.' Charlotte smiled. 'How lovely. I'd heard
of this being done in a family bible, but I've never
seen one. Miles, do tell me about them all.'

They sat together with Miles's arm round her
shoulders, their heads bent close as Miles pointed
to each name in turn.

'It begins with the birth of my great-great-grandfather, then his marriage and the births of his two children.'

'Is that his handwriting, do you think?'

'I'm not sure. I suspect it was a later generation who began the list, starting with names and dates as far back as he knew. See, the writing doesn't change until my own father wrote his marriage date and the birth dates of my brother, Christopher, and me.'

Charlotte looked up at him in surprise. 'A brother? You have a brother.'

Miles shook his head. 'No, not any more. He was killed in 1915 at Ypres in the Great War. See, here's his death date.'

Charlotte read the dates and felt the sadness behind the written words. 'The war to end all wars', they'd called the carnage of those years and yet now it was happening again.

'I think,' Miles said, bringing her thoughts back to earlier generations, 'it was my grandfather who started writing it all in this bible.' He pointed to the name Josiah halfway down the page. 'He would know his own father, Joseph, and he was old enough by the time his grandfather, Luke Thornton, died in 1835 to have known him too. He'd have been eleven. But look, Charlotte, this is what I wanted to show you – every generation – it's all boys. Luke had Joseph and Marmaduke, who never married because he died at twenty. Joseph had only one child, Josiah, and although Josiah had three children, again they were all boys; my father, Philip, and my uncles, Richard and Henry.'

'He only lived a few days,' Charlotte murmured pointing to Henry's name. 'How sad.'

'And it's even more sad that no one ever spoke of him. It wasn't the thing, you know, in those days to speak of the dead.'

Charlotte rested her head against his shoulder and whispered. 'We'll always talk about Philip. We'll keep his memory alive.'

Miles reached for his pen to write the last heartbreaking entry of Philip's death below that recording Louisa's death, but for a moment he hesitated. 'You see, I couldn't bring myself to enter Georgie's death. Not until we knew for certain. And now I'm so glad I didn't.'

Still he hesitated to begin writing. 'I wonder if I ought to write in the entry of Alfie's birth. I mean, he is Philip's son.' A small, wistful smile played on his mouth. 'But these austere gentlemen would never have entered an illegitimate child into the family bible, now, would they?'

'Darling,' Charlotte said softly, 'it's your bible now. You must write in it what you want to. Everyone around here knows Alfie is Philip's son. Even Alfie knows now. So, if you want to include him, you should.'

'Another son,' he murmured as he began to write with honesty.

Alfred, the illegitimate son of Philip Thornton and Lily Warren, born 30 June 1927.

Beneath that he wrote the details of Philip's death, adding, *As a result of his wounds.*

When the ink was dry he closed the book and turned to Charlotte. He touched her face gently. There was no need for words, not any more.

Despite his sadness at the loss of his son, whic they'd known for some time was inevitable, hi. overriding anxiety now was for the safe delivery of Charlotte's baby.

She could see his overwhelming love for her in his eyes and, now, she had no more doubts. Miles truly loved her.

She smiled and kissed him. 'And the next entry, my darling, will be a much happier one.'

He held her close and she felt his tears wet against her neck.

Sixty-Six

With cruel irony, only a week after Philip's death, Charlotte felt the first labour pangs. If only he'd lived another few days Philip would have seen her child born. But it was not to be.

Knowing that his wife's confinement could not be long away, Miles had asked the nurse to stay on another few weeks. Nurse Monty had beamed. 'I'd be delighted,' she'd said. 'I am a qualified midwife, too. My last appointment before coming here was to a Mrs Marshall in Lincoln, who had twins. Both born healthy, but a handful for a young mother.'

So Nurse Monty was on hand when Charlotte appeared out of her studio late one morning, clutching her stomach. 'Oh – oh. Miles – *Miles...*' she called and everyone came running.

Nurse Monty took charge with her customary

almness and organization. Charlotte was soon
n the room on the first floor that had been set
aside for the birth and where everything had
been ready for weeks.

'Shall I call the doctor?' Miles hovered anxiously
outside the door.

'There's no need for him to come yet,' Nurse
Monty said, forbearing to say that she could
manage to bring a child into the world without
the aid of any man, doctor or not. She was aware
of the circumstances within this household, however, and was sympathetic. The poor man had
lost one wife through childbirth and the present
Mrs Thornton was forty-one and this was her
first baby. There could be complications. Nurse
Monty was confident of her own capabilities, but
she was no fool. The nearest hospital was several
miles away and the doctor might be out on a
home visit anywhere over a widespread area if
called at the last minute. No, better to be safe
than sorry, was Nurse Monty's maxim. So she
added comfortingly, 'But it would be wise to let
him know that Mrs Thornton has gone into
labour, though we are in the early stages at the
moment.'

But even the knowledgeable nurse was caught
unawares by the speed with which Charlotte's
labour progressed. Nurse Monty had expected a
long, protracted labour, but within an hour, the
contractions were coming closely together.
Unable to leave her patient, Nurse Monty sent
Kitty with an urgent message for the master, who
was pacing the hall below. 'Send for the doctor at
once.'

'Sir – sir–' Kitty flew down the stairs almo
tripping in her haste. 'Nurse says can you send
for the doctor.'

Miles stopped in his pacing and stared up at the
girl, terror in his eyes.

''Tis all right, sir. Nothing wrong, but babby is
coming quicker than Nurse thought.'

Miles ran to the front door and dragged it
open, then he stopped and heaved a sigh of relief.
Dr Markham was climbing down from his pony
and trap outside.

'Bennet's on holiday,' he said, mounting the
steps. 'I'm acting as locum, so I thought I'd just
look in. How is she?'

Miles felt relief flood through him. 'Further on
than expected.'

'Ah, good – good. That's excellent.'

'Is it?'

'Of course, my dear fellow. Much less tiring
than a protracted labour,' Dr Markham said,
patting Miles's shoulder and then heading swiftly
to the stairs. 'We'll keep you posted, Miles. Try
not to worry.'

As Miles watched him go up the stairs, he muttered, 'You might as well ask me not to breathe.'

Only two hours later, Miles was allowed into the
bedroom to find his wife sitting up in bed, red
cheeked with her recent efforts but smiling
happily. The child lay sleeping in the crib beside
her bed. Miles took Charlotte in his arms and
kissed her tenderly.

'Thank you, my darling,' he whispered.

Wrapped in each other's arms, they wept tears

joy and then giggled helplessly like two naughty children when they thought of what Osbert's reaction to their news would be.

Very late that night, when the house was quiet, Miles Thornton lifted down the heavy bible and laid it on his desk. He opened it at the flyleaf and read again the entries, written in different hands down the years.

He took up his pen and began to write with a proud flourish.

On Friday, 5 December 1941, to Miles and Charlotte Thornton, the precious gift of a daughter, Louisa Alice.

He sat back and reread the words, cherishing the moment.

'A daughter,' he murmured aloud, his voice husky with emotion. He imagined he was telling all the people listed on the page, generation after generation of sons. Somewhere, somehow, he hoped they were listening.

'I have a *daughter.*'

The publishers hope that this book has given you enjoyable reading. Large Print Books are especially designed to be as easy to see and hold as possible. If you wish a complete list of our books please ask at your local library or write directly to:

Magna Large Print Books
Magna House, Long Preston,
Skipton, North Yorkshire.
BD23 4ND

This Large Print Book for the partially sighted, who cannot read normal print, is published under the auspices of

THE ULVERSCROFT FOUNDATION

St - Mary's ✓

This is a lovely reading I could not leave it down every one should read this book.